More books by S.M. LaViolette & Minerva Spencer

THE ACADEMY OF LOVE SERIES
The Music of Love
A Figure of Love
A Portrait of Love
The Language of Love
Dancing with Love
A Story of Love*
The Etiquette of Love*

THE OUTCASTS SERIES
Dangerous
Barbarous
Scandalous

THE REBELS OF THE *TON*
Notorious
Outrageous
Infamous

THE MASQUERADERS
The Footman
The Postilion
The Bastard

THE SEDUCERS
Melissa and The Vicar
Joss and The Countess
Hugo and The Maiden

VICTORIAN DECADENCE
His Harlot
His Valet
His Countess
Her Master
Her Beast
Their Master

This book is dedicated to all my wonderful readers!

Thank you, thank you, thank you for reading and buying my books! And a HUGE thank you for your wonderful letters, cards, and emails, which keep me motivated to write into the wee hours of the night.

Acknowledgements

They say it takes a village to raise a child. Well, it definitely takes a lot of wonderful, devoted people to launch a book.

Without the help of Brantly, George, Linda, & Shelly, none of my books would ever get out into the world. You are my Four Readers of the Bookpocalypse!

Dancing with Love

Minerva Spencer
writing as S.M. LAVIOLETTE

Crooked
Sixpence
CS
P
Press

CROOKED SIXPENCE BOOKS are published by
CROOKED SIXPENCE PRESS

2 State Road 230
El Prado, NM 87529

First printing December 2022
ISBN: 978-1-951662-57-8

10 9 8 7 6 5 4 3 2 1

Photo stock by Period Images
Printed in the United States of America

Chapter 1

London
1816

Miles Ingram shivered beneath his worn overcoat. This was the coldest year in memory and he might have worried that he'd lost all feeling in his hands and feet if he'd not spent the better part of the day having them trod upon by giggling schoolgirls stumbling their way through the quadrille.

Miles knew it could have been worse; he could have been teaching them the waltz, a dance that seemed to make silly young women lose what little sense they had.

All he wanted to do after walking the not inconsiderable distance from Russell Square back to his part of town—a dirtier, more cramped section of London—was throw back a stiff drink or two and soak his aching feet in a basin of hot water.

Rather than sinking into self-pitying depression Miles should be counting his blessings. Thanks to this newest teaching position, he'd earned enough money to pay the next six months on his lodgings and he even had enough left over to buy food.

Finding work as a dance instructor had not been as easy as he'd hoped—especially when he had to avoid taking work in the great houses of the *ton,* where his name, if not his face, would be known.

That left him with the daughters of bankers, merchants, and captains of industry. But even employment in those sorts of households wasn't assured. Many a mama took one look at Miles's face and sent him packing. It seemed he was too attractive for wise mothers to trust him with their wealthy daughters.

Miles snorted. As if dallying with young bits of fluff was something he thought about these days. No, most of his minutes and hours were consumed with the basic struggle to survive. Day-to-day life had become a constant grind since the school where he'd taught upon leaving the army—the Stefani Academy of Music and Art for Young Ladies—had shuttered.

The school's closure should not have taken Miles by surprise as there had been signs of financial instability for some time, but his optimistic—or simply foolish—nature had stopped him from accepting the truth. The only reason he'd been lucky enough to get his newest teaching position was because of his friend Freddie—Lady Winifred Sedgewick.

Freddie had been a teacher at the Stefani Academy—the mistress of deportment, manners, and elocution—along with Miles and five other instructors.

In the aftermath of the school's dissolution Freddie went back to doing what she'd done before taking her teaching position: matchmaking.

Although that was a term Freddie loathed, much preferring to call it *finishing young ladies and launching them into fashionable society.*

"It is a lowering way to make one's living," Freddie admitted. "But I've been pitchforked into the world of commerce with nothing else to sell."

Miles had grinned and eyed her tall, slender body up and down with a lascivious leer. "Well, not *nothing* else, darling."

Naturally she had ignored his randy innuendo. That was one of the many things he loved about Freddie: her unflappability.

"And what are *you* going to do to earn your bread, Miles?" she'd retorted.

"What do I have to sell other than my dancing skills?"

At the time Miles had been sprawled over a somewhat shabby wing chair in the parlor of the house Freddie shared with two other teacher friends, Serena Lombard and Honoria Keyes.

"At least you are a man, and men have options."

Options? Ha! He had only three as far as he could discern: marry a rich woman, teach dancing, or fling himself into the Thames.

Miles had kept those depressing thoughts to himself. "I suppose I could seek out a lonely, wealthy widow and barter this fancy package of mine."

Freddie had looked up from her needlework, which she was never without, her expression dry. "I shouldn't think that would bring you enough money to live on."

Miles had laughed. "Freddie! You're a cold-hearted wench. I guess there's nothing for it but to marry *you* and let you take care of me. I've always fancied being a kept man."

She'd made a sound that might have been a snort if it hadn't been so delicate and feminine. "You will marry eventually, Miles, and we both know it."

Her certitude had irked him. "Why should I? My brother already has two daughters and his wife is young and fertile; there will be loads more children in their future. Besides, even if Bevan doesn't have a son there's always Crispin. I am merely one of the spares and completely irrelevant."

Freddie had given Miles a less-than-convinced look but had, thankfully, abandoned the subject of marriage.

He couldn't help smiling at the thought of his dearest friend, who took excellent care of him, like a hen with one not particularly smart chick. And thank God for that, too. Because if Freddie hadn't steered Miles toward this current job he'd have needed to go to his brother and ask for his allowance.

Miles grimaced at the thought and shoved it from his mind. He hadn't needed to go to Bevan so there was no point in borrowing trouble.

"Damn it," he muttered as he trod on something hard and sharp and gave an undignified hop as pain radiated out from the ball of his foot. The parchment-thin sole of his Hessians no longer protected him much and his greatest fear these days was that his overworked feet and shoddy footwear would conspire to rob him of the only way he had to earn enough money to live.

He limped onward; now he would most certainly need to beg a basin of hot water from one of the kitchen servants so he could soak both feet the moment he got home.

But when Miles reached his lodgings a short time later, he found the pinch-mouthed landlord, Mr. Fisher, waiting for him in the cramped, dingy entryway.

He glared at Miles as if he'd shown up two hours late for an important appointment. "Ah, *there* you are."

"Yes, Mr. Fisher?" Miles used the same cool tone he employed to put pert students in their place and regarded the smaller man through narrowed eyes as he pulled off his gloves. They were the best pair he owned but were so thin and worn he could feel the cool breeze through them.

"You've got a visitor."

"Oh?"

"He's been waiting for nigh on *three* hours."

"Well?" Miles prodded. "Who is it?"

Mr. Fisher glanced around—as if somebody might be listening—and leaned closer, "He looks to have been *crying*."

Miles removed his hat and dropped his gloves in it. "In the parlor?"

"No, I put him in your rooms."

He scowled. "Why? I pay good money for use of the public spaces." Such as they were.

Fisher drew himself to his full height. "You needn't get all snirpy with me! He said he was your brother."

Miles didn't pause to ask him *which* brother. Instead, he rudely pushed passed Fisher, taking the steps to his third-story rooms two at a time, not wanting to imagine what was bad enough to make either of his brothers cry.

His heart pounded so loudly that he could barely hear the clatter of his boots on the wooden stairs.

If Bevan or Crispin had come all the way to London then something was wrong.

Terribly wrong.

Chapter 2

London
Nine Months Later

Mary Barnett had ignored her dead father's meddling for as long as she could.

It was humiliating to even contemplate the terms of Lucas Barnett's will, but time was running out. If she wanted to continue living her life the way she liked, then she would have to knuckle under and do her father's bidding.

And she would have to do it within the next six weeks.

"Oh, Da," she muttered. "Why did you have to do such a thing?"

But she knew the answer to that question: because he'd believed he knew what was best for her.

Mary had always understood that her father had loved her more than anyone else—even more than he'd loved his wife or Mary's much prettier and sweeter younger sister, Jenny.

"I've got you, darlin' and yer Ma has Jen, and we all have each other," is how her folksy father had explained the complex tangle of family loyalty and love.

Unfortunately, her father's love had left Mary with shackles for which there was only one key: marriage.

Mary could hear his justification for the oppressive clause, spoken in his peculiar, blended accent, the last vestige of a boy who'd been raised by an itinerant tinker with no single place to call home.

"It should be yer son—or maybe girl—who'll take over one day, Luvvie. I'll see to it young Jen is taken care of, but you, Mary? Yer a chip from yer Da's block. When ye marry, ye and yer man will take charge and grow things 'een bigger."

Lucas Barnett had refused to pay heed to Mary's argument that she didn't need—or want—a man, either to run his business or for any other reason.

"Everyone needs somebody, Mary. Everyone."

That might be true, but Mary didn't believe that person necessarily had to be a mate. Wasn't loving her father, mother, and sister enough?

15

Mary chewed her lower lip in frustrated fury and sanded the letter she'd just written to Sir James Woodson, a man she had briefly met during business negotiations in Lanarkshire.

The letter was beyond improper, but she suspected that Sir James—a portly, raw-boned widower of fifty with a freshly minted baronetcy—would look beyond the impropriety to the solution she offered for both of them.

During their business communications Mary had discerned that Sir James was without humor but he was kind and decent and he also satisfied her father's ridiculous requirement that she marry a man who was titled. Thankfully a mere baronet or even a knight would suffice as Lucas Barnett had not expected her to marry into the peerage.

Mary had endured enough derision from proper lords and ladies in her youth—during her single, loathsome Season—to give her a disgust of the entire class.

Sir James would be a practical, businesslike mate and they could live together without messy emotional entanglements. The only unfortunate aspect of marriage with Sir James was that he would likely expect an heir. As distasteful as it was to imagine engaging in physical relations with Sir James, she could bear the indignity if it meant avoiding the alternative, which was handing control of her father's companies over to her cousin Reginald.

She would die before she allowed that to happen.

Mary snorted at the uncharacteristically dramatic thought and was searching for a wafer to seal the letter when the door opened.

"Ah, here you are, my dear." Louisa Barnett said, as if she'd discovered Mary hiding in a cupboard rather than sitting in her own study.

Mary hastily dropped the letter into the open drawer and closed it before turning.

"Did you need something, Mama?"

Mrs. Barnett frowned, her eyes flickering up and down Mary's seated person. "I do wish you would not wear such a rag, Mary. Even at home." She heaved the sigh of a greatly put-upon mother. "But you don't have time to change, I'm afraid."

"Change? But why? We had no plans today." Mary smoothed the light brown muslin skirt of her perfectly serviceable morning gown. She tucked a loose tendril of flaming red hair behind her ear and frowned. "Or did we?"

"Oh Mary, how could you forget? We are meeting with Lady Winifred Sedgewick today."

"Lady Winifred Sedgewick?" Mary repeated stupidly, her mind racing like a caged ferret. "I'm not familiar with that name."

"She is here about you and Jenny."

"I'm sorry, but I have no idea what you are talking about, Mama."

Louisa clucked her tongue. "Surely you remember? About you and Jenny and the Season."

Her and Jenny? The Season?

Ah. Mary closed her eyes and shook her head. *Now* she remembered the brief conversation from a week or so earlier. "Oh mum, I never agreed to this."

Her mother winced at the name, which she considered common. "Why must you always be so *difficult,* Mary?" Louisa Barnett demanded in her carefully honed upper class accent.

Mary didn't know why the older woman tried so hard. No matter how many elocution lessons her mother took, she still sounded exactly like what she was: a social climbing cit trying to ape her social betters.

It left Mary feeling tired.

"Are you listening to me, Mary?"

"Yes, Mama."

"Now that a union with Sir Thomas Lowrey—Lord rest his soul—is no longer possible I *know* you must be looking for somebody. Especially as there are less than two months remaining before the terms of your father's will take effect." Her sour expression suddenly lightened. "Unless you've given up on that idea?" She clasped her hands together in a gesture that was both prayerful and thankful. "Oh, you *have,* haven't you? You will leave all that men's business to your cousin Reginald and finally—"

"I have not changed my mind about marrying to satisfy Da's will." Louisa flinched at the word *Da,* but Mary didn't care. "And I certainly have no intention of giving Reginald control of Da's companies. Or anything else, for that matter." J

"If that is the case then why do you have any objection to meeting Lady Sedgewick? You have six weeks to find a husband. Why turn away help?"

Mary wondered what her mother's reaction would be if she learned Mary had just offered herself in marriage to a man who was almost twice her age and whose baronetcy was so new the ink was scarcely dry. A man whose country accent was so thick they'd likely need an interpreter to officiate their wedding.

She smiled slightly at the thought but decided against telling her mother about Sir James. Not yet at least. She didn't need the headache such an announcement would likely cause.

But she needed to say something, so she said, "I told you I would marry by July fifteenth, Mama, but I didn't say I was prepared to engage a matchmaker."

"That is a vulgar term, Mary." Louisa Barnett's lips tightened in disapproval, not an unusual expression when she spoke to her eldest daughter.

"What *does* a person call her?"

"Lady Sedgewick. She is a *countess.*"

Mary could only stare.

"Don't give me that long-suffering look, my girl. After the last man you contemplated marrying, I shudder to think of what kind of fright you will end up with if I do not take a hand."

"Sir Thomas wasn't so bad," Mary said, although she didn't put much effort into her defense.

"*He wasn't so bad?*" her mother repeated in a voice louder than necessary. "Sir Thomas Lowell was not only a dullard, a drunk, an inveterate gamester, and likely *diseased*, but the man also died in the bed of his mistress! Thank God you'd not formally announced your betrothal."

Mary couldn't deny that what her mother said about Sir Thomas was true. He *had* been all those things—and more, besides. As for dying in his mistress's bed… well, Mary only wished that he might have waited to do that until *after* she'd married him and satisfied the terms of the will.

"I don't care about any of that, Mama. You know I am not looking for romance or love."

"I have never met a female who didn't want love and romance. You are an unnatural daughter, Mary. I don't understand what happened that left you so hardened."

Mary could have told her exactly—to the moment—when she'd abandoned any dreams of love and romance, but why bring up such an unpleasant memory when she'd worked so hard to hide it?

"As much as I'd love to discuss my failings as not only a daughter but a female, we were talking of this matchmaker—er, I mean countess. I don't need anyone's assistance to find a suitable husband."

"I know you don't care about being a societal outcast but your poor sister is suffering greatly. She was not invited to the Harrington ball and there are only a precious few weeks remaining and her first Season will end a failure. She is heartbroken."

Mary had heard Jenny crying more than once over the past few months and knew her mother spoke the truth. These blasted aristocrats and their petty cruelty! Oh, how she wished her younger sister was not so set on being accepted by people who would never love or cherish her as she deserved.

"If you believe Lady Sedgewick can help Jenny, then hire her, Mama. But is it even worth the effort with less than half the Season remaining? Why not wait until next year? In any case," she went on, not waiting for her mother's answer, "if this is about Jenny, then why must *I* meet with the woman?"

"Lady Sedgewick is here to address Jenny's situation and more besides."

"*More besides?* Why don't I like the sound of that, Mama?"

"The countess has connections we can only dream about, Mary."

"*Ton* connections are not what I dream about."

Her mother clucked her tongue. "How can you possibly not wish to take your pick of husbands from the finest men Britain has to offer?"

"You mean aristocrats who are so hidebound by pride they wouldn't lift a finger to stop themselves from starving? Men who'd rather *marry* their way out of their self-inflicted financial problems?"

For once, her mother did not take the bait. Instead, she cast some bread of her own on the water. "You claim to be a *businesswoman*," her mother spat out the word as if it were a fly she'd encountered in her tea. "Shouldn't you want to be informed before you make such an important decision?"

"Have no fear, I will be. It just so happens I gather my information from sources other than aristocratic marriage-fixers or scandal sheets."

"*You* might be satisfied with marrying some—some *ironmonger* from the provinces who was elevated to knighthood thanks to his war contribution, but what about your sister?"

"An ironmonger from the provinces was good enough for you, was he not, Mama? And Da didn't even have a title."

Her mother's eyes narrowed. "Don't ever make the mistake of believing our lives are in any way similar, my dear. *I* was not given a choice of whom I would marry."

Mary had no interest in delving into the subject of her parents' marriage, which she already knew had not been a love match.

"I am not standing in your way when it comes to this countess. If you wish to employ her for Jenny's sake, do so, mama. You do not need my approval." Mary glanced at the pile of correspondence on her desk, impatient to finish her morning's work.

"You are afraid to meet this woman."

Mary looked up from the desk. "I beg your pardon?"

"You heard me."

She didn't care for her mother's coy, sly look. It usually meant she was planning something: something that involved Mary.

"I don't fear her, Mama. Nor do I need her help. I shall find my own husband."

Louisa Barnett's face seemed to crumple. "Oh, Mary!" she cried, suddenly imploring rather than hectoring. "*Please* come meet her. I don't ask much of you, do I? You never accompany your sister and I to functions, you spend all your time with your precious secretary John Courtland and a host of vulgar businessmen, you didn't even make an appearance at Jenny's own ball here at Coal House. Won't you *please* do this one thing for me—for your sister? Please at least meet Lady Sedgewick. It shan't take more than a half-hour of your time."

Mary tapped her toe on the floor, an action her mother took for impending capitulation.

"Just this one time, Mary! I promise. Jenny is not the only one who would benefit from her acquaintance. You have only six weeks before—"

Mary would get no peace until she'd appeased her mother. She stood. "Fine, I shall meet her."

Her mother beamed. "I knew you would come to your—"

"But *only* to listen, and *only* about Jenny. There is to be *no* mention of the terms of Father's wretched will." Good God, that was the last thing Mary needed, not that people didn't speculate about her—thanks to her wretched cousin Reginald's big mouth, no doubt. "Give me your word on that, Mama."

Her mother bobbed up and down like an excited pigeon. "I would *never* mention such a private matter, Mary."

Mary bit her lip to hold back a snort of disbelief.

"Now, please, come along, she is waiting."

Mary headed for the door and then stopped, narrowing her eyes suspiciously. "Where is Jenny, since this is all about her?"

Mrs. Barnett waved her hand dismissively. "Oh, she is a mere child and has no idea about such matters."

Mary sighed but followed her mother from the room, gritting her teeth against the next half hour, wishing she'd not hidden the letter to Sir James Woodson in a drawer, but instead sent it.

Chapter 3

Mary didn't know what she expected a matchmaker to look like, but the woman in the Rose Salon was a pleasant surprise. Lady Sedgewick stood as they entered, displaying the ramrod straight spine of a woman who'd spent her formative years strapped to a plank.

Mary dropped a stiff curtsey, aware as she did so that an expert was appraising her performance. "Good afternoon, Lady Sedgewick."

"It is a pleasure to meet you, Miss Barnett." Her voice was low, pleasant, mellifluous; it was the type of accent Mary's mother could copy for a thousand years without ever mastering.

Lady Sedgewick positively *dripped* aristocrat and was beautiful in an icy, untouchable way. Her smooth, immaculately coiffed hair was a pale ash blonde and her skin the color of fresh cream. Her eyes were an unusual slate-gray that reminded Mary of a frozen lake in the dead of winter.

She was all muted tones and understated elegance and yet she had more presence than any woman Mary had ever met. She held herself like a queen, her sedate dove-brown clothing managing to appear rich rather than drab.

Mary's mother—who was garbed in an expensive moire silk gown festooned with Belgian lace—appeared overdressed and vulgar in comparison.

"Thank you so much for agreeing to meet us on such short notice, my lady," Mrs. Barnett gushed.

"It is my pleasure," the countess said, sounding astonishingly genuine.

The door opened and not one but three servants entered bearing refreshments. Mary experienced a pang of pity for her mother; Louisa Barnett would never understand that more was not necessarily better in the eyes of these aristocrats. Indeed, a woman like the countess would probably view her mother's efforts to impress her as proof of her low origins and social-climbing intentions.

"Will you pour, my dear?" Mrs. Barnett asked Mary.

She almost rolled her eyes; it was going to be one of *those* days. Mary was to be put through her paces like a performing circus animal.

She poured the tea, conscious of every clink and clatter. Good, it was just as well that Lady Sedgewick understood that she would have her hands full if she attempted to try and civilize a barbarian who couldn't even pour tea without making a racket.

Once everyone had tea and biscuits Mary decided to move matters along before any more time was wasted. "My mother tells me you are a matchmaker, Lady Sedgewick."

"Oh, *Mary*." Louisa's voice throbbed with mortification.

But Lady Sedgewick smiled—an expression that transformed her from an ice queen into a warm and attractive woman. "The term is as accurate as any other, Miss Barnett, and a good deal more polite than some."

The countess's poise went well beyond anything Mary could ever hope to achieve. The woman was grace personified and Mary couldn't help admiring her even though social elegance had never been something she'd considered important.

"I do felicitate matrimonial arrangements," the countess continued. "I also provide assistance and advice on navigating the somewhat treacherous waters of the *ton*."

"Deportment? Elocution?" Mary suggested.

"Yes, those as well, when necessary."

Mary quirked an eyebrow and the countess's striking gray eyes glinted with humor. "I do not think you require counseling in those areas, Miss Barnett."

The frisson of pleasure Mary felt at the compliment was irritating. What did she care if this woman thought her manners socially acceptable? They *were* socially acceptable—and why wouldn't they be? Mary had gone to the most expensive and exacting finishing school in the country. True, she'd left that same school at sixteen, but if three years hadn't been long enough to absorb the basics of polite behavior what kind of an idiot would that make her?

"I'm not sure what my mother has told you, my lady, but it is my *sister* who requires your assistance."

The countess nodded. "Mrs. Barnett mentioned your younger sister."

"Well then, you hardly need me here." Mary made to stand, but the woman's next words stopped her.

"I am here today on a matter that does not concern your sister." To Mary's surprise Lady Sedgewick's cheeks tinted a delicate shade of pink. The addition of the slight amount of color to her face made the countess look younger. It was also intriguing. Just what was making the cool, composed woman blush suddenly?

"Yes, my lady?" Mary prodded.

"Mrs. Barnett gave me reason to believe you are contemplating marriage. Er, rather quickly—six weeks was the term she mentioned."

Mary shot her mother a poisonous look that was wasted because Mrs. Barnett was pointedly ignoring her.

"I hope you will not consider me impertinent," the countess went on. "But I have recently been engaged by a new client—a gentleman of excellent character and breeding—who wishes to make himself known to you."

Mary frowned. "I—I beg your pardon? Did you say he wants to meet *me*? Are you sure it isn't my sister he's thinking of? I've not been to a social function of any kind for"—she broke off as she wracked her brain. Lord, when *had* she last been anywhere that didn't involve work?

"Well, not for years," she said.

"No, I am not mistaken. It is you he wishes to meet, Miss Barnett."

Mary knew she shouldn't encourage the woman, but she couldn't help asking, "Who is your client?"

"The Earl of Avington."

Mrs. Barnett made a cooing sound, as if somebody had just launched a particularly spectacular firework, and then turned as red as a brick when she realized what she'd done.

"An earl, Mary," she murmured, as if this would excuse her lapse in propriety.

Even with her vast fortune Mary had not attracted so much as a baronet during her one agonizing Season ten years earlier—not that she'd wanted to meet anyone at the time, given how deeply in love she'd been with her cousin Reginald.

But even though she'd not been looking for suitors, it had been a humbling and unpleasant experience. Not only had her merchant background worked against her, but her visible scars and prickly demeanor had ensured her permanent wallflower status.

Mary realized she was absently stroking the rough skin on her cheek and lowered her hand, looking up to meet Lady Sedgewick's placid, unreadable gaze.

"Are you quite sure the earl doesn't wish for an introduction to me so that I might make him known to my sister?"

"*Mary*," her mother hissed.

But Lady Sedgewick chuckled. Lord. She even *laughed* with grace and charm.

"No, Miss Barnett. He wishes to meet you."

So what if an earl wanted to meet her? It was surprising her name was still in circulation given her excessively private nature, but she was, after all, one of the wealthiest unmarried women in England. Or maybe this earl knew of her situation? It wasn't difficult to imagine Sir Thomas—loose-lipped from drink—sharing the mortifying details of her father's will in gambling hells all over London.

Whatever the reason for this man's interest, he was doubtless ancient, pox-riddled, and one step ahead of the dunners. An earl would need to be in desperate straits to suffer not only her lowborn connections but also her appearance.

Did she really wish to meet such a man? Why bother when she already had Sir James in mind? The old widower might not be the sort of man who made a woman's heart pound, but that was a positive attribute in her opinion. And he was a known quantity while this mysterious earl was not. Who knew what sort of a wreck the man might be?

Mary straightened her shoulders, ready to be done with this.

But before she could tell the countess she wasn't interested, her mother said, "Think of Jenny. With such a connection she would be welcome everywhere—by everyone. Is that not right, my lady?"

The countess hesitated, and then nodded. "The earl's family is very well-respected."

Her mother turned back to Mary, her gaze imploring. "Jenny could have everything you did not, Mary."

Mary held her mother's gaze until the older woman colored and looked away.

She turned to the beautiful stranger, who had watched their interaction with a coolly assessing gaze. "I don't recall hearing about the Earl of Avington before."

"He inherited after his elder brother—a married gentleman who did not spend much time in London—died last year." She paused and gave Mary a speculative look, as if wondering how much information to convey.

Mary could have told her it didn't matter what she said, any man she considered marrying would undergo a complete investigation. She was not a woman to leave important matters to chance.

"If Lord Avington is interested in meeting me, I'm going to assume it is with marriage in mind?"

Louisa made a distressed noise, but the countess didn't so much as blink at Mary's bold question. Mary liked the woman more and more.

"Yes, Miss Barnett, he is contemplating marriage."

"I will further assume that his interest in marriage is motivated by financial expediency?"

Louisa groaned.

The countess smiled slightly. "It is true that the earldom has experienced difficulties in recent years. He also has a large family to consider. In addition to his brother's widow and her daughters, the earl is responsible for two younger sisters, a younger brother, and a host of other dependents." The countess's forthright gaze flickered, as if something about this was uncomfortable or difficult for her.

If Mary had possessed antennae they would have been twitching. "Are you personally acquainted with Lord Avington?"

"I am," the countess said, her expression once again unreadable.

Well, that was interesting, but hardly surprising. Mary's slight acquaintance with the aristocracy had convinced her that they were all related to each other.

So, an earl wished to meet her, did he?

If Mary simply said, "Thank you, but no thank you," she would look like a selfish sister who did not care about Jenny's happiness.

But if she said *yes*, wouldn't that just complicate her life unnecessarily? After all, if Mary left right now, she could post that letter to Sir James and forget all about this penniless earl, his crumbling estate, and extensive family.

Mary opened her mouth to thank the countess for her time, but something else came out, instead, "Can you tell me something about the earl's family?"

"Ingram is the family name and they've lived in Gloucestershire for centuries. The earl's county seat, Avington Castle, is not far from the Forest of Dean and is considered one of England's treasures."

"Avington Castle," her mother repeated in an awed voice.

"Perhaps you might have heard of it?" the countess asked.

"Indeed I have," Louisa said.

Mary had not, but she could imagine it: it would be enormous, ancient, and in wretched condition. It would require a sum equivalent to that spent on the Peninsular War to repair. Maintaining it would be equally daunting thanks to falling agricultural prices, which would mean Mary's deep pockets would be expected to make up the difference.

Why was the earl's estate in such poor condition? Had the prior earl been unlucky? Reckless? Thoughtless? Was the earldom's destitution the work of just one man or the cumulative effect of generations of wastrels?

Was the new earl a drunkard? A gambler? A philanderer? Why was he looking to *her*? A woman so reclusive as to be a hermit. A woman *known* to be physically damaged.

"Why does his lordship not wish to meet my younger sister?" Mary asked bluntly, earning another scandalized look from her mother.

"The earl is disinclined to marry a woman just from the schoolroom."

Mary knew the man would change his *inclinations* quickly enough when he saw Mary and Jenny side-by-side. After all, what kind of man wanted an older, scrawny, and badly scarred heiress instead of a nubile, gorgeous, and charming one? Or perhaps he thought a homely, older woman would be so grateful for a husband that she would be grateful and biddable?

Mary allowed herself a small smile at the thought.

She glanced from her mother's hopeful face to the countess's unreadable one, her own thoughts on the letter in her desk.

If she married Sir James, she would know exactly what she was getting: a cit with humble aspirations. A man who wanted to engage in country entertainments and marry a woman who'd provide him with a few children to keep him company in his dotage.

Unfortunately, a marriage to Sir James would do very little to help Jenny.

But with the power of an earldom behind her, her sister would not have to choose from the dissipated ranks of the aristocracy, nor would she need to look lower, to the class of people she was *from*, but no longer *of.*

Marriage to an earl might also be useful in Mary's businesses. The right voice in the House of Lords could prove priceless in many ways…

Lady Sedgewick set down her cup and saucer and Mary realized the other woman was watching her, but not with impatience. Indeed, Mary thought she saw a glimmer of respect in her eyes. Or maybe she envied Mary her ability to make her own decisions—at least to a point. Because the truth was that Mary wasn't free; she was bound by love.

Not just love for her sister, but love for the life she lived. She *loved* the richness of her days, the mental challenges of managing and growing her father's shipping and mining empire, and she especially loved that she could pursue her private projects—like her trade schools—without having to seek approval from some *man*.

As much as Mary had loved her father, and as well as they'd got on together, Mary had dreamed of a day when she'd not been under anyone's thumb.

In the almost two years since her father's death, she'd had a taste of true independence. How many women her age, who were not widows, enjoyed such freedom? And all thanks to her beloved Da.

But then he'd snatched it away with his wretched will!

Mary swallowed bitter laughter as she considered how Da would have viewed her new opportunity. His Mary to become a countess? Lucas Barnett would have crowed it from the rooftops.

"Mary, darling?"

She looked up to find her mother staring, a deep groove of concern between her eyes, as if she dreaded what Mary might say next.

Lady Sedgewick's expression was kind, patient, and—if Mary wasn't mistaken—pitying.

Pity.

Heat crept up her neck and face; if there was one emotion she absolutely loathed, it was pity. If this impoverished earl could be audacious enough to dangle after Mary's fortune through a matchmaker, then Mary could be audacious enough to meet him face-to-face. She feared *no* man.

Besides, the earl would change his mind about which sister to marry quickly enough when he saw her and Jenny together. Her sister would make a lovely and gracious countess for Lord Avington.

She met Lady Sedgewick's cool gray gaze. "I have no objection to meeting his lordship."

Louisa Barnett could not hide her joy. "We can invite his lordship to dine with us on any evening when it is convenient for you to join us, Lady Sedgewick."

Mary had no intention of waiting on a dissipated aristocrat when it came to a matter as important as this.

"Actually, Mama, I should like to have this meeting sooner rather than later. In fact, it will have to be this week," she added, earning a glare from her mother.

The countess merely nodded. "If you would allow me to consult the earl, I will send you a message by tomorrow?"

"Yes, thank you, my lady."

"Please tell his lordship we so look forward to meeting him," Louise Barnett added, her eyes shining as she all but bounced up and down on the settee.

Mary had had enough. "I shall leave you to discuss the particulars with my mother, Lady Sedgewick."

The countess smiled up at her. "It has been a pleasure to meet you, Miss Barnett."

Mary experienced a sudden flicker of unease as she studied the countess's beautiful face. Was that triumph she saw beneath Lady Sedgewick's serenity? Triumph about a mere dinner invitation? No, ridiculous.

Mary shrugged aside her unease. One dinner meant nothing to her, but it would placate her mother and hopefully curb her meddling and nagging.

After she'd met this impoverished fortune-hunter—and horrified him with her mere appearance—she would send her letter to Sir James and have done with this whole farce.

Mary closed the door to the sitting room quietly and headed back toward her study, her mind already on the work that awaited her.

Chapter 4

Miles breathed through his mouth and tried not to touch more of the dingy carriage than necessary.

He'd had four separate lessons that day and had been dreadfully late getting home, which meant he'd had almost no time to bathe and change for dinner. He had hoped to walk to a more respectable area to hail a decent hackney. Instead, he'd been forced to stop the first conveyance that passed and had climbed inside without inspecting it.

As far as Miles could tell, he'd engaged the most ancient, ramshackle, and disgusting hackney in all of London. Perhaps all of England.

When he tried to shift his arse into a more comfortable position, he discovered his Hessian was stuck to something.

"Bloody hell," he muttered, yanking at his foot with increasing violence before it finally came free—along with a piece of the carriage floor stuck to the worn sole.

Miles gave a disbelieving laugh as he prodded at the debris with his other boot. That was when he noticed he could see the street through the gaps in the floorboards. Well, he supposed he should be thankful for the holes, which at least ventilated the carriage and carried away some of the pungent odor of vomit and worse.

Miles gave up on dislodging the scrap of flooring and sat back.

Even worse than the revolting carriage was his suspicion that he would be so late for dinner the door would be barred to him.

Perhaps that would be just as well.

Good Lord, how had he ever let Freddie talk him into this?

"Marriage—and quickly—is the only choice you have, Miles," she'd said. "Or do you wish to send your sisters off to be governesses? Or maybe Crispin could clerk at a counting house? But what of your Aunts Cordelia, Beatrice, and Mabel? Would you send them to the workhouse? And what of—"

Miles had lifted both hands to stop Freddie's verbal barrage. "All right, all right, I take your point. Lord, Fred, you're merciless, you know that?"

"And you are refusing to face the truth and are behaving like a child, Miles."

He'd laughed, but it hadn't held much amusement. "You're right. I *am* behaving like a child."

Miles had come to see her directly upon his return from Avington Castle, where he'd needed to spend the entire time reassuring all those relatives that she'd just mentioned that they wouldn't end up in the poorhouse before the year was out.

Freddie put down her needlework and fixed him with her piercing gray gaze. "You have done an excellent job hiding how dire your situation is, but I *know* you, Miles."

"*Pfft.* Dire is such an extreme word, darling. Matters are actually no worse than calamitous. Or perhaps disastrous."

She had ignored his attempt at levity. "I know Bevan has only been dead nine months, Miles, but you cannot put off marrying any longer."

That was true, he couldn't. He'd learned that much and more on his most recent perusal of the family ledgers.

Curious as to what Freddie was working on, Miles had tilted his head so that he could see what was in her embroidery frame: it was a magnificent vase of flowers, the blooms so real he swore he could smell them.

Freddie's needlework was not merely a gentlewoman's pastime; she sold her completed pieces to earn money. Miles only knew that because the same savvy shopkeeper who bought her work also bought his carvings.

The old man had been excited by Miles's diminutive horses, which he'd whittled almost compulsively since returning home from the war. He'd asked if Miles could carve chess sets.

As it turned out, Miles *could* whittle entire chess sets—quite nice ones, too—and the shopkeeper bought everything Miles made.

It was ironic, really. His only marketable skill—other than dancing—and he'd learned it entirely by accident while he'd been held captive.

The money he earned from his carvings often meant the difference between eating or starving. He suspected the same was true for Freddie and her needlework.

"Miles?"

"Hmm, darling?"

"Are you listening?"

"Yes, of course I am. Please, let us discuss my *dire* future."

"I have taken the liberty of drawing up a list of marriageable ladies for you."

Miles had laughed "Of course, you have. Go on, then, Fred. Let's have it."

She went to her writing desk and extracted a slip of paper from the top drawer.

Miles stood to take it from her and flopped back into his chair, his gaze flickering over the four names written in her perfect copperplate.

He grinned. "I see you've numbered them, Fred. Are they listed in order of something? Looks? Brains? Money? Weight?"

She was already back at her stitchery and didn't bother looking up. "Suitability. The one at the top being the most suitable."

"Fenella Sparks?"

"Miss Sparks is the only daughter of Joseph Sparks."

"Sparks? It seems like I've heard that name before," he mused.

"Cornish tin baron."

"Ah, yes, now I recall. So, tell me about this tin princess."

"Miss Sparks is very pretty and petite, dark brown hair and green eyes."

Miles snorted. "Because that's all I care about, eh, Fred? A woman's appearance?"

She glanced up from her work and blinked slowly, her gray eyes unnervingly sharp once they'd focused. Honestly, the woman could make him feel like he was still in short pants.

Miles had waved a hand. "All right, all right. Don't make your mouth go all flat and crinkly and disapproving at me. How old is Miss Sparks?"

"She will be eighteen in two months."

"Christ—seventeen? She's half my age, Freddie!" He shook his head. "No, I refuse to marry an infant. In fact, I don't want anyone younger than—" He stared at the off-white plaster ceiling above his head while he pondered. "Nobody younger than twenty," he said, listing his youngest sisters'—twins—ages. "And even that is probably too young. The last thing I want is a young, impressionable woman who will expect courtship, romance, and love."

Freddie made no response, nor did she look up. But Miles knew that *she* knew what he meant. Although they'd never spelled it out in words, they were two of a kind when it came to matters of the heart: neither of them had even a speck of interest in love, at least not the romantic kind.

Miles knew why *he* avoided affairs of the heart, but he'd never pried into Freddie's affairs to learn her reasons. They were close friends, but there were some things you didn't share even with your friends.

He turned his attention back to the list, trying to match the surnames with the industries.

"Barnett." He looked up. "As in Lucas Barnett the shipping magnate?"

"Yes, and mining. Mary Barnett is his eldest daughter. She is twenty-eight."

"Perfect so far. But why is she the last name on the list?"

Freddie didn't look up, but Miles would have sworn her already stiff shoulders became even stiffer.

"She is notoriously private and eschews society. I am not even sure she wishes to marry."

A woman who did not wish for marriage? Other than Freddie and their friend Lorelei, a bluestocking teacher from the Stefani Academy, Miles had never met such a creature.

And Miss Barnett didn't care for society, either?

That sounded bloody promising as Miles didn't much care for society himself, not that he would have any say in the matter now that he was head of his family.

Miles looked up from the scrap of paper. "If you don't think she wants to marry, then why include her?"

"Not only is she the wealthiest woman on that list, but there is a rumor that her father left a stipulation in his will regarding marriage," she stopped, her pale cheeks tinting an attractive pink.

"What it is?" Miles prodded.

"I don't know what it is exactly, but it has something to do with ownership of the companies passing to a male relative if she does not marry *soon*."

"Why are you blushing?"

"I am *not* blushing."

Miles smirked; oh yes, she was. "Tell me, Fred."

She hesitated, but then said, "If I am blushing it is only because I am ashamed to repeat such gossip."

"Go on."

"Miss Barnett was negotiating a marriage contract with Sir Thomas Lowery."

Miles's eyebrows shot up. "*She's* the heiress old Tommy had bamboozled into marriage?"

"Yes. Until his unfortunate demise."

Miles couldn't help laughing at the prissy euphemism. "Cocking his toes up in a brothel when he was all but betrothed deserves something better than *unfortunate demise*."

Freddie ignored his raillery. "Apparently she has very little time to satisfy the terms of the will."

Something she'd said earlier snagged his attention. "You're saying that she personally runs her father's empire?"

"Yes."

"Hmph. She must be an unusual woman."

"Indeed. It is generally believed her personal fortune is somewhere in the neighborhood of three hundred thousand pounds."

Miles whistled and Freddie winced. "Sorry, Fred. That is quite a respectable neighborhood."

"In terms of money, at least, she has no need to marry."

"You sound envious, my dear."

"I envy her position, but I do not envy her choices."

"What do you mean?"

"Right now, she is her own mistress in a way few women can even imagine." Freddie paused, a bleak look clouding her gray eyes. "But if she wants to continue doing something she obviously enjoys then she must jeopardize that freedom. After all, no matter how kind or reasonable a man appears, a woman will always become his property upon marriage and a husband will always be his wife's master under the law."

Miles studied her beautiful but undemonstrative face and wondered what had happened to her during her marriage to the Earl of Sedgewick, a man who'd been a few years ahead of Miles at Eton. From what Miles could recall of Sedgewick he'd been handsome, charming, and well off. So why had he left his widow both destitute and emotionally stunted?

As much as he would have liked to know, Miles would never pry into her affairs. If she wanted him to know, she would tell him.

"If Miss Barnett doesn't socialize, how does one meet her?" he asked.

"Fortunately for you, I met her mother—Mrs. Louisa Barnett—at a ball her daughter and one of my charges were attending and she invited me to tea tomorrow."

"Wait—I thought you said Miss Barnett didn't socialize?"

"This was her younger sister, Miss Jennifer Barnett."

Miles laughed. "Freddie, I'm confused. Are you saying Mrs. Barnett invited you to discuss finding a husband for the younger girl?"

"Ostensibly Mrs. Barnett has invited me to discuss sponsoring Jennifer. However, she raised the subject of Mary."

"What did she say?"

"She didn't say much—we did not get a great deal of time to talk—but the little she did confide convinced me that Miss Mary Barnett might be willing to marry if she thought it would improve her younger sister's chances."

"My goodness." Miles's eyebrows shot up. "That seems very... altruistic."

Freddie resumed her needlework. "The younger daughter is said to be quite lovely, Miles. I don't suppose you'd change your mind about an eighteen-year-old bride?"

"No child bride for me," Miles said, still chewing on the information that Miss Barnett would marry to better her younger sister's social position when she personally didn't care about society. She must be an interesting woman.

"There is one more thing, Miles."

"Ah, here it comes. She shrieks like a fishwife? Takes snuff in public? She—"

"She was injured as a child. Quite badly."

The smile slid from his face. "How?"

"She was caught in a house fire."

"Good Lord—was she badly hurt?"

"I understand she was fortunate—as far as such things go—but some of her scars are visible. I daresay that could be the reason why she doesn't care to socialize."

"Yes, the *ton* can be quite cruel about anyone who is less than perfect."

"Yes, they can be." Neither of them had ever been ostracized for their physical appearance, but they'd been stigmatized for being poor.

Freddie gestured to the piece of paper Miles still held in one hand. "The second name on the list, Harriet Skinner, might be of more interest to you. She is—"

"No, you needn't tell me about the others. I'll see Miss Barnett first, Fred. If you can arrange an introduction, that is."

If she had been surprised by his choice, she had not showed it. Nor had she wasted any time setting up this first meeting.

So, here he was only a few days later on his way to court a woman who might not wish to be courted. And he a man not interested in courtship. What a perfect pair they made.

But Freddie had the right of it when she said Miles needed to marry an heiress. It was shocking to consider marriage less than a year after his brother's death, but matters were indeed dire and he could not wait much longer or the people who relied on him would suffer.

Miles stared unseeingly at the lamps as they flickered past the grimy hackney window. Yes, he must have money—and a great deal of it—and he had only one thing to sell to get it.

**

If unpunctuality was not the *first* item on Mary's list of pet peeves, it surely came second.

She glanced at the hideous clock on the mantle—one of her mother's gaudier acquisitions—to confirm the time. Yes, Lord Avington was twenty-two minutes late. When she looked away from the ormolu monstrosity it was to find Lady Sedgewick studying her. Mary knew the woman was aware of her irritation—she'd certainly not bothered to hide it—and she expected the countess would offer some excuse or apology for her client's shameful tardiness.

But the cool blond woman turned her attention to Mary's younger sister Jenny, instead.

Jenny, thrilled to be dining with a *real* countess and a *real* earl—even one who obviously did not possess a pocket watch—was perched on the very edge of the settee, her pretty face flushed with excitement.

"When did you leave Mrs. Shipton's Academy, Miss Barnett?" Lady Sedgewick asked.

"I came home from Bath at the beginning of the year, my lady."

"And you were there for how long?"

"Four years, ma'am." Jenny's huge brown eyes, so like their mother's, flickered to Mary.

The hopeful look made Mary's chest feel tight and achy; her sister expected so little to be happy—just a place among the people whose ranks she'd been raised to expect to join. But the *ton* had consistently thwarted her sister's modest hopes and dreams and the only parties and balls Jenny had received invitations to were those held by the wives of merchants, shopkeepers, and the occasional banker.

You could change all that, Mary.

She knew that, but at what cost? A lifetime with a man who couldn't even show up for a free meal on time?

Mary pushed aside her irritation at the earl and gave her sister a reassuring smile. "Jenny is quite accomplished at the piano, Lady Sedgewick. She is also an excellent water colorist. That is one of her paintings over the secretaire."

Lady Sedgewick's cool expression turned to pleased surprise when she saw Mary had not exaggerated her sister's talent.

"That is exceptional, Miss Barnett." The countess gave Jenny a warm smile that made her sister's rosy cheeks even rosier.

The door swung open to reveal Yost. Their butler's face was impassive, even though he knew Mary's opinion of unpunctual behavior.

"Lord Avington, ma'am." His eyes lingered on Mary before flickering to Mrs. Barnett, who'd already leapt to her feet.

"Show him in, Yost."

There was movement in the hall behind Yost and then the most beautiful man Mary had ever seen entered the room.

Mary knew she should welcome him—even if he was deplorably tardy—rather than stare like a slack jawed yokel, but all she could do was gawk in wonder, as if a unicorn had pranced into their midst.

Beautiful was the only word for Miles Ingram, even though it was a word more commonly applied to fortunate women. And yet there was nothing feminine about the Earl of Avington.

For some reason Mary had expected him to be a slight, foppish man—like Sir Thomas had been.

She could not have been more wrong.

He was tall—at least a head taller than Mary's five-foot-two—and his broad shoulders tapered to narrow hips which were sheathed by skin-tight black pantaloons that showcased muscular thighs and well-formed calves.

Enormous, heavily lidded eyes a shade of blue somewhere between gentian and delphinium sat above high cheekbones, his dark blond lashes so long she could see them even from where she stood. Mary's own lashes were short and spiky. Indeed, the words *short* and *spiky* were probably perfect to describe her personality, too.

Mary realized her mouth was open and closed it, clamping her lips tightly to keep inappropriate sounds or drool from slipping out.

She cut a glance at Lady Sedgewick; the other woman wore her usual cool expression, seemingly untouched by the man's godlike appearance.

Did the countess have poor vision? Could she see *at all?*

Lord Avington's lips curved into a smile that robbed Mary of any remaining breath as he strode toward her mother, a tower of masculine loveliness who moved with an easy grace that was painful to behold.

Hysterical laughter simmered inside her. Good Lord! What could Lady Sedgewick have been thinking to bring such a paragon of physical perfection here to court her? Was she having a laugh at their expense? At *Mary's* expense? This man could not *possibly* be interested in marrying somebody like her!

Indeed, if he was going to marry anyone, it should be the countess, herself. The two of them together were almost blinding in their magnificence, two golden gods, both entirely at ease in themselves and comfortable with their place in the world. Mary had never seen a woman with more confidence than Lady Sedgewick and yet she *knew* the woman was dirt poor, not to mention long past her first prayers and probably older than Mary.

As for the earl...

Well, she'd never seen such a vision of male perfection before, not even her cousin Reginald—who until that moment been the most handsome man of her acquaintance—could approach this man for sheer flawlessness.

Mary swallowed the copious amounts of moisture flooding her mouth and widened her stance slightly, as if to brace herself.

Even if Avington was a babbling lunatic, he could marry any woman he wished—probably women who were *already* married flung themselves at him. Why, every heiress in England would prostrate herself at his feet, even without his title. Just what had—

"Miss Barnett?"

While she'd been working herself into breathless hysteria the blond god had come to a halt in front of her, his understated elegance making the over-bright gold leaf and rich plum sitting room look like it was trying too hard, which it was.

A slight frown marred his smooth brow, telling her it wasn't the first time he'd said her name.

"What?" she blurted rudely, vaguely aware of her mother flinching in her peripheral vision.

"I was just saying how pleased I am to meet you and your family."

It was difficult to look directly at him and she fought the impulse to shield her eyes.

"Er, yes," she mumbled. "The pleasure is ours."

And then he made it even worse by bestowing the same blinding smile he'd given her mother as he took her hand and bowed over it, his sculpted lips coming nowhere near her naked fingers before he released them.

"I apologize for my late arrival, I'm afraid I was held up."

Mary took shelter in behavior that had served her well over the years, both to hide her natural shyness and also to mask her insecurity: she launched an attack.

"You encountered highwaymen, my lord?"

The earl gave a startled laugh. "I beg your pardon?"

"You said you were *held up* I assume you meant you were accosted by highwaymen."

The room was utterly silent.

Jenny watched in wide-eyed wonder and Mary swore that amusement lurked behind Lady Sedgewick's cool gray eyes, while Mary's mother looked as if she were being physically tortured.

As for the beautiful creature standing before her? Well, he simply grinned: an easy, natural grin that transformed him from an angel into a something even more compelling—a *mischievous* angel, a cherub all grown up with a square, chiseled jaw and lustrous blond hair. Good humor danced in his ridiculously blue eyes and his full lips quirked up at both corners, as if he enjoyed being raked down by a scarred, long-in-the-tooth, waspish cit.

He leaned closer and Mary's heart flipped and flopped like a landed fish.

"I *wish* I could claim to have been set upon by footpads on my way to Russell Square but I'm afraid the truth is quite lowering. You see, I scorched my last decent neckcloth—a whopping burn right in the center of it. I couldn't even nip out to purchase a new one because all the shops were closed."

The earl fingered an exquisite snow-white confection at his throat and gave Mary a conspiratorial smile that had an effect not dissimilar to staring into a blast furnace at one of her father's foundries.

"I must confess it is never easy borrowing a replacement from the fellows who live at my lodgings." His eyes twinkled. "You see, in a house full of impecunious bachelors, linens are often the innocent victims of carelessly wielded irons."

Mrs. Barnett and Jenny chortled and even Mary couldn't resist smiling. Not only did he not bother hiding his poverty, but he also took the sting out of her shrewish question with his gracious response.

He had lovely manners. Quite the loveliest she'd ever seen. They matched his lovely person.

Mary had a sudden urge to cry.

Chapter 5

Miles swore he'd felt Mary Barnett's irritation out in the hallway before the butler had opened the door. He couldn't blame her. He loathed unpunctual behavior, especially as he was usually the one inconvenienced by it. A dancing master had very little right to expect timeliness from the people who employed him.

On first glance, Miss Barnett did not appear much older than her sister. Indeed, her small stature and slender build only served to emphasize the impression of youth. Her personality, however, was anything but waiflike.

While her sister and mother had accepted his smile and apology, she had held his feet to the fire, staring boldly up at him with eyes as green and hard as agates, although that description didn't really do them justice. They were a brilliant green that reminded Miles of stained glass on a bright day. Her gaze was piercing, all the more compelling for coming from such a diminutive person.

Her diminutive size was the only characteristic Miss Barnett shared with her sister, who was a dark-haired, dark-eyed little beauty who resembled their mother.

Mary Barnett was fair and freckled and had the sort of skin that seemed finer grained than other peoples. Her green eyes were enormous in her cat-like face and fringed with short, spiky lashes that were almost too pale to be visible.

And then there was her hair, which could not be described with elegant words such as auburn or russet. No, it was the unapologetically red orange of a raging inferno. It had been plaited and coiled into a heavy crown that shone like polished copper and overwhelmed her delicate features.

Despite its brutal imprisonment, corkscrews of color had worked their way free, the strands forming a fiery halo that made her stern, sharp features bear more than a passing resemblance to a Renaissance martyr.

Miss Barnett employed no curls or other devices to hide the rough-textured, crepe-like skin that emerged from the high neck ruff of her gown and covered the left side of her neck. While most of her face had been spared burns, the fire had licked at the smooth skin of her jaw and cheek.

She wore no glove to conceal the rippled skin of her left hand, a hand which was barely half the size of Miles's own. The skin on her other hand was smooth, her nails neatly trimmed and rounded, and a smudge of ink darkened her right index finger.

She was all sharp angles and burning intensity. And right now, that intensity was aimed at *Miles.*

Mrs. Barnett broke the awkward silence. "Shall we proceed to dinner?" Her eyes darted between Miles and her eldest daughter, as if Mary Barnett was a barrel of gunpowder that required careful handling.

"May I?" Miles offered Miss Barnett his arm for the short journey to the dining room and was more than a little surprised when she accepted.

The walked in silence to a vast cavern of a room that was dominated by an immense black table. Although the walls had their share of artwork in appropriate locations, the house—at least the parts Miles had seen—felt like a seashell that had no inhabitant. And yet this room, with its monstrous table and buffet, felt strangely... homey.

Miss Barnett noticed him staring at the table. "It is made from parrot coal—or you may have heard it referred to as cannel coal."

Miles ran a hand over the slick black surface. "I've never seen such a thing."

"If you look closely, you can see shells and the skeletal remains of fish."

"It is beautiful," he said truthfully, earning his first genuine smile from her.

"Thank you, my father had it made especially for Coal House. There is a bench in the garden that is also made from cannel."

Coal House. It was a name that made no apologies for itself or its owner, and it was as much a newcomer to Mayfair as its master had been. The enormous mansion straddled the ruins of two older properties—perhaps even three—and Miles felt a bit affronted on behalf of those demolished and already forgotten houses, which hadn't been grand enough for the departed Lucas Barnett to deign to occupy.

Miles shook himself, annoyed by the odd notion. He, more than anyone, should have no nostalgia for decrepit old buildings. Lord! The state of Avington Castle was enough to make him weep.

Whoever had arranged the seating—he suspected Mrs. Barnett—had possessed the sense to cluster everyone at one end of the table rather than stretching the group from end to end.

Miles was seated at the head with Jenny Barnett on his right and Miss Barnett on his left.

Dinner progressed as smoothly as could be expected between complete strangers who'd assembled for business of a most delicate nature. Freddie, an expert at generating and guiding conversation even in the most awkward circumstances, rose to the occasion.

"Mrs. Barnett told me you spent last summer in Brighton," she asked the younger Miss Barnett. "What were your impressions?"

Jennifer Barnett was sweet and unspoiled and her eyes sparkled under the countess's careful questioning.

As for her sister, Miss Barnett appeared to have recovered from her initial irritation and joined in the conversation if not as often as her mother and sister, certainly as pleasantly.

Mary Barnett was not a homely woman, but neither could a person call her pretty, even without the scarring. Her features—small and even—were unremarkable taken either by themselves or as a whole.

It was hard for Miles not to stare at her. Not because of her burns—although he knew they must have been agonizing—nor even because of her shocking orange hair and hard green eyes.

It wasn't her appearance so much as her *manner*—her vigor, for lack of a better word—that drew his gaze and was not something one encountered among the languid ladies of the *ton*, or people in general, for that matter.

Keen, cutting intelligence radiated from her like the unforgiving beam from a lighthouse lamp. When she fixed her bright green gaze directly on him Miles felt as though she was filleting away the bland layer of charm which insulated him from the world, the same way a layer of fat insulated a salmon from frigid waters.

It was a novel experience and not a comfortable one.

Men were fond of comparing women to flowers—beautiful as roses, sunny as daisies—if Miss Barnett were a flower, she would be a thistle: spiky and daunting and guarded.

"My lord?"

Miles turned from his contemplation of the forceful Miss Barnett to her younger sister, who was a cuddly bunny by comparison.

"Yes, Miss Barnett?"

Her fair cheeks blushed a becoming pink and her large chocolate eyes widened at his smile. It was a reaction Miles was accustomed to receiving from the opposite sex all his life. Well, except from Miss Mary Barnett.

"Lady Sedgewick said you were acquainted with the Duke of Wellington. Could you—could you tell us what he is like?"

"I wouldn't say I *know* him, Miss Barnett, although I do know what he was like to serve under. He was an exacting, but fair, commander. He could be abrupt at times, but he usually had adequate provocation." Indeed, Miles thought it a miracle how much the man had accomplished while fighting political battles in London at the same time he was fighting actual battles in the Peninsula.

"Is it true what they say about him being impervious to harm?"

"Oh, Jenny," Mrs. Barnett chided with a laugh. "Don't be silly—of course he could be hurt."

Miles smiled at her. "It is true that His Grace was fortunate in avoiding serious harm while, at the same time, not hesitating to put himself in great danger."

Miles didn't share that it had been the general's willingness to expose himself to danger in pursuit of the cause that had inspired him to take risks that had led to his being captured twice during the war.

To give Wellington his due, the General had not clapped Miles on the back and commended his bravery as the others had when he'd volunteered for the disastrous mission that had ended with not just captivity, but torture for Miles and death for his fellow soldiers.

No, Old Douro had given Miles a grim and serious look before saying, "May God go with you, Captain."

If God had gone with him on that endless ride through the dead and dying Miles had certainly seen no sign of him. In fact—

"My lord? *My lord?*"

Miles shook himself and looked up to find the others staring at him.

"Ah, I beg your pardon, ma'am." He smiled; the jaunty, charming expression as natural to him as breathing. "I apologize—gathering wool, you know."

Freddie's brow was creased with concern, Mrs. Barnett looked embarrassed, her youngest daughter, confused. And Miss Mary Barnett? Well, she was looking at him—for the first time that night—with an expression of actual interest.

Mrs. Barnett filled the awkward silence. "We shall leave you to your port, my lord."

Miles opened his mouth to protest the ritual—rather ridiculous under the circumstances—but then realized he could use half an hour to collect himself for whatever came next.

***

Mary listened idly while Jenny and Lady Sedgewick discussed the latest fashions from Paris, her mind back in the dining room.

She'd been unable to stop looking at Lord Avington during dinner. Had he noticed?

Probably not. He must be accustomed to people—especially women—staring at him. He was so attractive it was bloody ridiculous.

Mary smiled a little at the curse word. She loved using vulgar language, even if it was only in the privacy of her mind.

Her father had cursed like a sailor in front of her, although he'd tried to curb his crudity whenever he'd been around his wife.

"Yer Da's like a coin that's already been minted, luv. There ain't no changin' me now," he'd say after cursing at bad weather thwarting one of his ships, or the cost of timber, but never at a person—not even the lowliest employee. Lucas Barnett was a gentle soul when it came to his workers, if not to the titans of industry who sat across the bargaining table from him.

Mary couldn't help smiling as she thought about what her Da would have made of the male confection currently drinking port in his dining room.

She had inherited her looks from her father, although his hair had been more red than orange, his eyes blue rather than green. But he'd been small and wiry and angular, his skin as freckled as hers.

For all that he'd been born in the gutter, Lucas Barnett had purchased only the best, even though he'd not possessed the palate to appreciate it. So the bottle of port Lord Avington was enjoying right now probably cost more than a butler made in five years.

Her father would have been thrilled that his money had purchased the interest of an earl for his daughter. Indeed, he would have been tickled to have an aristocrat in his house, his only regret likely that Lord Avington was not a marquess or duke.

He wouldn't have cared that his lordship had only deigned to step foot into Coal House because of Mary's money, and it wouldn't have bothered him that the magnificent earl would never have given Mary a second glance if she's been poor.

While Lucas Barnett might have agreed that it was money that brought Mary and Lord Avington together, he was a romantic to the core and would have argued that what became of their acquaintance was up to them.

"Yer heart was burnt far worse than yer body, Mary. Ye think no man can luv ye 'cause of a bit o' rough skin. But ye were made for luv— just like yer Da. Yer loyal and fierce and passionate and ye need a loving soul to gentle ye. There be a man out there who can handle the reins easy like, luv. Jest make sure ye give him a fair chance when he comes 'round.'"

Jenny laughed at something and Mary glanced up at the merry sound. Her sister positively sparkled as she chatted with the countess. Jenny would be a natural success—a diamond of the first water—if she could only have the chance.

A chance the Earl of Avington could give her.

Louisa Barnett looked on fondly, her mother's gaze lacking the suspicion and frustration it did whenever she looked at Mary.

Mary didn't blame her mother. Jenny was a daughter Louise understood; Mary was a daughter who should have been born a son. She was an *unnatural female* who loved the same things her had father had loved—not slippers and gowns, but coal and ledgers and shipping schedules.

"Yer Ma luvs ye, Mary, she just don't understand ye." Her father would say whenever he relayed a message from his wife, who had often used her husband as an intermediary with their willful, prickly daughter.

Mary knew that if she'd been a poor girl—or the daughter of some other father—she would have needed to behave more in line with societal expectations. As it was, she was wealthy and the mistress of herself and her world. Her father had always wanted her to take over his businesses and had trained her for that eventuality. But he'd been a stubborn old goat and had wanted to have his cake and eat it, too. Hence the insulting and aggravating condition in his will—a condition that made her sick to her stomach even to think about it. As if his demand that she marry hadn't been bad enough, he'd forced her to take an aristocrat as a husband. He'd known how much she'd hated her one Season and had seen that she'd avoided *ton* entertainments in the years after, and yet he'd pitchforked her into that world, regardless.

Marriage to Sir Thomas Lowery, who'd been a gambler, rake, and fool, would have been tolerable as Mary could have ignored the baronet as easily as he would have ignored her. They would have lived separate lives and rarely crossed paths.

But the man in her dining room...

Mary's mouth flooded with moisture at the mere thought of the earl. She was, to her enduring shame, as susceptible to masculine beauty as any woman. No matter how much she might wish otherwise, it would not be possible to ignore Lord Miles Avington.

She'd had her inquiry agent investigate the earl. He was not rakish, profligate, or a fool. Indeed, he was the only peer she'd ever heard of who worked to support himself.

After seeing him—or after *he*'d seen *her*, to be precise— Mary knew it would be Jenny that Avington would want to court, regardless of what Lady Sedgewick had said. And who would blame him? Jenny wasn't just lovely, she was also sweet, loving, and kind. Exactly the sort of woman any man would want.

The very opposite of Mary in every way.

Mary would not make a fuss about the earl changing his mind. As far as she was concerned, they could all behave as if courting Jenny had been his intention from the beginning.

And she could post her proposal letter to Sir James first thing in the morning.

The door opened and her thoughts fled like startled mice as the earl entered the room.

It had been only thirty minutes since Mary last saw him, but already she'd forgotten the effect of his masculine beauty. At least on her. She tried to see past his astounding façade to the person behind it, but he was simply too dazzling.

It wasn't only his person that was lovely, his behavior both before and during dinner had been easy and gracious. He'd conversed on any number of subjects during their meal and had appeared to greatly enjoy himself even though Mary knew the conversation was hardly scintillating.

He was courteous and kind and would make an excellent husband for Jenny, even though at thirty-four he was more than fifteen years her senior. But then that had been the age difference between Mary's mother and father, and their arranged marriage had turned into a loving one, although she knew her mother had never fallen in love with Lucas Barnett.

The earl gently lured Jenny to the piano, offering to turn pages for her. He behaved as if her music was a gift better than diamonds or gold and she blossomed under his warm gaze.

Lord Avington was the type of man who made every woman he looked at feel like a queen.

Mary wondered if all that sunny, good-natured smiling and laughing was an act.

It had to be. After all, could anyone really be that happy?

Chapter 6

W ould you care for a stroll in the garden, Miss Barnett?"
Mary had been chatting with Lady Sedgewick and
hadn't heard the earl approach.

All eyes were on her while she goggled up at Avington. "Er, yes, that would be pleasant," she said, loathing the faint tremor in her voice.

"Here, Mary." Her mother hastened toward her, removing her own shawl and arranged it on Mary's shoulders without waiting for permission. The wrap was a lovely black velvet shot through with threads of peacock blue and gold. Mary thought it looked incongruous with her severe dark green evening gown, but to reject it would be churlish.

The earl extended his arm and Mary placed her right hand on his sleeve, wondering if he had deliberately engineered it so he would be looking at her unblemished profile which, if not exactly attractive, was at least not the stuff of nightmares.

Why was she even thinking of such things? She'd come to terms with her appearance years ago. And if he was disgusted by her scars, well… who wasn't? She didn't wish to look at burnt flesh either and avoided mirrors for that very reason.

Not only was there a full moon in the sky, but festive colored lanterns glowed along the garden paths and around the fountain in the center.

Mary smiled; her mother had created a romantic mood for this exact purpose. Was Louisa disappointed the handsome lord had asked her plain, damaged daughter to walk with him instead of her favorite child?

Well, she needn't worry; Mary had every intention of releasing the earl from any commitment he might feel he'd made to her. Now that he had seen Jenny, he would have come to his senses and changed his mind about which sister to court.

"Are you warm enough?" the earl asked, his voice as refined and attractive as every other part of him.

"Yes, quite." More than warm, especially on the side of her body closest to his.

He loomed over her and she hadn't realized how tall he was until he'd offered his arm. He gave the impression of lightness and grace and yet he was so… substantial. Indeed, her head did not reach his shoulders, which were broad and powerful in his closely fitted, if shabby, coat.

Once they were off the terrace and away from the house Mary stopped, removed her hand from his sleeve, and turned to face him.

The lantern nearest them had a vermillion glass cover and she looked up to find him transformed; his eyes an almost violet blue, his pale skin washed a dull red. The light created interesting, sinister hollows that made him resemble a different sort of angel—a fallen one.

Mary was disgusted by her foolish whimsy. He was no angel, fallen or otherwise. Any changes to his appearance were nothing but a trick of light and shadow.

"I should like to speak bluntly, my lord."

"I daresay you are quite good at that, Miss Barnett," he said, his voice laced with humor.

"I hope you will not be insulted, but I had one of my employees, Mr. Albert Ross—a man I know to be discreet and honest—gather some information about you."

His lips pulled up at the corners, giving a flash of white, even teeth. Mary's stomach tightened into an even smaller, harder knot at this further proof of his perfection.

"No, I am not insulted, nor am I surprised." His amused acceptance made Mary feel dirty, something she'd never experienced before when investigating a potential business partner's background.

Because that is what this was, wasn't it? A business arrangement: Jenny's money for the earl's name, social influence, and consequence, which, Mary had to admit, was not insubstantial even given his poverty.

Mary squared her shoulders; she would *not* feel guilty about investigating this man's character and past.

"Tell me, Miss Barnett," he said, "what information did you unearth?"

"In short, I learned you are an acceptable candidate for marriage."

He laughed. "Well, that's a relief."

Mary frowned, unamused by his levity. "The blood of your family is as blue as a person can possess, without being royal, and there has been an Earl of Avington for over three hundred years and a barony far longer." She paused, but he merely stared down at her, his posture relaxed, his face unreadable.

"I learned your brother was well-liked and a responsible landlord to his tenants, although his coffers had been too depleted by your father."

"What of me, Miss Barnett? What did you learn about Miles Ingram?"

"You joined the army in 1806 and were twice taken prisoner, you were held for nine months the first time and several weeks the second, during which time you were t-tortured."

He nodded. "Go on."

"You received medals for bravery in each case and sold your commission after the second instance. You returned to England but did not reenter polite society." And here came the part Mary found most interesting. "For almost five years you've been earning your living as a dancing instructor—part of that time at the Stefani Academy for Young Ladies. You only accept clients from the merchant class, thereby lessening chances of you being recognized by any members of the *ton*. You've lived frugally and quietly but now that you've inherited the title you must marry because your family's need for funds is immediate."

"Yes, that is all true."

Mary was relieved that he did not seem offended by her investigation nor her impertinent observations. That was just as well because she was about to get even more impertinent.

"Do you wish for a brief courtship, my lord?"

He chuckled and the rich, velvety sound swirled inside her and settled low in her belly. Really, the man was a menace to her peace of mind; the sooner she got away from him, the better.

"Yes, Miss Barnett, the briefer, the better."

While a speedy marriage was necessary for Mary, it was not what she wanted for her little sister. Jenny deserved to enjoy a lengthy, romantic courtship, regardless of how desperate for money Avington was.

"I should like Jenny to enjoy at least the semblance of a courtship before she weds. She is very young and a certain amount of wooing would please her greatly."

His eyes widened and he laughed.

Mary was not accustomed to being laughed at and found she did not care for the feeling. She drew herself up to her full height. "I'm afraid I do not see the humor in this, my lord. If it is money you need before—"

He lightly laid his forefinger across her lips.

Mary was so stunned by the intimate gesture that her brain temporarily seized with shock; nobody had *ever* touched her so casually in her life!

She'd just opened her mouth to administer a blistering set down when he removed his hand and smiled—a rather hard smile that was unlike any of the others that had graced his gorgeous face thus far—and then he compounded his disquieting behavior by taking both of her hands in his.

Mary gasped at his continued affrontery. "My lord! What do you think—"

"Shh." He gave her hands a gentle squeeze and—to her utter stupefaction—she stopped talking.

Just like a master bringing a dog to heel.

The thought was an arrow that pierced her surprise, and yet she seemed unable to do anything about it.

"It appears there must have been some mistake, Miss Barnett," Lord Avington said. "I thought Freddie, er, Lady Sedgewick, made it clear that it was *you* I came to meet tonight."

Freddie? The thought of that exquisite creature—Lady Sedgewick—possessing such an incongruous pet name momentarily distracted her.

"Miss Barnett?" He lifted his right hand—still holding both of hers with his left—and tilted her chin until she was forced to meet his eyes. "Did you hear me?"

Mary knew her mouth was open but couldn't seem to close it. Never in all her days had she been so casually handled by a stranger. And yet she could not make herself pull away.

Instead, she said through strangely numb lips, "Yes, Lady Sedgewick mentioned that it was me you were coming to see."

"Then why are you bringing up your sister?"

"Surely you have changed your mind after tonight?"

"What happened tonight?" he asked, his distracting thumb still resting lightly on her chin.

Before she could answer, his shapely lips curved into a smile of comprehension. "Ah, I see. You thought that I'd changed my mind because you twitted me about being late." He chuckled softly. "I will not turn tail and run at the first sign of danger. I am made of much sterner stuff, ma'am. Besides, I, too, abhor unpunctual behavior. You were right to take me to task."

And then he released both her chin and hands, leaving her feeling strangely bereft.

Mary shook her head, both to clear it and in disagreement. "No, not because of that," she said, stepping back to put some distance between them. "I thought you would change your mind because of *me.*"

His forehead furrowed in confusion. "Because of you?"

A sudden gust of anger blew the fog from her brain. Why was he forcing her to articulate the obvious? Was that his flaw—he lacked sense? Beautiful but no brain?

"I thought you'd changed your mind because of my appearance, my lord. Because of my *burns.*"

His eyebrows, which had been arched, now dipped low, flicking upward at the ends, making him look like a confused angel. "But I knew of your injuries before coming to dinner, Miss Barnett."

"I daresay you'd *heard* about them, but now you've seen me." And not even all of her, at that—but enough to guess just how damaged she was beneath her clothing.

His gaze moved over her burned cheek and neck and he did not so much as flinch at what he saw.

Good Lord he was polished! Or was he just so thick he couldn't put two and two together?

"I am sorry for the pain you must have endured, Miss Barnett, but I am not shocked or disgusted by your burns. Seeing you—and your sister—has not changed my preference in any way."

Yet again, he'd rendered her speechless. Was he lying? Brainless? Or did he have some other, less obvious, and more nefarious reason to prefer her over Jenny?

"Why me, my lord?" Mary waved a hand at his person. "Given your appearance and connections you could have any woman—wealthy or not—to be your wife. Your family coffers are stricken but your reputation—both yours *and* your family's—are sterling. Even I know that teaching dance would not harm your reputation so much as enhance it. It would be viewed as a charming eccentricity, an amusing anecdote you could share over dinner. So, please, I must know the truth: why me?"

"Freddie told me you didn't particularly wish for marriage but that you might consider it for your sister's sake. Is that true?"

Mary was momentarily surprised by his answer. "Yes," she admitted, not quite ready to tell him the whole truth.

"I also do not wish to marry but must do so for my family. It seems fortuitous that neither of us viewed marriage as a matter of romance, but rather expedience. I've only been in your presence a few hours but I can already see you are practical, which is another reason I believe we might suit. I want a more mature wife—a woman who will not expect things from me that I either cannot or don't wish to give."

"What things would those be, my lord?"

"Love, Miss Barnett. At least not the romantic sort."

Mary was more than a little taken aback by his declaration, although she couldn't have said why. Maybe because he looked so much like a romantic hero from a fairy tale that it surprised her to learn he wasn't one.

He grimaced at whatever it was he saw on her face. "Blast! I *have* put my foot in it, haven't I? I'm terribly sorry. You said you wanted blunt speaking and—"

"I'm not insulted, my lord, just surprised. I do want plain speaking; it is the only kind I like. The main the reason I've put off marrying for so long is that I *dreaded* awkward attempts at wooing and courtship and protestations of love."

His broad shoulders sagged slightly "Ah, I am pleased to hear it."

"Perhaps we might take a few minutes while we are alone and discuss matters?"

"Of course," he said. "Let us sit—it is very rude of me to keep you standing while I chatter on."

He was so *polite*. No doubt what he was really thinking was that he hadn't intended to haggle like fishmongers—either sitting or standing—in the middle of a garden only a few hours after meeting.

"There is a bench just through here," Mary said, leading him toward a seat that was surrounded by rose bushes.

Although it was large enough for her and Jenny to sit on without touching, it was a much cozier space with Lord Avington beside her. Not only did his muscular thigh press against hers, but Mary was close enough that she could smell an intoxicating mingling of the port he'd just consumed, a hint of cologne, and freshly starched—unsinged—linen.

She allowed herself a moment to savor the scent of him before clearing her throat. "I propose we approach this like any other business transaction and lay out our terms."

"Like bargaining for a horse?" He smiled down at her.

"Having never bargained for horses I cannot say," she said curtly, once again feeling as if he were laughing at her. "Shall we just agree that if there is no meeting of the minds then tonight will be an end to it?"

"Very well. Ladies first." He crossed his arms, and the action drew her gaze to his nearest hand, which was broad across the back yet shapely. Something about its sheer masculinity made her belly tighten.

"Miss Barnett?"

"Er," she wrenched her eyes away from his hand and looked up. "What was that?"

"I said you should lay out your terms."

"But if I go first, then you will have the advantage, my lord."

His blond brows arched and he raised his chin, the action turning his beautiful features haughty. "It is the gentlemanly thing to do."

"I am *not* a gentleman and disclosing my terms first will mean you have all the information when you list *your* terms."

"Good God! You're serious, aren't you?"

Mary pursed her lips.

"Very well, *I'll* go first, then."

"That wouldn't be fair to *you*."

He stared at her, his pleasant, courteous expression crumbling around the edges.

Mary was intensely curious to see what lay beneath his façade, but he quickly adjusted his social mask.

He sighed. "It would appear that our *negotiations* have broken down even before they got started, Miss Barnett."

"Do you have a coin?"

He snorted. "Are you going to *charge* me to hear your terms?"

That made her smile. "No, I will toss it to see which of us goes first. Do you have one?"

"A coin is about all I have," he muttered and then slid a hand beneath the snug lapel of his fitted coat and dug around before coming out with a coin, which he placed on her outstretched palm.

The metal was warm from the heat of his body and the weight of the coin was unusual. She angled it so that moonlight reflected off the surface.

"Is that Greek writing?"

"I should hope so, as it is a Greek coin."

"Why do you carry a Greek coin in your pocket?"

"It is my lucky piece."

Mary raised her eyebrows. "You believe in luck?"

"Doesn't everyone?"

"I don't."

"Not at all? Not a hare's foot? Some special piece of jewelry, some—"

"Nothing."

"I'm not sure I believe you, Miss Barnett."

"There is no such thing as luck, my lord. Or rather I should say people are responsible for making their own luck."

"Why that is utterly—"

"Logical?"

"I was going to say grim."

"Why grim?"

"Because such an outlook removes chance and serendipity from life."

"If fewer people believed in *luck* there would be far less reckless gambling and concomitant misery, my lord."

His lips tightened slightly, remind her that his father had beggared his family with exactly that sort of behavior.

"Touché," was all he said.

Mary shut up about *luck* and tossed the coin. "You may call it, my lord."

"I'll take the bird, Miss Barnett."

The coin landed with a soft *thwap* in her palm and she peered at it and scowled. "Hell and damnation."

He laughed. "*What* did you say?"

Mary ignored him, relieved it was too dark for him to see her blushing skin. With all her freckles, it was a gruesome sight.

"You win." She looked up to find him grinning. "Gloating is very bad form, my lord."

He rearranged his features into a mask of seriousness. "So then, *I* will go first."

"Perhaps you misunderstood, my lord? Listing your terms first will give me an unfair advantage."

"Quite right."

Mary gave a disgusted snort. "You are *such* a gentleman."

He smirked. "To the end." He faced forward, took his chiseled chin between his thumb and forefinger, and stroked thoughtfully. "Hmmm. Terms, terms, terms." His expression was almost pained—as if he were not accustomed to thinking so hard. His eyes slid toward her and he laughed.

"What is so funny?" she demanded.

"You."

"What do you mean?"

"You look so impatient—and suspicious.

Mary narrowed her eyes. "I'm waiting, my lord."

His teasing manner fell away. "My *terms* are very simple, Miss Barnett." He laughed, but this time the sound lacked any humor and it seemed to be directed at himself, rather than Mary. "Actually, there is only one: I need pots of money."

Mary waited for him to say more, but he merely sat there.

"Pots of money," she repeated flatly.

"Yes. Enough to take care of my family and tenants and make repairs and improvements to Avington Castle and its attendant tenant farms, all of which have been neglected for years." He cocked his head at her. "You are a woman of business, Miss Barnett—tell me, is *pots of money* a proper contractual term?"

She ignored his question. "And that is all you would require from me, pots of money?"

"After all that squabbling about who was to go first, I'm afraid I only have one *term*." He chuckled mirthlessly and said, "It is your turn, Miss Barnett."

Mary took a deep breath; it was time to confess her real motivation for marriage. "I don't know how much you know about me—"

"As I have neither the inclination nor the money to hire an inquiry agent, I know very little about you, Miss Barnett. Why don't you tell me what *you* would like me to know?"

Mary's face heated at the mockery in his voice, which had a distinctly hard edge to it.

Well, she'd wondered if the man ever did anything but smile politely and now she knew there was steel beneath his handsome exterior.

Her Da had always said Mary could goad a stone into an argument. It appeared she could also provoke the most courteous gentleman she'd ever met into icy anger.

"It is quite simple, my lord. I need your social status to aid my sister next year so that she might have a more successful Season." Mary hesitated and then plunged onward. "I also need a husband for business reasons."

"I don't understand?"

"Er, this will take a bit of explaining," she said. "Before my father's death we operated the company together. For the past two years I've managed it all myself—from his shipyards to his mines to everything in between. In other words, my lord, you should be aware that I have been, and will continue to be after I am married, an active rather than passive business owner."

"I can't imagine you being passive in any situation, Miss Barnett."

Mary studied his faintly amused expression and considered asking him just what he meant by that comment, but decided she didn't want to know.

"What Lady Sedgewick told you—that I'm contemplating marriage to improve my sister's social opportunities—is only part of the truth The other reason is that I need to marry to satisfy a condition in my father's will."

"What sort of condition?"

"If I want to retain control of his businesses, I need to marry within two years of his death." She cleared her throat. "The second year will be up in less than six weeks."

He chuckled dryly. "You've certainly left matters to the last minute, haven't you?"

Mary bristled at his amusement. "Actually, I'd been in negotiations with another gentleman who unfortunately passed away."

"Sir Thomas Lowery?"

Mary's jaw sagged. "How did you know that?"

"I wasn't certain until just now that the woman he was, er, *negotiating* with was you."

"You were a friend of his?"

"Hardly. But Sir Thomas could be quite indiscreet when he was in his cups." He hesitated and then added, "Which he was almost all the time."

Mary ground her teeth. "So, my situation is common knowledge, then?"

"I wouldn't say *common*, but people know."

If Lowery weren't already dead, Mary would probably kill him.

"So, your father has hinged your inheritance on marriage?"

Mary carefully considered her next words. She had never told Sir Thomas the entire truth, but... Well, why hold anything back at this point?

"My father left both me and my sister considerable heiresses. But if we don't marry, we will only ever receive quarterly allowances. Very, very generous allowances," she admitted, "but still allowances. There is a special clause in my case. If I don't marry, ownership of all the shares in my father's companies—the value of which is far greater than my inheritance—reverts to my father's nephew, who will only have to pay a quarter of every year's profits into a trust fund to maintain control."

The earl looked genuinely shocked. "Why would your father do such a thing?"

"It was his greatest wish that I marry." Even if it was against Mary's will. "He knew that if he left my inheritance in my hands that I would have enough capital to start my own businesses." She snorted softly. "He is the one who taught me how to think, after all." And he'd done such a good job with his will that there was no escape for her other than doing exactly what he wanted.

Or at least *mostly* what he wanted.

"Who is this nephew—er, if you don't mind me asking?"

She *did* mind. She minded all this idiocy, but it wasn't his fault that her private business was apparently grist for the *ton* rumor mill. "My cousin—Reginald Cooper—is already a minor partner in several of the companies." Mary hesitated and then asked, "Do you know him? Reginald has always aspired to move in *tonnish* circles, with some small measure of success."

"No, I do not, but then it's been years since I've socialized. So," he said, "if I understand you correctly, you stand to lose a great deal of money if you don't marry."

"Yes. And control."

"And control," he repeated, his lips twitching into a faint smile.

Mary bristled at his amusement. "I can see that you think that is what this is all about—control—but there is more to it than that. Reginald is a follower rather than an innovator. As arrogant as it might sound, my lord, I am a far better manager than Reginald could ever be."

"I believe you, Miss Barnett."

Mary was annoyed by the flush of pleasure she felt at his words.

"So," the earl said, "you've mentioned your reasons for marrying—your sister and your father's will—but you haven't told me your, er, terms?"

This was the part she was least looking forward to—not that any part of the discussion was anything other than distasteful.

Mary had no intention of mentioning that Lucas Barnett had stipulated a titled husband—why give him such an unfair bargaining advantage—but the other part of her father's requirement she could not, unfortunately, ignore.

"My father wanted the man I married to assume an equal share—and responsibility—in the companies."

The earl's eyes widened. "Are you saying—"

"You and I would operate them as equals."

"But I don't know the first thing about shipyards or mines!" He laughed. "Other than how to ride on a ship and burn coal, that is."

"I suspected that, my lord. I, on the other hand, have spent a good deal of my life learning the intricacies of my father's various enterprises."

His humor dissipated at whatever he saw on her face—likely poorly suppressed rage.

"As you've requested plain speaking, Miss Barnett, and given the conditions of your father's will, I can't help but wonder why you wouldn't seek a husband who is a man of business?"

"I have no intention of sharing management of the companies with anyone. If we were to marry, I would want to oversee all business decisions without any input from you and would require a promise to that effect."

He gave an unamused snort. "Is that why you've decided to choose a husband from among the *ton*? Because you believe we don't care to sully our hands with business and would be more likely to give you such a promise?"

"Can you deny that aristocratic men view themselves above both work and commerce, my lord?"

"I work and have done for five years, Miss Barnett. Some would argue that what I did on the Continent, along with thousands of my aristocratic brethren, was also a bit like *work*."

His scorn felt twice as cutting because it was well deserved.

It was time to tell the truth before things devolved any further. "My father's will also requires that I marry a gentleman. Specifically, one with a title."

His eyebrows shot up. "Ahhh. That explains why you entertained marrying Lowery. I must admit I thought your wits had gone begging to consider such a man."

Any remorse she'd been feeling dissipated at his sarcasm. "And you are such a better choice, I gather?"

"I might not know anything about ship building or mining, but at least you could count on me not throwing your father's businesses away at some gaming hell."

"That is actually my first term, my lord."

"What? My ignorance on the subjects of shipbuilding and mining?"

"Of course not," she said witheringly. "I meant that I would require you to leave the management of the companies to my sole discretion."

"But you said your father's will stipulated—"

"I know what I said."

"I see. You wish to contravene that clause—or at least the spirit of it."

Mary nodded.

"So, you would want me to do what, then? Sign an agreement that I'd keep out of your affairs? No," he said, answering his own question before she could speak. "Such a document would show you were trying to undermine your father's will."

Not to mention that such a document would have no legal effect given that wives were the chattel of their husbands, but Mary left that unpleasant truth unspoken.

Instead, she said, "I wouldn't require a document. Just your word on the matter, my lord."

"My word?" he repeated. "What's to stop me from seizing control of everything once we are married and locking you away in a sanatorium?"

Mary shivered as she met his suddenly hard gaze. "Nothing but your word as a gentleman."

"This hardly seems like the decision of a hardnosed businessman—er, businesswoman."

"Sneer all you want, my lord. What other choice do I have?"

He suddenly laughed. "Lord, I'll wager Lowery leapt at that offer, didn't he?"

Mary unclenched her jaw just enough to say, "Just like you, he had no interest in engaging in business."

Avington snorted but didn't comment. Instead, he crossed his arms, stretched his long legs out in front of him, and seemed to sink into thought.

His casual pose displayed his excellent figure to perfection and Mary couldn't resist the opportunity to ogle.

As she shamelessly gorged on his well-formed muscular body she couldn't help noticing the condition of his clothing. His garments were clean and meticulously maintained, but everything—from his highly polished Hessians to his snugly fitted coat—was obviously far from new.

Not that it would have mattered if he'd dressed in a grain sack with a bucket on his head; the man was simply breathtaking.

Mary had been around handsome men before—her cousin Reginald was almost as physically perfect—but never had she been around a man who possessed such an engaging personality to go with his good looks.

He was so very *sunny* yet there were hints of something darker beneath his veneer of sophistication—like at the dinner table, when he'd talked about the war.

Just looking at him reminded Mary of how she used to feel going to *ton* functions where she'd find herself surrounded by men who were so much more polished, attractive, and at ease than she could ever be. As humiliating as those balls and parties had been, she'd found herself drawn to those beautiful, confident men as fatally as a moth was drawn to an open, killing, flame.

Marrying such a man would be a disaster—she knew that with every ounce of her being—and yet she could feel herself inventing reasons why it would be far wiser to align herself with Lord Avington than the elderly, stolid Sir James.

Mary allowed herself one last visual pass up and down his body, her hungry eyes lingering on his thighs, which were so tightly encased in black pantaloons that he might have painted them on his body.

The earl looked up from his thoughts and caught her gawking. "You must have known that Lowery would have forgotten all about his promises once he exceeded whatever allowance you gave him and he needed more money."

"And you wouldn't go back on *your* word, I presume?"

Rather than look insulted, he smiled. "No, I wouldn't."

"And how do I know that?"

"Because my word means something to me."

"And you think Lowery's word meant nothing to him?"

"I *know* it didn't." He sat up straighter, tucking his feet beneath the bench and depriving her of her spectacular view. "Lowery owed money to dozens of people, many of whom had once been his friends." He gave her a taunting smile. "Or didn't you employ an inquiry agent to poke around in his past as you did with mine?"

"For your information, I used the very same man to investigate Sir Thomas. I knew he had... problems." The last thing Mary wanted to confess was that she'd been desperate enough to overlook all the negative information that Ross had discovered because she'd been running out of time. But judging by Avington's smug smirk, he'd already guessed that for himself.

"How do I know you'd keep your word?" she asked, wanting to wipe that annoying grin from his face.

If anything, Avington looked even more amused by her rude question. "For one thing, I do not suffer from an addiction to hard spirits, reckless wagering, or cards. Nor do I owe money to half the *ton*."

"So, you would agree to leave the management of the companies to me, then?"

"No, I'm not saying that at all." He ignored her exasperated hiss and continued. "I'm saying that if I give you my word on something, you can rest assured I will keep it. As for the clause you are trying to circumvent; I could not agree to do something which would ignore a dying man's last wishes—even though I never met your father. And before you rip up at me," he said when she opened her mouth, "which I can see you are raring to do, let me explain."

"Fine," she said tightly. "Explain."

"I have no reservation against working. Nor do I look down upon business and commerce. If we were to marry, I would not only feel honor bound to abide by your father's wishes, but I might actually enjoy it."

"*You* would be interested in learning about ships and coal," she said, making no effort to hide her disbelief.

"I daresay I would find it quite stimulating."

"Stimulating."

"Yes, stimulating."

"You can't treat managing massive companies like a hobby, my lord. It isn't always easy or enjoyable, or—indeed—*stimulating* like horse racing or—or an afternoon at Gentleman Jackson's."

He grinned. "Oh, come now! Commercial endeavors cannot possibly be as stimulating as boxing, but certainly more stimulating than cocking or bear baiting."

Mary scowled. "You think the management of my father's businesses is a source of amusement, my lord?"

"No, I think the oversight of businesses which probably employ hundreds, if not thousands, of people is deadly serious, Miss Barnett. But I think your insistence on belittling and disparaging me is amusing. For a woman who wishes to marry in less than six weeks you certainly don't seem interested in facilitating your goal. Or are you speaking to me this way because I'm merely one of several applicants for the position?"

"That is hardly your affair," she shot back, irked beyond sense at his good humor.

Predictably, he laughed at her incivility. "True enough. So then, back to your terms."

"I don't see the point in continuing with our discussion when you have already rejected my first term."

"Don't I have the right to know *all* the terms?"

"To what end, my lord?"

"I need all the information if I am to make an intelligent decision."

Mary huffed. "I don't think—"

"Is this how you negotiate your shipping contracts, Miss Barnett? By folding at the first obstacle and running away from the table? Isn't there such a thing as proposal and counterproposal?"

She gritted her teeth. "Fine. My second term is that I *propose* a fifty-fifty division of fungible assets upon marriage, which would eliminate the need for allowances," she said the word with all the disdain she felt. "As *pots of money* is your only motivation for marriage, you should know the value of my personal wealth varies from day to day, but—aside from the business assets—I estimate it to be approximately half a million pounds."

She cut him a glance, but he didn't appear to have moved since the last time she'd looked. Why did he not speak? Was fifty percent of her inheritance not enough? Did he want it *all?*

"Is that it, then?" he asked after a long, uncomfortable moment of silence.

"No. My third term is that I would require our marriage to be a business arrangement."

His forehead furrowed. "What exactly do you mean by that?"

She sighed. "Once again, it hardly seems necessary to go into greater detail if you are opposed to—"

"*Once again* I don't have your extensive experience in the world of business, but in—let's say horse trading"—he cut her a mocking smile— "it is common to state the terms of the exchange fully before demanding a response."

Mary heaved an exasperated sigh. "Like you, I want no, er, romantic entanglement. I wish to go about my life and allow you to go about yours. I will continue doing what I have been doing for the last two years since my father's death."

"Which is?"

"I spend time at all my businesses and travel to consult on new opportunities. I take servants with me so that all is proper and I always bring my secretary, John Courtland."

"So… how do you envision our marriage functioning?"

"Both of us would be free to live our lives the way we choose, provided we do not embarrass the other." Mary hoped her meaning was clear enough. Namely, that she didn't care if he kept a dozen mistresses but she certainly did not want him to flaunt them in front of her. "It is my intention to spend most of my time in Bristol or Falmouth. You are free to use any of the six houses but I assume you would prefer the London residence or your family estate."

"Bristol and Falmouth are where your father's principle businesses are located?"

"Two of them, but I also have houses in Plymouth, Glasgow, and Liverpool."

"Indeed? We need hardly see one another, then."

It wasn't a question, but she nodded.

"Two people living together, but not, er, side-by-side."

Mary's brow furrowed. Why was he smirking like that? Was he driving at something? "Yes, my lord."

"So, scarcely a marriage at all, in other words," he said, a cheerful smile on his face but a hard glint in his eyes. "You will be the Countess of Avington but you will operate all those businesses the way you've done for years."

Mary bristled. "Is that what is bothering you? That your *countess* will engage in trade?"

"Putting aside the fact that such behavior will have a deleterious effect on your first stated goal for marrying a peer—promoting your sister's interests—I can't help but wonder where, in your plan, there is time for children and family?"

"Children?" she repeated stupidly.

He cocked an eyebrow. "Yes, Miss Barnett. Babies. Offspring. The fruit of our loins."

Mary's face heated at the word *loins*. "You did not say anything about children when you stated your terms, my lord."

"I beg your pardon, Miss Barnett, but I didn't think that children *were* considered a term or in any way negotiable."

"It is a contract, my lord," she said icily. "That means everything is up for negotiation."

He shook his head in disbelief.

For some reason, her chest tightened with shame, and that bothered her. Why did she feel ashamed when this oversight was *his* fault.

"Well, then," he said, his gaze holding her pinioned. "I suppose this will be the first alteration to our negotiation. Is that the proper term?" he asked coldly, not waiting for an answer before saying. "Yes. I would expect children from my wife. At least I would require that we both made *rigorous* attempts to have children." He lifted one eyebrow. "Is that another term? Should I enumerate exactly how I would go about putting a child inside you, Miss Barnett? Do you need details as to how often I would want to come to you and—"

"Please *stop*, my lord. I don't need such m-matters enumerated."

His lips twisted, although he looked less than amused, and he raked her body from head-to-toe-to-head with a gaze so heated that the air crackled. And then he smirked and said, "That is a pity."

Mary was beginning to rethink her assessment of the earl as a smiling, empty-headed, happy-go-lucky angel.

Chapter 7

As Lord Avington seemed content—indeed amused—to merely watch Mary squirm and blush, she knew it was up to her to move the uncomfortable conversation along.

"You said *children and family*," she said.

"Yes, if I am going to get married, I would like children. I would like a family. Do I need to state an exact number, Miss Barnett? Is that a term?" he asked, smiling politely. "I can't help noticing you appear very surprised by what is rather a common expectation from a marriage."

"I assumed because you had a younger brother, and did not mention children earlier, that it wasn't a concern." She swallowed and cleared her throat. "It is part of the reason I was interested in Sir Thomas."

"Ah, yes, he had children from his first marriage."

She nodded. "Two sons and three daughters from his prior *two* marriages. He was a widower twice over."

"I see," he said, his face suddenly unreadable. "Does your request for plain speaking stretch to this subject, Miss Barnett? Or is this matter too… delicate?"

Mary had to strenuously combat the urge to turn and run from the garden.

Instead, she assumed an expression she hoped was suitably jaded and said. "I am an adult, my lord, not a child. Speak freely."

"Did Sir Thomas agree not to bed you, Miss Barnett?"

Mary experienced a sudden desire to slap his handsome, smirking face, but she'd goaded him into this, hadn't she? "I made it clear to him that carnal relations were not part of the arrangement."

"And he accepted that, er, *term*."

"He did," she admitted tightly.

If Mary had to pinpoint the second most humiliating moment in her life it would have been seeing the gratitude—mixed with revulsion—in Sir Thomas's drink-yellowed, blood-shot eyes when she had taken him aside—away from their solicitors—and informed him that he'd never be expected to warm her bed.

"Hmmm. Well, it seems we have reached a second bar to any agreement, Miss Barnett. I may not wish for romance and love, but I do want children—and not only for the purpose of creating an heir. We Ingrams value family greatly. Right now, I have seventeen relations living at Avington Castle."

"And that is something you like? Having your family all living with you?" *And off you*, she thought, but did not say.

"Although it is a serious responsibilty to provide care for all those people on the proceeds of a destitute estate, I do not find my relatives a burden, if that makes sense. I love them all and have benefited in untold ways from growing up in a large, tightly knit family. You are right that my younger brother would ably fill the position of earl, but I would wish to try and fill it myself, first." He smiled.

Once again it was difficult to breathe.

The feelings that churned within her at the thought of making children with this man were so conflicting it left her light-headed. He was too gorgeous—too perfect; just imagining him seeing and touching her damaged body was mortifying enough that she'd been relieved when he'd not mentioned an heir as one of the reasons for needing to marry.

That said, the thought of *having* such a man's children was frighteningly intoxicating. She was not an inhuman monster who only loved working. She'd been ten years old when Jenny had been born and had adored having a baby to love and cherish.

But to engage in such intimacies with a man like the earl?

She swallowed. That was something she couldn't think about right now. Not with him sitting right there in all his magnificence and looking at her.

Far better to think about it in the privacy of your own room. In your own bed.

"Is my desire for children an insurmountable request, Miss Barnett?" the earl asked, his question thankfully interrupting the painfully erotic imagery that had exploded in her mind's eye like a pyrotechnic display.

Mary opened her mouth, but nothing came out. What was wrong with her? She was no milk-and-water miss! She'd gone nose-to-nose with some of the most terrifying industrialists of the age and had come away victorious.

The earl stared at her for a moment longer, and then said, "It is up to you, Miss Barnett. Just say the word and I will thank you for the company, the fine meal, and take my leave."

Mary met his serious gaze. If she said *yes*, then she could avoid not only yet another embarrassing disclosure, but also more meetings like *this*, where she was routed by a pair of perfect cheekbones.

If she said *yes*, she could post that letter to Sir James first thing tomorrow morning and probably be married within the week.

Sir James would probably want children, too. He was a childless widower with a baronetcy to pass along, not to mention tens of thousands of pounds sterling.

But, unlike the Earl of Avington, Sir James was a mere mortal—as homely as Mary in his own way—and possessed all the sexual allure of a pair of thick woolen stockings. He would get her with child with the same dull, practical determination he went about sinking a shaft for one of his Lanarkshire mines.

If she said *no*…

It shamed her to admit it, but the thought of engaging in the sexual act with Lord Avington was as thrilling as it was terrifying.

You want him, just admit it, Mary. You want to possess *him—like an art collector slavering over an especially rare and exquisite painting.*

Mary gritted her teeth at the irritating yet accurate thought.

She met the earl's patient, questioning gaze and amazed herself by saying, "I am amenable to ch-children."

He nodded, but she couldn't tell if her answer had pleased or disappointed him.

You'd better tell him now, Mary… It will only be worse the longer you wait…

She had to clear her throat twice before she could speak. "But before we talk any more about the matter there is something else you need to know, first."

***

"Yes, Miss Barnett?" Miles said, almost afraid to hear what the indomitable woman came up with next. Already he was bloody astounded that she'd believed they would marry and live as strangers. What sort of person—man or woman—wanted to live their life without the prospect of sex or children or intimacy?

Bloody hell.

While Miles had no mistress at the moment, he'd always enjoyed a healthy and active sex life, even during those often-nightmarish years when he'd served in the army.

He might not expect romantic love from the woman he married, but he most certainly expected physical intimacy. He also expected fidelity and would give the same in return, although he somehow doubted Miss Barnett would believe a male aristocrat capable of such behavior, especially as Sir Thomas had died in his mistress's bed.

Miss Barnett's mouth twisted miserably. "I believe you deserve to know that I am not a virgin."

Miles had to admit it wasn't what he'd been expecting. As prickly and standoffish as she was, he would have wagered a hundred pounds—not that he had it—that she was untouched.

Clearly there was more to Miss Barnett than just business.

"Nor am I, Miss Barnett. That is not a stumbling block to forging an alliance with you."

She nodded, lifting her chin in a defiant gesture that plucked at his heartstrings for some reason. Mary Barnet was not, he suspected, a woman who showed weakness often.

"But your insistence on living separate lives *does* present a problem. Especially when it comes to having a family. While I understand your need to travel, we'd need to live in the same city—the same house—at least part of the time."

She pondered that for a moment and then said, "How long, do you think?"

Her question amused him, but for once, he restrained his teasing nature. "Women do not always get enceinte with each—"

"I am aware of that," she said quickly. Even in the moonlight he could see she was a bright red, as if she'd just been dipped into scalding water. "I like to have things organized, my lord. I need schedules and timetables. I need *order* in my life."

Miles was actually beginning to enjoy himself.

"What do you suggest then? A breeding schedule according to your estrus cycle? In the world of horse breeding—"

"You are purposely being obtuse and obnoxious," she said, scowling at him. "You *know* I am simply trying to conceive of an arrangement that will work most efficiently for both of us."

"This isn't a business amalgamation, Miss Barnett. This is our *lives* and if we were to have children, we need to consider the sort of household we'd be bringing them into. It seems to me you are suggesting we meet only long enough for me to impregnate you and then we live separately.

"Is that so bad?" she asked, sounding almost plaintive. "Don't a great many aristocratic marriages function that way—with both parties fulfilling their duties and then pursuing their own ends?"

"I cannot deny that a great many marriages operate exactly like that," he said. "But I don't wish to be part of one."

"You've already said you don't want love. But now you are throwing up hurdles to my suggestion of a business arrangement. What *do* you want? Are you sure you wish to marry at all, my lord."

I don't he wanted to shout, but of course he did not.

"What I would like," he said icily, "is to have access to my wife's bed without having to schedule an appointment."

Her dark green eyes glittered with dislike and Miles could not blame her.

"I'm sorry, that was inexcusable." Miles inhaled deeply and then exhaled, forcing himself to put aside the anger that had simmered inside him from the moment this woman had greeted him earlier that evening as if he were a feckless rake who'd just slithered—unpunctually—into her life like a reptile.

Instead, he thought about what she was offering, which was enough money to save the earldom and his family. She was amenable to children, if not exactly delighted by the prospect. She didn't expect love, courtship, or romance from him. It all sounded so perfect that it should have suited him better than a custom coat made by Weston.

Why then, did it leave him feeling so bloody bleak?

***

Mary had never felt so grubby and common in her life. She'd devised a plan that would give them both what they wanted, and Lord Avington was staring at her as if she'd just flung a bucket of manure all over him.

She opened her mouth to tell him to go straight to the devil, but he spoke before she could force the words out.

"I'm sorry, Miss Barnett," he said again. "Not just for my callous statement, but because what you said made perfect sense."

Mary's jaw actually sagged.

The earl grinned. "Now there is an expression I've not seen on your face before."

"You'll have to forgive my shock as I've never heard those words come out of a man's mouth before. At least not in that order, and not directed at me."

His laugh was a genuine, joyous sound that caused havoc in her chest. "Yes, I daresay you've had to tolerate all sorts of male bullheadedness."

Mary would have put it more succinctly—and in less socially acceptable words—but, instead, she merely nodded.

"I am good friends with six women whom I met while teaching at a school, so I think I have a better idea than most men how the world treats intelligent women. To speak plainly, I propose we live together as man and wife and raise any children we have like two parents who respect—and perhaps even come to care for—each other."

The thought of this man ever coming to care for her left her breathless. It was impossible for somebody who looked like *him* to care for somebody who looked like *her.*

In her limited experience, homely women and handsome men rarely came together out of choice. And when they did, the men made the women's lives miserable—just like her cousin Reginald did to his plain but once wealthy wife, Joan.

Of course, poor Joan would not be nearly so miserable if she'd not made the catastrophic mistake of falling in love with Reginald.

Mary could hardly blame the woman since she'd made the same mistake herself, once—and with the very same man.

That was a mistake Mary had no intention of making ever again. With any man.

"When you travel to your various mines and shipyards I would travel with you, Miss Barnett. I stand firm on that point."

"Why?" she demanded.

"First, because it is the only way I would be able to learn about your businesses."

If he had stopped there, Mary would have been annoyed enough, but then he said, "And the second reason is that I will not have my wife travelling all over Great Britain alone with another man, regardless of whether or not he is your employee."

Nettled, Mary shot back, "But you may be alone with other women?"

A divot of annoyance formed between his glorious eyes. "I am a man, Miss Barnett. It does not reflect ill on me to be in the company of men or women alone."

"I suppose that goes for your mistress, as well?" Mary instantly wished she'd kept her mouth shut.

His angelic features suddenly turned hard and stern. "Is that something else you discovered from your investigations, Miss Barnett?"

Mary pursed her lips, refusing to answer and subject herself to more chiding.

"I am actually relieved you've raised the subject of mistresses. Once I am married, keeping me sexually satisfied will be my wife's duty, Miss Barnett. And her satisfaction will be my responsibility." He smiled. "A responsibility I will take very seriously, by the way."

The images his words and heated stare evoked were torrid ones. Mary knew what a man looked like when he made love—how intensely physical the activity was—and she couldn't help imagining Lord Avington's beautiful face distorted by passion as he slid into her body.

She shoved aside the distracting image and forced herself to hold his mocking gaze. She desperately wanted to say something to wipe the arrogant smirk from his face but didn't trust herself to speak without sounding like a breathless ninny.

"Other than your requirement that I violate the terms of your father's will—which I will address after a moment—I find everything else you've said both reasonable and generous. Indeed, I feel as though I will be bringing very little to the bargain."

Mary thought he must be jesting but, for once, he wasn't smiling.

"I know you said you are considering marriage partly because of your sister. I must emphasize that I cannot guarantee Miss Jenny the husband of her dreams."

"I realize that," Mary said.

"What I *can* promise you is that she will be invited to any function she desires. The Ingrams are poor in money but we are rich in connections. However, we will need to do more than just marry."

"What do you mean?"

"You and I would need to brave the *ton* ourselves if we are to be of any help to her. That will mean parties and balls and any number of frivolous entertainments—at least until she has been accepted. Freddie has indicated that socializing is anathema to you.

"It is, but I am willing to engage in a certain amount of frivolity in order to make Jenny a success."

He snorted. "You make it sound as appealing as a slow march to Tyburn."

She tucked a spiral of escaped hair behind her ear. "That is as accurate a description as any I can come up with, my lord."

"Cheer up," he said, "the happy news is there is hardly any Season remaining this year and we might get by with very few public appearances for now. I do feel obliged to confess there are some ceremonies you won't be able to avoid."

"Such as?"

"Your presentation to the Queen, for example."

Mary's entire being revolting against the idea of being cinched into an eighteenth-century gown and groveling at the feet of a sneering monarch.

He laughed. "Judging by your expression, that might be enough to make you reconsider whether any agreement is possible between us."

"You are wicked to laugh at me, my lord."

"Yes, I am a heartless brute," he agreed, "Best you know that beforehand."

"Surely a presentation is something we might put off until next year?"

"If we married *after* the Season ends then presenting you won't be an issue. How much time do you have to comply with the will?"

"A little over five weeks." A horrid thought assaulted her. "I won't be expected to host things like country house parties and hunt balls and such, will I? Not only do I need to travel a good deal, but I have no idea how to organize such things." Her voice had risen by the end of her confession.

The earl took her hand in both of his, the action spurring her heart into a gallop. "Do not worry yourself, Miss Barnett, I daresay your mother is experienced at the management of a large establishment and she will have my aunts and sisters to help her."

"My mother?" Mary squawked. "You would wish for *her* to live at your country house?"

He gave her an exasperated look. "Of course your mother and sister must live with us. I've already said how much the Ingrams have always valued family and Avington Castle has far more apartments than occupants."

"I just thought you meant *your* family," Mary said lamely.

"Your family will be *my* family if we were to marry."

His words caused an unexpected warmth in her chest. He would want her family—people who had coal dust under their nails—to live in his grand ancestral home?

Hope for a possible future with this man sprouted inside her—a tiny and fragile sprout, but it was hope just the same. He would never love her—or perhaps even like her—but at least he did not seem determined to despise her.

But then she remembered his refusal to comply with her first term and her newly sprouted hope shriveled. She refused to hand control of her businesses over to any man, even one as attractive and alluring as the Earl of Avington.

"We still need to address the issue of my father's will, my lord."

Chapter 8

Miles bit back a groan. He had no idea how long they'd been out in the garden—a century, at least—but his nerves felt raw from the encounter, and he knew, regardless of how emotionless she seemed, that hers must be, too.

"I daresay you are overwhelmed by all of this, Miss Barnett. We needn't discuss everything tonight—"

"Overwhelmed?" She seemed to double in size. "I am no vaporish miss."

He chuckled wearily. "No, those are not two words I would use to describe you."

"What two words would you use?" she asked, arrested.

The woman certainly did not pull her punches. "Clever, determined, fearless, to name a few."

"That is three words."

Miles smiled. "That's why I'm a dance teacher rather than a maths teacher; my addition and subtraction skills have always been abominable."

She looked distracted rather than amused by his jest. "I want to settle matters tonight, my lord."

Of course, she did—she liked schedules and predictability.

"I cannot violate the spirit of your father's request, Miss Barnett. However, I *can* promise that I wouldn't interfere in matters I do not understand, and that I would be willing to learn from you and accept your lead."

She chewed her lower lip, her face thoughtful.

As she pondered, Miles studied her.

Miss Barnett was a tough, self-contained little thing and Miles couldn't help wondering if she was only this standoffish and curt with him, or if her behavior extended to everyone.

He didn't get the impression of great closeness with her mother. As for her sister? Well, she clearly loved the girl if she was willing to marry to benefit her, but love did not always mean closeness.

She looked up and met his gaze. "It is not ideal, but I can respect your reasons." She swallowed and added, as if against her will, "I believe you will keep your word."

Relief washed over him. Until that moment, Miles had not realized how much he'd hoped they might find some common ground. She might be humorless, prickly to the point of unpleasantness, and intent on shattering every expectation society would have for his countess, but he admired her directness and honesty.

He smiled at her. "Well then, we have made progress."

"It seems to me that we've done more than that; we've reached an agreement." She cut him an uncharacteristically hesitant look and said, "I hope you don't think me forward, but do you require more time to consider our discussion?"

Miles *did* think her forward—and he bloody well resented her for it, too. He desperately wanted more time. But what reason could he give for any delay?

"Don't *you* wish for some time to consider, Miss Barnett? Even a few days? A week?"

"No."

Miles swore he heard a cell door clanging shut.

Her expression—so honest and open only seconds before—suddenly shuttered. "If you'd rather not—"

"Please, Miss Barnett—don't view my hesitation as a lack of interest. It is not. I am extremely interested. It is simply that I am not accustomed to making important life decisions in the blink of an eye."

She eyed him somewhat grudgingly. "You wish for some time—a week? Two?"

Would a week be enough to become comfortable with the idea? Not really. He suspected even a year would not be ample.

"You know something about my past and family, Miss Barnett. I should like to know something of yours."

She frowned at his question, and Miles would have wagered a pony that she was trying to figure out how sharing information might put her at a disadvantage. She was, through and through, a businesswoman.

"My background is mundane and uninteresting."

"I doubt that. Your father was a self-made man who became one of the richest men in the country and you, a lady, now run his empire. That sounds the farthest thing from mundane. It is an unusual calling for a gentlewoman. Perhaps as unusual as being a dancing master is for an earl. Please. Won't you tell me a little about yourself?" He snorted softly. "We've already been out here so long everyone will be wondering if we've fallen asleep. What are a few more minutes?"

She heaved a sigh. "Oh, very well.

He couldn't help feeling a little amused by her ungracious reaction. Perhaps he'd been spoiled, but women usually did not view conversation with him with quite so much reluctance, if not outright revulsion.

"I worked with my father every day—six days a week—from the time I was sixteen until his death almost two years ago." A tiny, fond smile flickered across her lips and disappeared.

"Sixteen? That's a bit young, isn't it?"

Her sharp, fierce features became even more intense and she shot him a pugnacious look. "I wanted to work for him earlier, but we made a bargain when I was twelve. I would go to school until I was sixteen and after that—if I still wished to work for him—I could leave school early, provided I agreed to endure a single Season in London when I came of age."

Miles smirked at her use of the word *endure*, but let the matter be. Instead, he asked, "What kind of work did you do?"

"He made me start at the bottom."

"Lord! Never say you were an iron worker or coal miner?"

She laughed and the sound was unexpectedly girlish and feminine. "No, nothing like that, but I had to begin as a clerk, doing the same work as the lowliest of his clerical workers." She suddenly dropped her direct gaze to her hands. "I daresay my promotions were easier won than the others; I don't delude myself on that score. But I worked hard and earned them all the same."

Miles did not doubt that for a moment.

They sat in companionable silence, her probably recalling her father and Miles taking the opportunity to observe the woman he suspected would become his wife. He was accustomed to women who worked—how could he not be after years spent teaching in a girls' school with so many female teachers? But working as a merchant clerk? Especially in the all-male bastions of mining and shipbuilding?

He'd never met any other woman who'd done that.

Miles wasn't a stranger to heiresses—indeed, he'd been betrothed to one years before. But Elizabeth Everton had been nothing like Miss Barnett—at least he hoped to God they were nothing alike.

He shivered at the unwanted memory of Elizabeth, whom he'd not thought about in years, and shoved her back into the room where he'd locked her.

Another door in his mind, one that he'd also believed locked, suddenly opened and Pansy looked out at him.

The sharp stab of grief stole his breath away.

Oh, Pansy.

It had been a long, long time since he'd allowed himself to think of her. But still not long enough.

"My lord?"

"Hmm?" Miles looked up into questioning green eyes, his lips automatically flexing into a smile. "I'm sorry, Miss Barnett."

"You had a rather sad expression on your face."

"Sad? Me?"

As was her wont, she ignored his attempt at humor and said, "Yes, sad. What were you thinking about?"

Her question—inappropriately, *invasively* personal—momentarily robbed him of speech. They had only met a few hours earlier and she believed herself entitled to his innermost thoughts?

As he held her inquisitive green gaze, Miles knew that he would have to become accustomed to such forthright behavior if he married her. When Miss Barnett wished to know something, she just came out and asked it.

"I was thinking about my brother Bevan," he lied.

He could see by her expression that his answer did not satisfy her, that it had not been comprehensive enough, and that she wanted to ask *what,* exactly, he had been thinking about Bevan.

Miles wondered just how good her inquiry agent was. Did she know about Pansy and Elizabeth and what had happened on that cold winter day all those years ago?

The thought of her sending strangers to poke about in his past made Miles feel a distinct lack of charity toward her. But then she was prepared to give the man she married hundreds of thousands of pounds—not to mention entrusting him with her future—so it would be foolish to enter such a union without some investigation, especially given the number of destitute peers who preyed on unsuspecting heiresses, lurking at the edges of the *ton* like hungry bottom feeding fish searching for an overlooked morsel.

Not that Miss Barnett was unsuspecting; not in the least.

"Were you close to your brother?" she asked.

Miles felt another flash of irritation at yet another personal question but quickly suppressed it. He was the one who'd wanted to become acquainted, wasn't he?

"We were very close when we were children but not in recent years. My brother did not approve of my work, and I did not have much leisure time to visit Avington, although I made the journey home at least twice a year."

"When did you last see him?"

"Two weeks before his death." Indeed, Miles's was consoled by the fact that the visit had been one of the best they'd had in years, so at least there'd been no bad blood between them.

He saw she was waiting for more and said, "Shortly after my visit he caught a chill that took hold and killed him within days." Miles still could not believe it. Hale, hearty Bevan, dead from the sniffles.

Miles looked away from his thoughts into her green eyes, which were as sharp as a kestrel's. That's what she reminded him of; a small, fierce hawk.

Could he marry her? If he did, could two so very different people find if not happiness, then at least contentment, together?

If he didn't marry her, he'd need to do this again—albeit he doubted he'd ever have a conversation as shockingly direct as this one with any other heiress.

The thought of their unconventional *negotiation* made him smile.

But it also made him tired. He did not want to go through this ordeal—in any form—again.

She had made up her mind and was ready to commit. It did not behoove him to behave like a missish schoolgirl.

Miles met her raptorlike gaze. "I do not need more time, Miss Barnett. I am honored to accept your terms."

"Are you sure, my lord?" As brisk and businesslike as she tried to appear, Miles could see anxiety behind her piercing eyes. She might have a hard shell around her, but she had a soft underbelly just like any other living creature. The last thing he wanted to do was pick and prod at her where it would hurt.

And so he gave her one of his most charming smiles. "Yes, I am very sure."

She gave an abrupt, businesslike nod. "I accept your terms as well, my lord."

Miles experienced a sudden tightness in his chest, a pain that centered on his heart, until it was difficult to breathe.

So, this was it. After all these years, he was really going to do it: sell himself for money.

His stomach pitched with nausea, and he forced a rather strained smile and stood. "I've behaved badly keeping you out here so long."

"You didn't keep me. I am responsible for my own behavior, Lord Avington."

His smile became a bit more natural. "Of course you are."

"Besides," she said, standing and brushing off her skirt. "It was my preference to sit here for an hour rather than let this process drag out over weeks."

Miles was surprised to find he agreed. Their negotiation might have been vulgar and unconventional, but at least the matter was settled in a fraction of the time it would have taken to court and woo another woman.

There was only one thing left to do.

Miles sank to one knee, and took one of her hands in his, the burned hand, he noticed absently, and said, "Miss Barnett, will you do me the honor of becoming my wife?"

She sucked in a breath and her lips parted in surprise, the unstudied expression making her look rather pretty. "Yes, my lord, I will." Her voice, naturally low and somewhat scratchy, was almost hoarse.

Miles raised her hand to his mouth and allowed his lips to touch her skin, which he'd not done earlier. After all, they were now betrothed and kissing her hand was his right.

The burned skin was as soft as a newborn babe. He wondered if she had much sensation in her hand. He also wondered how much more of her was damaged beneath her clothing.

Miles pushed the thought away; he would find out for himself in five weeks.

He released her fingers and stood. "I will endeavor to be a good helpmeet, Miss Barnett."

Her lips curved in a determined, not entirely convincing smile. "As will I."

If Miles were cut from the same cloth as Mary Barnett—a woman who asked the questions she wanted whether they were acceptable or not—he would have asked her what she was thinking to make her look so grim.

But of course, he did nothing of the sort.

Chapter 9

Mary was sitting at her desk, working on the cost estimate for lock construction on the new canal when the door to her study opened.

She looked up, expecting to see Yost or one of the footmen. Instead, it was Lord Avington.

Mary scrambled to her feet. "My lord, what—"

He shut the door and locked it. And then he turned and strode toward her.

"What is going—"

"Hush," he murmured, placing his finger over her lips the way he'd done once before.

And once again she obeyed him without hesitation.

"I've been thinking about those *terms* of yours, Miss Barnett."

"Y-you have?"

He nodded, his gaze strangely menacing. Mary took a step back and bumped into the chair behind her, her heart beating twice as fast as it had a few seconds before.

"I've decided on a new term for our agreement."

"Er, but we already—"

Mary made a mortifying squeaking sound as he slid his hands around her waist—large, warm, powerful hands—and lifted her, turned her around, and set her onto her desk, all in one smooth motion.

"Before I commit to marrying you, Miss Barnett, I've decided that I want a sample of what you have to offer."

"S-sample?" she squeaked.

"Mmm-hmm." He stepped back and fixed her with a burning gaze, fisting his hands on his hips.

Without her permission, Mary's eyes lowered to the front of his pantaloons, which his cutaway tailcoat framed just like a painting. And what a work of art he was.

Mary's breathing roughened as she took in his erection thrusting against the thin material. He was long and thick and far more intimidating than she recalled Reginald being.

"You told me you were not a maiden, but you didn't tell me exactly how much experience you have when it comes to pleasing a man, Miss Barnett." His hand dropped to the front of his pantaloons and he stroked himself over the fabric.

This time Mary could muster no words. Instead—mortifyingly—her sex clenched so hard that she dropped her hand to her mound, as if that would stop the sudden eruption of pleasure.

Mary gasped as a spasm gripped her body and arched her spine. She bit her lower lip to stifle the primal moans threatening to escape and ground the heel of her palm against her throbbing core.

This cannot be me!

And yet she could not stop herself.

Wave after wave of joy rocked her body, until she could no longer contain her bliss. She cried out—uncaring what Lord Avington might think of her—shamelessly broadcasting her pleasure for anyone hear.

"Very nice, Miss Barnett." His voice penetrated the haze of satiation that shrouded her like a warm, protective cocoon. "Open your eyes and look at me."

Go away, she wanted to shout, and yet she instantly obeyed.

The earl made an approving noise deep in his chest and grinned, a terrifyingly fierce, erotic smile unlike any he'd worn the evening before. "Were you thinking about me when you came?"

Mary gasped and his grin turned to a stern glare in an instant. "Answer me! You wanted plain speaking, didn't you?"

She struggled to spit out even one word. Y-yes."

His pupils flared. "What a good girl you are. Tell me, do you touch yourself often?"

"No!" she blurted.

His eyes narrowed.

"N-not terribly often," she amended.

"How often?"

"Perhaps once a week—no more than twice."

"Mary."

"Oh, *very well!* Most nights, my lord. There are you happy?" she demanded.

He nodded slowly, menacingly. "That makes me very happy, indeed."

Marcy couldn't help preening.

"From now on, there will be no more of that, are we understood?"

"But... *why?*" Rather than sounding forceful, as she'd hoped, she'd sounded... whiney.

"Why?" he repeated, his eyes widening with shock. "Because what is beneath that skirt is now mine. That is why. Are we understood?"

Her jaw sagged. She wanted to argue—to remind him that had not been one of his terms—but, instead, she found herself nodding dumbly.

"Good girl," he said.

Rather than annoy her, the words were like a gentle caress.

"Now lift your skirts, spread your thighs, and show me what I shall be getting."

Mary made a strangled yelping sound.

"Hush and do as you are told," he ordered briskly, his full lips compressed into a stern line as his eyes bored into her. "I should have requested a full inspection last night." His nostrils flared. "I'll want to touch and lick the merchandise, as well."

Mary goggled. He *looked* exactly like Lord Avington, but surely there must be some mistake?

"Don't make me repeat myself, Miss Barnett," he barked in a voice that caused her to yank up her skirts with trembling fingers.

They both turned to look down at what she had bared.

For the first time in memory, Mary didn't worry about her unsightly scars or how they would look to another person.

No, she didn't think of anything but the needy, demanding pulsing between her legs.

"Ah, beautiful," he murmured, stepping close enough that he could stroke and caress her pale, freckled thighs with his elegant, tapered fingers, his gaze hungry, as if Mary were the most desirable thing he'd ever seen.

"Soft like satin," he muttered. And then slowly, inexorably, he pushed her legs wider, opening that most vulnerable, private part of her to his hot blue gaze.

"Just a touch," he whispered, parting her folds with a single finger. He groaned, the sound vibrating through her body. "So wet and hot," he hissed, sliding the rough pad of his thumb over her swollen nub while penetrating her with his middle finger. "I can't wait to put myself deep inside you, Mary, and fuck you until you scream out my name in—"

Mary gasped and jerked upright in her bed, her eyes flying open as yet another powerful burst of pleasure exploded inside her. Her thighs clenched and she shivered as each wave of bliss washed over her. "My God," she groaned, blinking into the darkness, her lungs finally unseizing as she gasped and filled them with air.

Mary swore that she could smell him—that clean linen and sunshine scent that had teased her nostrils while they'd sat side-by-side on the garden bench.

She had never had a dream so vivid, so... erotic.

Her nightgown had twisted around her waist and realized her hand was still between her tightly clenched thighs. She yanked it away, mortified to discover her fingers were soaked with her own juices.

"Argh," she groaned, flopping onto her back, and heaving a sigh. This was worse than bad; this was terrible. She'd not even known the man an entire day and she was already dreaming about him. What would she be like after she'd actually married him? Shared a bed with him?

Perhaps he will be a selfish, lazy lover like Reginald had been?

Mary snorted. Not likely. She thought about how gentle and kind he'd been with Jenny, how attentive and courteous he'd behaved with her mother.

No, he was nothing like Reginald.

"Oh God, what have I done?" she whispered into the darkness.

He'd insisted he wanted children, a family, a harmonious relationship with his wife. While a man like Miles Ingram might be able to live alongside a woman like Mary without becoming infatuated or— God forbid, falling in love—Mary was all too aware of her own limits.

She was *already* infatuated with him and it had been less than a day.

She would never be able to resist him, no matter that she knew only pain and humiliation would await her. She would fall in love with him—not just the potent lust that already burned up her veins—and his eventual rejection would *crush* her.

None of that could be allowed to ever happen.

There was only one way to save herself and that was to make him change his mind—not about the marriage, of course—but at least his expectations of their marriage.

Right now, he thought they could live their lives side-by-side in companionable amity.

Mary had an easier time believing that she would be the toast of next Season than believing she could live with Miles Ingram as his *friend*.

Fortunately, Lord Avington was an aristocratic man who lived by a code of honor. No matter how much he might come to dislike Mary, he would never break their betrothal, so she was safe in that regard.

She would spend the next five weeks convincing him that the *last* thing he wanted was domestic tranquility with her. By the time Mary was finished with him, he'd beg her to move to one of her houses in the provinces and never darken his doors again—especially not the door to his bedchamber.

He would marry her and they would both get what they needed from the union.

But it was a matter of survival to avoid spending one more minute with him than was necessary.

And she'd spend each of those minutes ensuring that he hated her.

Only then would she be safe. Only then would she ensure that her life—her future—was truly her own and without awkward, dangerous emotional entanglements.

Which was exactly what she had always wanted.

Wasn't it?

***

Mary's eyes were gritty and raw from her sleepless night. She desperately wished that she'd not agreed to meet Lord Avington at Lady Sedgewick's so early, but they had only a few weeks to plan, so they would have to make the most of their time.

Besides, the sooner she launched her *campaign*, the better.

Mary didn't know what she'd expected the countess's house to be like, but she certainly hadn't visualized the cool, reserved woman living somewhere so warm and welcoming.

The décor in the cozy townhouse managed to be both shabby and stylish and Mary knew the faded carpets and threadbare furnishings were far more in keeping with aristocratic houses than the expensive, brand new furniture her mother insisted on stuffing the rooms with at Coal House.

There were paintings everywhere, some jammed so closely together you could scarcely see the wall behind them.

All in all, it was utterly charming and she felt immediately at home in the small parlor where the gruff elderly servant led them.

"Come and see Mr. And Mrs. Vickers," the earl said to her as Lady Sedgewick spoke quietly to the servant on some matter.

"Turkeys!" she blurted. "I have not visited many aristocratic houses, is it the norm to keep domesticated fowl in one's back yard?"

He laughed. "Lord no! The Vickers are pets and belong to the owner of the house."

"Oh, this is not Lady Sedgewick's house?"

"No, Freddie is a tenant here, along with our mutual teacher friend, Miss Lorelei Fontenot. The house belongs to yet another former teacher, Honoria Keyes. She leases the property as she is now married to Lord Saybrook, the Duke of Plimpton's heir. Perhaps you have heard of her? She is a quite well-known portraitist."

Mary supposed that would explain all the art on the walls. She was intrigued by the thought of a female painter and opened her mouth to ask more questions, but then recalled what she was supposed to be doing: alienating him.

"I haven't heard of her and care nothing for paintings, or artwork, in general," she said.

His pleasant expression slid from his face. "You don't care for art?"

Before Mary could contrive an offensive response, Lady Sedgewick closed the door and sat in a chair across from a settee.

Mary lowered herself onto the sofa and the earl sat beside her, his big body occupying more than half the small space.

She moved away from him, toward the arm of the sofa, making no effort to be subtle.

The earl's nostrils flared and a red mist spread over his sculped cheekbones. "You were saying that you didn't care for art," Avington prodded, clearly not finished with the subject.

She cut him a dismissive look. "I am too busy for such frivolity and have far better ways to occupy my time."

It was a barefaced lie, but he wouldn't know that Mary rarely missed a Royal Academy Exhibition.

The earl laughed. When she didn't join in, he frowned. "You are speaking in earnest."

Mary met his shocked blue gaze and said, "Yes, my lord, I am a philistine. That's what you are asking, isn't it?"

Before he could speak, Lady Sedgewick cleared her throat and said, "Thank you so much for agreeing to meet with me at my home,

Miss Barnett. I would have come to Coal House but there are several matters that are keeping me close to home today."

Thankfully, Avington turned away from Mary, his irritation dissipating as he faced their hostess, a genuine smile curving his lips. "It is always a pleasure to see you, darling."

Mary's jaw tightened at not only the endearment, but also at his easy and open affection.

Which she was already doing an excellent job of destroying any chance of ever enjoying herself.

The countess smiled at Mary, "No doubt you were surprised to see a pair of turkeys strutting about in my yard."

"Yes."

Mary's face heated at her rude, monosyllabic answer. She'd not counted on feeling such embarrassment when she'd formulated this plan.

The countess's faintly startled look shamed her into expanding her answer. "I actually have a keen interest in poultry."

The other two stared at her.

"I suppose you could call it a hobby," she blithered. Well, it probably was the closest thing she had to a hobby. She didn't play the piano, do needlework, or go shopping like her sister and mother.

"What sort of an interest?" the countess asked.

As Mary looked from one perfect face to the other, she couldn't help wishing that she'd kept her mouth shut about what was likely considered a peculiar hobby, but it was too late to take her words back.

Besides, Mary loved talking about her birds. Just this once she'd be pleasant.

She had weeks yet to launch her rudeness offensive.

"When I was little one of my father's ship captains brought me two breeding pairs of miniature fowl—they came from the island of Java. Because of their diminutive size they are frequently kept aboard ships, where space is at a premium." Mary smiled, as she always did whenever she thought of her birds. "I've had over four hundred birds from those first two pairs."

"Four hundred?" the earl said. "Good Lord! Where do you keep them all?"

Mary turned to Lord Avington and then wished she hadn't. They were seated so closely on the small settee that their faces were barely a foot apart. He'd been beautiful by candlelight; by sunlight, he was breathtaking, the blue of his eyes startling and his handsome features enhanced, rather than diminished, by the faint lines around his mouth and at the corners of his eyes.

Quite honestly, it hurt to look at him.

Her reaction to his appearance irritated her and made her remember why she needed to remain vigilant when it came to being rude. "I haven't kept them all, of course," she said sharply enough to make him recoil. "I have only thirty-five birds and I keep them at Coal House. My father had a lovely structure built for them to blend in with the garden—a pagoda, it is called. It is situated in the very back of the garden." She didn't bother to mention how much her mother hated having a henhouse in their yeard.

"How interesting," he said, his words sounding genuine, as was his expression.

Mary ignored what was obviously a peace offering and turned to the countess. "I offer breeding pairs to any of my workers who have the space and inclination to raise their own birds." She hesitated, and then added, "They are not just good for eggs, they are also affectionate creatures and make amusing pets." Her face heated at that admission.

"I, too, was delighted to learn that fowl make good pets," the countess said, surprising her. Mr. and Mrs. Vickers are not only a delight to observe, but they recognize people and even have their favorites."

"Freddie is Mr. Vickers's favorite," the earl said in a confiding tone. "Indeed, I believe that poor Mrs. Vickers is suspicious that you are trying to cut her out with him, Fred."

The countess gave him look of fond exasperation and turned to Mary. "Perhaps I might see your birds the next time I am at Coal House?"

"I would enjoy showing them off to you," she said, not lying. Just because she was going to be rude to the earl didn't mean she had to be rude to all his friends.

"I would like to see them, too," the earl said.

Mary gave him a tight smile. "Of course, my lord."

Rather than appear offended, as she'd expected, humor glinted in his eyes, as if he were amused by her stiffness toward him.

She would need to redouble her efforts.

The door opened and the same servant as before entered with a tray of refreshments.

Once tea and biscuits had been distributed, Lady Sedgewick turned to Mary and said, "Miles has indicated you've both agreed that I should take charge of the preparations for your wedding as well as organizing your social schedule?"

"Yes, please," Mary said, genuinely grateful. "I think that would be best."

"And you wish to get married within six weeks?"

"Er, five at the latest. Will that be a problem?"

"No, not at all. Unless you are hoping for a large town wedding, then—"

"That is the last thing I want," Mary assured her.

"Do you mean you don't want to get married in town, or you don't wish for a large wedding?"

"Either, actually." Mary glanced at the earl, wishing he'd step in.

"Miss Barnett and I discussed getting married after the Season and both agree that is best. As for avoiding a large town wedding, there is a lovely chapel at Avington Castle."

"May I make some suggestions?" the countess asked.

"Please do, my lady."

"I wish you would, Freddie."

Mary and the earl both spoke at the same time.

The earl chuckled. "I think what we both are saying, my dear, is that we desperately want you to tell us what to do."

"You should send the announcement to the newspaper today— shall I write it and send it off for you?"

"I can do at least that much," Avington said.

"Even if you get married in the country, you should host a ball in town to celebrate your betrothal. As we are short on time, you could have it a few days before you depart for Avington Castle."

"A ball might be difficult considering I don't have a large house to host it in," the earl said.

"That is generally the bride's family's responsibility."

They both looked at Mary.

"I'm sure my mother would be delighted to assist with planning such an event." That was understating the matter. Louisa Barnett would be over the moon when she learned her daughter was going to marry the earl. Mary had not divulged that information last night as she'd been too exhausted to cope with the orgy of excitement that would commence when her mother heard the news.

The countess took a little notebook and pencil from the needlework basket beside her chair. "How many guests can the Avington chapel accommodate?"

"No more than two hundred."

"Two hundred!" Mary repeated. "I thought you said *small?*"

"I probably have that many relatives alone, Miss Barnett," Avington said. "I hope you don't intend to invite any friends or family of your own?" he teased.

The countess gave Mary a sympathetic look. "I know it sounds like a great many people, but two hundred guests is actually quite modest. We shall have to be very selective with the invitations. Do you have a large family?"

"No. Just my cousin, his wife, my mother, and sister."

Mary would have liked to leave Reginald's name off the list—indeed, she would be overjoyed never to see his face or think about him for the rest of her life—but her mother would never allow that. Neither of her parents knew what Reginald had done to her, Mary had made sure of that. The last thing she'd wanted was pity. She'd wanted revenge, and soon—with this marriage—she would have it.

The thought made her smile.

"Once the betrothal announcement is in the newspaper you will be flooded with invitations," the countess said.

How amusing. All the invitations poor Jenny had wanted would suddenly come *flooding* in because of an announcement in the newspaper.

"Everyone will be most interested in meeting you," the countess went on to say.

Mary didn't point out that most of those people had had ample opportunity to meet her a decade earlier and had showed no interest.

"It is my recommendation that you—and his lordship—accept as many invitations as possible."

Mary frowned. "I beg your pardon?"

Before the countess could answer, the earl spoke. "We don't have to run ourselves ragged, Miss Barnett." He gave her a wry smile. "We shall have all of next year to do that." He glanced at the countess. "Isn't that right, Freddie—we can ease into this?"

Lady Sedgewick didn't look like she agreed. "The more you can attend the better."

"I will attend three functions each week," Mary said.

The earl and countess exchanged a look.

"And absolutely no balls," Mary added.

For the first time, Lady Sedgewick's unreadable face showed some emotion: displeasure.

Avington laughed, but there was no humor in it. "No balls? Are you including our own betrothal ball in that prohibition, Miss Barnett?" He was smiling as pleasantly and blandly as ever but his eyes were blue ice.

"Our betrothal ball is the first and only ball I'll attend."

There was a moment of strained silence, and then Lady Sedgewick nodded. "Very well, I shall select three invitations every week if you would like."

Mary nodded.

The countess jotted something in her book and then turned to the earl. "I know we will have to wait for next year to launch Maria and Penelope, but it couldn't hurt to allow your sisters to stretch their wings at a few gatherings. Could you bring them to the city for a few weeks, Miles? And perhaps your brother, too?"

The earl hesitated and glanced at Mary.

It pained her to realize that he wasn't sure he wanted to expose his family to her hostility, but then that meant her plan was working, didn't it? Shouldn't she be happy?

"Of course, the twins and Crispin should come to town. They will be eager to celebrate my impending marriage," he said, smiling grimly.

Lord Avington's sisters were around Jenny's age but neither had come out due to financial constraints. His youngest brother, Crispin, was at university, although she supposed he might be out for the summer.

"You will like my sisters, Miss Barnett," the earl said, unbending a little. "And they will get along swimmingly with young Miss Jenny."

"You will have friends with you when you attend *ton* functions," Lady Sedgewick assured her, still a bit frosty, but visibly trying.

"Very well," Mary said, and then forced herself to add, "As long as they don't expect me to abandon more important business to entertain them."

The warm, sunny room was suddenly frigid.

Mary's cheeks burned and she felt vaguely nauseated.

After a long, excruciating silence, Lady Sedgewick cleared her throat. "Would you be free to pay a few calls, Miss Barnett?"

Morning calls. Bile rose in Mary's throat just thinking the words, the sickness in her stomach intensifying. She'd hated those humiliating visits almost more than balls and parties.

"Lord Avington and I have meetings with our solicitors for the next few days. So, no morning calls this week." Not to mention she had a great deal of work to do with her secretary on the canal project in Lanarkshire, which was coming to fruition at the worst possible time.

The countess set down the small notebook. "I'm afraid I must have misunderstood you, Miss Barnett."

Mary met the woman's cold gaze and almost shivered. "In what way?"

"I thought you were interested in furthering your sister's social aspirations."

"I am."

"Then attending functions—even balls—and making social visits are the least of what you must do."

"Fine. I will clear my schedule next week. I'll make morning calls on the same days when I must attend evening functions." Mary paused, and had to force herself to add, "Better to ruin three entire days than part of every day."

The countess's full lips tightened, but she merely nodded rather than hurl the Staffordshire shepherdess on the table beside her at Mary's head. "I will consult with your mother on these matters and have a schedule for you by next week."

Mary darted a quick glance at the earl, who'd been quiet throughout the tense exchange.

His gaze was already resting on her, and his once-warm blue eyes were bleak.

By the time five weeks was at an end Lord Avinton would not be able to bear looking at her, not to mention actually touching her.

Mary should have been happy, or at least relieved. After all, her plan was working like a charm.

Instead, she felt like weeping.

Chapter 10

It had only been four days since Mary and Lord Avington had agreed to marry and already she missed the simplicity of her former life.

Take right now, for instance.

A mere three days ago she would have been ensconced in her study with her secretary, John, happily reading the latest batch of reports from Liverpool.

Instead, she was sitting across from a ridiculously attractive stranger whom she'd been insulting at every opportunity.

Interestingly—and worryingly—he'd suddenly stopped responding to her snappish responses and barbed questions yesterday. Ever since, he'd been cool, but no longer rigidly angry.

Mary worried about that. Had he simply had enough? Or was he up to something?

The earl cleared his throat. "I've sent for the last five years of ledgers for Avington Castle and they should be delivered to you within the next few days. They will give you a good idea of the estate and which items are most pressing."

Lord Avington's words were music to Mary's ears. One of the few aspects of this marriage that she still looked forward to was exploring her new home in the years ahead. Well, if he didn't bar the gate against her.

She might begrudge her husband-to-be access to her body, but she was grateful that her money would be used to restore a castle that guidebooks called one of the most fascinating in Britain.

"I look forward to learning about the property," she said, unable to make a sneering response for some reason. "I understand it is considered one of England's treasures."

A genuine smile flickered across his face. "It was… once. I suppose it could be again." He left the words, *with enough money* left unsaid. "The books date back to 1588, which is when construction was completed, and are worth perusing for their historical value alone."

"Is that not a little late for castles?"

"It is, indeed. It is one of only a handful of such structures built during the Elizabethan period. I believe architects call it a *revival* castle which makes it sound as if it isn't a *real* fortification. Tt was seized by the Roundheads during the Civil War and used as a garrison, so although it was built by a wealthy ancestor with hunting, feasting, and frivolity in mind, it was briefly used for military purposes." He hesitated, and then said, "I would be happy to come and look over the ledgers with you when they arrive."

The offer was both humbling and painful. Humbling because his generosity with her—a woman who'd been as unpleasant as she could contrive—touched her. And painful because she knew she'd have to reject it.

Mary studied her fiancé of seventy-two hours, attempting, and failing, to read the truth in his eyes. She was no more accustomed to his face and body than she'd been that first evening. If anything, she was more in awe of his perfection.

Nobody—no matter how attractive and confident and self-assured—liked to have an offer of assistance thrown back in their teeth. It might be the final straw and make him stop trying.

Mary forced herself to say, in the most bored, patronizing tone possible, "That would be most helpful, my lord."

Rather than flinch at her blatant insincerity, the corners of his magnificent eyes crinkled with amusement and he assaulted her senses with one of his wit-scrambling smiles.

"What is so funny?" she demanded, her face heating. What sort of man thrived on insults?

He refused to answer her impertinent question. Instead, he gestured to where her mother, sister, and Lady Sedgewick sat, discussing flowers or orchestras or some other frippery. "It sounds as if the ball will be quite grand."

Mary scowled. She was already exhausted hearing about the ball and her impending wedding and her mother and sister had only known about it for a few days. Thank God it would only last a few more weeks. If this had carried on for months, she would have run mad.

"My mother would like nothing more than to speak of ball or wedding matters from the moment she wakes until her head hits the pillow. In fact, I would not be surprised to learn she talks of it in her sleep."

He laughed and Mary gave him a grudging smile.

"My sisters will be thrilled to join them," he said. "They and my brother and my Aunt Mercy will arrive next week. I made arrangements to put them up at the Clarendon." His warm, confident manner faltered slightly.

Mary didn't need to be a mind-reader to guess at the source of his faint flush: money. The only time she'd seen him become stubborn and unreasonable was yesterday and briefly today at their settlement discussions, which had eaten up almost six hours each day.

Both times he'd become short tempered it had been about money.

"We have already agreed to generous jointures for all my dependents and more than generous dowries for my sisters. Upon marriage I receive *half* ownership in each of the companies—and the income they generate, which should be more than enough to discharge my obligations and not only repair Avington Castle, but build an entirely new castle if I am so inclined. If you wish to settle your personal fortune on future children, that is fine. But to give half to me in addition to everything else seems… excessive."

Mary had turned to the two teams of solicitors. "Will you excuse us, please?"

The four men—two of hers and two of his lordship's—had evacuated the room with alacrity. The earl's solicitors had been red faced with embarrassment and Mary knew that her presence at such negotiations was not only highly unconventional, but also deeply distressing, not just to the earl's lawyers, but to the earl, himself.

Mary snorted. Too bad; they'd do well to become accustomed to her presence at any and all discussions pertaining to her or her businesses. Lord Avington, included.

She'd turned on him the moment the men were gone. "I am weary of your resistance on this point, my lord."

"As I said, it seems excessive."

"It is not excessive," Mary said, speaking to him in a tone of voice she had *never* used on anyone before—no matter how menial. "You will discover—once you learn more about these business enterprises—that while they yield a profit, it is not always regular. Often that money needs to be immediately invested to yield larger results. You cannot count on it as a stable source of income. So, you will need a *regular* source of income—hence the division of my inheritance. My *dowery* in other words. You had your chance to set your terms the night we made our agreement. It is too late now."

Rather than argue, he stared stonily at her.

Mary flung her hands up. "I find your reaction to such a simple division of money asinine."

His already haughty expression turned arctic at her tone and Mary's heart skipped wildly. Who knew he could look so stern and dangerous? So much like the man in her deliciously erotic dream, in fact.

"Asinine?" The word had frost on it.

"Yes, and embarrassing. Why do you think I made such an issue of this to begin with? Can you imagine how excruciating it would be for me to give my husband an allowance—as if he were my *child*. It would be unbearable and humiliating. Or perhaps we could just have your bills sent to me?" She gave a scornful laugh, refusing to be daunted by his cold, aristocratic stare. "Do you think I care to give my time to such matters—to become so. . . *entangled* in your affairs? Bills from your tailor? Your club?" *Your mistress*, Mary wanted to shout.

Thoughts of Lord Avington with a mistress seemed to be overwhelming all others these past few days, which made her even angrier. Especially since it was all her fault that she knew anything about the matter. She should have stopped Mr. Ross rather than allow him to continue his investigations. Now she knew more about the earl's current lover—Lady Celeste Copley—than she'd ever wanted to. Indeed, she knew that he'd gone to her only last night.

Had they talked about Mary? Laughed about her? Planned their liaison around the upcoming nuptials?

Mary ground her teeth, full-blown furious at the jealousy that licked at her at the mere thought of this relative stranger with another woman.

What was wrong with her? She was doing everything in her power to drive him away forever. So what if he had a mistress? All the better. She should be encouraging him to have a dozen.

The earl stopped his pacing and stood a mere foot away, his hands clasped behind his back in a distinctly military posture as he glowered down at her. If he thought to use his size to disconcert or pressure her, he was greatly mistaken. Mary had held her ground when faced with belligerent iron workers and arrogant ship captains, an angry lord was nothing.

Mary glared up at him. "*Looming* over me shall not change my mind, my lord."

The words hung between them like the echo of a gunshot. When they finally dissipated, the only audible sounds were Mary's harsh breathing and the loud ticking of the mantle clock—until Lord Avington threw back his head and laughed.

"You are right, Miss Barnett," he'd said, when he'd finally curbed his mirth. "I expect I will be saying that a great deal in the years ahead. Let us call the solicitors back into the room and I shall agree to an equitable division and we can move on."

His easy, smiling capitulation had taken the wind from her sails. Her own anger had taken longer to dissipate.

She was still annoyed now, hours after the meeting.

His reactions were often perplexing, to say the least. Laughter in response to an argument was completely foreign to her. And smiling in response to insults was mind boggling.

Was he so shallow and stupid he didn't even notice her cutting remarks?

Or was there something else—something more worrisome— going on beneath his handsome mask?

She couldn't keep her gaze off his long, elegant body as he lounged on the divan across from her. Did nothing matter to him? Was there nobody or no ideal he would fight for? He'd been in the army, of course, but even his comments about that period of his life had been dismissive and languid. Wasn't such behavior an indication of a lack of depth?

He met her censorious look and his shapely lips curved, his smile lush and promising. He was truly painful to look at and her reaction to him did not appear to be getting better each time she saw him. No, if anything, it was worse. Even when he wasn't with her, she thought about him. True, it had only been a few days, but she'd never experienced this—this *profound* distraction before.

Not even with Reginald when the two of them had been lovers.

Mary grimaced at the unwelcome thought. She'd have to face her cousin and his wife soon enough—after avoiding the pair as much as possible over the last ten years. She already knew the invitations had gone out to them for both the ball and the wedding.

"Do you enjoy reading, Miss Barnett?"

She looked up from his muscular thigh, which was garbed in buff pantaloons today. "Erm, reading?"

"Yes, books."

She ignored the jolt of annoyance she experienced at his easy teasing. "I read a great many journal articles pertaining to mining, manufacturing, and scientific innovations."

"But do you read for *pleasure?*"

What was he getting at *now.* "I do not read fiction or poetry, if that is what you are asking."

"You will have to give me a reading list so that I might educate myself, Miss Barnett."

She snorted.

"What? You don't believe that I am interested?"

"In mines and shipyards? No, my lord, I do not."

His eyelids lowered slightly, but his lazy smile did not falter.

Mary felt her skin prickle under his gaze—as if he found her an object of amusement.

"It's your turn, now, Miss Barnett."

"My turn to do what?"

"To ask *me* a question. After all, that is why your mother and Freddie have us sitting here together—so that we might get to know one another."

"Must we, my lord?"

"Must we what, Miss Barnett?"

"I am not interested in pointless chatter."

Instead of jumping to his feet and telling Mary to go to the devil, the earl merely smiled; it was that same slow, sensual smile that sent a painful jolt of pleasure skirling through her midsection.

"I daresay pointless chatter will be one of my few contributions to our marriage, Miss Barnett."

Mary couldn't help snorting. She met his eyes and they stared at each other in silence. Her heart fluttered in her chest like a butterfly beating its wings against a high wind and palms were suddenly damp. Mary knew—with a painful flash of clarity—that she didn't care how wrong her attraction was, nor how it was likely to cause her a great deal of pain.

Nor did she care *what* was beneath his façade, or even if there *was* anything at all but his gorgeous person: she wanted him.

She wanted his *person*. She wanted to possess him the way many women yearned for fine gowns or expensive jewelry.

And the thought of taking him into her body and having his child beneath her heart for nine months?

Mary swallowed noisily and blinked her eyes, as if that would banish the torrid sensations such an image evoked.

She *wanted*, and she knew the gnawing, greedy want she felt would only get worse before it got better. If it ever did.

Never had she wanted anything as badly as she wanted this man.

***

Never in his life had any woman looked at him with such scathing disregard.

Miles almost laughed. But he didn't because he'd begun to suspect his laughter irked her. She was not a frivolous woman. Actually, that was understating matters to such a degree as to be ridiculous; she rarely smiled or showed happiness or enjoyment in anything. Although, he had to admit, she had seemed quite pleased by his offer of estate ledgers.

Well, he thought with a bitter twist of his lips, it was a bloody good thing she liked ledgers because that was the only bride gift he could afford to give her.

Not that she appeared to want anything from him except his family escutcheon—for her sister—and his promise not to meddle excessively in her business *or* her life. Or touch her.

Two lives lived separately. Isn't that what she'd wanted? Well, she'd capitulated to his demand for children and a *normal* family life, but—based on her behavior these past few days—she would make him pay for it every step of the way.

And based on the sour, almost agonized expression she wore whenever they were in proximity, she sure as *hell* didn't want to spend any more time with him than she had to.

Well, the feeling was mutual; just thinking about bedding her gave Miles a headache.

Interestingly, the only thing that gave him any hope at all was her confession that she wasn't a virgin. Didn't that hint at passion? Perhaps somewhere inside her there was a woman who might like to talk of matters other than ledgers? If so, maybe Miles could find her if he was patient enough.

That was probably only wishful thinking.

She was probably exactly what she appeared: a cold, emotionless woman whose only interest in life was making money.

After all, look at her reaction to his offer to peruse his family's ledgers with her. They weren't just a compilation of expenditures; they were his family's history.

She'd looked at Miles as if he'd just offered to dunk her head in a horse trough.

Mary Barnett no more needed his assistance to comprehend his family's pitiful ledgers than the average woman needed help pulling on a glove.

Miles had already seen her mental acuity in action during the excruciating meetings with their solicitors, when she had insisted on opening the company books to him.

While he was not experienced in such matters, he was certainly educated enough to realize the sheer scope of her father's holdings and her obvious expertise.

She was correct in believing that he was ill-equipped to offer help in the management of those businesses. And she was probably correct in believing that he'd never be able to comprehend all of it. But he'd be damned if he didn't even try.

Besides, all of it seemed very interesting to him. Certainly more interesting than sitting in Lords and bickering endlessly.

Miles liked the thought of learning something that yielded an actual, tangible result. If you engaged in shipbuilding, you'd have a ship at the end of your endeavors.

If you engaged in assembling the necessary votes to pass some pet piece of legislation, you'd end up with a bill that bore no resemblance to the cause you'd spent months championing.

Miles studied Mary Barnett—she'd not invited him to use her Christian name and perhaps she never would—as she stared fixedly at the intricate carpet between them. Her jaw was moving slightly, as if she might be having an internal argument—something that was not unlikely given how much she seemed to enjoy conflict.

Miles couldn't help wondering what she was thinking. He wished he could ask her, the way she just came right out and asked him the things she wanted to know.

He opened his mouth to do so, but then shut it without speaking.

Miles suspected he might not want to know the truth, especially if it was thoughts about him.

Chapter 11

The effect of Miles's betrothal was immediate in some ways, one of which being his treatment at the hands of his creditors. Men who'd dunned him since his brother's death—and Bevan and their father for years before him—were now willing to extend more credit, forgive interest, and do everything and anything that would maintain the connection between themselves and this new man: a man who would soon have access to one of the greatest fortunes in England.

The sum required to settle his family's debts was obscene—unthinkable, really, although Miles forced himself to think of it daily.

First and second mortgages on the London House—which he'd not stepped foot in for decades as it had been leased all that time—and not two but three mortgages on the estate in Yorkshire. Loans on every piece of art and every article of value—furniture, silver, jewelry.

While using Miss Barnett's wealth to settle those massive debts made Miles feel ill, spending her money on himself—or at least exploiting the new credit available—was impossible.

Miles knew his resistance was futile. The truth was he *had* to spend it, at least some of it.

His family were arriving soon—his two sisters, at least two aunts, and Crispin—and they would all require clothing.

Miles himself looked like a bloody street urchin in his holey boots and threadbare garments and yet he couldn't bring himself to purchase new boots, coats, linens, and the dozen other items he'd done without for years.

He was so bloody ashamed whenever he thought about spending her money on himself.

Despite his shame, he was *determined* to hide his feelings from his relatives as the last thing he wanted was for them to feel guilty that he'd bartered himself for their pleasure.

Oh, they all knew that he was marrying for money, of course. But they didn't need to know just how much he hated selling himself, not to mention how much the woman he was marrying hated *him*.

They would be arriving tomorrow, and Miles had no earthly idea what to do with them. Which is why he was—yet again—haunting

Freddie's comfortable parlor, even though the poor woman was already swamped managing the details of his upcoming ball and wedding.

"You write more letters than anyone I know," Miles said as he strolled toward his favorite chair and dropped into it.

"Most of these are not personal," Freddie said. "And I must credit *you* for at least four of them."

Miles frowned. "Me?"

"Yes, news of your betrothal has set off a veritable avalanche of requests for my services."

"Well, always glad to be of assistance. Are you accepting them all?"

"No, I'm afraid I've got my hands full with your affairs at the moment. But you didn't come here to discuss my clients, Miles."

Miles sighed. "No, I didn't. I know you've never met them before, but I came to ask if you'd help with Pen and Maria when they come to town?"

"You know I'd love to meet your sisters and help in any way I can. What did you have in mind?"

"They will need clothing—as will my aunts and Crispin—and none of them have ever spent time in London. I know this sounds terribly similar to what you do for a living and—"

"Don't be foolish, Miles, you are my friend and I would love to help." She gave him a charming, warm smile. "Besides, shopping for clothing is not exactly a chore." Freddie opened her notebook—the one she was never without. "So, they arrive tomorrow?"

"Yes. I daresay they'll be exhausted." Not only from the journey but from being trapped in a coach with two of his elderly aunts, who'd insisted on coming to chaperon their nieces.

"I shall meet them at Coal House on Wednesday when they come to dinner, perhaps I might discuss a shopping expedition with them then? If they are amenable, we could go as soon as Friday," Freddie said, flicking back and forth between pages and making a small note.

"I'm sure they will be."

Miles smiled fondly at her and turned back to the basket. All the silks were on cards, separated by color and shade. Freddie was very neat and organized compared to his sisters, whose needlework baskets always resembled colorful bird nests. Speaking of birds… He picked up a dainty pair of scissors that had been cunningly fashioned as a long-legged bird—a stork or crane or some such. The tips of his fingers barely fit into the gold rings. He turned them on their side to get a better look. They were intricately detailed, right down to individual feathers, and quite beautiful.

He chewed his lip; did Miss Barnett do needlework? Would she like a pair? He could not see her bent over a tambor, for some reason. But didn't everyone need a pair of scissors? He would like to get her *something*, even though he knew he would be buying the gift with her own money. He frowned at the thought.

Miles lifted the scissors. "These are lovely."

She jotted something in her book and closed it before looking up. "Those belonged to my grandmother."

"Do you think Miss Barnett would like a pair? She likes birds, after all."

"I don't know—does she enjoy needlework?"

Miles grimaced. "Lord, I don't know." He replaced the scissors, suddenly feeling rather foolish.

Freddie lowered herself next to her basket of silks. "I have a few things I want to say."

"Uh-oh. I know this tone. You are about to give me a raking."

"Have you spoken much to her, Miles?"

He thought about the other night and his attempts to learn more about her. And her subsequent comment about *pointless chatter*. "Only about business."

"Have the two of you made any plans?"

"You mean about the wedding?"

"No, I mean *before* the wedding."

"Lord, Fred—what kind of plans?"

She sighed. "Surely you cannot be so dense?"

Miles's face heated. "She wishes this to be a business arrangement, Freddie. You heard her; she has consented to three engagements per week, and she told me specifically that she did not care for any false courtship. What the devil does that leave?"

"False courtship is one thing, Miles, but actually getting to know your wife a little is quite another." She grimaced. "I know she appears… prickly"—she ignored Miles's bitter hoot of laughter— "but you must understand that she would have had a terrible time all those years ago during her single Season."

Yes, he could only imagine how the *ton* had treated her.

He sighed. "You are right. I will try harder to be more understanding."

"Good. As your sisters and Crispin will be here, why not make up a party? How about a night at the theater? A day trip to Richmond?"

He grimaced at the thought of throwing together people who didn't know one another. But they would need to know each other eventually, wouldn't they?

"How about Vauxhall Gardens? Isn't that something good for all ages?" he asked.

"Excellent suggestion."

"Would you come, Fred?"

"Of course I will, I am employed by Mrs. Barnett."

"Yes, but I would like you to come as my *friend* rather than my soon-to-be mother-in-law's employee."

"What possible difference could that make?"

"Now it is *you* who are being dense, darling. I want you to enjoy yourself and relax, not work."

"I enjoy myself more when I work."

Miles rolled his eyes. "Stubborn."

Freddie picked up her embroidery frame and Miles could see she was working on something different today, no longer the vase of flowers. "You could arrange a barge party to take everyone," she suggested.

"I could, using Miss Barnett's money."

"Miles!"

He looked up at her sharp tone.

"This behavior is unworthy of you."

"What is unworthy? Not wishing to strew her money around with largesse—as if it were mine? As if everyone in London wasn't perfectly aware of what I am doing and why? Lord." He let his head fall against the high back of the chair.

"Do you think being ashamed of what you are doing is somehow making things better?"

Miles ignored the question.

"Really, do you? Mary Barnett is fully aware of the bargain she has made, Miles, a good deal of that bargain is you lending her family the consequence they desire. You can best go about fulfilling your part of the deal by acting as if you *do* believe her family deserves the welcome of the *ton*—even in the face of her aggravating and inexplicable hostility toward you," she added, more to herself than to Miles. She shook herself and fixed him with a glare. "Dispense with your foolish, ridiculous, and damaging masculine pride. You owe that much to her."

Miles knew she was right. He had no idea why he was so childish about the money. It was, after all, *why* he was marrying her. He'd not sugar-coated his offer; he had *spoken plainly*. Then why did he feel like such a dog?

"Matters will be awkward enough given how obstinately Miss Barnett is behaving. Your stiff, standoffish attitude will only make things worse. Especially if you behave so in front of your family and they see how you feel about the arrangement. Do you wish to make them feel guilty for your sacrifice?"

"Of course not," he snapped, returning her glare.

She gave him a satisfied, cat-like smile. "Good, that is better. Very lordly, in fact."

He laughed, all the irritation draining out of him. "What a witch you are, Fred."

Her gray eyes flitted over his person. "You sound like a lord, but you still look like an impoverished dancing master."

The woman was relentless. Miles looked down at the scuffed toes of his Hessians, boots so old no amount of polishing could make them presentable. He sighed. "Fine. I shall go shopping tomorrow."

"Go today."

He had to laugh. "You've already made this match, Freddie. You needn't work so hard anymore on my behalf."

Suddenly her magnificent eyes were sad. "You are my friend, Miles—my best friend. I want you to be *happy*. Can't you understand that? I know Mary Barnett would not be your first choice of wife," she hesitated and her pale cheeks darkening to a deep rose. "She is not replacing any other in your heart, is she?"

Miles stared at her, wondering if this was her way of asking if it was *her* he loved. It wouldn't be so odd; he'd wondered the same thing a time or two himself. Did he love Fred? Was he *in* love with her?

Had she asked him about love because *she* loved *him*?

No, Miles couldn't believe that. Although he knew nothing about her marriage, she'd made it clear she would never marry again. Nor did she take lovers. *That* he knew because she had once told him so.

The conversation had taken place the first year he worked at the Stefani Academy. He and Freddie had stayed late at the school to help Portia Stefani and the other teachers with the upcoming Christmas celebration. When their friends had left to go hear an author acquaintance of Lorelei's speak, Freddie had begged off and Miles had accompanied her home. She'd invited him inside, offered him a glass of surprisingly good brandy—a last vestige from Honoria Keyes's father, who'd once owned the house—and they'd ended up together on a settee before a crackling fire.

They had talked for what must have been two hours, and then Miles had kissed her and, for a moment, she had responded. But only for a moment.

He'd released her when she'd suddenly stiffened. He'd opened his mouth to apologize, but she'd stopped him.

"Please, don't say you're sorry—I'm not. I wanted to kiss you as much, if not more, than you probably wanted to kiss me."

Miles had wanted to do a damned sight more than kiss her for a very long time—but he'd kept his mouth shut and let her speak.

"The truth is, that is all I want, Miles. I do not take lovers and I'm not interested in marriage." She'd smiled to soften her words. "I value you greatly as a friend. I hope what has been simmering between us does not jeopardize our friendship."

It was the only time either of them had acknowledged the attraction they felt for each other. Miles still believed she was one of the most beautiful women of his acquaintance, but he'd stopped thinking of her as a potential lover. She'd been right—they were friends, best friends. Given their pasts and the way they looked at life they would have never suited each other as anything more.

Miles would do anything for her—take a bayonet through the chest, give her his last coin—so he supposed he must love her. But *in* love with her? No. Although it had been so long since he'd felt that emotion, that he doubted he would even recognize it anymore.

"Are you asking me if I'm in love with Celeste, Freddie?"

Not surprisingly her color deepened at the mention of their mutual friend and his erstwhile mistress and Miles was instantly ashamed by his behavior.

"I'm sorry, darling. Just because you're my friend doesn't mean I should mention such sordid subjects in your presence."

"You know you may always say anything to me, Miles." She held his gaze for a moment longer and then lowered her eyes to her work.

Miles thought their conversation was over, but then she said, "Take the time and make the effort to get to know Miss Barnett, Miles. I feel certain you won't regret it."

Miles chuckled, stood, and strode over to her, dropping a chaste kiss on her cheek. "Yes, ma'am. Now, I'd better be off if I'm to obey your orders to engage in an orgy of spending."

Freddie put aside her needlework. "I shall walk you out."

Out in the small entry way Miles picked up his hat and cane and glanced down at his worn boot. He held out his foot and turned it from side to side. "I can't say I won't be happy to see the last of these old fellows. I've not had a new pair of boots since... Hell, I can't recall." He let his foot fall to the floor with a soft thump.

"Miles?"

He turned to Freddie. "Yes, darling?"

"It will be all right." Her expression was oddly tense, as if *she* were the one who needed reassuring. Was she feeling guilty about brokering this match, even though he'd asked her to? Or was it something else she was feeling.

Miles could not bear to think of what that might mean—not now—and he pasted his most charming smile on his face. "It is *already* all right, Freddie. It's better than all right and it's also far better than I ever hoped for," he said, not entirely lying. "I'm just being a spoiled child because I enjoy all your coddling." He grinned and held out his arms, as if to display his person. "The next time you see me, I shall be togged to the nines! I'll be an entirely new man."

At least on the outside, he would.

Chapter 12

Mary was in the back garden when a footman approached with Lord Avington following along behind him.

"Hello Miss Barnett," her betrothed said when she turned from the bench where she'd been watching her birds and reading one of the recent reports on Baltic lumber tariff issues.

"Good afternoon, Lord Avington," she said, her eyes drawn to her footman's red face.

"Don't scold poor Nathaniel," the earl said, reading her expression far too easily for her comfort. "I made him bring me out here when I heard you were with your birds." He flashed her a winning smile. "You did mention letting me see them," he reminded her.

"Of course." She nodded her dismissal at the red-faced footman, who was under standing orders not to disturb her when she was with her birds, which was the only private time she allowed herself.

She set aside the report and watched as the earl approached the cluster of fowl.

He pointed to Heather and Peony, who were dust bathing companionably in a pot that had, until half an hour ago, held some sort of flower. "You must keep your gardener busy."

She ignored the comment. "Did we have an appointment, my lord?"

The earl turned away from the birds. "No, we did not."

He must have purchased new clothes and it was like the final touch on a masterpiece painting—the addition of a gold frame.

Ugh! She wanted to run and hide. He was simply too perfect. She must have been stark raving mad to think she could marry this man and hold him at arm's length. Even when she avoided him thoughts of him dominated her waking and sleeping hours with increasing frequency.

"I won't take up much of your time," he said, no longer smiling as he'd been a moment earlier, making Mary feel as if she'd been responsible for dimming the sun. "I came to ask you to Vauxhall Gardens next week."

She frowned as she tried to recall the schedule she'd received from Lady Sedgewick. "Oh. Is that one of the three outings?"

His lips twisted into an odd smile. "No, this was something additional."

"Ah."

"If you don't fancy Vauxhall, we could take a ride out to Richmond and have a picnic." He hesitated and added. "These would be entertainments for us and our families, to get to know each other. Intimate affairs."

Mary ignored the joyous leaping she felt in her chest at his words. He wanted her to get to know his family…

Stay with your plan, she ordered herself.

"You did say you liked plain speaking," she reminded him.

"Yes," he said after a long pause. "I did say that."

"Would you be terribly bothered if I declined your kind invitation? You could always take Jenny and Mama."

He smiled tightly. "No bother at all, Miss Barnett. And yes, I will ask your mother and Miss Jenny."

Hector suddenly crowed and the earl turned to look at the diminutive rooster. "Well, he's quite the lad, isn't he?" he said, smiling at the glossy black bird, whose plumage was blazingly iridescent in the sunlight.

Mary couldn't help smiling as she looked at her prize rooster. "Yes, Hector is one of a kind and the result of a decade of careful selection."

"Do they all have names?"

"Don't you name your horses?" she shot back.

His eyes seemed exceptionally blue as he stared at her. "I want to make an amendment to our *schedule*. Not Vauxhall," he assured her when she opened her mouth. "But I do want to take you for a drive in the park tomorrow. I've purchased a curricle for our journey to Avington Castle."

Ah, yes. Mary had tried to put that out of her mind. It had been yet another idea of Lady Sedgewick's that they travel from London together—to get better acquainted. Mary had not been able to fabricate a suitable excuse.

You are a liar, a voice in her head laughingly accused. *You are dying to be alone with him for almost three entire days.*

Mary ordered the voice to shut up and turned to the man still standing and waiting in front of her.

"What time?" she asked.

"In time to be part of the afternoon strut."

Mary digested that information, nodded, and then forced herself to say. "Very well, I shall add that to my weekly calendar."

He bowed. "I look forward to seeing you tomorrow, Miss Barnett."

Mary nodded and then watched him leave; his figure as magnificent from the backside as it was from the front. When he disappeared around a hedge and out of sight, she felt an intense, sharp pang.

She had to fight the urge to run after him—to beg him to reconsider his offer to host a party at Vauxhall Garden.

Mary shook away the foolish notion and turned back to her report. She had no time for parties, she was already falling farther and farther behind.

But when Mary tried to resume her reading, she found it impossible to concentrate for some reason.

***

"She said *no*?" Lorelei Fontenot demanded, lowering her biscuit back to her plate without taking a bite.

Miles swallowed his mouthful of food before saying, "I did ask her mother and sister and they will attend. I've engaged a barge to—"

"Is the woman demented?" Lori asked sharply.

Miles scowled at his over-excitable friend. "May I remind you that *woman* is to be my wife, Lori."

"Oh, don't come all *lord of the manor* with me, Miles."

Before he could respond, not that he was sure he knew what to say, Freddie cleared her throat and said, "Lori." She didn't raise her voice or even give the younger woman a chiding look, but—miraculously—it seemed to be enough.

Lori flung up her hands. "Fine. I was being obnoxious—I'm sorry, Miles. But *even so*," she persisted, "Surely somebody needs to tell her that such behavior is not acceptable? I'm the rudest person I know and even I wouldn't do such a thing!"

Miles and Freddie exchanged amused looks and he knew she was thinking the same thing as he was: Lori would absolutely do such a thing—and much worse.

"I see the way you two are looking at each other," Lori said, her lips pursing with irritation. "And yes, I *might* do something like that. But not to you, Miles. You are lovely. You are all that is good about your wretched, horrid, overbearing gender."

Miles laughed. "On behalf of men, everywhere, I accept your compliment."

Lori was not diverted. "Tell him, Freddie! Tell him that he must speak to Miss Barnett and explain why she must put herself out, at least for the sake of her sister and mother, who will end up looking downright odd if they arrive at Vauxhall Gardens without her."

Freddie sighed, set down her cup in its saucer, and said, "Lori is correct, Miles. I know you don't wish to hear it, but Mrs. Barnett has engaged me to launch her daughter *and* to see that this wedding goes off smoothly. If Miss Barnett will not come out and socialize—"

"But she does socialize," Miles interrupted. "Just last night we went to a dinner party at Lord and Lady Davis's house. Tomorrow we will be going to the Linwood dinner. And later this week we will be attending a Venetian breakfast."

"Her three functions a week," Freddie said flatly.

It wasn't a question, but Miles nodded.

"Three functions?" Lori repeated. "What does that mean?"

They both ignored her question.

"You will need to explain—gently—that she needs to make appearances at functions planned by her own family and yours, Miles."

He gave a disbelieving snort.

"Would you like me to talk to her?" Freddie offered.

"Or me?" Lori said.

He gave a genuine chuckle of amusement at the thought of Miss Barnett and Lori squaring off against each other. He could sell tickets and make a fortune on such an event. "Er, as much as I'd like to foist this off on you, Fred, I must decline." He grinned at Lori. "And as entertaining as it is to imagine you and Miss Barnett in the same room together, my dear Lori, I respectfully decline your offer, as well."

"So what are you going to do?" Lori asked, taking her fourth macaroon and dunking it into her tea.

"I'll talk to her tomorrow when I take her driving in Hyde Park." He gestured to the soggy mess she'd made of the biscuit. "That is disgusting, by the way."

She grinned and popped it into her mouth, chewing enthusiastically before swallowing and then saying, "May I come along on your drive tomorrow?"

This time Freddie joined Miles when he laughed.

***

After leaving Freddie's house Miles took his new curricle and pair out for one more drive before tomorrow, when he'd be taking Miss Barnett out for the first time.

He'd bought the entire rig from Viscount Elton, who'd been desperate for a quick sale after a bad run at the tables.

"You've landed in a bed of roses, haven't you old man," the viscount had taunted when the money had changed hands and they'd retired to Whites—where Miles was once again a member—to share a drink.

Miles had ignored the other man's crass comment, which had been tinged with more than a little envy. Elton himself had been angling for an heiress for years. But no man who cared for his daughter would allow her to marry the dissolute viscount, no matter how desperate he might be for a title.

"I know her cousin—Reg Cooper," Elton went on, undaunted by Miles's clear disinterest in discussing Miss Barnett with him. "He was all set to hold his breath and take the plunge with her... oh, this must have been nigh on ten years ago," he added, as if Miles had asked.

Miles finished his drink and set down his glass, wishing he'd never agreed to tarry with Elton, although he couldn't regret the purchase of the curricle and pair as the fool was undoubtedly a good judge of horseflesh.

As he prepared to stand Elton said, "Cooper said she was burned all the way down and twice as eager to make up for it." Elton said, causing two men who'd joined them—both friends of Elton and too young for Miles to have known at school—to snigger.

Miles moved before he'd realized what he was doing, knocking the table into the other two men and closing his hands around Elton's neck and jerking him out of his chair before pinning him to the wall full of books behind him.

"You've got a big mouth, Elton," he snarled, squeezing his fingers tighter and ignoring the three or more sets of hands that closed around his upper arms and attempted to tug him off the other man. "If I hear another word out of you about Miss Barnett—or her family—ever again I'll shut your mouth for you. Permanently."

When he released his grip Elton slithered to the floor, red faced and gasping.

Miles was vaguely aware of a jumble of voices behind him, but his head was buzzing so loudly he couldn't make out any words.

A hand closed around his arm and he whipped around.

"Steady on, Avington," a familiar voice warned.

He blinked away the red haze and saw it was the Marquess of Saybrook, his friend Honoria's husband.

"Saybrook," he muttered, glancing around and grimacing at all the attention he'd garnered.

"Come. I'll walk out with you," the marquess said.

Once they were out in the street the other man turned left and Miles followed without comment. Not until their club was out of sight did Saybrook ask. "Where are you headed next?"

It took Miles a moment to recall what his plans had been. He felt scorched by his own fury; not since the war had he lost control of himself like that. "I need to stop at Weston's and then on to Hoby."

"I'll go with you as far as the tailor," Saybrook said. "I've been meaning to order a few new waistcoats. Shall we walk?"

It was only half a mile to Weston's shop on Bond Street, so the men struck out in that direction.

Saybrook, who had been badly wounded by shrapnel during the war, walked with his uninjured side toward Miles. He was fair-haired, blue eyed, and as handsome as a Greek god on the one side while the other was an unmoving mass of scars.

Miles had known the other man for years—indeed, Saybrook had rescued him the second time he'd been taken captive during the War. Their history was a complicated one and only recently had they become better acquainted.

"I take it Elton was being his usual charming self?" Saybrook said after they'd walked in silence for a while.

"Yes, I shouldn't have let it get to me."

"You just bought that rig of his, didn't you? His curricle and those spanking chestnuts?"

Miles nodded.

"I thought about bidding on them myself," he said and then laughed. "But Honey has pointed out—quite rightly—that I shouldn't purchase every single horse I fancy. At least not until we build another extension on the stables."

"Didn't you just build on more stalls?"

Saybrook laughed good naturedly. "Yes. Fortunately, there is no law that says I can't always build more. Well, no law except my wife, that is."

Miles smiled at the thought of Honey ever denying her husband anything he wanted. The two were so besotted with each other it would have been nauseating if he didn't like them both so much.

"Thanks for stepping in back there," Miles said.

"Of course," Saybrook said. "I heard what Elton said. You had every right to rough him up—to do more, in fact."

"It is unfortunate that the man is such a notoriously poor swordsman and shot. If I challenged him, I would be viewed as a cold-blooded killer." Miles sighed. "I should have stayed long enough to give him the opportunity to slap a glove in my face."

"Elton is a craven little toad. I doubt he has the stones to stand up for himself."

What had infuriated him more than Elton's crack was the fact that Miss Barnett's own cousin had been so indiscreet. Miles was not looking forward to meeting the man who'd been Miss Barnett's lover—or at least one of them.

"I had a chance to speak to Miss Barnett at the Davis's dinner party last night," Saybrook said.

"Oh?" Miles had been seated at the far end of the table from Honey and Saybrook, but he'd noticed the marquess enjoying a lively chat with Miss Barnett. She'd actually smiled at the other man. Miles had half a mind to ask Saybrook how he'd managed that feat, but kept his mouth shut.

"She's a fascinating woman," Saybrook went on. "I was especially interested in her views on the Baltic tariff issue. I'm on a committee that Lansdowne has formed and we are reviewing the matter."

Miles knew that. He'd only recently assumed his seat in Lords, but he knew there was a large—and growing—faction who were proponents of Adam Smith's *laissez-faire* theories. Now that the war was over, many believed the sky-high import taxes—on lumber as high as 275%—should be relaxed, if not entirely eliminated.

Naturally Miss Barnett, as one of the nation's biggest shipbuilders, would be behind such legislation.

"She has agreed to provide me with some information that will help argue the issue." Saybrook cut Miles a sideways look. "Er, I hope I didn't overstep discussing such matters with her?"

Miles laughed. "I doubt you could stop her," he said. "Not that I would wish to," he added, not entirely truthfully.

It was uncomfortable to be marrying a woman who openly dealt in trade. But Miles wasn't sure if he was embarrassed by her actions or shamed by her superior knowledge. That, he knew, was a subject he would need to give some serious thought to.

"She is an impressive woman," Saybrook said.

"She is, indeed."

The other man hesitated, and then seemed to come to a decision, and said, "It used to bother me to think of Honey engaging in business."

Miles gave him a surprised look. "But she is an artist. Although it is unconventional, it is hardly unheard of for women to be painters." Female titans of industry, on the other hand, were rare—indeed, Miles couldn't think of another.

"That is true," Saybrook said, "but it bothered me to think of her spending hours—over many weeks—closeted with the men she painted." He snorted. "She's recently been commissioned to paint Old Douro, you know."

Miles stopped and turned to the other man. "I did *not* know that! How splendid."

Saybrook couldn't keep from grinning, the lopsided expression charming. "Wellington contacted her himself, quite an honor from a man we both know likes to delegate all but his most important correspondence to his secretary. In any event, I am very proud of her, although of course I can take no credit for any of it. She is a genius without any help from me or anyone else."

"She is," Miles agreed, clapping a hand on Saybrook's shoulder. "But you are to be commended for having the wit to choose such a brilliant wife."

The two of them laughed and recommenced their journey.

"I can't wait to congratulate her," Miles said. "Unless I'm not supposed to know?"

"No, I am not talking out of school. She was going to tell Freddie and Lori about it, I'm sure you will hear it from her own mouth at the Linwood dinner party—you and Miss Barnett are coming, are you not?"

"We are."

"So, you will not mind if I mention Miss Barnett's contribution to Lansdowne?"

Miles couldn't help thinking that the marquess had been very clever to mention Honey's achievement before asking him such a question.

In all honesty, the thought of his future countess's name being bandied about in a discussion on tariff's—a subject which would become ugly and heated—was not something he could bring himself to like. But he *was* proud of Miss Barnett for her knowledge and expertise, even though—just like Saybrook, he'd had no hand in any of her brilliance.

He turned to the other man and said, "Not only is it not my place to decide to whom or about what Miss Barnett speaks, but I have to admit that I am—like you—rather proud to ally myself with such an intelligent, talented woman."

It was too bad Miss Barnett didn't feel the same about him.

Chapter 13

The door to Mary's office swung open hard enough to bang against the wall, causing her secretary John—who'd been in the middle of listing his suggestions for improvements at the new colliery they'd just acquired—to startle and jump to his feet.

Mary frowned at her mother, who was standing in the doorway and breathing heavily, her skin flushed, her hair ruffled. "Mama, what is—"

"I want a moment with my daughter, Mr. Courtland," her mother said grimly, her gaze riveted on Mary.

Mary nodded at her secretary. "We can finish this later."

Poor John scuttled from the room in record time, closing the door soundlessly behind him.

Mary gestured to a chair. "Won't you have a—"

"Why, Mary? That's all I want to know. Why?"

"Why what?"

"Lady Sedgewick tells me that you have rejected Lord Avington's suggestion for an evening at Vauxhall Gardens."

"Oh. That." She replaced her quill in the standish and sat back in her chair. It, like the desk, had belonged to her father and both were too large for her, but she loved using them despite that.

"You have always been... willful, but your behavior recently is excessive even for you. Why are you treating his lordship with such disdain?"

"This is not a love match, mama, and the sooner you stop expecting such behavior the sooner—"

"It does not need to be love to include common courtesy, Mary."

Mary blinked at her raised, harsh tone. "You know how I despise such trifling activities. Why can't you and Jenny just go in my place and leave me in peace?"

"Why can't you think of somebody except yourself for once?"

Mary's temper, which had been simmering for days—more at herself than at her mother's disapproval—finally boiled over. "This entire farce of a marriage is for somebody else!"

"What is *wrong* with you? How did I err so in your upbringing? You have a handsome, kind, personable man and all you do is rebuff and reject his every overture of friendship."

"That is an exaggeration. I went with him for a drive in his new curricle only a few days ago."

"Don't even remind me," her mother wailed. "You insisted he take your *secretary* along with you! To Hyde Park!"

Mary shrugged. "What of it? John sat in the groom's seat, not in my lap. Besides, Lord Avington has evinced an interest in our family's business. He can hardly find a more informed man to tutor him than John."

Mary had hoped that the act of inviting her secretary along on a drive in Hyde Park would be the thing that would have put her beyond the pale in the earl's eyes.

But—if anything—he'd appeared even more amused than usual.

Yet again, Mary had seriously misjudged the man. If she felt sorry for anyone, it had been poor John, who'd felt like a fish out of water each time the earl had stopped the curricle to converse with a friend—of which he appeared to have hundreds—and had taken pains to introduce her secretary to each and every one of them.

"You are ruining everything, Mary. *Everything.*" Her mother dropped her head into her hands and then, to Mary's utter horror, burst into tears.

"Mama!" She leapt up and hurried around the desk and took her mother's arm. "Please, sit."

When she slumped onto the sofa Mary crossed the room, tugged on the servant pull, and then returned to sit beside her mother, patting her shoulder ineffectually while she cried.

Such emotional outpourings were anathema to her. The last time she recalled crying herself was from physical, not emotional, pain— while she'd recuperated over the weeks and months following the fire.

Not even when Reginald had all but stripped her bare for the amusement of his friends had she shed a tear.

Don't get angry, luv; get revenge, her father had been fond of saying.

Of course, Lucas Barnett had meant his business opponents, and not his own family. But if her father had ever learned what Reginald had done not only *with* her, but *to* her, he would have killed his nephew with his bare hands.

Mary had had no way to get revenge upon her cousin a decade ago, and so she had settled for showing him how little she cared about him and what he had done to her.

The one good thing to come from her father's burdensome will had been the chance to finally exact her pound of flesh from her cousin.

Her lips twitched into a smile as she imagined Reginald's face *now*. He wouldn't be smirking knowing that his chance at gaining an equal share in Barnett Shipping and a host of other lucrative ventures was being yanked from his grasp. In less than three weeks Mary would snatch hundreds of thousands of pounds from his greedy fingers.

For the first time in over a decade she was looking forward to seeing him again.

The door opened and a footman entered, shaking her from her pleasant thoughts. "Send for Tripp," she said.

Tripp was her mother's maid, a phlegmatic woman who'd been with Louisa Barnett since before she'd married Mary's father. Tripp would know how to settle her frazzled nerves.

Her mother grabbed her hand when Mary stood. "You must stop this, Mary. Please. I beg of you."

She looked down into the other woman's red rimmed, bloodshot eyes and sighed before lowering herself back onto the settee. "You don't understand, Mama. I cannot simply stop working entirely. You saw how much time Papa spent on his businesses. Now they are *my* responsibility."

"I know that, Mary. But to turn down an offer to socialize with your betrothed's family? You cannot do that! You will make your sister a laughingstock. You will make Lord Avington a laughingstock."

"Surely you are exaggerating, Mama. I do not see how—"

"Please. You only need to play your part for a few more weeks."

Mary pulled away and stood, pacing the rug, her frustration on the subject pouring out in words, "That isn't true and you know it. There will be next year to contend with. If I do not put my foot down now, I will find myself overtaken by all this—this pointless... vapidity. The same way you would not wish to sit in on a meeting at the shipyard, I do not wish to give my life over to one pointless social event after another, Mama." She stopped her pacing and threw herself into her chair.

Her mother stood and came toward her, for once, her expression was not judgmental or critical, but sad. She took Mary's hands. "This man will be your husband for the rest of your life. You will live with him and his family. The same way you would not insult or alienate a prospective business partner you should not treat the earl this way. He is far too polite to ever say anything. You must make this right, Mary." She gave her hands one last squeeze and then turned to go.

When the door closed behind her Mary dropped her head in her hands, as her mother had done earlier. Rather than sobbing, she groaned.

This was turning out to be much more unpleasant than she'd anticipated.

Although some of it had been amusing. Her lips twitched into a reluctant smile as she recalled Lord Avington's face when she'd shown up for the drive through Hyde Park with John Courtland in tow. Shock had seized his gorgeous features for a heartbeat before he'd given her the pleasant, warm-eyed smile he always bestowed on her.

Mary was aware of the looks they'd received as carriage after carriage had stopped to exchange greetings. Part of her had been ashamed by her behavior. But another part had wanted him to say something—to *do* something—rather than just smile.

She knew in her heart of hearts that he was horrified at having to marry her. She told herself that if he'd shown his disdain, she could have borne it better than his relentless courtesy.

But her mother was right; she'd need to live with the man for the rest of her life—even if they didn't do so in the same house. She might want to alienate him, but she didn't want to insult his family and make him hate her.

Mary sighed, reached into her desk, and took out a sheet of parchment.

And then she wrote a letter to Lord Avington begging his pardon and asking if it was too late to accept his invitation to Vauxhall Gardens.

Chapter 14

Lord Avington leaned toward Mary and said, "I am delighted you changed your mind and decided to accompany us to Vauxhall Gardens." His expression was as blandly pleasant as ever, as if she'd not rudely rejected him first. "Have you been there before?"

"My father used to take us at least once a year." Indeed, Lucas Barnett thought an evening at Vauxhall Gardens was the pinnacle of sophisticated entertainment.

"Was he from London?"

"He used to say he was from everywhere. His father was a traveling tinker and they were always on the move. He spent most of his time in the North after he acquired the first parcel of land and established a colliery, only moving to London after I was ten years old." Mary glanced across at her mother, who was talking quietly with Lady Sedgewick. She knew Louisa Barnett could not actually *hear* the conversation, but she wondered if she could somehow sense her eldest daughter was discussing the mortifying subject of Lucas Barnett, coal baron.

To say her mother did not think that her husband's past an item for polite conversation would be an understatement. Sometimes Mary wondered if her mother was relieved that her husband was dead. Oh, Louisa had been fond of him, after a fashion. But nothing like the way Lucas had adored and worshipped her. Her mother had cringed and winced often in his company and, if he were alive tonight, he would be dominating the conversation with his laughter, loud talk, and overwhelming personality.

Lord Avington's aunt—either Beatrice or Mabel, Mary could not tell them apart—asked his lordship something, forcing him to turn away.

Mary watched him from beneath lowered lashes while he spoke to his aunt, his expression as kind and attentive as ever. He looked at everyone that way.

He even looked at *Mary* the same way, despite her obnoxious behavior.

She had decided to give her *plan* a brief rest tonight. More for her sake than for his. It was hard work being so unpleasant and she simply couldn't bear to behave like a churlish shrew in front of his younger siblings and aunts.

Not only was being detestable taking a toll on her, but she'd received a rather unpleasant piece of information earlier that day when Mr. Ross, her inquiry agent, had paid her a visit.

And it was all her fault for allowing the man to go on with his investigation into the earl's private life even though there was no longer a need for it.

Spying on him made Mary feel just as boorish and common as the *ton* believed her to be. But she couldn't stop herself; her desire to know more about him, to see beneath his handsome, perfect mask, was a burning, unquenchable hunger, no matter how unappetizing the truth was turning out to be.

"His lordship went to a Lady Celeste Copley's house twice this past week," Ross had reported, his normally pasty face flaming. "Er, in the evening," he'd added, just in case Mary hadn't understood what he'd meant.

Mary knew very well who Lady Copley was. She'd come out the same year as Mary and had been hailed a diamond of the first water, her unblemished ivory skin and rich raven curls often said to be the true inspiration for Byron's *She Walks in Beauty*.

Mary couldn't even hate Lady Copley because the woman was kind and sweet and had been one of the handful of people who'd acknowledged her that dreadful Season.

Mary's lips twisted into a bitter smile. So, Mary's glorious husband-to-be had a lover as beautiful as he was.

And as poor.

Mary had heard a rumor that Horace Beckworth—a wealthy and crude industrialist who was facetiously called the Tin King of Cornwall behind his back—was courting the lovely widow Copley.

Could that possibly be true? If so, it was the stuff of great tragedies: two beautiful, cultured people forced to marry the social equivalent of street curs.

Mary stared at her betrothed as he spoke with his aunt, but another vision filled her head, one of the earl holding the exquisitely beautiful widow in his arms, the two of them naked and passionately entwined, their perfect bodies slicked with sweat.

She made sure to punish herself with the painful image before dismissing it.

Were they just lovers, or in love? Would they have married if Lord Avington hadn't needed money? Did they lie in each other's arms and discuss the sacrifices they both had to make? Did they compare stories of their hideous but wealthy intendeds?

Ross's report had sickened her. The ferocious burn she felt in her stomach at the thought of him with the dark-haired beauty—or any other woman—told her that it was already too late to fight the overwhelming desire she felt for him.

She wasn't worried about falling in love, of course, but she imagined that obsession—or the desire to possess—could be just as painful.

She should have married Sir James. He was homely and unexciting and safe. They could have merged their fortunes and produced a child or two with little emotional mess or fuss.

Indeed, she should have married just about *anyone* else.

But she had chosen Lord Avington and she would not, could not, give him up. She had seen a beautiful, mesmerizing flame and had—even with her experience with fire—reached for it. And now she would burn—was *already* burning.

Mary looked at her husband-to-be's elegant profile and considered today's disturbing news. Would he continue to go to Lady Copley after they were married?

Would his smiling expression alter if she were to ask him such a question?

Or perhaps she should amend their marriage contract—add another term about the subject of lovers?

The thought of how that would scandalize her solicitors made her smile.

Just then, Avington turned back to her. He tilted his head, quizzical. "You look amused, Miss Barnett?"

It was, Mary realized, as close as a gentleman like himself would come to asking her what she was thinking.

"I am thinking how much I am looking forward to an evening at Vauxhall Gardens, my lord."

His smile was blinding and his skin flushed slightly, the involuntary response demonstrating just how much her words had pleased—or, more likely, had surprised—him.

"Well, jolly good," he said. "I'm not much of a hand at organizing entertainments, so I'm glad to have come up with something to please you."

Mary could only hope he never found out just how pitifully little he needed to do to please her.

***

Miles decided the barge ride had been an excellent idea. Their party was large, but he'd hired a luxurious vessel that accommodated all his guests with room to spare.

In addition to a collection of younger people hand-selected by Freddie there were Miles's twin sisters, Pen and Maria, his brother Crispin, Freddie, Louisa, and Jenny—both of whom had invited Miles to call them by their Christian names while his betrothed still had not.

Well, at least Miss Barnett had changed her mind about attending tonight, so he supposed that was progress.

She'd also been far less... acerbic.

Vauxhall Gardens was widely regarded as a romantic location, so perhaps they might spend some time wandering the darkened pathways and get more comfortable with one another.

Miles ignored the mocking laughter in his head and turned back to his bride-to-be.

Miss Barnett wore yet another of her dark, concealing gowns, this one a forest green that flattered her brilliant eyes. Even so, the cut of the garment was decades too old for such a young woman. Sometimes he wondered if she purposely went out of her way to make herself appear unattractive.

"How have you been spending your time since we last saw one another?" He'd last seen her at dinner a few nights earlier. Thus far their engagements had only included smaller gatherings. He was grateful to Freddie for choosing so wisely for them.

"I seem to have been caught up in wedding arrangements, as much as I have tried to avoid it." She sounded so bitter that Miles couldn't help smiling.

"What sort of arrangements?"

"Lady Sedgewick request that I accompany her to be fitted for my wedding gown."

"You do not find shopping for finery an enjoyable pastime?"

"It is not my first choice of how to spend my time." She gave a soft, unladylike snort. "Nor even on a list, if I were to make one."

"How *do* you like to spend your leisure time—apart from your birds, that is?"

"Well, there is the current canal scheme that is finally coming to pass."

"But that is work. What do you do for *pleasure*, Miss Barnett?" She gave him an exasperated look but said, "I am planning an addition to a school." The words were abrupt, as if the admission embarrassed her.

"What sort of school?"

"It is just a charity I am interested in. Surely you can't want to hear about it."

"I wouldn't ask if I wasn't interested."

"As you probably know, most orphanages or foundling houses merely apprentice out their students."

Miles nodded.

"Unlike those schools—which send children into factories or jobs like chimney sweeping—we train ours in crafts and trades that are in great demand and can command a higher wage." Her expression had become animated and she looked very pretty with her flushed cheeks and sparkling green eyes.

"What kind of things do they learn?"

"Right now, we have a wheelwright, a saddler, milliner, and mantua maker. I have wanted to erect more housing—twice as much as what we currently have—and build a stable block with a forge so that we might employ a blacksmith and farrier. My plans have been on hold until recently." She cut him an almost shy glance. "Construction is set to begin immediately after we are married." She suddenly blushed, and that's when Miles knew her school was yet another reason that she was marrying him: she needed control of her money for her expansions.

"This sounds like a quite a venture. What gave you such an idea?"

"Supporting schools is not so unusual."

"No, but most women would simply donate money and leave it at that."

"Ah, but that is most women of *your* class."

Here it was, the subject that was never far beneath the surface: their disparate backgrounds.

"You are correct, Miss Barnett, I speak from limited experience. But that does not mean I am judging you. Will you tell me how you came up with such an idea."

Miles thought his words pleased her, although her sharp little face was not easy to read.

"I spent almost a year recovering from my... injuries. I was nine years old and restless and tucked away from the world." Her gaze flickered to her burned hand. "The nurse who cared for me was from the very worst part of London, from a place where some of the streets didn't merit names. The woman could not read, but she told me stories of growing up in St. Giles and it was like hearing tales from a foreign country. It was fascinating yet horrifying and I became obsessed with one day seeing it for myself."

"Good Lord! Don't tell me you've gone to St. Giles? Nobody in their right mind enters such areas unless they must."

"Plenty of people—women and children among them—*have* to enter those parts of the city, my lord."

"I certainly hope you're not one of those women."

She frowned. "Of course, I go to visit my school."

Miles felt chills even though the weather was warm and pleasant. "That is an extremely dangerous and foolish—"

Miles felt a soft touch on his shoulder and looked up to find Freddie behind him. "I'm so sorry to interrupt, but Jenny was curious about one of the buildings with a rather large park. I thought you might know its identity?"

Had she been listening to their conversation and sensed an argument? Ah, Freddie, always looking out for him.

Miles glanced down at Miss Barnett, who was staring at him with a look of thinly veiled hostility, as if she'd known what he was going to say and had relished the confrontation.

He might have agreed to her *terms*, but he'd not agreed to allow his wife to go traipsing through the most dangerous parts of the city.

Miss Barnett could rest assured they were not finished discussing the subject of St. Giles. But it could wait until another day.

"Will you excuse me, Miss Barnett?"

"But of course, my lord."

∗∗∗

Lady Sedgewick took the seat the earl vacated. "Are you enjoying the barge ride, Miss Barnett?"

"I am," Mary said. She'd been enjoying the argument that had been brewing and regretted that the countess had put a stop to it. Well, Mary had the rest of her life to bicker with Lord Avington, didn't she? "Do you go to Vauxhall Gardens often, Lady Sedgewick?"

"In recent years I've gone numerous times in a chaperone capacity. Tonight is the first time I've gone for pleasure since the year I made my come out." She smoothed the skirt of her gown, a plain but well-made lavender that had last been fashionable ten years before.

"How long have you been a widow, my lady?" Mary had no idea if the question was rude, but she was exhausted from trying to walk a proper path. Besides, she was curious about the other woman. Especially when it came to her relationship to Lord Avington, which appeared to be a close one.

"My husband died eight years ago."

What Mary really wanted to know was her age, but even she knew that was ill-mannered so she asked "Were you married long?"

"I was married for four years." She gave Mary a bland smile. "I married Lord Sedgewick when I was seventeen."

So, she was a little older than Mary. What sort of peer left his widow so destitute she was forced to work for a living? Did Lady Sedgewick have no family to care for her or take her in?

"Are you from London, my lady?"

"No, my family is from Dorset. My brother is the Earl of Wareham."

Ah, interesting. Was there some schism in the family? Or perhaps Lady Sedgewick simply did not wish to live under somebody else's roof and under a man's thumb. Mary could certainly understand that.

"You met Lord Avington at a school where you both taught?" Mary knew the answers to all of this and more, thanks to Ross. But what else was there to speak of? Lace? Gowns? Floral arrangements?

"Yes, I taught there for five years. Until recently, I lived with two other teachers."

Mary knew about her erstwhile roommates, both of whom had made exceptionally advantageous marriages.

"So, now you live alone?"

"Lorelei Fontenot, who taught composition and literature at the same school has come to share my home. She had been living with family in Cornwall. Her brother is a vicar and has four children and is expecting a fifth. Miss Fontenot decided there was not enough room for her. She is a vibrant young woman who needs the stimulation of the city," Lady Sedgewick smiled fondly. "I am very happy to have her with me."

The friendship between the teachers must be strong. Mary envied them their ties; she hadn't made many friends—well, any, really—since leaving school. And even at school she had not become close to anyone, not when she'd only wished to leave and work for her father.

Mary wanted to hear about the countess's experiences teaching school, but the earl's twin sisters, Maria and Penelope, joined them and the chance for personal conversation was at an end as the topic turned to the evening ahead.

***

Miles had secured three adjacent tables in the dancing pavilion, where they consumed platters of the obligatory ham, strawberries, and bottles of champagne. He was currently seated between Jenny and her best friend, a young woman named Patricia Fenton, the daughter of Peter Fenton, who owned at least a quarter of the mills in Britain. Young Patricia couldn't string two words together without giggling.

Jenny, however, was a refreshingly unspoiled young woman who responded to his questions with sensible answers.

Even so, Miles found chattering with two eighteen-year-olds exhausting. After dancing with each of them, he saw that Miss Barnett was alone at her table.

"Would you care to dance, Miss Barnett?"

"Thank you, but I do not dance."

Miles cocked his head. "Not at all?"

"Not at all."

He studied her rigid profile as she stared out at the dancers. "May I ask why?"

"Because I prefer not to make a spectacle of myself."

"How is dancing making a spectacle of oneself? If it is because you are not an accomplished dancer then I feel compelled to remind you I can offer you lessons at a great discount off my usual rate."

Rather than smile or laugh, her eyes narrowed. "Is dancing important to you, Lord Avington? Is it something you wish you had laid out in your terms?"

Miles ignored her tone—which was that of an employer chastising an upstart employee—and smiled. "Since you do not care to dance, perhaps you would take a stroll with me?"

Her lips parted in surprise. "A walk?"

Miles enjoyed her momentary disequilibrium far too much. "I shouldn't think we need a chaperone, but why don't we ask our resident expert before we set off?"

Freddie and Mrs. Barnett looked up when they approached.

"Miss Barnett and I are going for a walk." He looked at Freddie as he spoke.

"It is a lovely evening." Which was her way of saying a walk was unexceptionable.

Louisa thrust a bundle of fabric into Miles's hands. "Would you give this to Mary, my lord?"

Miles took the gauzy green and gold shawl, wondering idly if Mrs. Barnett always chose her own wraps to flatter her daughter's clothing. He placed it over Mary shoulders, aware of how she shied away from his fingers as they brushed the sleeves of her gown. She did not like to be touched. Well, at least not by him.

"Have you walked in the gardens before?" he asked as they made their way through thinning crowds, not far behind several other couples.

"Every now and again with my parents, but never alone with a gentleman."

"You will be quite safe with me. I shall keep to the better lighted paths."

They walked in silence. Just when Miles thought they might continue that way, she spoke.

"I had an opportunity to speak with Lady Sedgewick on the barge ride."

Miles's mouth curved into a smile at the sound of his friend's name. "She is reserved, but a lovely person once you get to know her. By the way," he said after a pause, "I just discovered that one of my former teacher friends—Serena Lockheart, neé Lombard—carved one of the benches in your garden at Coal House."

"Really? Which one?"

"The one you were sitting on while you enjoyed your fowl."

They walked under a trio of lanterns that marked a fork in the path. Miles led her toward the right, staying within sight of two couples ahead of them.

"How interesting," she said, her voice lacking its characteristic hostility. "For some reason it surprises me that a woman would carve such a massive thing."

"It is her preference to work on large projects. Although she is a slightly built woman, she wields the tools of her trade to remarkable effect."

"I don't believe I've heard of a female sculptor before."

"There aren't many."

"And what do you think of that?"

He looked down into her eyes, which were dark and mysterious in the dim lighting, her small face triangular, like a cat's. She certainly was a tiny thing, something he forgot until they stood close like this, her head barely coming to the middle of his bicep. Why, he could pick her up and—

The vision that invaded his mind was sultry and visceral; a fleeting, seductive image of holding her hips in his hands while he entered her, her head tipped back to expose the vulnerable 'V' of flesh beneath her chin and—

"My lord?"

They'd stopped walking—or *he'd* stopped. He also had an erection.

The devil! How bloody inconvenient, not to mention odd as he'd not entertained thoughts of bedding her. Strangling her, yes, but amorous thoughts? Hardly.

Well, whatever the source, it was unfortunate.

He cleared his throat and pasted on a smile. "I'm sorry, you were asking about Serena." Miles impressed the hell out of himself by recalling what they'd been speaking of before his erotic interlude had scrambled his wits. "I suppose I am something of a male bluestocking." He smirked at her disbelieving snort. "Oh, you don't think there is such a thing? It is true. I've spent several years working with remarkable women. It is my experience that women can do most things men can do, and often better or quicker or with less fuss. Only when it comes to physical strength do men have the advantage." Miles cocked his head. "Why are you looking at me as if another eye has sprouted from my forehead, Miss Barnett?"

"It is not often you will hear a man admit to such radical beliefs. In fact, I believe you are the first."

"Oh come, surely your father must have held similar beliefs. He would not have left his businesses to you otherwise."

"But he left them to me conditionally, didn't he? And the condition involved a man."

"Perhaps he made those conditions for some other reason, and not because he doubted your competence."

"Perhaps. But I doubt he would have done the same had I been a son."

Unfortunately, so did Miles.

They'd reached the end of the path—which had several benches, all occupied—so they turned back the way they'd come.

"Will all your teacher friends be coming to our wedding?" she asked.

"I'm afraid Annis—who was once a language arts teacher and is now the Countess of Rotherhithe—cannot come as she is in a rather delicate way, but the others will attend either our ball, the ceremony at Avington Hall, or both." He didn't tell her how several of them had responded when they'd heard he was marrying an heiress.

Serena, whose husband was obscenely wealthy, had written to offer him a loan with repayment terms so generous as to be laughable. She had, most eloquently, implored him not to sacrifice himself for money.

But a loan would do Miles no good, because he would only need to repay it—no matter how generous the terms.

And won't you need to repay the money you are taking from Miss Barnett? a niggling voice demanded.

He looked down at the woman walking beside him. Although this interaction had been more pleasant than most, he doubted that it meant anything significant. For reasons unknown to him, she held him in aversion and there was no currency—not the offer of children or family or companionship—that Miss Barnett would accept from him.

Miles was struck with the chilling realization that he would live out the rest of his life in debt to her.

They walked back to the pavilion in silence.

Chapter 15

Mary sat beneath the shade tree, too distracted to read the prospectus she'd brought along with her. Instead, she watched Jenny and her best friend, a featherbrained ninny named Patty Fenton whose incessant giggling grated on Mary's nerves. They were blushing and stammering under the attention of Lord Avington's younger brother, Crispin. He was a very attractive young man, although he couldn't hold a candle to the earl, at least not in Mary's opinion. Or perhaps it was only that Crispin, at nineteen, was still unformed while his brother was a man who'd seen the world and had faced death on the battlefield.

Mary shoved the earl out of her thoughts and glanced at the watch pinned to the bodice of her gown. Barely an hour had passed since they'd arrived at Richmond, which meant there were several interminable hours still to be endured.

This was the second entertainment this week, not counting the Vauxhall Garden excursion. Mary had to admit that hadn't been as taxing as she'd feared. It did not escape her that the reason it had been more tolerable was because she'd called a temporary cease fire in her campaign of incivility toward Lord Avington.

Unfortunately, that was over. It was back to a full-on offensive, in both senses of the word.

"Shall we take a stroll, Miss Barnett?"

Mary looked up and lifted her hand to shield her eyes from the sun, as if she didn't recognize the voice perfectly well.

Lord Avington had purchased new clothing and the effect on her nerves was both unwelcome and extreme. It was lowering how susceptible she was to snug fitting pantaloons, shiny Hessians, and a well-tailored clawhammer coat. In her own way, she was every bit as pathetic as Patty Fenton with her giggling.

"Unless you are still reading," he said, making her realize she'd been staring—and probably drooling.

"I would like to walk." She put aside her reading and picked up her bonnet and he helped her to her feet. Not until she'd taken his hand did, she realize it was ungloved. The pads of his fingers were rough, and this wasn't the damaged hand.

136

"What is it, Miss Barnett?"

Mary dropped his hand when she realized she was still holding it, staring. "You have callouses, my lord. You must indeed be a vigorous dancer if even your hands show signs of hard work."

He laughed, the sound like warm honey poured straight into her veins.

He held his hands out before him, as if he'd forgotten what they looked like.

It was shocking to see just how mutilated the left hand was, the once elegant fingers misshapen and twisted, the burned, scarred skin far worse than that on Mary's hand. She wanted to ask what had happened, but she'd been so beastly to him that she did not deserve to ask such a personal question.

"I get callouses from carving—or whittling, I suppose it would be called."

"You must do a great deal of whittling."

An odd expression flickered across his face and she could not read it.

"I've been doing a great deal these past few years but I shan't do so much in the future." He smiled wryly and Mary wished she knew what he meant.

"What sorts of things do you carve?"

"I started off just carving birds, flowers, and other animals, but these past few years I've been carving chess sets."

"Chess sets? What do you do with them?"

"I make them for a man who sells them in his shop." He hesitated, and then added, "A friend of mine paints them as I have no skill in that department."

To think of the earl engaging in manufacturing, no matter how small scale, was shocking.

"You are surprised to discover I dabble in commerce."

"A little."

"Well, teaching dancing is not as lucrative as one might think." His smirk told her that he was jesting.

"Where did you learn to carve?"

"In Spain. Do you like to play chess?" he asked, changing the subject with an abruptness that was uncharacteristic.

"I have never learned."

"I will teach you. It is thought to be an excellent game for battle. And is not business a form of battle?"

"I suppose it can be. Ideally, there shouldn't be a winner and a loser, both parties should get something out of the deal."

They crested a slight rise and below them was a large pond teaming with waterfowl.

"Oh, how lovely," she said, her eyes darting from the ducks to the swans to a gaggle of fat geese waddling along the shore.

"These are Pen Ponds. Would you like to sit?" He gestured to a bench near the water.

They sat and Mary couldn't help smiling at all the quacking and squawking. "They are rather noisy, aren't they?"

"Sometimes there are far more of them. Look," he pointed to a small clump of hawthorn scrub in the middle of the pond.

Mary gaped. "Is that a heron?"

"Yes, they build their nests on those tiny islands."

"I've read about them but haven't seen one before."

"Are you a bird watcher?"

"Just a casual admirer." Mary wished she had more eyes to watch all the birds at once.

They sat in silence, until Mary turned and realized that Lord Avington was looking at her, rather than the birds.

Her face heated when she realized she'd unthinkingly put him on her bad side. "If this is tedious, we can go."

"No, I am quite enjoying myself."

"Are you a bird fancier, my lord?"

"I like the birds, but I like watching you enjoy them even more."

His words warmed her, which immediately irritated her. "I thought we'd agreed to dispense with courtship and romancing, my lord."

"Does our agreement prevent courtesy or kindness or enjoying one another's company, Miss Barnett?"

She ignored his question and turned back to the birds, no longer tranquil and happy, intensely aware that he was watching her.

"Why are you so *angry* at me, Miss Barnett?"

Mary turned on him. "Why aren't *you* angry?"

"What is there to be angry about?" he asked, sounding genuinely perplexed.

"Doesn't it infuriate you that you're being forced into marriage with somebody like me? A scarred, on the shelf heiress who will never fit into your world. A woman you don't know and likely wouldn't like if you did?"

His look of startlement was oddly satisfying. "Perhaps you are underestimating your appeal?"

"No, I'm not, my lord. And this is not an issue of self-esteem or the lack of it. The truth is that I don't think I'll find you of interest, either."

He gave a bark of laughter.

"How could I?" she demanded, yet again nettled by his response to an insult. "We have nothing in common."

"You don't know me well enough to make that judgement—you haven't even tried to know me."

"Do you enjoy engineering projects? Does examining profit and loss in a company and conceiving of a way to improve one and decrease the other keep you awake at night? Would you rather read a patent application than a poem? Do you despise idle chit chat, card playing, dancing, balls, house parties, or prancing about on parade in Hyde Park?"

He stared at her; his breathtaking blue eyes unblinking.

"I'm going to assume your answer to all those questions is a *no*, my lord. And yet mine is a resounding *yes*."

He snorted softly. "How much you presume to know about me, Miss Barnett, especially as you've done everything in your power to avoid actually spending time with me."

Mary didn't bother to deny it.

"You want this marriage as much as I do and yet you're behaving as if I'm forcing myself on you."

"I *want* it?" She made a bitter sound. "No, my lord. But I do *need* it. That doesn't mean I need to surrender to my fate without expressing my dissatisfaction. Or if not openly expressing it, at least not smiling vapidly and pretending that I'm elated by being given no choice in my future if I want to retain the fruits of many years' worth of labor."

"Smiling vapidly," he repeated, more to himself, and then fixed her with a hard look. "And what does all that *railing* and hostility achieve, pray? Except to make everyone uncomfortable?"

"Maybe being forced to marry for money or because of a dead man's desires *should* make other people uncomfortable."

"Well, you've certainly achieved your goal, then."

Mary ignored the dig. "You cannot really be as resigned to your fate as you appear?"

"Believe it or not, Miss Barnett, I don't spend my waking hours lamenting our impending marriage, as you appear to do."

His cool smile enraged her. "That is such twaddle!"

"And what makes you think I am railing against my fate?"

Mary could no longer hold her tongue. "Can you honestly tell me you wouldn't rather marry somebody else—anyone else—other than me?"

His eyebrows shot up. "I can honestly say that is a strange question, Miss Barnett."

"You must think I'm a fool."

"*I* must be a fool because I have no earthly idea what you are getting at."

Suddenly his puzzled, beautiful face was more than she could endure.

"Wouldn't rather marry the woman you've been voluntarily spending evenings with—Lady Celeste Copley—if she had my money?"

***

Miles flinched away from her, fury and disbelief overwhelming the confusion he'd been feeling only a few seconds before.

"My God! Are you *still* investigating me, Miss Barnett?"

"Well, I hardly saw it in a crystal ball, my lord."

An awful silence inserted itself between them and for a moment Miles imagined doing the unthinkable: jilting a woman.

He gave an unamused bark of laughter, glaring at the person who'd driven him to such shameful, dishonorable contemplation. "I could understand you prying into my background before we met and discussed our expectations that first night. But the fact that you are *still* having me—what, followed?—when we are to marry in less than two weeks?" He snorted. "*That* I cannot accept. Tell me, ma'am, will this continue after we are married, too?"

Her face darkened at his accusation and her green eyes glittered with anger and something else: jealousy.

It was the first time since Miles had met her that he truly found her unattractive. Not because of the burns on her cheek, but because of the ugly emotions pouring out of her in waves.

She ignored his question and asked one of her own, "Can you deny that you went to her on the very day that we settled the details of our marriage contract? Should I expect you to stop at her house after our betrothal ball or on the eve of our wedding? Will this continue after we are married?"

"*Enough!*" he thundered, getting to his feet. "I refuse to justify my actions or provide you with a detailed list of whom I visit and why and when." Miles's heart was pounding painfully against his ribs and he felt as if some sort of seizure was imminent. Not since those wretched weeks in Spain—when he'd been beaten and burned and mutilated—had his anger manifested itself so physically, so viscerally.

"Do you think I will ever be able to make you happy, Miss Barnett?"

Her brow furrowed. "What do you mean?"

"I meant exactly what I said. Can I make you happy? You don't wish to spend any more time with me than you must. You were visibly revolted at the thought of bearing my children and having a family with me. If we go through with this marriage, will you be miserable for the remainder of your life—of *our* lives? Will you make *me* miserable?"

Her lips parted, but no words came out.

"Mary!"

Miles jolted and turned to find Jenny, Maria, and Crispin converging on them.

"It is time to play croquet,' Crispin called out merrily. "We need the two of you."

Miles took a deep breath and held it for a moment before expelling it, not sure whether he was grateful or disappointed that their interruption had stopped him before he had done something that was irreversible.

Chapter 16

Miles was still fuming about the row he'd had with Miss Barnett at Richmond three days later when he hopped out of a hackney in front of Celeste's house.

Were Miss Barnett's spies watching him even now? Would they run to her and tattle that he'd visited Celeste?

Considering the true purpose of his visit today that would be irony, indeed.

Miles knocked on the front door of the modest townhouse and didn't have to wait long before Mr. Towson, the male half of the married couple who managed Celeste's household, opened the door.

"Good evening, my lord. Lady Copley is expecting you."

Before the servant could lead him to Celeste's sitting room the woman herself appeared at the head of the stairs. "Miles, how lovely to see you. Do come up." She turned to her servant. "Please send up tea, Towson—and some of his lordship's favorite biscuits."

"Of course, my lady."

Miles took the steps two at a time and kissed her on the cheek when he reached the top. "Mmm, currant biscuits. Are you trying to fatten me up, Celeste?"

"No, I'm trying to get rid of them before *I* eat them. You are early," she said as they entered her cozy sitting room, which was decorated in pale grays and pinks and was as delicate and exquisite as the woman herself. "I thought your sisters would keep you occupied until midnight with more shopping."

"They tried." Miles handed her the small parcel he'd brought with him. "To be honest, I abandoned poor Freddie with them at the modiste's."

Celest laughed. "That is naughty of you, but I daresay they are happier without their brother there to mortify them. And Freddie could handle a pair of giddy young ladies in her sleep. Now, let's see what you've brought me," she said, carefully unwrapping the brown paper.

She gasped when she saw what was inside. "Oh, Miles! These are exquisite!"

He flushed at her praise. "Thank you. I think they are some of my best."

142

"Indeed they are! Do you know what colors you would like?" she asked, holding the tiny wooden hen closer to the light.

"Can you make her that lovely iridescent black you sometimes see in ravens and crows? As for the cockerel I was thinking rust red, white, and black."

"That sounds lovely. These details on the tailfeathers are quite extraordinary, Miles." She grinned at him, her eyes sparkling with enthusiasm. "These will be a pleasure to paint."

The door opened then and an older woman entered with a tray of refreshments.

"Ah, thank you, Mrs. Towson," Celeste said, carefully returning the carvings to their wrappings before turning to the tray.

"Do you think you can have them done in time?" he asked once the servant had shut the door.

"You are leaving in a week?"

"Yes, a week tomorrow."

"That should be plenty of time for them to dry."

"Thank you for doing this on such short notice, Celeste." Miles knew she mixed up her own paints for the wooden carvings. They were not watercolors like those she employed in her paintings but composed of pigments mixed—of all things—with raw eggs.

"So, how have you been?" he asked. "Anything new and exciting to report since my last visit?" That had been scarcely a week ago, when he'd collected the two chess sets she'd finished painting. Usually, Miles took their work to the shopkeeper himself, but this time he'd taken them to Freddie, who'd delivered them along with some of her own work.

"As a matter of fact, I do have news," she said, handing him a plate with three of the promised currant biscuits. "I have accepted Mr. Beckworth's offer of marriage. The announcement will be in tomorrow's *Gazette*."

"Ah, congratulations!"

Miles had known that Celeste had been seeing the wealthy industrialist for the last few months, but he was surprised matters had developed so quickly.

He and Celeste hadn't been lovers for over a year. Miles knew many people believed they were still intimate—including his wife-to-be and her nosey inquiry agent—but the truth was that the amorous portion of their relationship had been brief and far less fulfilling than their subsequent friendship.

Miles had recognized the jealousy in Miss Barnett's eyes and knew he could have assuaged it by telling her the truth. That is what he *should* have done, but he'd been too angry. And resentful.

And part of him—a small part—had enjoyed finally causing her a measure of pain after she'd done nothing but pick and snipe at him for weeks.

But that satisfaction had been short-lived and he felt ashamed by his behavior. Not only was it cruel, but it was less than helpful to building any sort of rapport with his wife-to-be.

"Miles?"

"Hmm?" He looked up from his thoughts to see that Celeste was holding out his cup of tea. "Ah, thank you. So, are you happy, my dear?"

The smile she gave him looked remarkably similar to the one he gave people all day long.

"It is for the best," she said, avoiding answering his question directly. "He is kind and generous and I think we will find contentment together."

"Congratulations." Miles meant it. Celeste's existence was even more precarious than his own.

Her deceased husband, Viscount Copley, had been a gregarious, well-liked man who'd been unable to pass up a wager, horse race, or card table. Her annuity was so tiny that the money from the chess sets they made together was critical for her survival and Miles knew she'd worried after he announced his betrothal.

Until Celeste, Miles had never gravitated toward extraordinarily beautiful women. Pansy, whom he'd loved with every particle of his heart and soul, had been beautiful to Miles, but he'd known, objectively, that she'd been handsome, at best.

Although Celeste was the most classically attractive woman he'd ever seen, she did not put a great deal of value on her appearance. It was her dismissal of her outer shell that had attracted Miles to her.

Indeed, Celeste was essentially the female equivalent of him: a perfect physical specimen.

Well, at least perfect by society's shallow standards.

He'd been relieved to meet somebody who knew that physical perfection, and the reactions it provoked, could be as much a curse as a blessing.

Even his teacher friends—all attractive women in their own ways—sometimes mistook Miles's exterior for *him.*

Only Celeste had looked past his outer shell to the person within. Back when they'd still been lovers, she'd said something that had stayed with him. "If one puts too much stock in one's appearance, then one is left with nothing when one's beauty fades."

Miles did not want to be that person when he was old.

He wasn't the cleverest or most interesting man, but he wanted to be treated as something more than an ornament. And it was especially burdensome to be regarded as a storybook hero when he was the farthest thing from it.

He was just a man, and a very flawed one at that.

Not only did a handsome appearance fade, but it also influenced normally rational people far too much.

Mary Barnett was an excellent example of that.

She didn't trust him, and a big part of that was because of his appearance. She resented his looks, but he had seen the acquisitive gleam in her eyes. He was a trophy of sorts and she was not immune to wanting him.

But that didn't mean she liked him. Indeed, he thought the very things that drew her to him were the same things that made her angry. She didn't like being attracted to what was essentially a glittering object.

Miles could understand the suspicion and—to a certain extent—dislike she held for attractive men.

Not for a minute did he deny that his people—the *ton*—were cruel and shallow. He knew her brief period among them a decade before would have been brutal.

It was also clear, from his unpleasant exchange with Elton, that she'd been betrayed by a man for the amusement of his cronies.

To protect herself, she'd erected a high, thick wall around her heart. Whether Miles could chip a way through—or even if he wanted to after that unpleasant argument at Richmond—was something he'd not yet decided.

"You are very quiet today," Celeste said, setting down her cup and saucer. "Is something wrong?"

"No, nothing wrong," he lied. Miles didn't want to talk about the thoughts plaguing him, so he said, "That wasn't the first time Beckworth asked you to marry him, was it?"

"No."

"What changed your mind?"

"Will you think badly of me if I confess that I am partially motivated by fear?"

"Of course not. Fear of poverty?"

"There is that. But I am only thirty and already my looks are losing their luster. If I am going to remarry, I had better do it sooner rather than later. Besides, Horace and I enjoy one another's company and he does not care that I cannot have children. It is not a grand passion, but then I allowed my emotions to convince me to marry Copley, so grand passions are vastly overrated in my experience."

Miles smiled, saddened by his friend's experience with love. Would he have become disillusioned with Pansy if they'd been allowed to marry?

He hoped not, but then he would never know.

"It is not only about Horace's money," she said, "although it will be pleasant not to fret about the future. I also think that marrying outside the *ton* is not such a terrible idea. There are so many unhappy marriages among the people we know. Perhaps our very differences will make for a more satisfying and interesting life."

Miles sipped his tea as he considered her words.

"It is true the difference between Beckworth's and Miss Barnett's backgrounds and ours is vast, but not, I think, insuperable. I respect Miss Barnett and believe we might, in time, make a life together." If he could ever chisel through that thick wall.

She paused and then said, "I received this in the mail a few days ago."

Miles recognized the invitation she held up; it was for his and Miss Barnett's betrothal ball.

He wondered how Celeste's name had slipped past Freddie. Or perhaps Mrs. Barnett was responsible for the invitation?

Not that it mattered. He wasn't prepared to cut Celeste's acquaintance just because they'd shared a bed briefly a year ago.

Miles knew the Duchess of Merton was on the guestlist and he and Dolly had been involved for almost a year. If he started striking the acquaintance of women he'd once been lovers with, they'd have to weed out several more names on the list.

"I hope you've accepted the invitation," he said.

"I was prepared to decline it, but then Beckworth told me he'd been invited and asked if I was attending. It seemed awkward to explain why I wouldn't"

"You should," Miles said. "We cannot avoid one another in the future nor do I want to."

If Miss Barnett took issue with the matter, Miles had no doubt that she would let him know about it.

Chapter 17

Mary was worn to a frazzle by the evening of the betrothal dinner and ball.

The only good thing about the weeks between the announcement and the party was that her mother and Jenny had been so consumed with preparations for the ball—and their removal to Avington Castle immediately afterward—that they'd only occasionally harried her with annoying questions like: "You must be so happy! How could you *not* fall in love with Lord Avington? Don't you feel fortunate to be marrying him? Isn't he just the most wonderful gentleman you've ever met?" And so on, and so forth.

Other than Avington's brief loss of control at Richmond Park that day—when she'd not only made the grievous error of exposing her jealousy of his mistress, but probably also the lust she bore him—Mary had never seen him be anything but pleasant.

Up until that day she'd believed that she wanted to see emotion—any emotion—on his perfect face. But the truth was that his crackling fury had frightened her, and she had profoundly regretted goading him to that point.

Mary shivered at the memory. What would have happened if the others had not interrupted them that day? Would he really have done the unthinkable and broken their betrothal?

And her heart in the process.

Mary looked in the mirror, and then wished she hadn't. The dress she wore, a blue that was dark enough to be called navy, was the same design and fashion as all her other ballgowns, which was to say conservative and rather... well, why pull punches—the gown was ugly.

She'd been wearing the same sort of dress for years and hadn't given it a thought. But tonight, for some odd reason, she felt... frumpy. And insecure.

Mary scowled at her reflection. *Who are you trying to fool?* she silently demanded. *You know exactly why you are noticing your unfashionable gown. It's the same reason you've finally given into Kearny's begging and allowed her to dress your hair in a new, more fashionable, style.*

Kearny had woven her hair into an intricate crown, complete with delicate curls framing her face. She had to admit the style was flattering, but it was also that of a younger woman.

Mary opened her mouth to tell Kearny to pull it down and put it back up into its usual style when the door opened and Jenny entered.

Her face lit up when she saw Mary.

"Oh Mary!" She raised her clasped hands to her smiling mouth, as if confronted with some great treat. "You look *beautiful.* That new style of dressing your hair is so flattering.*"*

"Thank you, Jen. You look lovely—that gown is perfect on you."

Jenny smiled and pulled her eyes away from Mary's reflection to gaze down at the pale pink confection she wore, which made her creamy skin glow. The fabric was gauzy and floated around Jenny's slim form like a rosy mist. The bodice was cut lower than usual but nothing untoward given the current fashions.

Unlike Mary's own high-necked, long-sleeved gown, which bore a closer resemblance to a nun's habit than a ball gown. All she was lacking to complete the look was a wimple.

Jenny held out her arms. "Aren't these just the loveliest things you've ever seen?" She was sheathed to above her elbows in rose-tinted kid, the gloves reaching high enough that they left only a tantalizing band of flesh between the leather and the small puffed sleeves. They appeared to have fifty tiny buttons each.

"They are indeed lovely. But are you sure you want to wear those down to dinner; won't they'll take an age to remove?"

Jenny giggled. "Of course, they'll take an age, silly, but that is part of the enjoyment of wearing them."

"It is?" It sounded like an annoying waste of time to Mary.

"I'm so happy that Lady Sedgewick said I might wear something other than white, as long as it was not *too* bold."

"Well, it is certainly a perfect color for you—you resemble a rose about to bloom."

Jenny's cheeks tinted at the compliment and she ducked her chin, a shy gesture that always made Mary feel protective and vaguely anxious for her pretty, sweet little sister.

Mary had been almost ten when Jenny was born and she could still remember how thrilled both her parents had been to have another child after so many years of hoping. Not even the fact that Jenny was a girl had dampened her father's enthusiasm. But then her father had never made Mary feel bad about being a daughter.

"No son could make me as proud, Mary. Pretty and smart as a whip, ye are," he'd told her more than once. Yes, her Da had thought the sun rose and set by her. Mary wondered if such pure, adoring love had ruined her for any other man. Certainly, she could expect nothing of the sort from the man whom she had agreed to marry.

Mary pushed the pointless thoughts away and drew on her own far shorter and less elegant gloves, covering one hand that was permanently stained with ink and one that looked as if it had been melted.

"Crispin has asked me for the supper waltz," Jenny said, bouncing lightly on the balls of her feet. "Aren't you excited, Mary?"

"Yes, I'm excited," she lied, her stomach and chest were heavy with dread at the thought of the long night ahead.

Mary forced a smile and held out her arm. "Come, let us go and join the excitement."

***

"Lord Avington is late, Mary," Louisa Barnett whispered to Mary the moment she entered the drawing room, which was already milling with guests.

Late again, and on the evening of his own betrothal ball.

Mary tried to suppress her annoyance and failed. Was it too much to ask that he be punctual for a ball that he and Lady Sedgewick *insisted* upon?

"Ah, look who is here, Mary," her mother said in an overbright tone.

Mary pasted a smile on her face and turned.

It was difficult to maintain even a false smile when she saw who it was.

"Cousin Reginald, Cousin Joan. How glad I am that you could both come to town on such short notice," she lied, keeping her gaze on Joan rather than Reginald, her former lover.

They were cousins in name only as there was no shared blood.

Reginald had already been fifteen when Mary's Aunt Dolly—her father's only sister—had married Reginald's father. He was seven years older than Mary and so handsome that she'd always thought of him as a god come to earth.

Until she hadn't.

150

"We were *so* excited to hear about your betrothal, my dear cousin," Reginald said, forcing her to look at him. It shouldn't have been a hardship as Reginald had been the most handsome man of her acquaintance until she'd met Lord Avington. Indeed, the two men shared a resemblance in that they were both tall, blue-eyed, and blond. But the resemblance was superficial. Not only was Avington more attractive, but he was a far better person, something that was evident just by watching how he treated others.

Reginald made a show of kissing her on the cheek—aiming for the burned one but then pulling back at the last moment and kissing the other cheek, instead. It was not the first time he'd played that game, so it no longer hurt her.

"How in the world did you trick him into it, my dear?" he murmured in her ear, his breath moist and hot against her temple, his voice so low that only Mary could hear it.

"Thank you, Reginald," she said coolly, turning away from him to greet his wife.

Like Mary, Joan Hastings had been a considerable heiress, which was the only reason Reginald had married her. Mary knew that because Reginald went to no effort to conceal how much he despised his tall, thin, homely wife, who bore an unfortunate resemblance to a stork.

Mary would have felt uncharitable about that assessment if the woman had not been so unctuously unpleasant.

Joan towered over her gorgeous husband and beamed down at Mary, her eyes as cold and fixed as the long-legged bird she resembled, as if she were standing knee deep in cold water, waiting patiently for the kill.

Except now there wouldn't be a *kill* because Mary had thwarted her cousin. Thanks to her timely marriage to Lord Avington, Reginald would be forced to watch as thousands of pounds were snatched from his fingers.

Just thinking about that made Mary smile—a genuine expression rather than the pasted-on version.

"And the wedding will be at his lordship's castle—in his own family chapel, I understand?" Joan asked.

"Yes, that is correct."

"No doubt it will be a cozy affair, as such structures are generally quite small."

Mary assumed that was Joan's unsubtle way of asking how big the wedding would be.

"I don't know the actual number but I believe there will be slightly more than two hundred guests."

"Two hundred!" Joan repeated, her beady eyes opening wider. "That is far larger than I would have thought."

"Your lovely mother told us that *we* are going to be one of the fortunate guests who will stay at Avington Castle, rather than put up at an inn in the nearby village," Reginald said, his pale green eyes glittering with some emotion that Mary could not decipher, although she doubted it boded well for her.

Mary had never been capable of reading her cousin, which is why she'd easily, and with little persuasion, given him not only her maidenhead, but also her love.

Indeed, she had fallen deeply, helplessly in love with him and had remained in that state for six months, until the evening when she'd overheard him talking about her to his cronies at a ball.

Now, ten years later, it sounded hyperbolic to say that she'd felt like he'd torn her heart from her chest and ground it under his heel as he had described—in excruciating detail—the sorts of amorous activities he'd convinced her to engage in.

As if that hadn't been bad enough, he'd denigrated not only her person—shuddering when he'd described her body—but also her efforts to please him. Ending by comparing her to an ill-trained, but enthusiastic, whore.

Mary had not spoken to him for a week after that, taking to her bed with a not entirely feigned sickness. A sickness of the soul rather than the body, although one had certainly led to the other.

She'd allowed herself only that week to grieve what she'd lost— or at least what she'd believed she'd lost—and when she came out of her chambers afterward, she admitted him the next time he called on her and coolly informed him that she'd changed her mind about announcing their secret betrothal to her parents.

It had been the second time she'd heard his true feelings about her.

After that, they'd rarely seen each other. And when they did—at family dinners or other social occasions—she'd always been polite and distant.

She knew her parents had been concerned in the sudden cooling of the long-time friendship between her and Reginald, but they had never pressed her on the issue.

"I've not stayed in a castle before," Joan said with a nervous trill of laughter, earning a look of irritation from her husband.

Reginald had never tried to hide his disdain for his wife. Even though his own father had been a manager at Lucas Barnett's shipyard in Falmouth when he'd met and married Mary's aunt, Reginald had always behaved as if his origins were genteel. With his handsome face and easy manners, he'd had a great deal of success with his charade.

"I am delighted to hear that you will be joining us," Mary lied, wishing for the hundredth time that she and Avington were running off to Scotland to speak their vows over an anvil.

Reginald leaned inappropriately close and said, "Tell me, Mary, will there—"

Whatever bile he was preparing to spew was interrupted by the arrival of Lord Avington.

As annoyed as she was at his tardiness Mary's mouth went dryer than a Temperance meeting at the sight of her betrothed.

She would have felt ashamed by how transfixed she was by the vision that met her gaze, but every other woman in the room was gawping, as well.

It wasn't as if he'd purchased flamboyant clothing. Quite the reverse. His garments were the epitome of quiet elegance. He was dressed in dinner clothing, but unlike her cousin Reginald in his light green satin knee breeches and dark green coat, the earl wore black breeches and a black tailcoat, his waistcoat the color of fresh cream with embroidery the same violet blue as his eyes.

His white stockings displayed exquisitely formed calves—no doubt the result of many hours spent teaching dance—and he'd had his hair cut, his glossy golden curls in a flattering upswept Brutus.

Joan's lips parted and a soft, *oh* escaped her mouth as she stared across the room at him.

Mary bit back a smile as she turned away from the stunned woman.

Lord Avington finished greeting her mother and sister, and then his remarkable eyes flickered around the room and when they settled on Mary, he smiled.

And then it was *her* turn to sigh softly as he strode toward her.

***

Miles was late. Again. His wife-to-be wore a look of shock, as if she'd not expected him to arrive at all. Well, he owed her yet another apology and was likely to receive yet another bollocking.

He smiled as he approached Miss Barnett. "I deeply apologize for my tardiness but would understand utterly if you refused to grant it," he said, kissing the back of her gloved hand.

"Highwaymen again?" she asked with an arch lift of one flame red brow.

"Believe it or not, I was set upon by footpads right outside my lodgings."

Several people spoke at once, asking what happened.

"Two men jumped me as I was walking toward the livery stable. I was fortunate that a groom heard the commotion and the two men ran away when he charged into the fray."

"You weren't hurt, I hope?" a tall, thin woman who looked remarkably like a stork asked.

"Er, only my pride—and my clothing." He grimaced. "That was the reason I was late. I had to return to my lodgings and change my torn coat and scuffed breeches." This he addressed to Miss Barnett, who was staring at him with a strange expression on her face. Was that concern? No, surely not.

"Not to worry," he said to his rapidly swelling audience. "I am as fit as a fiddle." He turned his attention to the man and woman Miss Barnett had been talking to. "I'm afraid we've not been introduced," he said, hoping to move matters away from his unfortunate delay.

Miss Barnett said, "This is my cousin Reginald Cooper and his wife Joan, Lord Avington."

Miles lifted Mrs. Cooper's hand. "A pleasure, ma'am." He inclined his head at her husband and managed to force the word, "Cooper," from between his stiff lips.

So, this was the swine who'd debauched Miss Barnett and then denigrated her to his cronies, was it?

As much as he yearned to punch Cooper in the face, Miles had to admit the man was a handsome devil. But there was an unpleasant gleam in his eyes that Miles could not like, and he could read the other man's knowing, sardonic gaze as easily as a book. Cooper was smirking, clearly amused that Miles had bartered himself for money.

Well, so he had.

He'd also done Cooper out of a fortune in the process. That made him grin.

He put the distasteful man from his thoughts and turned to Miss Barnett. "I received a letter today from my aunts and they bade me to extend felicitations to you and your family and tell you they are looking forward to your arrival."

His betrothed gave him a pained smile. "I am looking forward to meeting them all, as well."

An awkward silence followed her tepid assurance and Miles had to bite back a smile. Poor Miss Barnett clearly had some idea of the maelstrom of wedding excitement awaiting her at Avington Castle.

"When do you leave for your estate, my lord?" Mrs. Cooper asked.

"Four days hence." Miles turned to Miss Barnett and caught her giving him a pensive look.

He was driving her in the new curricle—just the two of them this time, without the downtrodden Mr. John Courtland.

Miles couldn't help smiling as he recalled that memorable drive in Hyde Park with Miss Barnett and her secretary. The woman might be prickly, rude, and annoying, but she was also amusing and unexpected.

He would have never suggested two entire days alone with Miss Barnett. It had been Freddie's idea.

"You need to spend some time getting to know one another," Freddie had insisted. "And it is unexceptionable to go together. Your man and her maid can travel behind with the baggage. It is perfect."

Miles had laughed at the description of a journey that was likely to end with neither of them speaking to the other. He'd tried to argue with her, but it had been futile. What Freddie wanted, Freddie got.

"I adore weddings," Mrs. Cooper cooed, the misty-eyed expression sitting strangely on her rather sour-looking countenance. "I've never participated in the planning of one before."

A faint flush spread across Miss Barnett's cheeks and a quickly suppressed look of dread flickered across her face. She slid Miles an uncomfortable look—one that held… *entreaty?*

He almost laughed out loud. Miss Barnett seeking rescue from *him?* Who would have believed it possible?

Miles knew he should simply ignore Mrs. Cooper's unsubtle hint, but Miss Barnett deserved a bit of her own medicine, didn't she?

So he gave the Cooper woman one of his most gracious smiles. "You must join us earlier. I know my aunts would welcome the help," he lied. They would want to string him up for disturbing what was likely a complicated guest arrival schedule.

Cooper and his wife exchanged a look and it was Cooper who spoke for them. "Er, we would not wish to impose—"

"It would not be an imposition to have you sooner—quite the reverse."

"That sounds delightful, doesn't it darling?" he asked, the endearment sounding as unconvincing as his wife's gentle cooing. "We shall set out the day after you—that will allow you and Mary to arrive and settle in before us."

Miles met Miss Barnett's accusing glare and winked. "Excellent."

His aunts would skin him alive, if his wife-to-be didn't do it first.

Chapter 18

Have you been to Avington Castle yet, Miss Barnett?" the Duke of Plimpton asked Mary.

Mary knew it was something of a coup that the elusive and extremely eligible duke had accompanied his brother and sister-in-law—the Marquess of Saybrook and his wife, the portrait painter Honoria Keyes—to their betrothal celebration.

"No, Your Grace, I've not yet had that honor. Lord Avington has assured me that his family have been in a frenzy of activity to, er, how did he put it? *Polish up the old pile* before my arrival."

The duke smiled, the expression crinkling the skin around his dark gray eyes and transforming his stern, severe features into something far more approachable.

"You are familiar with the property?" she asked, shaking her head at the footman's offer of more oysters.

"I've not visited in many years, but I recall it being very lovely."

"Are you related to Lord Avington?" Why not? Everyone else in the *ton* seemed to be.

"There is a connection on my wife's side, but it is very distant." Of course there was.

"I'm sure it seems as though we are all related," he said, reading her mind with enough clarity to make her blush. His gray eyes held a glitter of humor and his thin, mobile lips pulled up slightly on one side, making him resemble a mischievous boy rather than a daunting duke.

He had the most amazingly changeable face. One minute he looked entirely average—of medium build and height, medium brown hair, and neat but unexceptional features—and the next he could be warm and animated or intimidating and reserved.

Although he wasn't as handsome as Lord Avington, he emanated an air of dignity that immediately identified him as somebody of consequence.

"Will you be going to your country estate at the end of the Season, Your Grace?" she asked, deciding it was her turn to make conversation.

His gaze flickered down the table quickly—so quickly she almost missed that they landed on Lady Sedgewick. She also couldn't help noticing his mouth tightened, his slight smile replaced by an equally faint frown. "I only just arrived a few days ago. I have a daughter who will be eighteen next Season so I came to town to engage the services of the Countess of Sedgewick for next year."

"She is a miracle worker," Mary said.

"So I've heard from my sister-in-law." His serious expression softened as his gaze settled on Honoria Fairchild née Keyes. "Lady Saybrook had hoped to help launch Rebecca but she will be expecting a happy event."

"Well, I'm sure you'll be very happy with Lady Sedgewick."

"Evidently her schedule is already full for next year." His lips curved into a chilly smile. "I am hoping there will be an unforeseen opening in her busy calendar."

Hmm, *that* was interesting. Was there some sort of friction between the starchy countess and the stern duke?

A very pretty lady—whose name Mary had forgotten—claimed the duke's attention and Mary allowed herself to steal a quick glance at Avington.

He looked entirely at home, laughing and smiling and entertaining his enraptured dinner companions, both of whom sparkled under his attention.

"I believe you and I have actually conducted a great deal of business with each other over the years—through two of our companies, Miss Barnett."

Mary startled and wrenched her gaze away from her betrothed at the sound of her other dining partner—the Earl of Broughton's— comment.

Mary had never met a person with albinism before and to say Lord Broughton was striking was an understatement.

Even at the dinner table he wore round, dark spectacles which made his pure white skin all the more dramatic. He would have been an attractive man regardless of his coloring, but his snowy complexion combined with his classical features made him bear more than a passing resemblance to the statute of Apollo in her family's garden.

Mary shook herself when she realized she'd been staring, and not just because he was gorgeous. He'd also committed the grievous faux pas—at least according to Mary's mother—of mentioning business at the dinner table.

"Which companies, my lord?"

"I am a partner in Harrington and Bow Shipping in Bristol."

"What a remarkable coincidence. You are partners with Callum Bow."

"For many years."

"Callum is quite a character and was a dear friend of my father."

He was also a jovial, working-class Scotsman and one of the most gregarious, outrageous men she'd never met. It was difficult imagining him and this stern, beautiful aristocrat as partners.

Indeed, it was difficult imagining the earl engaging in commerce at all.

"I've known Callum for years," the earl said. "He was the captain of my very first vessel."

"His first ship was the *Invincible Maiden*, was it not?"

He grinned and the expression transformed him from an untouchable ice sculpture into a warm, vibrant man. "You have a good memory. We sold her a few years back—to Alec North, as a matter of fact."

Mary laughed. "You know Alec?"

He lowered his voice slightly and leaned closer, as if he were about to say something he didn't want their neighbors to hear. "Who in our business does not know him—or at least know *of* him?"

"My father was very fond of telling the story of how Alec lost one of his ships—I can't recall the name just now—in a race to Bermuda."

The earl gave her a conspiratorial grin. "The name of the ship was the *Petrel*. By pure coincidence, I was on it during that disastrous race."

"Good Lord! That must have been exciting. Won't you tell me about it? I've only ever heard the story second—or third, rather—hand."

Broughton cut a sheepish look around the table. "It isn't the most appropriate tale for a dinner party—"

Mary leaned closer, an answering smile on her face. "I won't tell anyone, if you don't, my lord."

***

As Miles stood in the receiving line beside his somber-looking fiancé he couldn't help contrasting her grim smile with the expression she'd worn at the dinner table an hour earlier.

He was still astounded by the transformation that had come over Miss Barnett's face during the meal. Just what had she been talking about with Portia's husband that had made her smile and laugh so much?

He'd rarely seen Broughton so animated before, either. Indeed, the man usually spoke less than the ice statute he so closely resembled. And yet their two heads—one a shocking white the other a brilliant copper—had been bent together, the pair as thick as thieves as they snickered and chattered like children.

"Lord Avington?"

Miles looked over at his mother-in-law-to-be, who stood on one side while they received guests, Miss Barnett on the other.

"Yes, ma'am?"

"Lady Sedgewick says it is time to open the ball."

He greeted the couple in front of him and then whispered to Miss Barnett, "It is time for the opening dance."

"Take Jenny with you."

Miles blinked. "I beg your pardon?

"You heard me," she muttered, and then turned to the next person. "Good evening, Mr. Beckworth, it is a pleasure to see you again. "

Miles's head jerked up at the sound of Celeste's lover's name. He'd never met the man face to face and was curious.

"Beckworth, a pleasure," Miles said.

"Avington, it is nice to meet you… finally." The industrialist gave Miles a look that said he knew *exactly* who he was, and his thin lips were twisted into a wryly amused smile. His features were too heavy and harsh to be handsome, but intelligence shone from his pale blue eyes and he had the sort of bone-deep confidence that made a person notice him.

"Thank you for coming tonight," Miles said, and then turned back to Miss Barnett and hissed, "I cannot take your sister out to open *our* betrothal ball."

"I told you weeks ago that I don't dance."

They greeted two more guests and then the earl leaned down and said, "I want to speak to you. Right now."

"We're rather busy at the moment." She nodded and smiled at more guests in the seemingly endless line.

Miles waited until they'd passed and then whispered, "If you don't come outside right now, I will sling you over my shoulder and carry you out like a sack of flour."

Her jaw dropped, her expression of stupefaction more than a little gratifying.

"Will you excuse us, ma'am?" Miles said to Mrs. Barnett, before his betrothed shook off her surprise and commenced arguing.

"Of course, my lord." Louisa gave her daughter a worried glance.

Miles took Miss Barnett's upper arm and guided her toward one of the French doors that led to the terrace.

The minute Miles shut the door behind him, she whipped around on him.

***

Mary's heart was pounding so loudly she had to raise her voice to be heard over it. "How *dare* you threaten me that way?"

"Why are you being so difficult?"

"Difficult? *Difficult?*"

"Yes, *difficult*," he shot back, even louder, clearly not caring if anyone overheard them.

"Just because a woman doesn't conform to your notions of— of—" she scowled up at him, unable to find a word that sounded right.

"Civility? Courtesy? Common *decency*? I merely asked if you would open our own betrothal ball with a dance and you reacted as if I'd struck you."

"You knew my position on dancing, my lord."

"My God! It is *our* betrothal ball, Miss Barnett."

Before she could answer he smiled and nodded to couple who must have been walking in the garden and had likely overheard their bickering.

"It is good to see you again, Lady Norton, Lord Norton."

The instant the door closed behind them, the earl spun around and hissed in a low voice. "One dance, Miss Barnett. All you need to do is dance with me one time."

There were over four hundred guests invited to the ball. Four hundred people who would be looking at them. At her. Speculating about what was hidden beneath her gown. Whispering. Laughing. Smirking.

Mary shook her head. "No. I told you weeks ago I never dance."

"You do know *how* to dance?"

"Yes, of course I do. I learned it at school."

"And you've danced before in public."

Her mouth tightened. "Yes, I did—ten years ago—which is part of the reason I have no intention of doing so now." He opened his mouth and Mary said, "Save your breath, my lord. I will not change my mind about this."

He stared at her in disbelief. "Do you regret this betrothal, Miss Barnett?"

"Are you really getting so exercised because I won't dance with you, my lord? Or is there some other reason? Should I put you out of your misery and jilt you, sir?"

His jaw flexed and he took a step toward her, hands clenching into fists at his side.

Mary swallowed at the anger coming off him in waves; he looked as though he wanted to strangle her.

***

Miles had to clasp his hands behind himself, not trusting himself *not* to throttle her.

"When we were at Richmond you asked me if I would rather have married Lady Copley if circumstances had been different. Do you recall that?"

She scowled. "Of course I remember."

"At the time, I tried to do the gentlemanly thing—even though you'd asked a less than ladylike question—and ignore your question."

She crossed her arms over her chest. "Yes, I remember that, too."

"I will tell you right now that I absolutely would rather have married Lady Copley had I been able to do so."

Pain and shock flashed across her face.

Rather than feel remorse, Miles felt even angrier at her for driving him to such cruelty.

And he felt disgust at himself for allowing it.

She sneered up at him. "Well, it is not too late, my lord! You need to simply say the—"

"I'd rather marry the street sweeper I saw this afternoon while walking down St. James," he said, raising his voice to be heard over hers. "Indeed, I cannot bring to mind a single woman I would *not* rather marry than—"

"*Miles!*"

Miles whipped around and encountered Freddie's shocked face.

Her stunned gray eyes slid from him to Mary. "Your voices can be heard inside."

His skin flamed under her appalled gaze. "Go back inside, Freddie. We will be in shortly."

She gave him one last look and then turned and left.

He filled his lungs to bursting and then turned to his betrothed. Before he could open his mouth to apologize, she lifted a hand.

"Don't."

"I will apologize if I wish to do so," he snapped. "My behavior was abhorrent and I deeply, *deeply* regret what I said."

"You did not hurt me."

"That doesn't matter. I should not have spoken so. Doubtless you wish to—"

"I wish to continue with our betrothal, my lord. I wish to marry."

He shook his head wonderingly. "But *why* when you obviously hate me?"

"I have eight days left before the wretched clause takes effect. Do you really believe I can find somebody else—somebody I won't dislike even more—before then?"

Miles gave a helpless laugh. "It's reassuring that you believe there is somebody out there you might hate more than me." As he looked down into her hostile, guarded gaze Miles wanted to tell her to go to the devil with every particle of his being, but he was too bloody exhausted to start the process all over again.

So instead of walking out of her house for the last time, he said, "You and I will both remain in the receiving line and Crispin and Jenny will open the ball."

She jerked out a nod and Miles held out his arm.

Without another word, she placed her hand on his sleeve, and they returned to greeting their guests.

Chapter 19

I know I lack your experience in such matters, Miles, but aren't you supposed to be charming me with delicious flattery rather than glaring across the ballroom at somebody else?"

Miles startled at the sound of his partner's voice and glanced down to find Lorelei smirking up at him. Unlike Miss Barnett's eyes, which were the dark, mysterious green of a primeval forest, Lori's eyes were the unnerving green of a cat. And right now they were glittering with mischievous glee—an expression that always boded if not ill, then at least discomfort, for the object of her teasing.

"Fishing for compliments, my dear?" he teased. "You look beautiful this evening, Lori. But then you already knew that." Miles aimed for light, casual mockery but fell woefully short of the mark.

"Oh, poor, poor Miles, that was not very convincing. You are not your charming self—what has happened? Who were you glaring at? Your Miss Barnett?" Lori twisted her head, not caring that she threw his steps off in the process.

"Well, look at that!" Lori said, her loud voice more suited to a cock pit than a ballroom, "She seems to be engaged in a rather heated discussion with Gareth." Lori snorted and turned back to him. "I've never seen that man speak to anyone other than Serena."

"He's great friends with Oliver." Oliver was their friend Serena's son from her prior marriage, and the lad was something of a mathematical prodigy, much like his new stepfather, Gareth Lockheart.

"Oliver is twelve, Miles. And the two of them don't talk; they play with *toys* together."

"Oliver is extremely mature for his age—not to mention far better behaved than you've ever been"—Lori laughed at that— "and he and Lockheart don't play with *toys*. Those are automata they build."

Lori rolled her eyes. "Yet more masculine infantilization."

"*What?*"

She chortled—yes, a chortle as Lori would never giggle. "You should see your face, Miles."

"What about it?"

"It's revolting how beautiful you are. You know that don't you?"
Before he could answer—although what the devil could a man say to

that?—Lori charged ahead in her headlong fashion, "Somehow you manage to make even befuddlement look attractive."

To his intense displeasure, he blushed.

Yes, he knew he was attractive, but Lori always managed to make him feel *guilty* about his appearance.

"Oh, stop it! Now you look like a puppy that's been swatted on the nose with a newspaper."

"Is swatting puppies something you are in the habit of doing, Lori?"

"Did you know the Duke of Plimpton came to the house a few days ago?"

Miles was grateful for the change in subject, no matter how dizzy her conversational gyrations left him. "What of it? The house belongs to Honoria and she is the duke's sister-in-law."

"Thank you for explaining the obvious to me, Miles. Wherever would we poor women be if you men weren't available to simplify life's complexities for us?"

Miles laughed. "I'm sorry—you were trying to make some point?"

"I *know* Honoria is married to the duke's brother, thank you very much. I was at their wedding. I hate to disappoint you, but Plimpton did not come all the way to London to attend your ball, no matter how amusing it has been to watch you and your betrothed bicker like a pair of homicidal siblings."

"Lori—"

"And His Grace didn't pop in at our house just because he wanted to admire a modest, perfectly average townhouse, either."

Miles found his gaze wandering to Miss Barnett—who was looking remarkably pretty and animated while talking to Lockheart. Just what the devil was the man saying to make her look so happy?

"Are you paying attention, Miles?" Lori asked.

He dragged his gaze back to his partner. "Er, yes."

"Plimpton wants to engage Freddie to oversee his daughter's coming out next Season."

"Ah, that will be a feather in her cap. Plimpton is excellent *ton.*"

"Freddie told him *no.*"

Miles did a double take. "Really? Why?"

"She won't tell me. I thought you might be able to winkle it out of her."

"Why would I do such a thing?"

She made the sort of rude noise a person shouldn't make in a ballroom—or anywhere else, for that matter. "Good Lord, Miles! You *cannot* possibly be so incurious."

"I didn't say I wasn't curious. But Freddie and I haven't managed to remain such good friends by prying into each other's business. If she wants to tell me her reasons, she will. What?" he asked when she glared at him. "Why are you looking at me like that?"

"You can't really be so obtuse?"

"Let's just pretend I am, shall we?"

Lori jerked him closer—the little beast was *strong*—and hissed into his cravat, "We all know that Freddie is in love with you Miles. You cannot be in earnest about marrying this Barnett harpy?"

Miles pulled back and glared down at her, meeting her scowl for scowl. "I'm not going to dignify your second comment. As to your first assertion, you are wrong. Trust me."

Rather than look chastened—as she should have—or scowling, as he'd expected, she simpered up at him. "*Grrr*, but I do adore this new, stern side of you, Miles." Her eyelids lowered over her remarkable green eyes and she flared her delicate nostrils. "You make me feel positively *naughty*. As if I might need some… discipline." She fluttered her long black eyelashes.

Miles shook his head at Lori, who was openly grinning up at him. "You are a vixen and I eagerly await the day when you meet a man who will take you in hand—or over his knee—and give you the discipline you so richly deserve and require, Lorelei."

She snorted. "Trust me, darling, that man hasn't been created yet." She hesitated, but then her gaze slid over to the Duke of Plimpton. "Although if I was to go willingly over any man's knee…" She shivered slightly. "His Grace looks like he has a very firm hand. I'll wager he could—"

"Hush, you strumpet."

She cut Miles a saucy look. "Why Miles, was my naughty talk making you—"

"Don't make me take you outside, Lori. I will do it," he warned.

Lori laughed. "You are blushing."

"I am not," he retorted, even though he could feel his face flaming. "You are a bloody menace to any man's peace.

"I try," she admitted with a proud tilt of her chin. "But back to the subject of Plimpton."

"I wish you wouldn't."

"All jesting aside, I find him a very intriguing man. In truth, the only thing I don't care for is his status."

"You don't want to be a duchess?"

"Lord no. A more constricting, stuffy, boring way of life I cannot imagine. Can you visualize me attending *ton* parties and playing the *grand dame*, Miles?"

"No."

She chuckled. "Me neither. But back to you, my dear—"

"Lori—"

"Will you be terribly miserable, Miles? I know how you've always avoided this folderol and now—well, you'll be well up to your neck in *ton* idiocy next year, won't you? And with a stubborn woman who won't even dance the opening set at your own betrothal ball!"

"That is my wife-to-be you are speaking of," Miles said quietly, no longer amused.

"I'm sorry," she said after a long moment. "I shouldn't have said that. I am just worried about you. You've spent most of your life avoiding society and now you've been pitchforked into it against your will."

"It is true that I will have to spend next spring in town and engage in the usual frivolities, but it will not be so taxing now that I won't be the one doing the hunting." Or being hunted.

Miss Barnett would suffer far more than Miles would. As angry as he was about her refusal to engage in one dance, he had to admit she'd done everything else she'd promised to do, and even a bit more. He'd seen her love for her sister, so he knew she'd put up with it all for Jenny.

Just as she would put up with Miles in order to retain control of her father's businesses.

It seemed like everything in her life was a negotiation or transaction of some sort. Why did that thought depress him so? Why did—

A face across the room jumped out at him, smashing his thoughts to flinders.

Miles stared at the eerily familiar features as his brain struggled to find the right name.

Beautiful...

Golden hair with pale, cornsilk streaks...

Sky blue eyes...

Full, bow-shaped coral—

Good God!

Miles's feet suddenly refused to take another step.

"Miles?" Lori whispered, her short, sharp fingernails digging into the back of his hand. "What is wrong? *Miles?*"

He blinked, horrified to discover that he'd stopped moving while the music was still playing.

Miles collected himself quickly and guided them out of harm's way, narrowly avoiding a collision with another couple.

"I beg your pardon," he murmured, aware that several of the couples around them had given him questioning stares, not to mention the startled look he was getting from his own partner.

"Is aught amiss, Miles?"

He shook his head, avoiding looking at the corner of the ballroom where he'd seen a face that only appeared in his nightmares.

Lori was like a ferret for such things. If she saw him even glance in Elizabeth Everton's direction, she'd somehow know who he was looking at and she would want to know why seeing her had upset him.

"I'm sorry," he said, smiling down at Lori.

"You turned as white as a ghost." Her sharp gaze flickered over the part of the room where he'd been looking when he froze. Her fingers suddenly clenched painfully tight, especially the one that was holding his injured hand.

"What is it?" he asked, heart in his throat.

"Is that Viscount Severn over there?"

Miles blinked. "What?"

"Viscount Severn! Is that him? Quick!"

He followed her gaze to where a man of medium height with excessively broad shoulders and striking black, shoulder-length hair was talking with five or six young bucks, all of whom appeared to be regarding him with reverent awe.

"Yes, that is Severn." The notorious viscount had a foot propped against the wall behind him, powerful arms crossed over his broad chest, a twisted smirk on his harsh features as he watched somebody on the dance floor, although Miles couldn't tell who he was looking at.

"So," Lori said softly, staring at Severn with an expression of fascinated revulsion. "*That* is the King of the Rakes, is it?"

Miles snorted at the old nickname. "I'm not sure he deserves that name after all these years. Nor am I sure he deserved it at the time. He was no worse than a dozen others when it came to behaving badly."

"You know him?"

"We were acquainted, but I wouldn't say I *knew* him. I haven't seen him in years—at least fifteen—but I heard he'd recently returned. Apparently, his grandfather is in ill health and has finally summoned him home from banishment." He cut Lori a glance. "I'm surprised you know of him; you would have been a mere babe when he was up to his tricks." He smirked at her glare, aware that her tender age—she was the youngest of their teacher friends—was a sore spot with her. "I often forget what an infant you are, my dear."

She scowled up at him. "I am four-and-twenty, Miles. That is scarcely an infant."

"How did you recognize him?"

"I saw him in Mr. Humphrey's window," she admitted.

She was referring to Humphrey's Print Shop, which usually had the very best caricatures—not to mention the most scandalous ones—in London. Not only did they generate excellent parodies of current events, but they also printed some of the most salacious gossip sheets that flooded the streets.

"Tell me what you know about him?" Lori asked, her eyes still fastened on the man in question. At least she wasn't the only one looking at Severn. Every set of eyes in the room kept sliding toward the infamous lord.

"He was a few years older than I was at school, so I don't know much."

"You must have known his brother, too."

"Yes, I knew his brother."

"Were they really identical?"

"In appearance, yes. In behavior, they couldn't have been more different."

"Perseverance and Stand Fast Severn," Lori said in a wondering ton. "What sort of names are those for English peers? And don't say *Puritan*, Miles, because I know that. I also know the Severn family split into two branches more than a hundred years ago. Why would the ones who remained *here* choose such names."

"I believe their mother was very religious."

"Do you think it's possible that the rumors were true—that Stand Fast killed Perseverance?"

Miles stared at Lori until she turned away from the man in question, clearly waiting for him to answer. Whatever she saw on his face made her blush. "You think that is an indelicate question, don't you?"

"I think people's fascination with Sev's death—and Fast's part in it—is unspeakably cruel. Back when I knew the twins, they were very close—inseparable. Whatever happened to his brother I'm sure it caused Severn a great deal of pain."

For once, she was not the irrepressible Lori he knew. Instead, she pulled a face. "I'm sorry. I know that was rotten of me. But—"

"But you could sell a juicy story about Viscount Severn for a great deal of money to your friend Mr. Parker?"

Lori managed to shock everyone else so often that it was more amusing than it should have been to shock *her* for a change.

Her eyes looked like green marbles and her full lips parted in an expression that made her look younger and far less jaded than normal. "How did you know about Parker?"

"I didn't know it for certain until just now." He glared at her. "But I suspected there must be some reason you suddenly had a mania for attending *ton* events when you'd turned your nose up at such things in the past."

"You *tricked* me." Her jaw tightened. "You—you *rat* you."

"Ha! Me a rat? I should say the shoe was on the other foot. Does Freddie know you've been using her good name to get you into balls and parties so you can collect dirt for your pet newspaperman?"

"For your information, Freddie knows exactly how I earn my money. And I'm offended that you'd believe that I'd use her like that!"

"Hush, Lori. You are drawing looks," he ordered quietly, astounded when her pretty lips snapped shut.

The instant she realized that she'd obeyed him without question, she opened her mouth, doubtless to deliver a proper blistering.

Thankfully the dance came to a halt before that could happen.

Lori cut him a filthy look and would have flounced off the dance floor but Miles caught her hand and firmly placed it on his arm.

"Behave," he hissed through his smile. "After all, you wouldn't want to be the subject of those same gossip columns tomorrow, would you, darling?"

She glared up at him from beneath lowered lashes but didn't try to pull away. "What a fine skill you have, Miles—speaking without moving your lips."

Miles grinned, and this time it wasn't entirely feigned. Getting the better of Lori wasn't a regular occurrence; he intended to enjoy it. "Let me escort you back to Freddie."

But the instant they were off the dance floor she yanked her hand away and gave him a frosty smile. "I beg your pardon, *my lord*, but I've important matters to attend to."

Miles watched as she flounced away, not surprised when she went in the direction of Severn.

For a moment, he pitied the viscount. He wouldn't wish Lori on anyone in her current mood.

But Lori wasn't his concern and he had plenty of his own problems to deal with.

Miles glanced over to where Miss Barnett still seemed perfectly happy chattering away with Gareth Lockheart. Good, she was occupied.

He looked around for Elizabeth and was unsurprised to discover that she was looking straight back at him.

Waiting for him.

Chapter 20

"—so you see this new form of hoist has eliminated the need for—"

"Oh dear. Hoists, Gareth? *Again?*" The feminine voice came from behind Mary and Garth Lockheart, who'd been studying a drawing that Lockheart had sketched onto a piece of paper he'd torn from a tiny notebook.

Mary turned to find Serena Lockheart and Lady Honoria Saybrook smirking indulgently.

She knew her face would be a shade of red that clashed with her hair. "Er, I'm afraid the subject of hoists is one I raised, Mrs. Lockheart. I asked your husband about a problem we've had in our Bristol shipyard and—"

Mary broke off when she caught sight of her mother over Lady Saybrook's shoulder, her face a mask of horror at hearing Mary utter the word *shipyard* in a ballroom, to a marchioness

"Er, in any case, Mr. Lockheart has been most helpful," she finished lamely.

Gareth Lockheart stepped into the breech. "I was telling Miss Barnett about the lift I made for your larger sculptures, Serena." The brilliant industrialist was an extremely handsome man, but there was something about him that was strangely lifeless, at least until he spoke to his wife

Mrs. Lockheart gave her husband a look of mock severity. "I'm afraid you overlooked something, Gareth."

He turned and squinted at his drawing. "What?"

Mrs. Lockheart laughed. "Not the hoist, Gareth."

The gorgeous man glanced around in confusion before comprehension dawned. "Oh, I say! I forgot our dance."

"You did. But you can make that up to me right now, dearest, because another set is about to begin."

Mary almost laughed at the look of misery that flickered over Lockheart's face as he stared at the couples assembling on the dance floor.

"Er, not a quadrille." He made a small, barely audible whimper. "Please, Serena."

His wife laughed. "No, my dear, I am not so foolish. It is a country dance—we only need to follow the leader's steps."

Lockheart sighed and turned to Mary. "Shall I messenger those plans to your yard in Bristol?"

"Thank you. I will write and tell them to expect it."

Before Mary could invite Lady Saybrook to take the seat that Mr. Lockheart had just vacated, Miss Lorelei Fontenot suddenly appeared and dropped into the chair.

"I hope I'm not interrupting anything," she said, staring at Mary in a way that seemed more than a little aggressive. Without turning to look at Lady Saybrook Miss Fontenot said, "Simon wanted to talk to you about... something, Honey. You should go to him."

Even Mary could hear the lie in her words.

The marchioness gave her friend a hard look, which the other woman ignored, and then smiled at Mary and said, "Will you excuse me, Miss Barnett?"

"Of course, my lady."

Lorelei Fontenot hardly waited until the other woman was out of earshot before saying, "What, exactly, is your dispute with Miles."

Mary bristled at the other woman's tone. "I don't know what you mean."

"Yes, you do. You take pleasure in goading him."

"That is not true."

"Yes, it is," Miss Fontenot shot back. "Take this business of refusing to dance the opening set at *your own ball*." She leaned closer, her gaze so sharp it would have inflicted a lethal wound had it been a blade. "You know that refusing him is only causing gossip. You won't have to cope with the effects of your behavior, but he will."

"What do you mean?"

"You must know they're already putting bets in the book at Miles's wretched club."

"That is hardly my fault."

"It is *exactly* your fault for giving them something to wager about."

"Men never need a reason to wager."

Miss Fontenot ignored her comment and said, "You are punishing him because you want him—badly—and you are angry at yourself." She leaned even closer. "And you are terrified by the strength of your own desire."

Mary flinched away from the other woman, her heart suddenly thrashing uncomfortably in her chest. "You don't have the slightest idea what you are talking about."

"Oh, but I *do*, Miss Barnett. I've watched woman after woman after woman fall in love with Miles. Or at least they fall in love with his handsome façade and then they get angry when they discover he is a living, breathing person with his own wants and desires and flaws, not a prince from a fairytale."

Mary scowled, infuriated by the other woman's accusations, which were far too close to the truth. Not that she would ever admit it. Instead, she asked, "What, exactly, is your point?"

"Miles might appear strong and indestructible, but he can be hurt. He is a damaged, angry, terrified man who has never been allowed to live his own life. Most importantly, he's never been allowed to love where he wishes. His family and their needs have always come first with him."

Mary could only stare.

"I understand that you, too, are being forced to marry?"

Mary jerked out a nod, and then wished she hadn't. Why did this woman believe she was entitled to such answers? And why was Mary—who was no wilting violet—allowing Miss Fontenot to run roughshod over her?

Because she sees you as you really are. You want Lord Avington badly and you punish him for your own desire.

The admission—even in her own mind—was so painful that Mary flinched away from it.

"Just leave me be," she said, ashamed by the tremor in her voice.

Miss Fontenot leaned closer and hissed, "Did you know that Miles almost got into a duel because he defended your honor at his club?"

"*What?* No, you are lying!"

"It is the truth. Viscount Elton made some disparaging comment and Miles took him to task for it."

Elton. The name brought a nauseating rush of humiliation with it, even after all these years.

Miss Fontenot nodded, as if Mary had spoken. "Miles has approached your upcoming marriage the way he confronts all his responsibilities: with dignity and grace. Meanwhile, you have taken every opportunity—from what I've seen and heard—to jab and pick at him because you want a reaction, don't you? His very equanimity bothers you. It irks you that he doesn't seem to care for you any more than he does any other person in his life." She lowered her voice. "You want him so badly you ache with it, don't you?"

Mary opened her mouth to hotly deny her accusation.

"Do not waste your breath, Miss Barnett. I am right and we both know it."

Miss Fontenot nodded sagely when Mary shut her mouth. "Good, now that you are no longer lying to me—or yourself—we can get to the meat of the problem."

Good God! She wasn't *finished?*

"You're in love with Lord Avington yourself," Mary accused, clutching at anything to shut her up.

Miss Fontenot snorted and gave her a scathing look. "And here I thought you were clever." Her piercing eyes seemed to bore into Mary's flesh. "Stop inflicting your anger, insecurity, and frustration on my friend, Miss Barnett. Miles has had rotten luck and deserves somebody who can return his affection and give him love and—"

"He doesn't want love! He told me that in no uncertain terms," she retorted, and then wished she'd kept her mouth shut when Miss Fontenot laughed, the derisive sound like nails scratching on Mary's skin.

"And you actually *believed* him? Good Lord, you *are* a fool, aren't you?"

Mary began to stand. "I won't sit here and be—"

Miss Fontenot grabbed Mary's wrist and yanked her back down. "You *will* sit here and listen to me or I will make such a scene in the middle of your family's ballroom that your sister will be fortunate to receive an invitation to a cock fight in Whitechapel by the time I am finished."

"What do you want?" Mary ground out through clenched teeth.

"If you cannot give Miles love and companionship, then release him from this farce of a betrothal."

Miss Fontenot's command clanged in Mary's ears like a pot striking a flagstone floor.

Release him, release him, release him . . .

The two words echoed repeatedly.

When Mary didn't answer, Miss Fontenot nodded, a smug, knowing gleam in her eyes. "Yes, I can see you intensely dislike the thought of losing him."

Mary didn't think she'd ever hated a woman more than she did Miss Fontenot.

"It is not too late to salvage this betrothal, Miss Barnett. Miles is yours and he has a very forgiving nature and loving heart. But even he can be pushed past the point of forgiveness."

"Is that some sort of threat?"

Miss Fontenot heaved a sigh of exasperation. "Don't be a ninny. Just make sure you deserve him." Her penetrating green gaze burned into Mary for a long, uncomfortable moment, and then her eyes, surely her most striking feature, widened with understanding.

"What?" Mary demanded.

"You aren't just obsessed with him. You *lo*—"

"I do *not!*" Mary snapped loudly enough that several people around them turned to stare. "I most certainly do *not* love him," she whispered furiously, glaring at the horrid, awful, prying stranger.

A stranger who was starting to grin.

And then chuckle.

Miss Fontenot nodded, as if Mary had said something. "You love him."

Mary opened her mouth to tell the woman to shut up but suddenly Miss Fontenot's gaze darted to something over Mary's shoulder.

"Damnation!" she muttered.

Mary turned to see what had upset the other woman, but all she saw were dancers.

"I have to leave. *Now,*" Miss Fontenot said. "But before I do, I want to make sure we understand one another?"

"I don't know what you are—"

Miss Fontenot squeezed Mary's arm so hard she gasped. "Do we understand each other?" she repeated in a menacing whisper.

"Yes!" Mary yelped, even though she could no longer recall what she was agreeing to.

"Good." Miss Fontenot leapt to her feet and rushed off, shoving past other guests so roughly as to make enemies for life as she hurried toward the door that led to the cardroom. Before she entered the room, she reached out and tapped the broad shoulder of Lord Stand Fast

Severn, the peer whose recent return to England had been flooding the gossip columns.

Severn spun on his heel, saw who it was, and scowled.

Evidently Mary wasn't the only person who'd taken Miss Fontenot in dislike.

Unfortunately, a handful of guests drifted in front of the angry viscount, obstructing Mary's view.

What in the world had *that* been about?

Mary shook away her curiosity and slumped in her chair, strangely exhausted.

Lord Avington needed *love*? Surely Miss Fontenot was wrong about that.

After all, the earl had made the absence of love a term in their marriage contract.

Hadn't he?

Mary frowned as she tried to recall her conversation with Avington, when he'd mentioned not wanting wooing and romance.

But had he said anything about love?

Or had it been *Mary* who'd brought up love?

She stared unseeingly at the dancers, wracking her brain to recall exactly who had said what that night.

Chapter 21

W hat are you doing here, Miss Everton?" Miles demanded of the woman he still had nightmares about.

Elizabeth Everton's plump, bow-shaped lips curved into a smile of delight and she blinked her huge, blue, and frighteningly empty eyes at him. "Miles! How lovely to see you. It has been *ages!*"

Not bloody long enough.

"What are you doing here?" he repeated. "You are supposed to be in America—in Boston." He lowered his voice, which had begun to rise. "Your father gave us his *word* that he would keep you there."

Tears welled in her magnificent eyes. "I heard about dearest Bevan's death from Mrs. Foxworthy. You must remember her? Our housekeeper at Derring Manor?"

"Yes, I remember her," Miles said grimly. Indeed, how could he forget? The housekeeper had been the one who'd given Elizabeth her alibi the day Pansy had died.

"Mrs. Foxworthy wrote to tell us about Bevan. Tragically, Papa took ill and died not long afterward."

Miles stared into her eyes, searching for a sign that Elizabeth had done something to facilitate her father's death. After all, it was remarkably coincidental timing. "Did you kill him?"

Elizabeth's eyes widened and her chin quivered. It was like watching an actor step into character—that of the bereaved daughter. "Miles! How could you say such a thing?"

"Good God," Miles whispered, his gorge rising. "You *did*. You killed your own father."

"I am hurt that you could even think that."

Miles's flesh crawled as he stared into her Delft blue eyes, which were just as hard as the pottery they so resembled.

She stepped closer and it took every ounce of self-control he possessed not to flinch away.

"I had hoped that after all these years we might be able to look past that dreadful misunderstanding, Miles."

Ancient, long-buried rage exploded inside him, obliterating common sense or any sense at all.

Miles grabbed her upper arm and frog marched her toward the nearest exit, not caring who saw them.

She giggled nervously. "Miles! Where are you—"

"Shut. Up." His vision clouded with a pulsing red haze; his anger so pure—so hot—he felt as if his blood was turning to steam in his veins.

He didn't stop or speak until he reached the library. A quick glance around the large room proved it was unoccupied and Miles roughly shoved Elizabeth inside and slammed the door behind her before shoving her up against the glossy mahogany and caging her between his two arms.

"You were *never* to return to this country, Elizabeth! That was the only reason my father agreed to the travesty of a deal he made with yours. That was the *only* reason you didn't hang."

Miles recoiled as heat, desire, and a twisted mockery of love whirled in her darkened gaze. Her breathing was ragged, her magnificent bosom straining at the tight, low bodice of her gown. "*I* never made that bargain, Miles. Nobody ever consulted me," she hissed. "For more than ten years Papa incarcerated me like a prisoner in Boston. How long should I suffer for something I never did?"

"You are a *liar!*" Miles shouted, his fingers digging into the soft flesh of her arms hard enough to leave bruises. But he didn't care. He wanted to wrap his hands around her throat and squeeze and squeeze until the life drained out of her crazed blue eyes.

She seemed oblivious to any pain, her gaze cloying and suffocating as she stared up at him. "I came back as soon as I heard you'd inherited. I knew you would break your vow never to marry because you would *have* to. Because you are so honorable and good." Her eyes suddenly flashed with genuine emotion: jealousy and hatred. "Why in the world would you agree to marry such a homely, scarred little thing, Miles? I've returned to you, so put her aside. We can finally be together and—"

Miles thrust himself from her and backed away, but she followed him, matching him step for step, until a settee halted his escape.

"You really are insane, aren't you? I *loathe* you, Elizabeth." His body shook with the effort of containing his loathing. "Don't you understand that?"

Her sensual lower lip quivered and a single tear slid down her perfect cheek. "But I'm innocent, Miles. I never did—"

179

"You are a *liar!*" he roared, taking a step toward her, his hands tightening into fists. "If you don't—"

The door swung open and Freddie stood on the threshold, her wide gray gaze going from Miles to Elizabeth back to Miles.

"Lord Avington," she murmured calmly, only her flushed cheeks giving away her agitation. "Is aught amiss? Your rather hasty exit from the ballroom was... noted."

Elizabeth's features flickered through a dizzying series of expressions—like so many masks—and the one she finally selected had, once upon a time, utterly and completely fooled Miles: it was her doe in the forest façade, the very image of a harmless female in desperate need of protection.

She took a step toward Freddie and held out a hand. "We have not been introduced. I am Elizabeth Everton, an old and very close friend of Miles. I am so *pleased* to meet—"

Miles closed the distance between the two women with two long strides and slapped Elizabeth's hand away from Freddie's outstretched one.

"*Miles!*" Freddie gasped.

"Don't *touch* her!" he snarled, towering over Elizabeth's diminutive form for a long moment before striding toward the door and yanking it open. "*Get out* of this house right now before I drag you by the hair and kick you down the steps into the street." He lifted a hand and pointed a finger at her. "If you know what is wise you will *never* come near me or anyone I care about ever again. Now, *out!*"

A smug, sly glint flickered in her wide blue eyes—satisfaction at turning him into a beast, no doubt—but it was almost instantly masked by regret and sadness.

"Naturally I will leave, Miles. I'm so sorry to have come where I'm not wanted." She nodded at Freddie and sailed from the room; her head held high but her shoulders convincingly slumped in defeat.

Miles slammed the door behind her and filled his lungs as an almost suffocating wave of nausea swamped him.

"Good Lord, Miles. What in the world was that all about? Who is that woman?"

Miles stared into Freddie's concerned gray eyes and shook his head, too sick to speak.

Instead, he reached for her with shaking hands, swallowing repeatedly to keep from vomiting.

Freddie stepped into his embrace without hesitation. "What is it, Miles?" she murmured into his shoulder. "You look as if you'd seen a ghost."

Miles wrapped his arms around her and squeezed so tightly that she grunted, but he couldn't make himself loosen his hold even though he knew he was hurting her.

"Thank God you came when you did, Fred," he whispered shakily into her hair, which was scented with the lavender she grew and harvested herself.

Miles closed his eyes and filled his lungs with her familiar, calming scent, his heartbeat gradually slowing.

He had no idea how long they stood that way—surely no more than a minute or two—as the rage drained out of him, leaving him feeling weak and exhausted. He was finally regaining control of his faculties when he heard the library door open behind him.

Miles knew even before he turned around who it would be.

Chapter 22

People are staring, Mary. One of us must go and see what has happened."

Mary grimaced at her mother's frantic whispering, wishing she could ignore her.

But even somebody as socially inept as Mary knew that Avington's abrupt exit with the mysterious blond woman had attracted far too much attention, and not of the good sort.

She felt the weight of hundreds of eyes; curious, prying eyes that were wondering why the two golden, beautiful people had all but sprinted out of the ballroom together.

"I'll go," Mary muttered. If nothing else, it would get her away from all the eyes.

It was scarcely any better out in the corridor, where a quick glance at the small clusters of people up and down the hallway told her that onlookers had gathered hoping for more gossip.

Jared, Mary's favorite footman, unobtrusively drifted up beside her. "They are in the library, Miss Barnett," he murmured, without her even needing to ask.

"Thank you," Mary said just as quietly, ignoring the curious stares as she made her way toward her favorite room in the house, both fearing and dreading what she would find there.

When she reached the landing the beautiful blond woman from the ballroom was sashaying toward her, a smug, private little smile on her face until she discerned Mary. The pained look of concern that seized her exquisite features was so genuine that Mary thought she must have imagined the sly smirk.

"Oh, Miss Barnett! I am so relieved to see you."

"I'm afraid you have the advantage of me," Mary said coldly.

"My name is Elizabeth Everton and I am a very dear friend of Miles." She pulled a face. "I apologize if our reunion made us a spectacle. I'm afraid he was overcome by emotion at seeing me. It has been some years. I had the misfortune of conveying the news of my father's death. Miles was... well, distraught would not be too strong a word."

Mary had seen his face when he'd all but dragged the blond woman from the room and *homicidal rage*—rather than *distraught*—was how she would have described the expression distorting his normally tranquil visage.

"Lady Sedgewick is comforting him—you know how close they are," the woman said in a confiding tone that made Mary's face heat.

"Excuse me, ma'am," Mary said, suddenly eager to get away from her.

Don't go in there, Mary. Go back to the ballroom. You can return with the Everton woman and quiet the wagging tongues.

But Mary had always admired those generals who'd gone on the offensive rather than those who'd practiced prudent retreat.

She would have the truth of the matter, by God. And she would have it *now*.

But when she flung open the door and saw Avington with his arms around Lady Sedgewick, she honestly wished that she had turned tail and run as fast as Napoleon fleeing from Russia.

No doubt she was the very image of homely stupefaction—mouth gaping, eyes round—while the beautiful countess met her gaze over Avington's shoulder.

"Miss Barnett," Lady Sedgewick said, her polite mask instantly sliding over the expression of anguish.

The earl's broad shoulders stiffened beneath his exquisitely fitted coat—a coat that *her* money had paid for—while he embraced another woman.

He stepped away from the countess before turning, his godlike features unreadable, his normally vivid blue eyes strangely colorless.

"Miss Barnett. I apologize for the spectacle I doubtless made."

"Who is that woman? My mother did not invite her and none of us know her."

He opened his mouth, hesitated, and then strode to the door and held it open. "Will you excuse us, Freddie?"

"Of course." The countess gave Mary a look that was filled with commiseration rather than guilt.

Once the door closed behind her, his lordship flipped the lock and then slowly turned to face her.

"Please sit." He gestured to the settee in front of the fire.

Mary crossed her arms and hugged herself, staying right where she was. "Is that something I can expect to find myself confronting often, my lord?"

One of his light blond brows lifted. "I'm sorry?"

"You embracing other women in my house."

Even though the light in the room was dim, his pupils shrank to tiny dots and his attractive features tightened until he looked stern and rather terrifying. "What are you implying?"

"Do I really need to explain what I saw?"

He took a step toward her, until she had to tilt her head to an uncomfortable angle to meet his icy gaze. "I think I'd like to hear it from your own lips."

"Is Lady Sedgewick yet another mistress?"

"You think I am the sort of man who would make love to his mistress in his betrothed's library on the night of his betrothal ball?"

Mary swallowed at the soft menace in his tone. "What conclusion am I supposed to draw, my lord?"

"If you thought me a man with even a vestige of honor you could not believe I would do such a thing." He cocked his head. "But then you have picked at me since the very first evening we met, haven't you?"

She opened her mouth to deny it, but he stepped close enough that she could smell the intoxicating scent of clean man mingled with the faint odor of starch. Mary stared at his cravat, refusing to meet his gaze, suddenly frightened. Of what? Him? Herself?

He took her chin and forced her to meet his gaze.

His eyes were truly magnificent, the numerous blues combining in a way that evoked endless summer skies and bottomless blue seas. There were crow's feet at the corners and evidence of dark blond hairs poking through his pale skin. His lips were works of art, the upper thin and shapely while the lower was plush and pouty, tiny crescents bracketing the corners. And then—so faint it looked like a blond hair trailing over his skin—was a long, thin scar that ran from beneath his lower lip down his chin.

"Why are you so prickly with me… Mary?"

Mary got gooseflesh at the sound of her plain name coming from those exquisite lips.

The earl did not wait for her answer. "I know you view me as just another dissolute aristocrat who cavorts with his mistresses and cares for nothing but his own pleasure. Do you want to change your mind about us, is that why—"

"No!" Mary bit her lip, horrified by the loud, desperate syllable and the way it made him jolt.

She was especially horrified by the dawning realization in those eyes.

"I mean—"

"I know what you mean," he said softly, his hand sliding from her chin to her jaw—thankfully the unscarred side—his nostrils flaring as his eyes flickered over her face, his expression no longer perplexed or anguished.

His lips pulled up on the right side, his smile self-mocking as he clucked his tongue. "Poor, poor Mary."

Mary didn't want to know what he meant by that.

His smile grew both in size and wickedness.

And then he lowered his mouth over hers.

***

Miles's wits—so scattered only moments before—were suddenly as sharp and focused as a lighthouse beacon.

Matters that had perplexed him suddenly made sense. Miss Scowly Mary Bennett might dislike him, but that didn't mean she didn't *want* him.

Miles wanted to laugh and cry at the same time.

Why had it taken him so long to recognize the signs?

He knew it sounded arrogant, but he was accustomed to women becoming infatuated with him—or at least with his appearance. It would be disingenuous to say he didn't realize he was attractive to women. And there was no denying that both men and women were attracted to beautiful things, whether those things were other people or expensive clothing or fine horseflesh.

Personally, he'd never understood how a man or woman could want another person so *badly* based only on their appearance. He'd been friends with Pansy for years before they'd fallen in love, and the attraction had been mutual. He'd wanted her physically, of course, but he'd also cared about what *she* had wanted.

The acquisitive glitter in Mary Barnett's eyes told him that she wanted him despite believing him to be a man of limited morals and low intellect—despite her best judgement, in other words.

She was buying him as surely as she purchased lumber to build one of her ships—or any other object she wanted.

As much as she might like to pretend that the two of them were in similar, desperate circumstances; they were not.

It would be far easier for a wealthy heiress to find a destitute peer than the other way around. When it came to their arrangement, Miss Mary Barnett held all the cards and they both knew it.

Well, all the cards except one.

And so Miles played his one card and lowered his mouth over her coral lips and kissed her.

His intention was to punish her, to give her what she wanted but withhold the most essential ingredient to making love: passion.

But then she gave a muffled gasp and opened herself to him, parting her surprisingly full, soft lips and welcoming him inside. In the blink of an eye all his cold, calculating plans flew out the window.

Miles tugged off his gloves, flung them aside, and cupped the back of her head—rather than her fragile throat, as he'd envisioned so often—tunneling his fingers into her heavy crown of hair, the strands as wiry as the copper they so resembled.

He slid his other hand around her waist and pulled her closer, using the tip of his tongue to trace the plush cushion of her lower lip, which he'd admired on far too many occasions.

She gave a soft, barely audible grunt that took his cock from half-hard to full mast in a matter of seconds.

Miles caressed from her waist to her lower back, his fingers resting on the swell of her surprisingly lush arse. He held her head at the right angle and invaded her, gradually sweeping deeper into her wet heat, stroking the sensitive insides of her lips, the hard slickness of her gums and even the fine serrations of her teeth, until she was boneless in his arms.

She might have had another lover—perhaps even more than one—but it was obvious to Miles that none of them had valued kissing.

Although she eagerly welcomed his tongue, her responses were clumsy and awkward, her own tongue darting shyly into his mouth, her slim body trembling with need or excitement or both.

The effect of her obvious desire was explosive, and Miles ground his aching prick against her belly, the sensation making them both groan.

Take her, the selfish, dishonorable part of his mind urged.

Miles visualized laying her out on the gaudy gold settee, lifting her gown, and thrusting his pulsing shaft into her tight, wet heat. It had been almost a year since he'd had a woman and the satiation of his desire would smash every other thought from his mind and grant him relief.

At least temporarily.

She wanted it every bit as much as he did. The door was locked and nobody would know.

But she was his betrothed and this was a function in their honor, not some back alley where strangers exchanged money to couple under cover of darkness.

When Miles took her for the first time, he wanted the luxury of hours, not minutes, to savor the experience. He wanted to invade and enslave her with pleasure; not engage in a quick, angry fuck in her mother's library.

And it would indeed be quick because they couldn't spare even five more minutes. They needed to get back to the ballroom ten minutes ago.

It was that last thought that brought him back to himself.

Gently, slowly, and reluctantly, he disengaged, until he could see her slitted green gaze and slack, swollen lips, twin spots of red on her pale cheeks.

Miles allowed himself one last caress of the surprisingly full hips hidden beneath her dreadful gown.

"As much as I desire you at this moment, Mary, I'm far too angry to make love. At least too angry to do you justice."

She jolted at his words and he noticed for the first time that her small hands were clutching his lapels in a death grip.

Miles lowered his hands over hers when she would have jerked away.

"Shhh. Don't run away. Sit with me a moment. It's time we clear the air. I have some explaining to do, and there are a few things you should know about me."

**

Mary stared at Lord Avington's lovely coat—which she'd wrinkled irreparably with her grabbing—rather than his lovely face.

The earl had kissed her—had caressed and explored her—and it had been even more magnificent than Mary had allowed herself to imagine.

187

His touch was tender and yet she'd felt the strength he'd kept in check.

He'd not lied when he said he wanted her—*her,* plain, burned Mary Barnett—she'd felt hard evidence of his desire against her stomach.

"Come sit." He led her to the dreadful gold silk settee, waiting until she was seated before going to the decanters her mother kept filled, even though her father was no longer alive to enjoy their contents.

When he returned, he held two tumblers of amber liquid.

Mary took one and tipped the entire contents into her mouth.

He chuckled. "Easy, darling."

Mary told herself it was the brandy that warmed her, rather than his endearment. He called everyone *darling;* it did not mean anything special, no matter how pleasurable it felt.

He took her empty glass, set it aside, and then sat beside her, a faintly rueful expression on his face. "I take it you still wish for plain speaking?"

"Always." No matter how much she might not like it.

"Lady Sedgewick and I are not, and never have been, lovers. We are very close friends and nothing more. As for Lady Copley, we were briefly intimate, but haven't been lovers for over a year." His eyes narrowed. "I visit her, but not for the reasons you believe. We are friends and we also are business partners. She paints the items I carve. That is how we both supplement our incomes. I should have told you the nature and extent of our relationship when you brought her name up at Richmond, but I was... angry, so I behaved like a child. Will you forgive me for that, Mary? And yes, I've taken the liberty of calling you by your Christian name and would ask you to do the same."

"You want me to call you Mary?"

He couldn't have looked more shocked if she'd punched him.

"What?" she taunted. "You didn't think I possessed a sense of humor?"

"Well, it's the first evidence I've seen of it."

Mary snorted and gave him a grudging smile. "I deserved that."

"Yes," he agreed. "You did. But I was not finished with my *air clearing.*"

"Go on."

"Do you forgive me for misleading you about Lady Copley?"

Mary was so relieved she could have wept. But she merely nodded and said, "Yes."

"I do not love her—I've never loved her. I am not sacrificing myself for my family by giving up the woman I love. I take it that is what you were thinking?"

Mary's first impulse was to deny it, but then she noticed the smudges beneath his glorious eyes. He was exhausted and he was offering her the coin she claimed to like—plain speech—she owed him the same.

"Yes, that is what I'd believed."

"My heart is not committed to any other woman." He paused and looked awkward. "Er, by the by, Lady Copley received an invitation and I wanted to warn—"

"I saw her," Mary said. She cut him a sheepish look. "It may have been part of the reason I was so hostile."

"You have no need to be—she is marrying Horace Beckworth."

"I know."

He fixed her with a stern look, and it was remarkably like the expression he often wore in Mary's naughty nighttime fantasies. "I don't have a mistress. I don't *plan* to have a mistress. And I won't like it if *you* take a lover. Understood?"

"Understood," she croaked, feeling a little lightheaded.

"Good." The earl threw back the rest of his drink, set down the glass with a thump, and said, "This next story is not so easy to tell. The woman you saw me with tonight is Elizabeth Everton, she and I were betrothed more than a decade ago."

"I recognize the name."

"From your investigations?"

She nodded.

"Did your agent tell you why the betrothal ended?"

"No, just that Miss Everton had changed her mind."

"I will tell you the truth, which is something I'd been honor bound *not* to share until tonight—until seeing Elizabeth again for the first time in over a decade." He stood and gestured to her glass.

"No thank you."

He refilled his—twice as much as before—and resumed his seat. "As you already know, my father had a problem with cards." He laughed bitterly. "Actually, he had two problems. One, he couldn't stay away from gambling hells. And two, he was a dreadful card player.

"When he inherited the title, the earldom was healthy. After twenty-five years with him at the helm every single item that hadn't been entailed had been sold or mortgaged."

He looked down at his glass and turned it around and around in his hands, his mouth compressed in an unhappy frown.

"One of the last things he gambled away was a substantial parcel of land that was critical to generating enough income for the estate. It was a neighboring property that had come into our family's possession two hundred years before through marriage, so there was also a large manor house on the land."

He took a drink and then continued grimly. "The man who won the property—James Everton—immediately moved himself and his daughter into the house. Have you heard of him?"

"He made his fortune in munitions, didn't he?"

Avington nodded. "My father had lost a great deal to Everton and not even the vast swath of land was enough to settle his debt." His eyes darted restlessly, as if he were searching for an escape "But Everton proposed a solution. He wanted his daughter to marry into our family and agreed to forgive all the debt and return everything except a life estate in the house if I agreed to marry his daughter." He met her gaze. "I was not engaged, but there was an unofficial agreement between myself and Lady Pansy Wargrave. It is her father and mother you met earlier tonight, the Duke and Duchess of Wargrave. They have three sons but Pansy was their only daughter. We grew up together as our mothers had been great friends since girlhood."

Mary experienced a sick, creeping sense of dread the longer she listened. She wanted to tell him to stop—she didn't need to know this ancient history—but another part of her couldn't resist and she held her peace and listened, frozen with morbid fascination.

The earl cleared his throat, finished his glass of brandy, and glanced yearningly toward the decanter before resuming his story. "Pansy and I had been in love for several years, but her mother and father had asked us to wait until she was twenty and had experienced life in London before we announced our betrothal." He swallowed hard. "When I told her what I needed to do—well, I'm sure you can imagine it was unpleasant, but we'd both been raised to accept familial expectations." He shrugged, gut-wrenching pain flashing in his eyes.

"Elizabeth's father wasn't satisfied for us to just marry, he wanted to wait until the Season began and have a huge, grand ceremony in St. George's." He gave a bitter laugh. "He wanted the entire *ton* in attendance. My parents were delighted to wait—after all, the money began to flow once our impending connection to Everton became common knowledge. A few weeks before we were all to remove to London, we hosted a house party—bigger than any we'd had in years." He paused and inhaled deeply, his expression one of pure misery.

"You don't have to tell me this," Mary said.

"Yes, I do. If I don't, you will be prey to all sorts of rumors, almost none of which are true. And there are other... reasons. But I'm getting ahead of myself."

He shoved a hand through his hair, his gaze distant as he looked into his past. "Pansy came to the house party, along with her mother and father—they were my parents' closest friends and to not invite them would have caused unwanted speculation. Although we had never acted on our love, we were young and I'm sure we did a poor job concealing our emotions."

His lips, which she now knew were unspeakably soft, curved into an unhappy smile. "It was winter and there was a nearby pond our family had skated on for generations. That year it hadn't quite frozen through enough to safely use by the time the party began. But by the second week we'd had another freeze and my mother planned nighttime festivities by the pond. The servants would erect a pavilion, there would be food and drink, and we would skate. It was to be the last gathering before we departed."

He took a deep breath before continuing. "The day before the event, Pansy received a message from... somebody. The footman who handed it to her didn't know who it was from and the message itself was later lost. In any case, Pansy took her skates and had one of the grooms saddle her favorite mare. She then rode out to the pond, went skating, and fell through the ice and died."

"Good God," Mary whispered.

"One of our servants—a stable lad—told my father that he'd seen Elizabeth and Pansy both skating on the pond the afternoon she died. He said their voices were raised, but he hadn't lingered and didn't know if they'd been arguing. When my father confronted Everton, his housekeeper swore that Elizabeth had not left the house that day. The message to Pansy had disappeared and without any proof, it was our stable boy's word against Elizabeth herself and her housekeeper."

"But you think—"

191

"I *know* she lured Pansy out to that pond and killed her." He leaned toward her, his eyes the hot blue of the center of a flame. "I wasn't the only one; Everton knew it, too and you could see the guilt in his eyes. He agreed to take her far away—to America—if we did not press the matter. He pointed out—quite correctly—that we did not have enough evidence. He said he would use every pound in his possession to destroy us if we tried to have her arrested and brought to justice."

"And what about Pansy's parents? The duke and duchess?" Mary asked.

Miles briefly closed his eyes, his face a mask of misery and shame.

"I wanted to tell them, but my father argued there was no point in airing our suspicions—that they were only that: suspicions without proof. He insisted that we could hardly accuse a man like Everton of covering up a murder on the basis of a stable lad's words. But I *knew* the most persuasive factor in his decision was that Everton forgave the debt and signed over the property just as he'd agreed to do if Elizabeth and I had married." He shook his head, his eyes bleak. "My father sold his soul and helped Pansy's murderer escape justice to pay his gambling debts."

Mary swallowed, considering her next words carefully before she finally spoke. "And so you joined the army."

He nodded. "I could not bear to look at my father—or my mother, who surely knew the truth, too. I think that living with what they'd done drove them both to early graves. I don't think Bevan ever knew—at least he never mentioned it."

"Why did Miss Everton come here tonight?"

"She is not right in her head, Mary. Her father died and now there is nobody to control her." His jaw shifted from side to side, his gaze distant. "I was not aware until tonight that she had returned. Now that I know, I will engage somebody to make sure she stays away from Avington Castle." He gave her a stern look. "I know this sounds hysterical, but you must never, ever agree to meet her—not even somewhere public. She is cunning and quite mad."

"You believe she would kill for you?" she asked, unable to keep her disbelief from her voice.

"She is… obsessed. And mad." He met her gaze, his handsome face suddenly haggard. "She has told me that she still wants me—that she has returned to England for me." He swallowed. "You must take care, Mary. Your life might be in danger. She has killed once to have me; she could very well kill again."

Chapter 23

Mary was looking at the latest reports from the Sunderland shipyard when there was a knock on her study door and Yost entered. "I'm sorry to disturb you, Miss Mary, but his lordship is here."

Mary blinked, her brain slow to change paths from deliveries of oak and Scotch Pine to her betrothed.

"Er… Where is he?"

"He is waiting downstairs with his carriage. He said he's come to take you for a drive."

Mary stared for a moment, confused. They'd had no meeting planned for today. Indeed, the house was in a flurry of packing in preparation for their departure tomorrow.

Miles would know that, so this must be important. "Tell him I'll be down in a few minutes."

The butler left and Mary removed her spectacles, pulled off her sleeve covers, and put the reports away in a drawer before locking it.

Her maid was already waiting with one of Mary's new carriage gowns laid out.

"Mr. Yost said you were going for a drive with his lordship," Kearny said.

Mary eyed the teal-blue and ivory ensemble—which she had never seen before—and nodded.

Several gowns had been delivered over the past few days, all of them chosen by Lady Sedgewick, whom Mary had entrusted with the selection of her new wardrobe. Although she knew it had hurt her mother's feelings, Mary simply didn't trust Louisa Barnett's propensity for frills, lace, and ribbons. Lady Sedgewick, on the other hand, had impeccable taste and knew what Mary liked.

As Kearny dressed her in the smart teal-blue gown, Mary thought about the last time she'd seen the earl—four nights earlier, at their ball, when he'd kissed her and confided the truth of his past.

Her feelings toward him had changed that night.

Whether because of his confession that he'd had no mistress since they met—and no intention to have one in the future—or the fact that he'd entrusted her with the most painful part of his past, she didn't know. But suddenly she saw her behavior since they'd met in a new, far harsher, light. She needed to stop punishing him for her own insecurities. While neither of them had wished to marry, he was treating her honorably and she owed him the same.

He didn't love her—or probably even like her—but he'd shown the other night that he desired her. That would have to be good enough.

And if Mary committed the not-so-unthinkable mistake of falling in love with him? Well, she could cope with that event when and if it happened. Why ruin her life anticipating disaster?

The hat Kearny placed on her head was ridiculously tiny, just a twist of straw and a colorful collection of silk blooms.

Mary could not deny it suited her.

Half boots in a matching teal kid and an exquisitely beaded reticule—made to look as if it were composed of peacock feathers—completed her ensemble.

"Thank you, Kearny," Mary murmured, staring at her reflection with wide eyes. Why, she looked almost... pretty.

Could a colorful gown and a few silk flowers really make such a big difference? The neckline was still high and the sleeves still long, and yet...

Mary realized she was staring and wrenched her gaze away from her reflection and made her way to the foyer, her head in a bit of a daze.

The earl's eyes went gratifyingly wide as he stared at her.

Was that approval she saw? Or just relief that she could be polished up enough not to embarrass him?

"That color suits you," he said. "You look very pretty."

"Thank you," she mumbled.

"I hope I didn't pull you away from something too important?"

"No, no, I was just looking at reports that come in once a week from the various offices."

Outside at the curb was a glossy black carriage with lovely cane-work and bright yellow wheels, the black leather hood lowered in deference to the sunny, warm day.

Mary hadn't paid attention to the equipage the last time he'd taken her for a drive, the day she'd insisted on bringing John along with them, back when she'd been more interested in embarrassing the earl than enjoying his company.

"We won't need you, Poole," he said to his groom after handing Mary up and sitting beside her. "You may return to my lodgings."

When the groom released the horses, they were clearly eager to bolt, but the earl handled them so deftly the carriage rolled smoothly away.

Lord Avington—*Miles,* she reminded herself—had looked godlike in his new evening clothing the other night, but today he looked almost suffocatingly masculine in his snug buckskins, blue clawhammer, and top boots.

They rode a without speaking, until Mary realized they were not headed in the direction of Hyde Park.

"Where are we going?"

"I lied about a drive in the park," he admitted, and then reached inside his coat and pulled out a folded piece of parchment, which he handed to her.

Mary's eyes widened when she saw what the document was.

"A special marriage license? But… I don't understand?"

"It occurred to me—rather stupidly and belatedly—that these wedding preparations were causing you no small amount of, er, apprehension." He jerked his chin at the document she held. "This is a way to put an end to all that. We might be marrying for the purposes of our family, Mary, but we can at least choose the sort of ceremony we have to suit ourselves."

Mary was too stunned to speak. She stared at the document, trying to understand what he was offering her, and why. She'd never seen a special license before but she knew they were not easy to acquire. Indeed, they were a privilege of rank.

When she remained silent, he said, "Yesterday I paid a visit to a small church not far from where we are right now and spoke to the vicar. He is prepared to perform the ceremony at our convenience."

Mary stared at his profile as he negotiated a busy intersection, deftly integrating with the flow of traffic before turning to her. "The decision is yours, Mary."

Her mind raced as he drove them through the city—presumably toward the church he'd mentioned. "Does this have anything to do with Miss Everton?"

"A little," he admitted. "But really I just thought about the fuss waiting for us at Avington Castle and thought perhaps this one time that maybe Freddie did *not* know best." He smiled at her. "Maybe, just once, you and I might know what suits us. We will be spending a good part of next year doing what suits others, after all."

"What would you like to do?" she asked.

Rather than answer immediately, he considered her question for a moment before saying, "I would like to marry you in my family's chapel. It is a magical little church and I think you would like it. I would also like our two families to have that chance to celebrate with us."

"I agree," she said. "I have been reading up about your estate. The ledgers you brought me have been almost like reading a history book, in some ways. And I'm intrigued by this church and how your ancestor went about building a Catholic chapel with the king's approval, even though it was illegal at the time."

He grinned at her, an expression that sent her pulse racing. "He must have been a charming rascal to have swung such a thing."

Mary smirked. *And the apple did not fall far from the ancestral tree*, she might have said.

"I am glad you wish to wait, Mary." He set his hand over hers and smiled down at her. "Not only am I pleased that we will marry at Avington, but I'm looking forward to our drive together."

For once, Mary was honest—with him and herself—and allowed her pleasure to show. "So am I, my lord."

Chapter 24

Their brief carriage ride yesterday had given Mary a taste of what this longer journey would be like.

Intimate was the most accurate word she could think to describe it. Just the two of them together—Avington's large, warm body pressed up against hers—their servants and baggage following behind them in a separate coach.

It seemed far too *intimate* to be proper, but Lady Sedgewick—the architect of their removal to Avington Castle—had assured her that driving to Gloucestershire together was perfectly acceptable.

"You can take the journey in gentle stages," the countess had said. "That will give you ample opportunity to enjoy yourselves and you will still arrive in plenty of time to join the festivities without being drawn into the more tedious aspects of the planning." She'd smiled at Mary. "You don't have to worry about a thing, Miss Barnett. Your mother, Lord Avington's aunts, and I will take care of everything for you."

The countess had not been exaggerating; she had even chosen Mary's wedding gown.

"Are you warm enough, Mary?" Lord Avington asked, making her startle with the use of her name. Would she ever become accustomed to it? She could easily visualize herself at the advanced age of eighty, still jumping when he spoke to her.

"Yes, thank you."

He turned slightly toward her, so that he could see her while keeping his eyes on the road. "Does it bother you that I use your name?"

Bother wasn't really the right word. *Stimulate* would have been more accurate, or perhaps *excite*. Every time he said *Mary*, he set off bubbly, tickly prickles all up and down her body.

Of course, she could hardly admit that.

"No, it does not bother me."

His smile said that he didn't believe her for a moment. "Won't you please call me Miles?"

She hoped the ignominious gulping sound she made was masked by the rumble of the curricle wheels. "Yes, thank you."

"Well?" he asked, cocking his head, a playful glint sparkling in his eyes.

"Well, what?"

"Let me hear you say it."

"It."

He laughed. "Very good! Now say *Miles* for me."

She cut him an exasperated look. "Miles."

"See, that wasn't so difficult. I think you are almost smiling."

Her lips—which had been twitching—pulled into a grudging smile, as much as she tried to stop them.

"I received a letter from my aunt Beatrice and she said your mother and sister have already been a great help with the wedding preparations."

"Yes, my mother sent me a letter detailing the plans in excruciating detail. So much so that it was almost as if I was already there."

He laughed.

"You could have gone earlier and left me to travel up alone," she said. "But then I suspect you are a little cowardly as well, my lord—er, Miles," she amended at his stern look.

"More than a little cowardly," he admitted, grinning without shame. "In all seriousness, I needed to stay. There were many items on the pre-wedding list that Freddie assigned me, and even now I'm not sure I have ticked them all off. Besides, the first time you see Avington Castle must be with me beside you. Not to mention I was looking forward to this long drive together and the chance to become acquainted."

Mary had been both dreading and anticipating this journey. Most of her dread had been that she wouldn't be able to hide her feelings for him if they were in such close proximity. Now that she was sitting so close, she knew she'd been wise to worry.

Well, what did it matter? He was already perfectly aware of her desire for him. That was both mortifying and a relief.

Mortifying because she'd not wanted to fall for him so quickly and easily, as countless others doubtless had. And a relief because she could initiate a permanent ceasefire in her campaign against him.

From beneath lowered lashes Mary watched his strong hands flexing slightly on the reins, which he handled with a deftness that reminded her of how they'd felt on her body the night of the ball.

She quickly looked away.

"I have an idea," he said, interrupting her erotic musing. "Why don't we alternate asking each other questions. I will go first," he said, not waiting for her to answer. "Tell me what business you remained in London to address."

Mary slid him a curious look, not sure if he was serious.

He nodded encouragingly.

"It's not very interesting," she warned. "At least not to most people."

"I will soon be your husband and your business partner," he reminded her, as if that very thought didn't haunt her thoughts every thirty seconds. "I am interested in what interests you." He lifted his eyebrows at her skeptical glance. "Give me a chance, Mary."

A cease fire, Mary, the wiser, kinder voice in her head reminded her.

"The three men representing the canal syndicate came to London to discuss the acquisition of the last piece of property, which had been problematic for so long we'd considered possible route variations."

"Why was the purchase of it so difficult?"

"There were several reasons…"

Mary's tentativeness soon gave way to enthusiasm when she realized he *was* interested, or at least that he paid attention enough to ask intelligent questions. While it was clear the subjects were new to him, it was equally evident that he would learn quickly enough.

Only when they rounded a tight bend in the road and she saw the turn off for their first stop—she had studied a map of their route prior to leaving London—did she realize she must have been talking for some time.

She broke off in the middle of a lengthy monologue about lock construction. "I'm sorry, you really must stop me when I bore on like that."

He slowed the horses and cut her a chiding look. "You were not *boring* on, Mary. I asked because I am interested and I found your explanations not only enlightening but fascinating."

His words—which sounded heartfelt—warmed her. Perhaps they might rub along together better than she had ever hoped?

At least when it came to business, she quickly amended.

He guided the horses toward the inn courtyard, where a young man trotted out to meet them.

Miles hopped down and turned to help her. "Rest your hands on my shoulders." He said, and then encircled her waist with his hands and lifted her as if she were no heavier than a feather.

Mary finally understood what the phrase *to swoon* meant.

He set her down and gave her a concerned look when she staggered back a step.

"All good?" he asked.

She nodded abruptly, grateful that the innkeeper came bustling out just then.

"Good day to you, my lord!"

"The same to you, Foley. The lady would like to freshen up and please bring us some lemonade and a half pint of ale."

"Right away, my lord." The innkeeper beamed at Mary. "This way, ma'am."

Mary was accustomed to receiving preferential treatment when she traveled, but nothing compared to the way people treated an earl. She would have said they fawned over Avington—*Miles*—but it wasn't obsequiousness so much as a genuine pleasure at seeing him.

Their baggage coach arrived shortly after Mary had washed her face and the inn maid had kindly brushed the dust from her bonnet and spencer.

"Thank you," she said, handing the empty glass that had held chilled lemonade back to the hovering servant.

Avington turned to her and smiled. "Refreshed?"

"Yes, thank you."

"Ready to continue in my yellow bounder? Or do you wish to ride in your far more luxuriously sprung coach?" He squinted up at the sky, which was no longer the brilliant blue of that morning. "There are some clouds gathering but nothing terribly menacing. I don't think we have to worry about rain for a few hours yet, and it will be a blessing to dampen down some of this dirt," he muttered, glancing at his driving coat which was liberally coated with dust.

When she hesitated, uncertain as to whether he was making the offer because he wanted her gone, he leaned close and said, "My preference would be for you to stay with me, but I don't wish to be selfish if you are choked by dirt."

Not surprisingly, his warm words disrupted her breathing and prodded her heart into a gallop. It was more than a little concerning how much she liked the feeling.

Mary looked up at the source of her pleasure and anxiety and said, "I'll go with you... Miles."

***

Miles lifted her into the carriage, marveling yet again at how tiny she was. Not only was she short in stature, but she was slight and wiry and reminded him of the miniature fowl she favored.

As much as she appeared to adore her chickens, Miles suspected that was a comparison she might not care for.

"Now, it is your turn to ask a question," he said glancing down at the neat and tidy little person beside him. A person who would be his wife in less than a week.

It stunned him that the thought no longer terrified or depressed him—not since the night of the ball, when he'd finally seen past the thorny hedge of incivility that she'd always kept between them.

Miles knew that he should have been annoyed and disappointed by the true nature of her feelings toward him—frustrated sexual desire—and furious that she'd put him through such hell these past few weeks to punish him for eliciting those emotions, and yet he couldn't bring himself to remain angry with her.

Nor could he suppress the growing desire he felt for her. Discovering the passion—for *him*—that simmered beneath her cold, prickly surface both excited and flattered him. After all, she was an impressive woman whose regard bestowed distinction.

One's first impression of her was that she was tiny and fragile and in need of masculine protection.

But Miles knew better than most how deceptive her exterior was.

In truth, her inner core was as hard as tempered steel, and she possessed the acute intelligence and merciless campaign instincts of a miliary genius.

She was a perfect example of how Mother Nature sometimes concealed the most dangerous predators in small packages, like hornets or wasps.

Their lives together would doubtless be uncomfortable, tempestuous, and maddening, but never boring.

"Why did you decide to become a dancing master?"

"As opposed to what?" Miles asked.

Her lips parted, but—for once—she did not have a quick retort.

"My options were not exactly myriad," he pointed out.

Her brow furrowed and he could see she was weighing her words, something he'd not seen her do often. "Surely you might have taken some government position?"

"I might have done before I joined the army, but after I came home—" he broke off and shrugged. She continued to regard him curiously, so he sighed. "Plain speaking?"

"Yes, please."

"After the army I found it difficult to—" Miles struggled to find the words that would be truthful but not make him appear to be some sort of mental and emotional wreck, which is what he had been back then.

You promised her plain speaking.

So he had.

"After the army—specifically after I was captured and tortured—I found it difficult to concentrate for long periods of time, which rendered me useless for either diplomacy or any other work that required attention to detail."

"You strike me as one of the most diplomatic people I've ever met."

"Only because you are one of the least."

To Miles's surprise and relief, she laughed. Not a feminine tinkle of genteel amusement, but a low guffaw that was almost guilty-sounding, as if laughter was sinful.

"That was rude of me," Miles said.

"Well, I asked for plain speaking."

"But not insulting speaking."

"I don't find it insulting to hear the truth."

"You are a singular woman... Mary." Miles couldn't help enjoying the flush the mere use of her Christian name caused. "That is the first time I've heard you laugh."

"I find that hard to believe."

"It is true."

"Are you saying that I am humorless, my lord?"

He opened his mouth to deny it, but then saw the glint of amusement in her bright green eyes.

Miles grinned appreciatively and her gaze slid away from his, as if she couldn't bear to see him happy.

"Miss Barnett?"

"Yes?" She stared at her skirt, which she was smoothing with abrupt motions.

"Look at me."

Her jaw flexed, as if she needed to force herself to do something unpleasant. When she finally looked up, her cheeks were flushed, her face... determined.

Miles struggled to decipher her expression. Anger? Revulsion? *Fear?*

"Why do you sometimes look at me with such dislike?"

"Is that what you think? That I *dislike* you?"

"I don't know," he admitted truthfully. "I cannot understand why you sometimes look away from me, as if it *pains* you to meet my gaze."

"I look away from you because I simply cannot bear it sometimes."

"What do you—"

"You are so—so *perfect* that it is almost overwhelming. Indeed, it hurts my eyes, my lord."

It was his turn to laugh. "That is absurd."

She didn't smile or laugh with him. "No, it isn't. Why don't you ask some of your female friends if what I am saying is absurd."

"So, that is why you look away? Because I am too perfect?"

She shrugged; her defiance obvious in the tilt of her chin. Also obvious was her embarrassment at such an admission, the color that blazed in her cheeks made her appear vibrant and pretty.

Before he could pursue the ridiculous subject, she glared at him and said, "You never answered my question. Are you trying to deflect?"

Miles laughed. "It's no great secret why I became a dance master. I'm not clever enough to support myself at a card table, I cannot mend things or make things—indeed, I discovered my utility was extremely limited. Not only was I unsuited to being entombed inside all day, but my only other skill—killing Frenchmen—was not greatly in demand here in England."

Miles experienced a pang of shame at the unease that flickered across her face at his crude pronouncement. But then she was the one who always insisted on plain speaking, wasn't she?

"As things turned out, I stumbled into my first job purely by chance. I was in a pub, drowning my sorrows, when I encountered Ivo Stefani—have you heard of him?"

"The concert pianist?"

Miles nodded. "He was, in the parlance of the street, *stewed*. He was also ranting about his wife, the English climate, and the idiocy of trying to teach the piano to giggling schoolgirls. He was especially incensed that his dancing master had just run off with a student. Thankfully the catastrophe hadn't occurred with any of the young ladies at the Stefani Academy, but a private student the dance master taught on the side. In any event, Stefani offered me the position on the spot."

And a right arrogant, obnoxious arsehole *he'd* turned out to be, too.

But Miles kept that information to himself.

"Was your family upset by your decision?"

"Bevan was furious that I chose to work rather than live on an allowance."

"Did you refuse the money because of what had happened with Miss Everton?"

Miles flinched slightly at the name but nodded. "Bevan wasn't just hurt and confused; he was also concerned that I would shame our family. As it turned out, very few people recognized me. I'd been away for years by then and my face was no longer familiar to most of the *ton*." Miles saw that she was smirking and said, "You find that difficult to believe."

"Yes."

"Perhaps you find me prettier than most other people, Mary?"

Her cheeks darkened slightly, but she ignored the bait.

Miles continued his story. "Unfortunately, Stefani abandoned the school and went back to Naples, taking much of the prestige with him." He frowned. "It's ridiculous, really, because Portia is every bit as good a musician as he was, but she lacked the reputation. The academy might have survived Ivo's desertion if he hadn't left a heap of debts for Portia to contend with. But he had, and she was forced to close her doors less than a year later."

"You mentioned that you sold your carvings. How did that come about?"

Miles waved his finger in a chiding gesture. "Now, now, Miss Barnett—I believe I've answered more than one of your questions. It is my turn."

Chapter 25

The afternoon flew by in a pleasurable blur as Mary and Miles exchanged interesting tidbits of information about their lives. By unspoken agreement they avoided any questions that might lead to more serious—and contentious--subjects. Miles could not recall the last time he'd had such an enjoyable drive.

Unfortunately, they were still a few hours from the inn where they would stop for the evening when the skies opened up.

Miles stopped the curricle on the side of the road and hastily put up the hood. He found two carriage rugs in the wooden box that usually doubled as a seat for a groom but today held an enormous picnic basket stocked with enough food to supply a regiment.

He wrapped the blankets around Mary's legs before climbing back up and taking the reins from her. She was small, but she was strong and had given him a derisive look when he'd asked if she was sure she could hold the horses.

He clucked his tongue and gave the pair their heads.

"How far are we from the inn?" she asked.

"Too far to ride in this sort of downpour," he said. "There is a much closer village where we will have to stop for the night. The inn there is rustic, but it will be better than driving in this."

"Do you think John Coachman will know to stop there?"

"I should think he would." It was Mary's servant who drove her traveling coach, so he didn't know the man. Still, it didn't take a great deal of sense to guess they would have found a place to stay given the sudden change in weather. "Are you cold?" he asked when he noticed she was shaking.

"A little."

Moisture clung to the curly red strands that had escaped her bonnet and even her eyelashes—almost white, but exceptionally lush— were beaded. The rugs were keeping her feet and legs dry, but the rest of her garments glittered with droplets rain.

He opened his coat. "Come closer to me."

She hesitated.

"I will make sure to put you at a proper distance before we reach the inn," he promised.

She scowled at his teasing but inched closer, until her small body was tucked alongside his.

"Put your arm around me."

She did so and Miles wrapped the coat around her and held her with one arm, shifting so that he could comfortably hold the reins.

Her teeth chattered.

"You *are* cold."

"I'm always cold," she admitted, shivering. She paused and then said, "You are astoundingly *hot*, like a furnace."

"It is gratifying to be of use."

"Don't let it go to your head."

Miles found himself grinning like a fool.

They drove in silence for a while, the rain falling harder, until he was forced to slow to a crawl or risk careening off the windy road into the ditch.

Mary's shivering gradually receded and Miles was pleased when she didn't move away.

"Have you ever driven in rain like this before?" she asked.

"I've been in far worse weather."

"When you were in the Peninsula?"

"Yes. The storms might not have been worse, but the roads certainly were after several thousand cavalry and foot soldiers churned it all." Miles drew back on the reins. "Good Lord, what's this?" he muttered as four men on horseback surged out from a thicket of trees onto the road.

Rather than simply cross the road, they ranged themselves across it, forming a human and horse palisade.

And then two of them raised their right arms in a chillingly familiar gesture.

"Get down!" he shouted, shoving Mary over his lap as a loud *crack* split the air and a hot searing sting creased the side of his face.

The second bullet struck the black leather hood's frame, and a third shot struck the horse on the right. Equine screams filled the air and Miles forgot about the men with guns as the horses broke into a run, charging directly at their aggressors.

They got close enough to see the men's startled faces when one of the men lifted a pistol and fired. Fortunately, his shot went wild as his horse reared and he struggled to hold on.

One man didn't move away in time and Miles's maddened pair collided with the horse and rider with a force that jackknifed the light carriage to the side, ripping the reins from Miles's hands with enough friction that his hands burned even through his gloves.

The sound of cracking wood joined that of screaming men and horses as the curricle slid down the steep embankment.

Miles wrapped his arms around Mary and held her tight as the world spun and everything went to hell.

Chapter 26

M ary? *Mary?*"
Mary blinked and stared into the darkness, struggling to breathe as something crushed her chest.

"Wh-where am I?" she asked, the words a hoarse grunt.

And then the darkness and weight lifted and Miles's face came into view, drops of rain hitting the hot skin of her face.

"The men are looking for us," he whispered, his voice barely audible over the rain. "Do you feel pain anywhere?" he asked, slowly lifting off her, his eyes darting around as he pushed up into a crouch.

Mary flexed her arms and legs and winced at the sharp burn on the back of one of her calves that felt like a cut or scrape, but nothing too serious.

"I'm fine." Although she'd be aching tomorrow and probably a mass of bruises, if the soreness she was feeling was anything to go by.

"Can you stand?"

Mary pushed to her feet and Miles took her arm and helped her, her sodden garments hampering her worse than any of her aches and pains.

They were behind a small stand of trees and all she could see in any direction was more trees. And rain. Lots and lots of rain.

"You carried me here?" she asked stupidly when she realized the carriage was nowhere in sight.

"I thought it best—before they came looking for us, which I daresay they will after they stop arguing."

"Arguing about what? Surely, they must want to get away before somebody else comes along and discovers what they've done?"

"If they were common highwaymen that is what they would do. But then if they were common highwaymen, they wouldn't have shot at us and driven the curricle over the embankment *before* trying to rob us."

"Who do you think they are?" Mary asked, a sick feeling building inside her.

He pushed his wet hair off his forehead. "One of them is dead and I overheard the other three shouting at each other. One wants to leave immediately and report to the woman who hired them, one wants to run and forget about the money they are owed, terrified they've killed us, and one of them wanted to climb down the hillside after us and see if I, at least, might still be alive."

She gasped. "A woman hired them? Do you think—"

"I think it is Elizabeth Everton."

"Good Lord! What are we going to do?"

"I shouldn't think they'd want to return to Elizabeth empty handed. We should assume they'll decide to brave the steep hillside and weather and investigate." He gestured to a large oak a few feet away. "Can you climb? The foliage is thick enough to conceal us if we go high enough and the tree is tall, so we should be able to have a look around."

"You don't want to run?"

"I'm not sure how far the nearest habitation is," he admitted. "The visibility is already awful and in a few hours it will be dark. I think the wisest choice would be to hide until they give up and leave. Then we could climb up to the road and hope for a passing carriage— perhaps even our baggage coach, if they are far enough behind us."

Mary wiped the rain from her face and nodded. "I can climb."

"Good girl." He laced his fingers together and crouched. "Let me give you a leg up."

***

They had made their way up five or six large branches and Mary was scrambling to reach the next one when Miles whispered, "Stop, Mary. I can hear voices, hold still."

She froze instantly, still standing on his thigh, which she'd been using as a stepping block.

Barely a minute later one of the men stopped almost directly beneath their tree, removed his hat, smacked the rain off, and clapped it back onto his head. "This is bloody stupid, Donny. They could be ten feet away from us and we'd not see them in this weather."

"What do you want me to do about it?" the other man— presumably Donny—snarled. "You heard Barry, we can't go back until we finish the job."

"Barry is mad! We were supposed to nab the bloke, not shoot at them and drive them both over a bloody cliff."

Donny made a noncommittal sound and shrugged, clearly not interested in disparaging whoever *Barry* was.

"Christ!" the first man wailed. "Paul is *dead*! What am I supposed to tell me sister? That I got her son killed? Bloody hell! I never shoulda taken this job and I shoulda never brought that young fool along with me.

"He was a man of eighteen, Petey, he made his own decision. You just tell Sally that Paul was a hero and he died tryin' to put food on the table."

"She'll want his body to give him a decent burial. We can't just leave him in a shallow grave at the bottom of a ditch!"

"You heard Barry. We can't go hauling a corpse back with us, Petey. Use yer head!"

Petey grumbled to himself and then said, "How long are we supposed to hunt for these two?"

"As long as Barry wants us to."

"They might be half-way back to Lonnon by now," Petey whined.

"If they're on the road, the others will catch them. You need to keep your gob shut and your mind on the job, Petey. All your carrying on is getting' on Barry's nerves. You should just be grateful the bloke we want isn't squashed beneath that bloody curricle. I'd not want to face that bitch with such news."

The first man, Petey, was openly crying now. "I don't care about 'er. What am I going to tell Sally?"

Donald made a noise of disgust, grabbed his friend's arm, and yanked him along as he marched away. "Come on. The sooner we search this area the sooner we can head back to town and—"

A sudden, deafening crack of thunder drowned out the rest of whatever he said.

Miles tightened his grasp on Mary's waist and murmured, "Give it a few more minutes."

She nodded and they waited.

After several long, wet minutes had passed, Miles said. "Up you go."

He gave her a boost to reach the fat branch overhead and then waited until she was secure before pulling himself up behind her and leaning against the trunk, his legs dangling over either side.

"Lean back on me, Mary."

She hiked up her heavy skirts and inched backwards, until she was resting against his chest.

"Wrap your arms around your knees. Don't worry, I'll not let you fall," he promised when she hesitated.

Once she was nestled against him, he enfolded her in his coat and held her in his arms.

After a few moments he felt the tension drain out of her body.

"What are we going to do?" she asked quietly—no hysteria or fear in her voice, which made Miles smile.

"To be on the safe side let's wait up here until it is dark. You should try to get a little rest."

"What will we do then?"

"If they leave, we'll go back to the curricle. There is a hidden compartment for valuables beneath the chassis. It's possible the men have found it, but if they haven't there will be money and my pistols."

"That man—Donny—made it sound as if there are other men watching the road for us."

"Yes, that means we'll have to avoid the road." Miles racked his memory to recall what there was in the way of villages or farmhouses off this stretch of road, but he'd never paid much attention in the past.

Miles rested his chin lightly on her head and filled his lungs with her scent.

Her hair was wet and had come unpinned. Somewhere along the way she'd lost the pretty straw hat she'd been wearing and wiry tendrils tickled his nose as he held her tightly. Her lush bottom pressed against his spread groin and Miles was stunned to feel himself getting hard.

He almost laughed. They were soaking wet, cold, running for their lives, and stuck fifteen feet up a tree and he was getting an erection.

"I remember looking at the map of our journey."

Miles pulled his mind from the gutter. "You did?"

"Yes. There is a strip of forest that runs with the road, but there are farmhouses and even a small village on the south side of that."

"You remember all that?" he asked, failing to keep the skepticism from his voice.

Her body stiffened. "I retain an image of things after I look at them."

"Oh. How fascinating. Does that apply to anything, or just maps?"

"Anything."

Miles was impressed—and not a little envious. "It should be easy to orient ourselves once we find the carriage," he said. "We'll head south and stop for shelter at the first opportunity. If we need to, we can take smaller roads until we can reach a large enough town and seek the help of a constable or magistrate. No matter how wealthy Elizabeth is she can't have paid for enough ruffians to patrol every road looking for us."

"It sounds like she wants you alive." Miles heard her swallow.

"But those men said nothing about me." She shivered and Miles knew it wasn't only from the cold. He also knew that she would recall Pansy's fate.

"Shhh." Miles tightened his hold on her and kissed her temple. "I won't allow anyone to hurt you. We're going to get out of this. I promise you."

"We were both lucky to get away without any injuries."

They were *extremely* lucky—terrifyingly so. He didn't want to think about what *might* have happened.

Instead, he said, "I know it isn't going to be easy, but we should try to get a little rest. We'll probably have to walk through at least part of the night."

She nodded and snuggled into his arms.

Miles knew he wouldn't be able to take his own advice to sleep, so he allowed his brain to run through all their options to make sure there wasn't a better plan than the one they'd decided on.

He'd thought that she'd drifted off when she said, "I cannot believe this is actually happening to us."

"Tell me my ears deceive me; tell me that you don't actually sound *happy* about our predicament."

"Maybe not happy, but certainly… alive. After all, this doesn't happen to a person every day. You have to admit it's more invigorating than any *ton* function you've been forced to attend."

Miles snorted. "I am betrothed to a mad woman. Instead of having a betrothal ball to entertain you I should have simply dragged you up a tree in the pouring rain and hired pistol-wielding scoundrels to hunt us."

He felt her body shake with laughter. "Perhaps it will become a new craze next Season."

Miles chuckled, squeezed her gently, and kissed her wet, bedraggled head. "Get some rest, mad woman."

Chapter 27

M ary?" Large, warm hands gently shook Mary's shoulders. "It's time to wake up, darling."

She groaned and unwillingly opened her eyes and shifted, every muscle in her body sore and cold. She blinked as her vision slowly adjusted to the near darkness, the outline of branches and leaves taking shape around her.

"It is barely raining and there is a break in the clouds—just enough so that we have a bit of moonlight. We should take advantage of it and climb down while we can. Rub your legs and arms to warm up."

Mary jerkily massaged some heat and life into her legs and asked, "How long have we been up here?"

"Believe it or not, you slept for almost three hours."

Mary yawned. "I could sleep for another three."

He chuckled. "You would have been excellent on campaign."

Getting down the tree took considerably longer than getting up it had. Of course they were both sore and it was almost dark, so they had to go slowly to avoid taking a tumble. Even moving at a glacial pace Mary had multiple scrapes and cuts on her hands and knees by the time her feet were back on the ground.

Her summer cloak was sodden, as was her pelisse and the bottom foot of her gown, the clammy material unpleasantly cold around her legs

"Let's get at least your cloak and pelisse off you," Miles said. "My coat sheds rain excellently and is dry inside. I won't be cold," he said when she hesitated.

Not only was his coat dry, but it was also warm from his body and smelled wonderfully masculine. Mary wanted to live in it.

When they reached the edge of the trees, Miles uttered a curse.

"What is wrong?"

"The carriage—it was right here, I recognize this tree."

Mary stared up at the steep hill they'd come down, which looked terrifying from this angle. "Do you think they hauled it back up?"

"Doubtful. I think it is in there." He pointed to some dark, lumpy shapes off to their right.

Mary squinted. "What is that?"

"Brambles," he said grimly. "Go sit over there." He pointed to a fallen log. "There is no need for both of us to get torn to shreds."

"Here, take your coat, it will—"

"No, keep it."

Mary grabbed his arm as he turned to go. "What if they are waiting? What if this is a trap?"

"If they are waiting, it's me they want. You just hide until they've hauled me away and make your way to the road."

Mary scowled. "That's hardly reassuring."

His white teeth flashed in the gloom. "I'm just teasing. I think they are long gone. They were too damned loud to be able to hide quietly." He laid a hand over hers. "Sit tight and I'll be back. I promise."

She nodded reluctantly and he turned and walked away, quickly swallowed up by the night.

For a large man he moved incredibly quietly. Mary wondered, not for the first time, what he'd done in the war. If he'd been captured and tortured did that mean he'd been a spy? Weren't officers supposed to get treated with courtesy?

It occurred to her suddenly that she should be terrified and concerned for her life rather than speculating about Miles's past.

Perhaps he was right that Mary was a mad woman to be enjoying this clearly life-threatening ordeal.

Although the word *enjoy* might not be the right one. She was cold, wet, muddy, and starving.

But she still wasn't miserable.

Indeed, she felt remarkably... *alive*. Never in her life had—

"*Sssst.*"

Mary yelped and her head whipped up to find Miles towering over her.

"Sleeping again, were you?" he asked, sounding more than a little amused.

She ignored his jesting. "Did you find it?"

He held up his hands and she noticed there was a bundle in each, one larger than the other. "Success! The picnic basket was crushed but I managed to scavenge some fruit, bread, what I think must be ham, and cheese. I've tied it into the picnic blanket." He handed the food to Mary and kept the larger bundle.

"Did they find your hidden compartment?"

"No, they must be inexperienced highwaymen. I have the pistols and the money."

"Was the d-dead man in there, too?" she forced herself to ask.

"No, thank God. But the horses were both in there."

"Poor things," she murmured.

"Yes, I will make sure Elizabeth pays for that."

They stood in grim silence for a moment and then Miles seemed to shake himself. "Well then, are you ready to venture forth into the night, my lady?" he asked with determined cheerfulness.

"Lead on, brave knight."

***

An hour and a half later Miles was beginning to fear they'd left civilization behind them when they crested a slight hill and saw a large, building-shaped shadow looming ahead of them.

Not far from it was a much smaller shadow.

"Is that a cottage and a barn?" Mary asked, lowering the apple she'd been eating as they walked. They'd already eaten the cheese and bread earlier and were down to the chunk of ham.

"It looks like it to me."

There was a light in the smaller building and they both resumed walking, turning toward it. "It seems terribly late for farmers to be awake," she said.

"Yes, it does," he agreed. "But we've seen nothing else, so I think we should take a chance and ask for shelter."

"What are you going to tell them?" she asked.

"I'll just say we are Mr. and Mrs. Ingram and that our carriage had problems and we became lost in the rain. What do you think?"

"It sounds feasible. But I think I should put on my own clothing—just so we look less, er, disreputable."

"Are you sure? They are still quite damp."

"Hopefully I won't have to wear them for long."

Once they were both dressed, they headed for the cottage

"Who are you?"

The voice came from behind them and Mary yelped and spun around.

An older man stood just outside the barn, holding a pitchfork in one hand. The barn door was open and a crack and the dim light of a lantern glowed within.

"Good evening," Miles said, his voice calm and commanding. "I'm afraid we had a carriage accident and became lost in the rainstorm. We're seeking shelter for the night and some assistance getting to the nearest town in the morning."

The man grunted and shuffled toward them. "You coming from London?"

"Yes."

"That's a long ways off."

"Yes, well we took shelter for a few hours and then lost our bearings."

The man grunted again and set his pitchfork against the wall of the house before opening the door open and shouting, "Dotty!"

Mary jolted and Miles put an arm around her.

"Well, come in," the man said, waving them inside.

The cottage was comprised of two rooms, the front half mostly kitchen with a tattered wing chair off to one side. A blanket hung in a doorway that led to the back part of the house.

A woman was crouched in front of a hearth, stirring something in a pot.

"We got guests, Dot," the man barked.

Now that they were in the light, Miles couldn't help noticing the man's clothing was dirty and his person unkempt.

The woman, when she stood, proved to be cleaner and tidier, but every bit as threadbare.

"We can pay you for lodging and a meal," Miles said when the pair just stared at them, the man's eyes brimming with something that appeared to be hostility, while the woman just looked concerned.

"You think we wouldn't offer a stranger in need a roof over their head without money?" the man demanded belligerently.

"Not at all," Miles said. "I only offer as a token of our gratitude."

The man snorted and headed for the blanket-shrouded doorway.

Once he'd disappeared the woman crept closer, a tentative smile on her face. "You must be soaked if you were out in that rainstorm. Here," she held out her hands, "Let me take your pretty cloak and hang it up in front of the fire to dry. I've got hot water, so you can wash your hands and—"

Their host emerged from the other room holding a Baker rifle, and it was pointed at Miles. "You just put that bundle of yours on the floor—nice and slow—you, too, miss."

Mary lowered the picnic blanket, which only held the chunk of ham, now.

"You're making a mistake," Miles said.

"Put it on the floor!"

Miles slowly complied and then straightened up. "My name is Miles Ingram and I'm the Earl of Avington. This is my wife and we've—"

"Oh, I know all about you, *your lordship?*" the man gave an ugly chuckle and jerked his chin at the woman. "Go make sure he hasn't got one of those fancy pistols his sort are so fond of carrying."

The woman approached Miles fearfully and he smiled at her, forcing a pleasant expression onto his face when all he wanted to do was throttle her and shoot her husband.

"I give you my word that I'm unarmed."

"Search, him, Dot!"

The woman jumped and hastened to comply.

"Hold your coat open," the man ordered.

Miles did so and the woman removed his notecase, the envelope he'd kept tucked in the breast pocket of his coat, and a handful of coins.

Once she'd set everything on the table the man jerked his chin toward Miles's feet, "Now look inside *his lordship's* bundle."

With a look of remorse on her homely face, Dot took the bundle and unwrapped it on the table.

"Open that inlaid box, Dot."

She hesitated. "Gerald, are you sure—"

"I said *open it!*"

She opened the box with shaking hands.

The man—Gerald—whistled when he saw the pistols inside. "I'll bet those cost more than our farm, Dot."

Miles didn't think that was saying much, judging by the poor repair the house was in, but kept that thought to himself.

Gerald gestured to the other package, the one that contained the birds he'd carved for Mary. "Open that, too."

Miles cut a glance at Mary and gave her a wry look. "Just so you know, I was planning to give these to you tonight, after a wonderfully romantic dinner. I'd ask that you close your eyes, but—"

"You shut up," Gerald snapped, taking a step toward him.

Dotty tore open the brown paper and gasped as she lifted the cockerel from the wrappings. "Oh! This is beautiful," she cooed, turning it around in her hands.

"Thank you," Miles said, and then turned to Mary, who was staring at the bird with as much wonder as the farmer's wife.

"You made that, didn't you?" she asked.

"Yes. Just for you."

Her lips parted and her face suddenly puckered, as if she were about to cry. "That's why you went to see Lady Copley, isn't it? So she could paint them?"

"Yes."

"They are exquisite, Miles." Her eyes glittered as she turned to give the carvings a longing look.

"Don't worry, I'll make you more to replace these, Mary."

"I *told* you to shut up!" Gerald said, raising the gun until the barrel pointed at Miles's head.

"L-look at this Gerald," Dotty said in a quavering voice, her eyes darting between her husband, whose anger seemed vastly overblown for the situation, and Miles. "There must be fifty pounds in here, Gerald."

Gerald clenched his jaws and turned away from Miles with obvious reluctance. When he saw all the banknotes laid out on the table, he gave another of his whistles. "Oh, you'll swing for this, my fine lad."

Miles narrowed his eyes. "What are you talking about?"

"You can stop lying now. I know all about you," Gerald taunted. "You're a secretary for some lord or other and you and your woman here robbed him blind. And now you're running around, wearing fancy clothes, and spending all that money you stole and pretending that *you're* the lord."

Miles was impressed by the lie. What a clever way to get normally law-abiding citizens to do one's dirty work.

"I'm afraid you've been terribly misinformed."

"Is that a fact?" The farmer grinned. "You hear that, Dot? We've been *misinformed,*" he said, aping Miles's accent, or at least trying to.

"You needn't take my word for it," Miles said. "You will find out you are wrong when you bring us to the local magistrate and they corroborate my story."

"Oh, I'm not takin' you to the magistrate."

Miles felt an unpleasant chill trickle down his spine. "What?"

"I'm turning you over to his lordship's men and collecting the reward."

"Reward?" Miles repeated.

"Five hundred pounds."

Miles's jaw sagged. Five hundred pounds was a fortune to these people. Indeed, up until a month ago it had been a fortune to Miles, too."

"Why not take me to the authorities and let them sort it out?" he asked without much hope.

"Ha! And give up that money?"

"We will give you more than that if you help us," Mary said quietly.

Gerald laughed, and this time he sounded genuinely amused. "I'm sure you would. All I have to do is let you go?"

"Doesn't it strike you as odd that a peer of the realm would not want thieves taken before the law to answer for their crimes?" Miles asked.

"Naw, his sort is different than the rest of us. They don't like to air their troubles. He wants to deal with your thieving arse his own way." He smirked at Mary. "Beggin' your pardon for my rude language, *my lady*."

"Who is the reward for?"

The farmer scowled. "What?"

"If I'm the one who stole from this peer then why can't you let her go? She didn't do anything."

"I'm just getting paid to hand you over. And that's what I'm going to do."

Miles changed tack. "I see you've kept your Baker in tip top shape."

Rather than look pleased, as Miles had hoped, the other man's face twisted in an ugly snarl. "Oh, were you in the army, *my lord*."

"Yes, I was."

"An officer, I'm sure."

Miles nodded.

Gerald turned his head and spat on his own floor. "That's what I think about officers. This gun belonged to my son. It's all me and Dot got left of him—not even his body to give a proper burial thanks to his captain who accused him of cowardice and had him flogged so bad he *died* from it. We wouldn't even have this gun if his best friend hadn't stolen it and brung it back so we'd have something of his."

Miles kept his mouth shut. After all, what could he say that wouldn't make matters worse?

Gerald gestured toward the door with the tip of the barrel. "Walk single file out to the barn. You go first," he said to Miles. "You try anything stupid and she'll be the one who gets shot for it."

***

Mary shifted uncomfortably on the packed dirt floor and stared into the darkness. "Are you sleeping?"

"No."

She waited a moment and then asked, "Are you angry?"

He snorted. "Only at myself for underestimating that *bitch*."

Mary swallowed at the pure venom in his voice.

"I'm sorry, that was ill said." He sighed. "And I am even sorrier that I did not take Elizabeth seriously as a threat."

"You could hardly have guessed that she'd attack us in broad daylight on a public road and then enlist half the country to hunt us down."

"I'll admit I'm surprised by the sheer *scope* of her plan, but I should have expected some retaliation from her. I just thought—after what she did to poor—" His mouth snapped shut and his jaws clenched tightly.

Mary knew what thoughts were tormenting him. He'd be remembering how Elizabeth Everton had so cleverly—and secretively—lured and killed his beloved all those years ago.

"You couldn't have expected this full-frontal assault, Miles. None of this is your fault."

"Yes, it *is*. I shouldn't have driven you without at least an armed groom riding behind us. I underestimated her, and you are paying the price for it," he said, his voice pulsing with self-loathing.

Mary disagreed but could see it wouldn't do any good to try and convince him.

"I have a plan," he said. "It's not much of one, but when Gerald comes to untie us, I'm going to attack him and I want you to run, Mary. I'll keep him busy and—"

"I'm not leaving you."

"This isn't your problem, Mary. I insist that you—"

"I'm not leaving you."

He made a noise of pure frustration.

"Besides, how far do you think I'd get running from them with no money, food, or weapon?"

Before he could answer the door to the barn opened and Gerald stood in the doorway, the lantern he'd had earlier in one hand, his rifle in the other. He hung the lamp on a hook and propped the rifle against the door.

"We're hungry and Miss Barnett needs to use the necessary."

Mary's face heated at Miles's words.

"She can wait until morning—when I untie you both."

"It will be a mess by then," Miles warned.

"Won't be my problem," Gerald shot back, dropping to his haunches beside Miles.

"What are you doing?" Miles demanded when the other man unbuttoned his clawhammer coat.

"Not that it's any of your concern, but I'm taking your watch."

Miles laughed, "I should say that's very much my concern." His eyes lifted to something over Gerald's shoulder and widened slightly.

Mary, who was tied to a pole facing away from the door, twisted to see what Miles was looking at.

Dotty moved swiftly, not making even the whisper of a noise until she brought the heavy pot in her hands down on her husband's head hard enough to make Mary wince.

Gerald grunted loudly and fell over.

Dotty released the pot and it fell to the hard-packed floor with a dull clatter.

"He won't be out long," she said, dropping down to her haunches and examined her husband briefly—presumably for signs of life—before crawling to Miles and untying his hands.

"Thank you, ma'am," he said, staring at Mary with a wide-eyed wonderous expression while Dotty worked on the rope that held him bound to the post.

"Gerald wasn't always like this," she said when Miles's hands were free and she moved over to Mary. "Our boy's death turned him bitter and mean, but he doesn't deserve to hang. And I know that's what will happen if he turns you over to those ruffians."

While she was freeing Mary, Miles stood and strode to the rifle. He didn't point it at anyone, he just held it lightly and at the ready.

"Not that I'm ungrateful, ma'am, but why exactly are you helping us?"

She snorted softly as she worked on Mary's rope. "I used to work in the Duke of Norland's house. You're an aristocrat if I ever saw one." She pulled out the last of the knots and turned to Mary. "You, on the other hand... well, I don't know."

Mary smiled at her. "Thank you so much, Dotty. My name is Mary. Isn't Gerald going to punish you for this?"

Dotty brushed dirt off her skirt when they both stood. "I'll tell him it was the Harper brothers from the property next to ours. The same men who came here earlier tonight also went to see them. I don't think you'll have good luck getting shelter at any farm in these parts." She shrugged. "Times are hard and five hundred pounds is a fortune. I can't give you back the money or the pistols because then he'd know that wasn't the Harpers." She chewed her lower lip. "You can have the two birds if you want them."

Mary exchanged a quick look with Miles, who said, "You can keep them or your husband will wonder why they are missing. I will make Mary more. But could I have the letter you took from my pocket, please?"

"I doubt Gerald even noticed that," she said. "I'll run and get it. You'll need to tie me up inside the house to make it look good." She cut a glance at Mary. "I don't know how many people are after you two—and I don't care what you did," she added hastily. "But those men were hard—the sort who wouldn't hesitate to hurt somebody." Her gaze flickered to Miles. "I don't have clothes big enough to fit you, but if she wants, I have some of our son's clothes. He was small—slight, like me. They'd fit you and those men said they were looking for a man and woman dressed in fine clothes, not two men."

Miles nodded and turned to Mary. "I think it would be a good idea."

"So do I." She smiled at the other woman. "Thank you so much for helping us."

Dotty's haggard face darkened and she jerked out a nod. "We'd best hurry, Gerald could wake up any minute."

Chapter 28

Y ou've been very quiet," Miles said, stealing another glance at his wife-to-be, who'd undergone a rather startling transformation, from the top of her shorn head right down to the hobnailed boots on her feet. "Is something wrong?"

"Breeches are... different," she said, cutting him a sheepish look from beneath her battered tweed hat, her short gray-brown hair sticking out at odd angles.

"Different good, or different bad?" he asked, more than a little amused at the sight of her.

"I feel as if I'm not wearing any clothes. It's quite... distracting."

Miles could have told her that the way her generous bottom stretched the worn canvas breeches was distracting as hell, but he didn't want to embarrass her, so he just said, "You look fetching. But you didn't have to cut your hair. That trick with the ashes works well, you could have just tucked it beneath your hat."

"I've always wanted to try one of the short hairstyles but my mother all but came unhinged whenever I suggested it. She told me I was already shaped like a boy and if I cut my hair people might not be able to tell the difference."

"Trust me, darling, you don't look like any boy I've ever seen." He hesitated and then mischievously added. "You don't feel like a boy, either."

It was still too dark to see if she was blushing, but Miles swore he could feel the heat radiating off her.

"Do you think Gerald will hurt her?" she asked as they trudged their way through yet another field of barley.

"I think she knows what she is doing," Miles said. "And Gerald will be excessively grateful for her interference when he finally learns that he was about to hand the two of us over to a woman who has already killed at least one person and probably more."

"Do you really think she killed her father?"

"It seems too coincidental that she'd be returning right as I was going to marry."

"Would you really never have married if you'd not inherited?" she asked after a few moments of silence.

"I don't know," Miles admitted. "Even if I'd wanted to marry, I was hardly in the position to support a family."

"You might have taken your allowance and lived with your family."

"No, that was one thing I could not do. What about you?" he asked, not wanting to talk about it. "Would you have married if you'd been given the choice?"

She spoke without hesitation. "No."

"Not even for children?"

She waited so long to answer he thought she wasn't going to, but then she said, "I'd convinced myself that Jenny's children would be enough." She heaved a sigh. "I realize that probably sounds like an unnatural opinion for a woman to hold."

It did, but he didn't want to say that. Instead, he said, "I understand your hesitancy when it comes to marriage. I can't even imagine what it must be like to be a woman and have so little control over my life and person. I know from my friends that a good many men abuse that trust. But I will not, Mary. I hope you know you can trust me."

There was a long pause, and then, "Yes, I know."

***

It started raining again about an hour before dawn. Fortunately, they encountered a hay rick just as the scattered drops turned into a torrent.

Judging by the condition of the hay, it had been standing for several seasons.

"It looks to have been forgotten," Miles said to Mary, who resembled a miniature soldier who'd marched to the end of her tether.

"How can you tell?" she asked.

"Ah, there speaks a city lass. You see how brown the hay is?"

She nodded.

"It is old and not good for anything, so we shouldn't have to worry about anyone hauling it away and disturbing us. It will probably be terribly musty and dusty, however."

"I don't care. I think I could sleep while standing right here, in the rain."

"I will lay down my coat and you will rest for an hour or two while I scout the area."

Any exhaustion she'd been feeling instantly vaporized and her shoulders straightened. "If you aren't going to rest then I don't need to, either."

He set his hands on her shoulders, marveling yet again, how small and fragile she felt. How was it that she managed to give the impression that she was the size of an ox?

"You need to rest." He took her chin and tilted her face until she was forced to meet his gaze. He smiled and leaned down and kissed her.

Her lips parted with surprise.

"There, that is better," he teased. "No, don't get that mulish look that puts the fear of God into a mere mortal's heart. Please, Mary, just rest. There is no reason for both of us to go tramping about and I *promise* I will return."

"You *can't* promise such a thing if somebody accosts you at gunpoint," she said. "I don't want to split up." She caught her lower lip and worried it for a moment before saying, "I can keep going if you are with me, but if they took you... Well, I would just curl into a ball and give up."

Not only was Miles touched by the normally fierce woman's vulnerable admission, but what she said made sense.

"Very well. I will stay." He removed his coat and went about arranging their bed. "Hay is not as pleasant as it looks," he said as he laid out the picnic blanket and then, finally, the coat Dotty had given Mary. "It will itch wherever it touches your skin." He laid down first and then held out his arms. "Lay on me as much as you can and I'll shield you."

Her lip pulled into a smirky sort of smile—a type of expression he'd not seen on her face before.

Miles laughed. "I am not using it as an excuse to put my hands all over you, although I have to admit that *is* a benefit."

Her face went a fiery red and she gave a snort of disbelief. But she didn't argue and instead sank down beside him.

Miles turned on his side and patted his biceps with his hand. "Rest your head here."

Her eyelids were already at half-mast and she lowered her head without protest. Miles didn't think she'd even taken three breaths before she fell asleep.

Once he was sure she was deeply in the land of Nod, he carefully rolled onto his back, leaving his arm stretched out beneath her. He stared at the dark V of hay over his head, his thoughts sluggish from a lack of sleep.

He needed to get up. He wouldn't go far, but he had to see if there was a road or village nearby.

But maybe he would close his eyes just for a moment...

***

Mary woke with a sneeze.

"Bless you."

When she opened her eyes, she looked directly into the loveliest shade of violet blue.

Miles smiled. "Good morning. Or should I say afternoon?"

"What time is it?"

He reached into his pocket and took out his watch. "Almost noon."

"Oh, my goodness! Have you been awake all this time, waiting?"

"No, I fell asleep perhaps ten seconds after you and woke up only a few minutes ago."

Mary sagged with relief. "I didn't mean to sleep so long."

"Me neither, but we needed it. The good news is that the rain has stopped."

Mary looked out from under the sheaf of moldy hay and saw the sky was a shocking sapphire blue. "It looks like it never rained at all."

"I'll wager the roads around here will tell a different story. It's going to be mucky."

"What are we going to do? Do you think men will still be searching for us?"

"Unfortunately, yes. I think Elizabeth will have intensified her efforts rather than given up."

"So you think we are in danger as long as we're in this area?"

"Yes. I also think she'll have people watching the main road." And possibly the area around Avington Castle, too, but he didn't want to mention that right now.

"What do you think happened to our coach and servants?"

"She has nothing to gain by harming them. My hope is that they've gone on to Avington and sounded an alarm and that we will soon have people of our own looking for us. In the meantime, we have no money and no transportation and we're being hunted by people who have both."

"What should we do?"

"We need to get money, first. My watch and chain should fetch us a goodly amount—enough to get two seats on the stage for certain. Dotty said the closest sizeable village was Blount. If we can make our way there tonight, we might find a place to pawn them and get a room at an inn—if there is one. Unfortunately, we'll need to find our way into either Cavensham or Reading to take the stage."

"You don't wish to try and contact the local constable or magistrate when we get to Blount?"

"That would be what I'd normally do, but the way Elizabeth is throwing her money around I don't feel too trustworthy about strangers of any sort." He pulled a face. "I know that seems as if I'm being overly cautious, but—"

"I think we should err on the side of caution," she said. "Miss Everton has shown no sign of stinting in her pursuit of you."

"No, she hasn't," he agreed grimly. "Why don't we eat the last of the food Dotty gave us and be on our way?"

***

They followed a small, single-track road and ducked into the bushes and trees—and once into a field of barley—whenever anyone approached. As a result, they didn't get to the tiny village of Blount until almost six o'clock that evening.

The first thing they discovered was that the tiny pawnbroker shop wasn't just closed for the night, it had a sign in the window saying it was closed for the remainder of the month.

"So much for that," Miles muttered.

They did have one piece of good luck, however. There was a festival taking place on Blount's village green and it appeared to have drawn every person from miles around, flooding the tiny town's population.

"At least we don't stick out like sore thumbs," Mary said as they watched crowds of people milling in the streets and on the green, where tents and booths had been set up.

A handmade sign garnished with flowers announced the gathering was the "Annual Summer Fete."

Miles counted the few coins that Dotty had given them—which had come from his own pockets—and frowned. There was barely enough to buy them both dinner and breakfast.

He would have liked to have taken more money, but he'd suspected that Dotty would need every penny to mollify her husband when he woke with a pounding skull and discovered he was five hundred pounds poorer.

"We have enough here for a few meat pies," he said, smiling as he looked down at her sun-reddened nose and dirt smudged face.

"I've never been to a fete before." She stared wide-eyed at the rather shabby tents and tattered banners as if the paltry country fair were something from the *Arabian Nights*.

"Want to wander about?" he asked.

She cut him a worried look. "Do you think it wise?"

"Looking the way we do I doubt that even our families would recognize us. Besides, there is something to be said for hiding in plain sight. I look nothing like a thief trying to impersonate a lord." His expensive clawhammer was torn in several places and so smeared with dirt it looked like a rag. His pantaloons had not fared any better. As for the new boots that he'd had for less than two weeks? Well, they looked far worse than his old boots had done.

As for her? Miles was *positive* her own mother would not recognize her. The ash she'd rubbed into her hair to dull the brilliant color had gradually worked its way into the faint lines on her face, making her look like a one-hundred-year-old boy.

She regarded him with a skeptical look, her eyes roaming over him in an assessing fashion that had an unexpected effect on his body. Miles supposed he should start *expecting* that effect by now.

"It doesn't matter what you wear. You're still you," was Mary's judgment.

Miles laughed.

"But I think we should go and look, regardless," she said.

He nodded. "As you wish."

Before coming into Blount Miles had taken off his overcoat and hat and left them with her small bundle of clothes in a bush not far from the river, which is where they'd have to sleep tonight as they couldn't afford the inn, even if it had unoccupied rooms.

They edged around a wagon that was blocking the thoroughfare while two massive men unloaded barrels of ale.

"I'm surprised you've never been to a country fete before."

"I've never spent any time in the country other than to drive through it from one city to another."

Fair enough.

They passed a man who offered to sketch a portrait for a few shillings while you waited. Next to him was a booth packed with fresh blooms made up into gaudy bouquets. There was a fortune teller, whose purple cloth tent looked exotic among all the dun-colored awnings.

As they browsed the various vendors Miles kept an eye out for anyone who seemed to be watching the crowd rather than joining in the festivities, not that he was overly concerned given the number of bodies packed together. While it might have been easy for their aggressors to overpower them on an isolated road it would not be so simple in the middle of hundreds of people.

Gradually, despite their circumstances, Miles relaxed and enjoyed Mary's innocent—almost childlike—appreciation of simple pleasures like the dunking booth and three-legged sack race.

"Are you hungry?" he asked, after they'd stopped and cheered on a father and his young son, who'd been victorious over two swaggering farm lads.

"Do we have enough money?" she asked, her forehead furrowing with concern.

"We have enough for a few meat pies. What do you say?"

A quarter of an hour later they each had a pie and were sharing a pint of apple cider.

"Ooh, this is good," she said, taking a sip, and then quickly taking a second, larger gulp before handing him the glass.

Miles eyes watered slightly and he coughed. "Strong," he said hoarsely, "Go slowly."

But she gulped down her half, and then part of his before they returned the glass.

Miles decided that tonight might be a good time to be a bit tipsy as they'd be sleeping in a shrub by the river.

"There are some seats over there where we can sit and finish our pies," Miles said, gesturing to some unoccupied benches in the middle of the green.

But before they could sit down an officious looking woman bustled up to them. "You can't sit here, we're about to set up for the contest."

"What contest?" Mary asked.

"It is our annual dancing contest." She pointed to a miniature grandstand that was only large enough for nine people. "Our honored judges will select one winning couple—the best overall in four different dances—and they are crowned the king and queen of the fete and also win a prize."

"What sort of prize?" Miles asked.

The woman looked at him, did a double take, and then looked closer, her eyes widening.

Miles smiled and waited for her to answer his question.

"Oh," she said, and then tittered for no reason. "Er, the princely sum of three whole pounds."

Miles looked at Mary, who had stopped chewing, her cheeks bulging with pie.

"Three whole pounds," he repeated.

"Indeed. If you are in need of a partner, you can go to the booth and they will pair you with someone." She cleared her throat, swallowed twice, and then lowered her voice and said, "Actually, I might be able to—"

"Thank you, but I have a partner," Miles said, still staring at Mary, whose eyebrows had begun to descend as comprehension dawned.

Mary swallowed her pie and then opened her mouth—probably to argue with him and remind him that she *never* danced—but loud shouting cut off whatever she was about to say.

"You bloody well won't *arrest* us!"

A loud cheer followed the angry announcement and when Miles turned, he saw that a group of ten or more men were advancing on a man on horseback.

"Oh dear," the woman said, her expression suddenly fearful. "Not again."

"What is it?" Miles asked.

"It is another grain tax protest."

Miles winced as two of the men pulled the mounted man from his horse. "Where is the constable?"

"Gone, he and his man are off somewhere investigating a carriage accident thought to have been perpetrated by more of these *protesters*."

The man who'd been pulled from his horse somehow got away from his persecutors and grabbed onto his saddle. His mount was already skittish and reared, knocking him to the ground while the crowed jeered and laughed.

"Who is he?" Miles asked.

"Henry Sindall, he was overseer of the poor and not much liked here." She pursed her lips and shook her head. "If we are not careful, it will be like Ely all over again."

Ely was a town where violent grain riots earlier in the year led to five men being hanged and a dozen or so others sentenced to transportation.

Sindall finally grabbed his horse's bridle and ran, rather than rode, away from his attackers.

The mob, deprived of their entertainment, dissipated, most of the men filing into the town's only pub.

Their hostess shook herself and brought her attention back to the matter of the dance. "You must go to the booth and pay an entry fee if you wish to enter the contest."

"How much is it?" he asked.

"One shilling for each couple."

"When does it begin?"

She glanced at the watch on her bodice. "In exactly one hour and thirty-six minutes." She gave him one last yearning smile, glanced curiously at Mary, and then went off to direct the men who were hauling away the benches in preparation of the dance contest.

Miles dug around in his pocket and pulled out the remaining change. When he'd finished counting, he smiled. "What a coincidence!"

Mary gave him a suspicious look. "What?"

"I have *exactly* a shilling."

She snorted. "You cannot be serious."

"Would you like somewhere nice to sleep tonight? Perhaps something more than a meat pie to eat? Perhaps even a ride into Reading?"

"I thought we were supposed to be *hiding*, not dancing in front of the entire village, not to mention every farmer for miles around."

"Three *whole* pounds, Mary. It's a fortune."

"You *are* serious."

"A clean, warm, soft bed…"

"You said there's probably not a room left at the inn."

"A bath… Maybe even clean clothes…"

She laughed. "You said I was mad, but *you're* the mad one. You might be a dance teacher, but I've not danced in over a decade."

"It's as easy as falling off a log."

"Falling on my face, is more likely."

Miles grinned. "Darling, with me as your partner you could have flippers instead of feet and we'd still win."

"No."

"Bacon and coffee for breakfast."

She groaned. "No."

Miles wasn't as good as his older brother Bevan had been when it came to imitating various animals, but he wasn't the worst either.

He gave it his best shot.

Mary gave a bark of laughter. "Did you just make *clucking noises* at me?"

"What would your hens say if they ever discovered how chicken-hearted you were?"

She rolled her eyes. "*You're* the mad one," she insisted. "Besides, I could never dance dressed like *this*."

That was when Miles knew he had her.

Chapter 29

I can't believe I'm doing this," Mary said for the fifth or sixth time. "We will soon be eating a five-course meal in our private parlor at the inn," he promised her.

Mary ignored him and asked. "Are you *sure* I look decent?"

He held her at arm's length while his gaze moved over her in a way that sent arrows of lust careening through her body.

"I think your hair is rather fetching this way," he said. "When I was on the Continent it wasn't rare at all to see ladies with such short cuts. It suits you."

Mary felt her face—freshly scrubbed after a brisk dip in the river—heat under his smiling gaze. She gestured to her dress, which was dirty and wrinkled, no matter that she'd tried to clean off the worst of the mess. "What about my gown?"

"Look around," he murmured in a low voice. "We fit in quite nicely."

He was right; they didn't look any worse than many of the other couples waiting to take their positions on the makeshift dance floor.

"Well, what do you say?" Miles took her hand in his and Mary realized it was his damaged one.

Without thinking about what she was doing, Mary lifted it to her face so she could look at it better.

The long, elegant fingers were bent and misshapen, the joints larger than the ones on his other hand. Odd, circular scars covered every square inch of skin.

Mary looked up and met his gaze, his eyes—for once—serious and unsmiling.

"Burns from a cigar," he said quietly.

"Attention! Attention everyone!" a woman's voice rang out, making Mary jump.

They looked away from each other and saw the woman from earlier standing in the middle of the dance floor.

"Dancers in group one, take your positions now!"

Mary looked at the piece of parchment pinned to Miles's coat. It had the number *1* printed on it.

"This is us," Miles said. "Are you ready?"

She swallowed once, and then twice, and then nodded. "Yes."

He grinned. "Let's take our places."

I must be mad.

Her chest became tight as Miles escorted her to her position among the ladies, who'd already begun to form a line on the hard packed dirt that comprised the dance floor. She was breathing deeply but still couldn't seem to get enough air. Panic closed around her like a strap tightening around her ribs.

Rather than take his position among the gentlemen, Miles leaned closer and murmured, "Relax, Mary. Fill your lungs. Do it," he ordered more sharply when she hesitated.

Mary inhaled.

"Nice and full," he soothed. "Don't stop until you feel ready to burst. Good. Now release the air slowly, squeeze it from your body by tightening your stomach muscles." He nodded once she'd followed his instructions, although she found it difficult to command her muscles in such a way.

"Again," he said.

Mary did the same thing a second time.

"And again."

By the third time it was easier.

"Better?" he asked.

She jerked out a nod. And she *was* calmer, if not exactly calm, her hands barely shaking as she fisted them at her sides.

He stepped closer, until their bodies were almost touching, his expression gentle and understanding. "I shouldn't have forced you to do this, Mary. If you don't wish to, we can step aside."

"But you've already paid!" Before he could respond, she said, "And I can do this." It was just a country dance and she was no weak, wilting flower.

"I am fine," she said firmly when he hesitated. "You should take your place."

He smiled. "That's my girl."

His praise warmed her and the smile she gave him was, if not exactly a grin, at least genuine.

When he took his position across from her, she couldn't help comparing him with the men on either side of him. They were probably a good decade younger than Miles and they wore clothing that was cleaner, if not nearly as fine. They were handsome and fit, but even in his torn, dirty clothing, and with his face scruffy and unshaven, he still stood out like a pearl surrounded by gravel.

He smiled at her and Mary could almost feel the women on either side of her sighing.

"My name is Sarah," the woman on the right said, her eyes darting between Mary and Miles, as if she couldn't quite believe they were together.

Mary could have told her that she wasn't the only one.

"I'm Edgar Phelps and this is my wife Becky," Miles said when Mary wasn't quick enough with an answer.

"Are you new to Blount?"

"We've just arrived from London to work for Lord Binghamton."

"Oh! Which positions?"

"Footman and chambermaid."

"My aunt works in the kitchen at Briarley Park." She frowned. "But why are you here if their lordships aren't back from town yet?"

"We came early to receive instruction before the master and mistress arrive."

Sarah pulled a face. "That will be Mr. Leeland you'll be under. He's in charge while the family is in town. A regular dragon he is, or so my aunt says. My aunt is just there"—she pointed to a woman garbed in somber black—"I will introduce you after this round."

"Oh, er, yes. That would be grand," he said, cutting Mary an amusing look of mock horror when Sarah glanced away to talk to the woman on her other side.

Mary smirked. "Hoist by your own petard."

Just then the fiddler struck up the opening notes and the contest dancing master—rather than the lead couple—prepared to call out the first figure.

In another moment, for the first time in a decade, Mary was dancing.

Her body felt jerky and awkward at first—just as she'd felt all those years ago with the critical eyes of the *ton* upon her.

But rather than sneer or scoff—as many of her long-ago partners had done—Miles smiled at her, visibly delighted to be dancing with her.

Mary soon discovered that an enthusiastic partner made all the difference. It was an entirely new and invigorating experience. For the first time in her life, she could understand why people *enjoyed* dancing.

Dancing with Love

As the bouncy, carefree notes flowed from the humble country orchestra, Mary forgot she was garbed in a gown that was stained and tattered. She even forgot that a woman apparently wanted to either kill her or kidnap Miles, or both.

And she gave herself up to the music and the pure exhilaration of dancing with the handsomest and most accomplished man on the dance floor.

***

Miles hadn't known what to expect of Mary's dancing. Even if she'd once been competent, she'd not exercised her skills for ten years.

The country dance was not difficult—no quadrilles or cotillions in the village square—but the dancing master who called the figures had combined them in such a way that the resulting dance, while simple, required speed, dexterity, and grace.

There was little time for chatter, which was just as well because even Miles—who'd spent the last several years dancing—needed to use all his attention to focus on the figures. He'd never danced on anything but a dance floor and found the adjustments necessary for the less than even surface challenging.

It was possible their country cousins had the advantage of them in that regard, but if Miles was confident in one skill, it was his ability to dance.

The expression of determination on Mary's face was adorable. She was a woman who liked to win, no matter the situation.

Miles was delighted, but not surprised, to discover she was a graceful and fluid dancer. Mary Barnett was not the sort of woman to be undone by something as simple as dancing.

A quick glance at the other couples flanking them convinced Miles that they were, at least among this group, the most practiced pair.

When they joined hands for the promenade, he said from the corner of his mouth, "Smile, darling—we are supposed to be enjoying ourselves, not marching to the guillotine."

She snorted a laugh and her lips curved into a reluctant, but charming smile.

"You have been hiding your light under a bushel, Mary," he chided, right before he released her. "You are an excellent dancer."

The crowd was far more raucous than any found in a *ton* ballroom and various members cheered for specific couples and shouted prognostications. Before the exuberant dance was even half over Miles had broken a mild sweat.

The moment the final note had played Miles straightened up from the court bow he'd assumed, caught Mary's hand, and quickly led her away from the dance floor before the chatty Sarah could introduce Miles and Mary to her aunt.

Miles headed for an unoccupied bench that was situated in such a way they could see the tiny grandstand where the judges were conferring *and* watch for Sarah.

"They don't look happy," Mary said once she'd caught her breath, pointing to the judges, several of whom were gesticulating wildly.

"They certainly don't."

Two of the men pursed their lips in disapproval and turned their backs on the others.

"Those must be the losers," Mary murmured, and then looked up at him. "Do you think we'll move on to the final round."

"I don't doubt it for a second," he said. "But they won't announce their decision until they've seen all three groups. Oh dear." Miles grabbed her hand and pulled her to her feet.

"What is it?"

"I see dear Sarah and her aunt. Let's find somewhere more... private to wait."

"That will teach you for being a shameless fibber."

"I wouldn't have been forced to lie if you'd not been so tongue-tied."

"If you'd waited another few seconds I would have conceived of something much better than *chambermaid*."

"Such as?"

"Itinerant tinkerer."

He laughed. "But they might have wanted to see our wagon and wares and then where would you be?"

"Probably hiding, very much like we are right now," she admitted. "Do you happen to know Lord Binghamton?"

"Well enough that if he were home, I would have approached him for help. Unfortunately, I don't know anyone else in this area. Ah, here is a good place," he said, stopping beside a stone bench facing the pub where the angry protesters had retired earlier.

"Many of these people look hungry, Miles," Mary said quietly.

"There has been a great deal of hardship all over the country," he agreed.

"I don't feel right about possibly winning this contest when the money would make a critical difference to most of them."

"Unfortunately, we don't have a better option now. But this is a good reminder to us that we should make sure our own people are not rendered so desperate."

"Of course we should," she said. "But it is beyond individual stewardship. It is nearly four shillings for a pound of bread in some places. These tariffs are killing English people."

"But how can we compete with the nations of Europe with *no* protections at all?"

"The agricultural age is over, Miles," she said with a gentleness he found condescending. "Great landed estates are quickly becoming an anachronism and should be part of England's past, not its future. We must look to imports for foodstuffs and raw materials and concentrate on growing our manufacturing infrastructure."

"When you marry me, you will become part of one of those landed anachronisms, Mary."

She cleared her throat and then said, with uncharacteristic delicacy, "I have looked over your family's ledgers. May I—"

"Speak bluntly?" Miles guessed. "Please do," he said, not that he suspected he had much choice.

"Your father was a dreadful caretaker of his property, but even without his gambling the land could not generate enough to pay the maintenance that such a structure requires."

Miles knew she was right—he'd heard his contemporaries bemoaning their inability to earn enough to keep their estates vibrant and healthy—but it irked him to hear the opinion spoken aloud, especially by a person who knew nothing of the sort of life that was quickly disappearing for so many people—not just the wealthy and titled.

"What is your solution, Mary?"

"A combination of agricultural activity and investments in key industries. Also, relying on so many small farmers is not the most efficient use the land."

"I'm aware of that. But I don't wish to be the one to throw people from their homes to consolidate the properties."

She inhaled deeply, as if to say something, but then closed her mouth.

"Is that something you advocate, Mary? Dispossessing people of their homes? Their livelihoods?" Miles wasn't sure he wanted to hear her answer.

She took her time considering his question. "I have eliminated jobs at several of our manufactories and the word *unpleasant* does not come close to describing how that felt. But the truth is that gross inefficiency will eventually bring down the entire endeavor—whether a person is talking about agriculture or manufacturing. Isn't it better to sacrifice the few for the good of the many? I'm sure that is a subject that featured in many discussions at your university."

Miles couldn't help chuckling. "Yes, there were plenty of arguments regarding the *theory* of such matters but very little practical knowledge. Perhaps there will come a time when the subject of business will join the curriculum."

"My father always said that operating a successful business was not something that could be taught but must be learned by doing." She shrugged. "In any event, it is increasingly clear that our current methods no longer work for Britain. Food shortages and the escalating number of poor and homeless Britons should be reason enough to change our ways, but I suspect more blood—like that spilled in Ely—will have to be shed before we change course."

He leaned closer to her. "Such serious talk! We should be watching our competitors, identifying their weak spots, and discussing our strategy for the next round."

She laughed. "I have my hands full—or my feet, rather—just replicating the steps. However," she paused and bit her plush lower lip. "I must admit the few times I had a moment to glance at the other dancers I couldn't help thinking that none of the men were as polished as you."

"A compliment from *you*, Mary?" Miles teased, but— astoundingly—his face heated at the rare praise.

***

Rather than diminish, the crowd of onlookers swelled to twice its size by the time of the final round; it had also become noisier and more boisterous.

Miles couldn't help noticing that some of the men who'd gone into the pub earlier had come back out again but were considerably less stable. A clutch of five or six of them had gathered around one end of the makeshift dance floor and were jeering and heckling a pair of dancers so relentlessly that the couple finally fled.

Two of the judges approached the laughing group and must have said something because the men quieted down afterward.

Shortly after the round ended the names of the eight finalist couples were announced.

Sarah and her partner, a strapping but exceptionally graceful lad, were called first. The next four couples announced were from the other groups.

Small, cold fingers touched his hand and Miles looked down at Mary.

Her face was rigid with expectation and she was staring straight ahead, rather than at him.

He squeezed her hand lightly. His Mary was fiercely competitive and wanted to win more for winning's sake than for the money.

Miles liked to win, too, of course, but they desperately needed this money if they were to avoid spending another night sleeping out of doors.

"And the names of the final contestants are…"

The announcer drew out the moment and Miles was amused to note that Mary was standing on her toes, her body leaning forward.

"Becky and Edgar Phelps!"

Mary's face fell and her shoulders slumped and he distinctly saw her mouth the word *bugger.*

Miles laughed and lowered his mouth to Mary's ear. "Have you forgotten our names already? Smile, *Becky.*"

Her eyes went round with shock. "Oh!"

The crowd clapped and cheered for them and her face went pink with pleasure.

"Dancers take your places!"

Miles kissed her cheek and whispered in ear, "Luck, Mary."

***

As Mary stared across at Miles, she had the oddest sensation that he could see past her eyes and right into her brain, where he could peruse her thoughts and memories like so many books on a shelf.

She shuddered to think of the mortifying images he would discover. So many featuring a scarred, scrawny, and scared Mary

Barnett, the wallflower whom even other wallflowers had rejected that long-ago Season.

But rather than sneer or mock what he found, his clear, knowing gaze bolstered her and reminded her that she was no longer that frightened girl, but Mary Barnett, a woman who went toe-to-toe against the most ruthless industrialists in Britain. And won.

Suddenly Mary couldn't understand why she'd allowed a mere dance floor to cow her for so long.

She met Miles's patient, hopeful gaze and smiled. *Good luck*, she mouthed, humbly recalling that she'd once arrogantly denied luck's existence. Mary knew better now; meeting Miles had surely been the luckiest moment of her life.

It was soon clear they would need all the luck they could get if they were to win the prize money. While the earlier dances had been energetic and intricate, the dance master had clearly saved the most fiendish combinations of figures for last.

All the couples moved with surprising grace for a country assemblage, but when the eight pairs split into two groups of four, the steps became even more complex.

Mary was only peripherally aware of the confusion that overtook the dancers in the other square when a *right and left* was quickly followed by a *chain figure of four*.

A disappointed murmur from the crowd told her that somebody in the other group had failed to execute the tricky combination.

Although the four dancers in her own square finished out the dance without making a single misstep, Mary knew that—of the four of them—she was the weakest link.

Rather than feel shame that she wasn't as good as the others, Mary celebrated the simple, joyous fact that she was, once again, dancing.

When the dance ended and Miles took her hands in his, his magnificent eyes blazed with approval. "Well done!" he said, and then caught her up in his arms and swung her in a circle before setting her back down.

For once, Mary was able to accept a compliment without getting prickly.

***

Dancing with Love

As delighted as Miles was by Mary's open, easy enjoyment of the dancing, he couldn't help feeling nervous about the increasingly hostile onlookers.

"Let's get away from the crowd," he murmured in Mary's ear as the judges conferred with each other. Once they'd moved away from the thickest part of the throng, they turned to watch the muttering, disgruntled people who surrounded one of the couples who'd been in the other square. Miles recognized at least two of the hostile onlookers as men who'd helped pull the man from his horse earlier.

"Did you see what happened with those other dancers?" Mary asked.

"One of them misjudged the turn and there was a collision," he said. "Naturally their mistake threw off the other couple."

Miles thought it was unfortunate that the crowd favorites were the least skilled of the eight couples. He hoped the judges made a wise decision or they might have a riot on their hands.

Even as he entertained that thought, a trio of large, roughly dressed men approached the judges and soon there were voices raised in anger.

"This looks like it could become unpleasant," he murmured to Mary as more men drifted over to support the original threesome.

"Should we leave?" she asked, needing to raise her voice to be heard over the escalating din.

"You can't leave yet!" Somebody behind them yelled. "You two are surely the winners."

Miles turned to find one of the couples from their first dance. The couple was young—they couldn't be above five or six and ten—but what they'd lacked in experience they'd made up for in enthusiasm.

He smiled. "You were both very good, as well," he said, not lying.

Both the youngsters flushed with pleasure. Before the young man could answer, angry voices carried toward them from the judging stand.

"Yer only givin' it to 'em because she's Sindall's get!" one of the men shouted, earning several approving growls and grumbles.

"Sindall?" Miles repeated. "I just heard that name a short while ago."

The young man beside them scowled in the direction of the judges. "They must have decided for Joe and Ellie Martin. Sindall is Ellie's pa."

"The same Sindall who is the overseer of the poor?"

"Aye, or at least he was until he angered half the township with his greedy ways. They'd better not choose Joe and Ellie," the young man muttered, grabbing his girl's hand, and pushing through the crowd toward the judges.

Miles took Mary's hand, too. "Let's go."

She dug in her heels. "But what about the money?"

He pointed to the table where they'd paid their entry fee. Several big brutes had converged on the woman they'd spoken to earlier. As they watched, one of the men yanked the small lockbox from her unresisting fingers.

"We need to leave," he said. "We'll fetch our clothing and you can change back into your disguise and—"

"Well, well, well! Look what we have here," a voice said behind them.

Miles spun around, instinctively pushing Mary behind his back as he confronted two hefty strangers.

He squinted at the smirking men and then said, "I *know* you from somewhere." But he couldn't recall where.

"Not as good as yer *gonna* know us," one of them said, causing his companion to give an especially ugly laugh and leer at Mary, who refused to stay put behind Miles.

The fight with the judges had drawn more attention and people were surging toward the stand, nobody paying any attention to either Miles or the two men menacing him.

"Run, Mary!" he ordered.

"I'm not leaving you."

"Dammit! I said—"

She shoved up beside him. "I'm *not* leaving you."

"She can't hide from us—neither can you," said the laugher, reaching behind himself—doubtless to pull out some sort of weapon. "You might as well give 'er to us now." He grinned. "We'll take real good care of 'er."

Something inside Miles's head snapped.

And then everything turned red.

Chapter 30

One minute Miles was ordering her to run away and the next he transformed into some other man entirely and launched himself at the ruffian who'd been reaching behind him.

Mary watched in slack-jawed shock as Miles's fists flew, moving so fast they were a blur.

Even though the stranger had at least two stone on Miles, he simply could not get in a punch—he was too slow—nor could he move out of the way fast enough to evade the brutal pummeling.

Miles was relentless, like a battering ram with fists, hitting him again and again, until the bigger man dropped to his knees.

Miles staggered back, caught his breath, and was about to turn to the second man—who'd watched his partner getting beaten rather than stepping in to help—when the first man began to push to his feet.

Uttering a vile curse, Miles reared back on one foot and kicked the man in the head so hard Mary couldn't believe it didn't fly off his shoulders.

This time, the man stayed down.

The second aggressor emerged from his daze and reached beneath his coat.

"Miles! Watch out!" Mary shouted, the scene before her unfolding in sickening slow motion.

Without stopping to consider what she was doing, Mary rushed forward and kicked out with all her might, unconsciously mimicking Miles's action from a few seconds earlier.

Her kidskin boots had thin soles but thick, hard heels, and while she came nowhere near the man's head, she did kick his knee hard enough to knock herself backward.

The man gave an agonized yowl, clutched his knee with both hands, and hopped up and down on his leg as he wailed. He careened into the milling bodies behind him and then toppled like a felled tree.

Miles was on top of the fallen man faster than a starving dog on a piece of meat. He grabbed him by the lapels and savagely slammed his head against the ground again and again and again.

"Stop Miles!" Mary shouted, grabbing his shoulders, which was like trying to dig her fingers into bedrock.

She gave up on his shoulders and grabbed his hair, taking a big fistful and yanking hard. "We have to go—now!"

Mary had to wrench on him three times—pulling out no small number of hairs in the process—before he released the man's limp body.

"We must go!" Mary grabbed his upper arm with both hands and struggled to lift him to his feet.

Once he was standing, he turned and stared down at her, his eyes disturbingly empty.

Mary swallowed nervously and glanced around, wondering why nobody had stepped in to either help or break up the fight. That is when she realized there was brawling all around them. The violence that had simmered all night long had finally boiled over and swept the crowd like a fever.

People weren't just engaging in fisticuffs, they were also ransacking the fete booths and attacking the buildings that bordered the square, filling the air with the sound of breaking glass and shouting.

And then Mary saw it: flames and smoke where somebody had knocked a lantern over in one of the tents.

"*Miles!*" she shrieked, suddenly paralyzed with terror. "Fire!"

Miles blinked, as if waking from a deep daze, and shook himself. He dropped into a crouch beside the man he'd just beaten senseless and patted down his heavy coat before reaching beneath it and withdrawing a battered pistol, leather coin purse, and a small cloth bag. He shoved the gun into the waistband of his pantaloons, slipped the other items into his coat pocket, and then grabbed Mary's hand and pulled her in the wrong direction—toward the road rather than the river.

"What about our clothes?" she said, needing to run to keep up.

"We'll have to go the long way around. This is about to become a full-blown riot," Miles shouted back, pushing through bodies, most of which seemed to be heading *toward* the fray.

Toward the fire.

Mary clenched her teeth to keep from vomiting. They would burn—all of them—and nobody could stop it. The mob had taken on a life of its own and the air was so heavy with violence it felt like an electrical storm had settled over the village.

Miles dropped her hand and pulled her closer, holding her pinned to his side with one arm while pushing through the astounding press of bodies with the other.

"Where did all these people come from?" she shouted.

"This must have been planned."

The single road that ran through the small village was jammed with wagons, most of them rustic farm vehicles although there was one fancy high-perch phaeton.

The foppish driver was screaming while dozens of men rocked the phaeton with the clear intention of flipping it over. The young man clung to his carriage like a crustacean fighting against the pull of the tide.

The last Mary saw of him, he was still holding on when the carriage jolted onto its side.

Thankfully, the crowds thinned rapidly as they left the area around the square.

Miles loosened his arm and took her hand but didn't slow his pace. "We're not out of danger yet."

As if to punctuate his words, the roar of hundreds of voices raised in shock and anger came from behind them.

"What do you think is happening back there?" Mary asked breathlessly.

"Nothing good."

Neither of them spoke again until they could see the river.

"We can slow down," Miles wheezed.

They walked for a while in silence, thankfully not seeing another person before they reached the spot where they'd stashed their pitiful bundle.

Mary changed into her men's clothing quickly while Miles kept watch.

Soon, they were on the march again.

"I'm sorry we didn't get our prize money, darling," he said a short time later. "And I'm *really* sorry that we need to collect our things and keep going rather than get some rest tonight. I know how much you were looking forward to camping beside the river."

"I understand."

He chuckled and shook his head.

"What?" she asked.

"It's just that you're so… accepting."

"What is the point in *not* being accepting?"

Instead of answering her, he said, "You're a tough little thing, aren't you?"

"It does no good to complain."

"It never does, but that doesn't stop people from doing it."

Mary trudged along in silence, considering his words, not wanting to tell him that she wasn't complaining because she wasn't having a terrible time. True, she was hungry and sore and sleeping outside was uncomfortable. She was also more than a bit concerned that Elizabeth Everton might actually catch them.

But, at the end of the day, she was enjoying herself more than she'd done in years; quite possibly more than she'd *ever* enjoyed herself.

Mary didn't want to know what that said about her life.

She cut a surreptitious glance at Miles from beneath her lashes. The skin beneath one eye was red and puffy and the long, thin scab on his cheek—from where the highwayman's bullet had grazed him—had broken open and was bleeding. His clothes were dirty and tattered and his hair stood up in wild clumps, as if a woman had been yanking on it.

In short, he looked an utter and complete mess.

And yet he was more glorious than she'd ever seen him.

Mary briefly closed her eyes and shook her head; she wasn't falling in love with him.

She'd already fallen.

***

Miles and Mary weren't the only ones who'd fled Blount when the fighting began. Even though it was almost eleven o'clock by the time they made their way back to the main road it was jammed with farm wagons and people afoot.

"We could not have asked for better cover," Miles said as they trudged along. "How are you holding up, Mary?"

"I'm fine."

She was tougher than many soldiers he'd known, but there were lines of exhaustion around her eyes. She'd changed into her breeches and hobnailed boots, even though Miles knew it had been *him* the two men had recognized.

"You knew those men, didn't you?" Mary asked, as if reading his thoughts.

"They were the two footpads who accosted me in London on the night of our betrothal ball."

Mary gave him a startled look but didn't pursue the matter.

Coward that he was, Miles was relieved that she'd let it drop. What could he say to her? How could he ever apologize enough for the mess they were in?

They walked in silence for another half hour when Miles happened to glance down at Mary.

"You are dead on your feet," he said.

"I'm fine."

"No, we should stop and rest—even if just for an hour or so."

"I don't need to—"

"Would you like a ride?"

Miles and Mary both jolted at the voice.

Somehow a wagon had rolled up beside them and he'd not even heard it. Miles shivered; he needed to rest or he'd get Mary killed.

Before answering, he examined the driver—a man about his age—and his other passengers, a woman who was probably his wife and a young girl between them.

He looked at Mary and lifted an eyebrow. *What do you think?*

She hesitated a moment, and then nodded.

Miles turned to the driver and smiled. "That is kind of you."

"Where are you headed?"

"Reading."

"I can take you halfway."

That would cut down on their time considerably.

The driver and his wife were neat and tidy and their daughter had a pretty ribbon in her hair; they hardly looked like the sort who'd hold strangers at gun point, but then neither had Gerald and Dotty.

Still, their options were rather thin at this point.

"Thank you," he said. "We'd be grateful for the ride."

Not until the wagon stopped did Miles see there were two young lads sitting in among the crates of produce.

He smiled at the boys, tossed the bundles he'd been carrying into the back, and then turned to lift Mary by the waist.

When she stepped back and made a soft hissing sound, Miles recalled she was supposed to be a young man.

He *was* tired.

Once they'd clambered into the wagon, Miles handed her his overcoat and then tucked the other bundle behind her head. "You should try to get some rest."

It was an indication of how weary she was that she didn't argue.

Once she was settled, Miles closed his eyes.

And was immediately transported back in time, to Spain. His hands were tied, there was a cloth sack over his head which made breathing an agony, and he was crammed side-by-side with a dozen other prisoners—

Miles's eyes popped open and he was no longer the least bit tired.

He saw that the boys were watching him like two little owls, wide-eyed as they perched on sacks filled with early harvest crops like beetroot, beans, and cucumbers. The farmer and his wife must have decided to leave Blount, even without having sold all their produce.

Miles had no doubt that soldiers would soon descend on the village. When they did, they would punish first and ask questions later. The farmer had been wise to take his family and go.

He sighed as he stared up at the sprinkling of stars overhead. The last twenty-four hours felt more than a little unreal to him. Hunted by a woman who'd once been his betrothed, engaging in a village dance contest to earn money with a woman who'd refused to dance with him at their own ball—a contest he believed they would have won had the judging been fair—and now riding among turnips in a farm wagon.

He glanced over at Mary. Her head had rolled to one side and her lips were parted, her breathing heavy, even while her body jolted from the motion of the cart. She really would have been excellent on campaign.

Miles realized, with surprise, that he was smiling. While he was profoundly sorry that he'd underestimated Elizabeth's insane desire to possess him, he could not regret this time alone with Mary Barnett.

If not for this bizarre journey, he might never have scaled her defenses—not that he'd reached the top of them yet, but at least now he had hope.

It was all too easy to imagine how they would have grown further and further apart, until the chasm between them was impassable.

He knew they were in danger—life-threatening danger—but he'd not felt so free in a long, long time.

There must be something wrong with him.

But—for now, at least—he couldn't make himself stop smiling.

***

Miles must have dozed off at some point because he woke with a start when the wagon jolted to a stop.

The moon was still high in the sky so he couldn't have been asleep for long.

"Mary," he murmured, gently squeezing her shoulder.

Her eyes sprang open. "What happened?" she blurted.

He smiled. "Nothing. Everything is fine. I believe we must be at their farm. Let me go speak to them."

She nodded, rapidly blinking the sleep from her eyes.

Miles hopped down and then turned to help the two little boys, both of whom were as bleary eyed as Mary.

He set the second boy down as the farmer approached. "Thank you for the ride," he said, deliberately making his voice rougher and less aristocratic. "How far is it to Reading?"

"'Tis nigh on ten miles."

"Thank you. We'll be on our way."

The man cleared his throat. "You were the ones dancing." He jerked his chin to Mary. "That's the lass."

Miles could not think of any reasonable explanation for Mary's clothing, so he didn't bother trying. Instead, he said, "We don't want any trouble."

The farmer's wife came to stand beside him. "You can stay the night in my brother's cottage. You'll be safe there."

Miles stared, unsure of what to say. Why were these people helping them?

He remembered his manners and said, "Thank you, that is very kind."

The woman pursed her lips. "'Tis the Christian thing to do. The road isn't safe on a night like tonight. We couldn't turn you out." Having had her say, she shepherded her half-asleep children toward the small house."

"We've been robbed of our money," Miles said to the farmer. "You've no reason to believe me, but I will pay you once I return home—for both the accommodation and some of your food." He unlatched the chain from his watch and handed it to the man. "You can hold this as a guarantee. And if I do not keep my word then you will be able to sell it for a handsome sum."

The man took the chain but didn't look at it. Instead, his eyes flickered over Miles's bedraggled clothing, settling on his boots, and he nodded. "I'll hold it for you." He gestured to the wagon. "Take what you want from the crates and sacks. I'll get some tea from my wife. You're welcome to use whatever you find in the cottage."

"Thank you. I can help you unload," Miles offered. "Do you want to put all this"—he waved at the vegetables— "somewhere?"

"Aye, we've a root cellar. I'd be obliged if you'd help carry it down."

Miles climbed into the wagon and shoved the crates toward the tail end.

Mary glanced toward the farmer, who'd unhitched the horse and was leading it into the small barn. "You trust them?"

Miles jumped down and then lifted two crates with a grunt. "I do—although I've been wrong before."

Mary picked up a sack of beets. "They seem like honest folk."

"You don't have to carry that."

She nudged him with the sack. "Go on. Show me where to take this."

Miles huffed out an exaggerated sigh and started walking, too exhausted to argue.

Between the two of them, they unloaded the wagon quickly, and when they came up from the root cellar after the last load, they found the farmer had returned with a covered basket. "My wife packed this up for you."

"That's very kind," Miles said.

The farmer brushed aside his thanks and handed him one of the lanterns. "It will be another heavy rain tonight," he predicted as he led them past the barn to a field that was full of crops as yet unharvested.

Mary squinted up at the sky. The moon was still visible, but fat clouds had begun to drift across it. "Where did those come from?" she muttered, clearly irked.

The farmer just smiled and pointed to the far end of the field. "It will take about five minutes; just follow the path and you can't miss the cottage."

"Your brother-in-law won't mind us staying in his home?" Miles asked.

"He joined the army half a year ago and they sent him to India. You'll not be putting anyone out." The man hesitated and then said. "You're welcome to stay tonight and tomorrow, too, if you want. This rain will settle in and it will be too hard tomorrow to travel, especially on foot. I'm going into Reading the day after and can give you a ride in the wagon if you don't mind waiting."

As if to punctuate his claim, a large drop of rain hit Miles's nose.

"The fire is set with some wood in the box, but you'll need to chop more and there's an ax in the shed behind the cottage. There's a well by the shed and the water is good."

"Thank you. We are very grateful for your help."

The man paused, opened his mouth, but then just nodded and said, "Good night."

Miles and Mary stared at each other for a long moment once he'd walked away.

"Is this a trap?" she asked quietly.

Miles thought about the honest expression in the woman's eyes. "I honestly don't think so. Besides, there isn't much choice; it's stay in this cabin or sleep on the side of the road in the rain."

Rain which was already falling faster and harder.

Mary nodded. "This seems like an incredible stroke of luck."

Miles agreed. He could only hope it was the *good* sort of luck rather than the other kind.

Chapter 31

The cottage was just one room, sparsely furnished with a narrow bed, a table with two chairs, a screened corner, and a small cabinet and basin beside the hearth that obviously served as a kitchen.

Once they'd set down their bundles Miles turned to the basket and pile of vegetables on the counter. "Sleep or food?"

"I'm starving," she admitted. The meat pie had been delicious, but it had been hours ago.

"Me too. Er, do you know how to cook?"

Mary bit her lip and shook her head. "I'm sorry, but the extent of my cooking skills is pouring tea."

He lifted the cloth off the blanket and smiled. "Ah, that is very generous of her." He pulled out a small, soft sack that must be filled with flour. "You are in luck as I happen to be a hand at making perpetual stew."

"What is that?"

"The French call it *pot-au-feu* and there are other names for it—hunter's stew, for example—but basically it is just a soup you make with whatever you have on hand and then keep adding to the pot."

"How is it that you know how to cook this soup? I thought you had a batman?"

"I did have one and he is still with me, my valet Fowler, but he was not with me when I was held captive."

"Oh." Mary felt like an idiot. She wanted to say something—but what?

While she dithered Miles picked up the wooden bucket beside the door. "I'll fetch some water."

Once he'd gone, Mary wondered if she should ask him about his time in the army, or was it something they would never speak of?

You mean like the fire that left you scarred for life.

Mary frowned. An accidental fire was hardly the same thing as war. While it had been horrible—almost unbearable, in fact—she'd always known her mother and father were right there beside her. And as bad as the burns had been, there was never any real danger that she would die—unlike her uncle and six servants.

254

She didn't care to talk about that night—or the months afterward—but she would, if he asked. Maybe she should just ask him about the war?

Mary pushed the thought away for the moment and turned her attention to investigating the contents of the basket.

The farmer's wife had been more than generous and there was a small packet of tea, a half-full jar of jam, and a small chunk of salt-pork tucked in with some dried apples and the precious flour.

She felt a pang of guilt as she realized just how much these people had shared, especially during a time when many families were starving due to the outrageous prices of even the most basic food stuffs.

Well, they would send back a handsome reward once they were out of this predicament.

If you survive.

She scowled at the unwanted, defeatist notion and turned to more productive thoughts.

By the time Miles returned with the water, Mary had unearthed a teapot, knife, and a clay container filled with a fragrant mix of herbs.

"Are you sure it isn't too late to cook?" she asked, noticing the blue smudges under his eyes.

"I won't sleep," he said. "But you should if you can."

"I got plenty in the wagon. And I'm hungry."

Miles set about building a fire in the hearth and Mary filled the teapot as well as the big cast iron pot.

Once the fire was crackling, Miles washed his hands in cold water, dried them on a cloth hanging over the cupboard door, and turned to the food she'd laid out.

"Why don't you sit and keep me company?"

The next thirty minutes were among the most engrossing in recent memory.

Miles chopped vegetables, used a smaller pot with a slice of salt pork to fry onions, and then emptied everything into the pot of boiling water.

"What are you doing now?" she asked when he took the small cloth bag of flour and dumped most of it into the pot he had just used to brown the onions.

"I'm making doughboys. Ideally, I'd have more fat than this." He gestured to the greasy stain in the bottom of the pot. "But this will have to do." He added salt to the flour and then took a dipper of water. "Cold water is best to bind it. Then you just squash it until it holds together." He rolled up his sleeves, exposing toned, muscular forearms that were dusted with golden hair, and then shoved his hands into the pot and mixed the contents until it was a cohesive ball.

"Now, you roll it out." He shook the empty flour sack over the table, using every bit of the precious substance. He glanced at her. "No rolling pin?"

Mary shook her head.

"Then we'll improvise." He pressed the dough flat with his hands and then cut it into strips, which he cut crosswise.

"There," he said, brushing the flour from his hands. "Now all we need to do is wait until our vegetables are mostly cooked and then we add these last." He glanced at the kettle, which was belching steam, and raised an eyebrow at her.

"Whoops!" Mary jumped up. "I forgot all about it—you distracted me. I've never watched anyone cook before."

"What?" he asked in mock amazement. "Didn't you pester your family's cook when you were a child?"

"My mother would have had a fit of the vapors had either of us loitered in the kitchen."

"I have many, many fond memories of driving poor Cookie half demented as a child. Around Christmas Bevan and I would take turns distracting her so that we could filch biscuits and cakes and sneak dippers of her famous wassail. One year we drank so much that we passed out and missed the carolers."

She smiled. "How old were you?"

"Probably nine and ten."

"You were only a year apart?"

"Not even—only eleven months." Sadness flickered across his face. "Bev and I were like twins growing up. He was the one who purchased my commission using his own money after my father had frittered everything away."

"How did he have his own money?"

"Bev inherited a small estate from my mother's youngest brother, who'd died without children."

"Your father didn't want you to join the army? I thought that was the fate of the second sons of the aristocracy."

"My father didn't want to pay for a commission. He also thought I would be more useful staying at home and marrying."

"And you preferred war to marriage to an heiress?" she couldn't help asking as she closed the lid on the teapot to allow it to steep.

Miles sighed. "Even after the debacle with the Evertons my father didn't learn his lesson. He never stopped gambling. I saw how life would be if I stayed in England. Even if I managed to marry a wealthy woman my father would slowly but surely drain the coffers dry."

They were both silent while she found mugs and spoons, but it wasn't an uncomfortable silence.

"We have no milk, but there is some strawberry jam—would you like a little in your tea?" Mary offered.

"Why not?" he said, reaching for the jar.

Mary nodded when he offered her a spoonful, even though she didn't usually take sugar.

"Mmm," he murmured as he sipped the scalding beverage. "Tea makes everything better, doesn't it?"

"It really does."

They sat and drank their tea in companionable silence, the sound of the rain keeping them company.

***

As Miles finished his second cup of tea, he decided there must truly be something wrong with him to feel so contented while they were being hunted by a homicidal heiress.

"Will we leave tomorrow or wait until the farmer takes his wagon to town?" Mary asked, setting aside her empty mug.

"What would you prefer?"

She pondered his question a moment and then said, "As long as we are at Avington Castle in time for the wedding, I have no preference."

It worried Miles how much he liked her answer—as if she, too, were enjoying this time together.

He gestured to her feet. "Why don't you take off those boots and let me have a look at that blister you mentioned."

"Oh, you needn't do that. I can—"

"Shh." He moved his chair around to her side of the table. "Give me your foot. Mary," he said when she hesitated. "I know a great deal about foot care. Despite that bosh about an army marching on its stomach, I assure you that feet are what we used."

She heaved a sigh and lifted her foot. "Fine."

Even though he was careful, she hissed when he slipped the boot off.

Miles clucked his tongue and then gave a hiss of his own when he peeled off the thick wool stocking Dotty had given her and saw the heel of her foot was caked with both dried and fresh blood.

He glared at her. "Why didn't you tell me it was this bad? How were you able to even dance?"

She shrugged.

Miles cursed under his breath, carefully set her foot on the chair, and stood. He rooted through the cupboards until he found a small stack of old kitchen cloths.

He poured some of the water from the tea kettle into the basin, added enough cold water until it was a pleasant temperature, and then set the basin and cloth down on the table.

"Up you get. Take off those breeches," he ordered.

Mary took a step back. "No. You don't need to—"

"Don't be foolish," he snapped, suddenly furious—more at himself and bloody Elizabeth Everton than at Mary. "Do you want your heel to become infected?"

"No, but—"

"Let me help you, for pity's sake."

"It's just—"

"Mary."

She glowered up at him and Miles suddenly understood why she was behaving so stubbornly: it was her left side.

"Mary. It occurs to me you are concerned that I might see your burns. Is that it?"

Her face turned scarlet, and she crossed her arms over her chest.

Miles strode to the bed, which was covered by a faded old quilt, pulled it off and handed it to her. "Strip and wrap this around you. I'll turn my back," he said before she could argue.

Miles stared at the pot simmering over the hearth as he considered the woman behind him.

How could he convince her that her burns were something he no longer saw when he looked at her? It surprised even him how quickly he'd stopped seeing them.

"You can turn around now."

She was bundled in the quilt, only her bare feet exposed.

Miles sat and wet the cloth in the basin before lifting her left foot.

He sucked in a breath when he cleared away the blood and saw the huge blister.

"It has already popped," he said.

She nodded, her teeth sunk into her lower lip in a way that sent blood rushing to his groin.

Miles was disgusted with his body's reaction. The woman was in pain, for pity's sake!

"Miles?"

He blinked, wrenched his gaze from her mouth, and looked into her frowning green eyes.

"Hmm?"

"You were staring strangely. Is something wrong?"

"Nothing." He lowered her foot and then set the basin of water on the floor. "Put your foot in here for a while to soak. Let me see the other foot."

The blister on her right heel wasn't nearly as bad, but it was getting there.

Miles released her foot. "You should soak this one, too. You should let them dry out and then I'll tear up that tea towel to use as a bandage. You shouldn't put your feet into shoes tomorrow."

Rather than argue, Miles could have sworn she looked... pleased.

"Very well," she said mildly.

"We can take the ride the farmer has offered."

She nodded.

Miles stared at her and then swallowed. How was it possible that a worn old quilt could look better on a woman than the finest lace?

Her eyes were a remarkable shade of green—had they always been so... brilliant?

When she lifted her hand to push a strand of hair from her eyes the blanket slipped lower, baring one delicate shoulder. How had he never noticed that a dusting of freckles could be so damned attractive?

Mary cleared her throat and Miles met her puzzled gaze; one flaming eyebrow cocked in question.

"I need to go and get more water," he muttered, turning in his chair before standing, and then hurrying from the cottage.

***

By the time Miles had calmed his mutinous body and returned to the house, Mary was no longer wearing her seductive quilt, but garbed in her bedraggled gown and waiting eagerly for her supper.

The soup was watery and somewhat tasteless, but the doughboys were good. "It is usually better than this," Miles said, feeling oddly guilty about producing such a bland dish.

"I think it's good," Mary said, glancing up at him in between eager spoonsful.

He couldn't help smiling. "You have a healthy appetite for such a small woman."

She blushed and set down her spoon.

Miles clucked his tongue. "Don't get prickly or take offense. I'm relieved to eat a meal with a woman who doesn't peck away like a bird."

Rather than scowl at him, she smiled. "If I'm like any bird, then it would be a chicken. And my hens have healthy appetites." She used her spoon to cut one of the dumplings in half. "These are delicious. I cannot believe they are only flour and salt with a little fat."

"Why thank you, Miss Barnett. I'm afraid it is my only culinary specialty."

"One more than me."

When she finished the contents of her bowl, he gestured to the pot, which was still over the fire. "More?"

"Well… maybe a little."

"I'll get it," Miles said, when she made to stand.

"Thank you," she said. "Those carvings that Dotty kept—the chickens."

Miles filled the bowl before returning to the table. "Ah, yes," he said "I'd forgotten all about them with all the other excitement. What about them?"

"They were lovely—and so lifelike."

"Thank you. I can only claim the carving."

"I wish we'd taken them with us—they were much too nice to leave anywhere that awful Gerald will get to enjoy them."

Miles smiled at the thought of fighting over some carvings when their lives were at stake.

"Don't worry, I will make you more—an entire flock, if you like. Perhaps next time I can look at your birds more closely and get the colors right. I had to work from memory when I described their feathers."

She cleared her throat, and then said, "I'm afraid I've held some very ignorant beliefs for a long time."

"Oh?"

"I've been wrong to assume all aristocrats are, er, lazy. You work to support yourself and Lady Copley paints carvings to earn her way. And all your other teacher friends, too—like Lady Sedgewick."

"Well, plenty of us *are* lazy. But you are right that some of us work in the limited ways we can." He smiled at her. "I had a choice—I turned down my allowance—but many, many women of my class are left in a precarious situation."

"What happened to Lady Sedgewick, Miles?"

Miles didn't answer right away.

"Not that I want you to break any confidences," she said.

"I'm not hesitating to be coy," Miles said, "I'm hesitating because I do not know what happened."

"You seem so close."

"I think we are, but she is very private. Indeed, I'd have to say she is the most reserved person I know. I know nothing about her marriage other than her husband died several years after they married—the victim of some sort of freak accident. And that he left her very little to live on. She could have moved in with her brother, of course, but she is too independent for that." He paused and then added, "She, too, sells her work." He gestured to the waistcoat he'd been wearing for several days now. It had once been a lovely gold silk with tiny mallards but now it looked more like a dull gray silk with dirty London pigeons. "This is her doing and was a gift for my last birthday."

"I have admired several of your waistcoats. That is lovely work."

"It is. I'm saddened that it is ruined. I only wish Freddie did it for pleasure, rather than profit."

"I'm sure she enjoyed doing that for you."

Miles considered his next words carefully. "There is something I wanted to tell you about Freddy."

She stiffened.

"It is nothing like what you are thinking."

"How do you know what I am thinking?" she shot back.

He gave her a steady look.

"Very well, so I might have been thinking something like that. What is it that you wanted to tell me?"

"I had a small amount of money left from selling out my commission and I, er, well, I've enlisted the help of my friend Annis—the Countess of Rotherhithe and the only one of the teachers you've not met—to arrange that the money go to Freddie."

"Why did you have to go through your friend?"

"I knew if I tried to give it to Freddie outright, she would refuse it."

"Ah."

"In any case," he said, "I wanted you to know what I'd done rather than have you come across the information at some point and, er—"

"Jump to the wrong conclusion?" she said with a wry smile.

"It could happen," he said mildly.

"Point taken."

Miles sat back in his chair, patted his stomach with both hands, and heaved a sigh of contentment. "It wasn't the best soup, but at least we are full and have a roof over our heads."

"And nobody is shooting at us."

"Yes, there is that," Miles said wryly. "I must say that you've been a grand sport about all this."

"So have you."

"Well, not only is it my fault, but I spent a goodly chunk of the last decade slogging through mud and dodging armed men, so it isn't exactly new to me." He stood and added more wood to the fire and then went to look out the window.

"What do you see?" she asked.

"Not a thing—not even the moon." He turned on his heel. "Are you tired?"

"I should be, but I feel surprisingly alert."

"Well, there is a stack of old newspapers—the most recent one 1802—and a rather scruffy deck of cards. Would you like to read or play a game?"

"I don't know any card games." She paused and then added, "Or any games at all, really."

"*What?* Not a one? Not even Blindman's Bluff? Jackstraws? Sardines?"

She laughed. "Fine—I know how to play Sardines. Who doesn't. But that would hardly be any fun with only the two of us."

He lowered his eyelids and cut her a deliberately wicked look. "I think it might be quite lovely to be a sardine with you, darling."

She gave a dismissive snort, but her cheeks flushed.

"You must know at least one game, Mary. Please. If you don't, I shall weep for you."

Mary chewed her lip.

"A-ha!" Miles said. "You *do* know how to play something. What? Out with it."

***

Say 'no'! What are you thinking, Mary? a strident voice in her head demanded.

"Come, come. What game?" Miles asked.

Mary came to her senses. "Never mind."

He laughed. "Oh no, darling! You can't say that now. Tell me, what game? Something wicked? I want to know?"

"You'll think it is silly."

His eyebrows shot up. "Why Mary! I didn't think you cared what anyone else thought."

Mary was oddly flattered by his words, no matter that they were wrong—enormously wrong when it came to *his* opinion.

"Fine," she said, giving him an exasperated look. "It's called *Questions or Commands.*"

"Ooh, I haven't played that since I was a schoolboy."

"You know it?"

He laughed, but at least it wasn't mean spirited. "Darling, I think everyone in England knows that game. Did you play it at your girls' school?"

Mary opened her mouth to lie and say *yes*, but somehow that seemed even more pathetic than telling the truth.

"I never actually played it."

"Why not?"

"I had a roommate my last year and she was a very, er, popular girl. She'd hold after hours parties." She cleared her throat. "I was never invited—even though it was my room, too—but I heard them play."

A soft, sympathetic look flickered across his face, and she wished she'd kept her mouth shut. "You were unhappy at school."

It wasn't a question, but she nodded. "I thought it was as miserable as it could get. Then I had a Season in London. "

"Let's play the game."

"It's a stupid game. I'm sure you don't want—"

"I want to play," he said. "Who gets to go first?"

Mary snorted. "What? I thought gentlemen always let ladies go first."

"Ha! Not when it comes to games."

Mary snatched up the deck, shuffled it, and then dealt them both a card. "Highest card goes first."

Miles flipped over an eight and groaned. "Ah, that's not fair."

"No sniveling."

He laughed. "Go on, flip yours over."

Mary lifted only the corner up and peeked at it. And then it was her turn to groan.

"No sniveling," he echoed, grabbing the card and turning it to reveal a four.

"Ha!" he crowed.

"I'm so relieved that you aren't the sort of person who gloats when they win."

If anything, his smirk just grew larger. "Wait, there is something we need." He went to the brown earthenware jug their new landlord's wife had provided and pulled the bung. "We can't play a game like this while drinking tea." He tossed the dregs out of their mugs, gave them a quick rinse, and then poured in thick brown ale. "Have you had beer before?"

"Of course." Mary took a sip and forced herself not to pull a face.

He grinned and leaned back in his chair, tucking his hands under his arms as he stared at her. "Alright then, here is my question—"

"Wait! What is the forfeit?"

His eyes moved over her in a way that made her breathing hitch. "You can either answer the question or strip."

"*No!*"

He threw back his head and laughed. "Well, it was worth a try. How about this: If you refuse to answer, then you have to drink the contents of your mug."

"But you *like* drinking it."

"I like stripping off my clothes, too."

"Very droll," she said. "I know you're just trying to make me blush."

"I'm so good at it."

"Pick a forfeit."

"Fine. How about a smut on the nose?"

Mary rolled her eyes. "Now you've made it too easy. We'll drink the ale if we don't wish to answer. What is the question?"

"How many lovers have you had?"

Chapter 32

It wasn't the question Mary had expected. At *all*. She'd thought Miles would ask about the fire. While she hated that question, she might hate this one even worse.

She was about to reach for the mug of ale but she glanced at his face. He didn't look at all surprised to see her reach for the beer.

That nettled her and she yanked back her hand. "One."

He nodded slowly.

So, they were going to ask pointed questions, were they?

"Would you have married Lady Copley if you'd not inherited your brother's debts?"

He spoke without hesitation. "No."

Now it was Mary's turn to be surprised.

And astonishingly relieved.

"Was your cousin Reginald your lover?"

Mary's chest froze.

He covered her hand with his. "You don't need to—"

"Yes." She swallowed and took a drink of ale, the thick bitter liquid soothing her parched throat. She tried to tug away her hand, but he tightened his grip.

"Did he force you, Mary?"

"No."

He looked relieved. "Will you tell me what happened?"

May stared into his kind, beautiful blue eyes. "I thought he cared for me—we'd been close since his father married my aunt. Or at least I thought we were close. Close enough that I—I became his lover. I told him it didn't mean that he had to marry me, but he argued that he wanted to. That he loved me." She swallowed. "But then I overheard him at a ball—the last ball I attended until our betrothal ball, as a matter of fact—talking to his friends. They were mocking him for dancing twice with me, telling him he must have a strong stomach."

Genuine fury sparked in his gaze. "Swine!"

"He told them all that he'd s-seen me—seen my burns—and that I was fortunate my father was worth as much as he was. Even so, he'd said he'd had to close his eyes and think of England."

"Good God, Mary. I'm so terribly sorry!"

The words wouldn't stop pouring out of her. "I told myself that I was grateful to find out before we could approach my father about marrying."

"You're right about that! A narrow escape, I'd say. Did you ever tell your father what Cooper had done?"

"No."

"Why not, Mary? Surely he wouldn't have left his will the way he had if he'd known."

She pulled a face. "No, you are right about that. Unfortunately, he probably would have strangled Reginald with his bare hands and gone to gaol for murder." She shrugged. "I convinced myself that what had happened with Reginald was just business. He'd wanted a merger— our marriage—so he could gain control of the company. If he hadn't been so confident, so arrogant, he could have had everything." Mary shivered at the thought of her fortunate escape.

"I'm sorry you were betrayed that way."

"Me too." Mary was suddenly exhausted.

"You look weary to your bones."

"You are the first person I've ever told that story to."

"Good God! What a horrible secret to keep to yourself all these years."

"I feel... better, having told you."

"I'm honored that you told me."

Mary struggled to smother a yawn and lost. "I'm sorry! This has been such an interesting evening but suddenly I can't keep my eyes open."

He chuckled. "I can't imagine *why* you're so tired. You've only slept in a nasty hay rick, walked for miles, danced like a whirling dervish, and kicked a bloodthirsty ruffian."

"Well, when you put it *that* way."

"Why don't you lie down and see if you can get some rest."

Mary glanced at the bed. "There is only one—"

"Go ahead and take the bed. I'll sleep in the chair." He gestured to the wooden rocking chair near the hearth.

"But how will you sleep?" she asked, yawning so hard she could barely get the words out.

"I'm accustomed to sleeping in strange positions and awkward places. Why don't you take off your dress?" he said when she went to the bed and sat.

"In a minute," she muttered, waves of exhaustion swamping her. "I'll just sit a while and rest."

She lay down on her side.

"Just for a minute," she said again.

And then promptly fell into a deep, dreamless sleep.

***

Mary woke with a start, momentarily disoriented as her eyes darted around the dimly lighted room before the night flooded back to her—the dancing, the rioters, the kind farmer.

She turned over in bed and blinked at the pale gray light streaming through the window.

A quick glance around the room was enough to show Miles was nowhere in sight.

Mary yawned and pushed herself up in bed, which is when she realized she'd fallen asleep fully dressed. One foot had strips of old cotton cloth tied around it and the sight of it brought the night before back to her.

Miles had tended to her so gently.

And then they had played *Questions and Commands*.

Mary groaned. Why oh why had she told him about Reginald? *You wanted him to know or else you would have drunk the ale.*

That was probably true. Besides, better that he heard it from her than from some vile cad like Viscount Elton.

Mary swung her feet to the floor and stretched, which is when she realized there was a rhythmic thudding sound coming from somewhere.

When Mary shuffled to the window, her jaw sagged.

"My goodness," she said, rubbing the sleep from her eyes so she could see more clearly.

It was Miles, and he was chopping wood.

And he was naked from the waist up.

Mary mashed her nose against the glass, whimpered in pain, and pulled back slightly.

Unfortunately, he was too far away for her to get a good look at him. Not only that, but it was still raining outside, although not as heavily as the night before, and the sky was a slate gray.

He raised the ax over his head and the muscles in his waist, back, and shoulders rippled as he brought it down.

Mary gulped and then leaned closer, bumping her nose yet again. She swallowed convulsively, her mouth inexplicably flooding with moisture.

"Oh my," she murmured.

His poor pantaloons were threadbare and soaked and adhering to the curves of his bottom as tightly as skin to a grape.

As she stood and drooled, Miles turned and looked toward the front of the house.

Mary ducked behind the frame but then realized he'd been looking at something else, not her.

It was the farmer who came striding up.

She tensed and glanced around the small room for a weapon, her gaze falling on the poker that hung next to the hearth. She grabbed it and then ran back to the window, her heart pounding in her throat as she watched the two men talk.

After a moment Miles nodded at something the farmer said. The other man smiled and then turned and left the way he'd come.

With the ax held loosely in one hand, Miles strode toward the shed.

Mary expelled the breath she'd been holding. Was that it? Was the show over?

When he emerged from the shed a few minutes later he was wearing his shirt.

"Well, drat," she muttered, watching as he loaded his arms with wood.

Mary hurried to make herself look busy and when he opened the door, she was filling the kettle with water.

"Good morning," she called out.

"Ah, look who is finally up," he teased as he refilled the wood cubby beside the hearth.

"What time is it?"

"Just before ten. You slept a long time."

"Did you get any sleep at all?" she asked, pushing back her hair, which sprang out from her head like an orange Renaissance halo.

"A few hours," he said. "Mr. Gilbert—that is the name of our host, by the way—came to say that he must drive his wife to her sister's house. Evidently Mrs. Gilbert is a midwife and the situation is an emergency. He wanted us to know that he is still hoping to be back in time to drive into Reading tomorrow." He smiled. "And before you ask,

269

I really do believe he has to take her to her sister's house." He picked up the wooden bucket. "I will bring in more water so that we might both have a bit of a wash."

Mary watched him go; her brain still groggy from sleep. Until she had her first two cups of tea, it was hard for her to form words or concentrate. Seeing him half nude had not helped her mental processes.

By the time Miles returned, the tea was steeped and she was sipping a cup, without jam this time.

Miles filled the basin, set it near the hearth, and then poured himself a mug.

And then he sat there sipping it and smiling.

Mary grunted.

He laughed. "I take it morning is not your favorite part of the day?"

"No."

He grinned.

"You are entirely too happy," she muttered, scalding her throat on a gulp of tea.

"I found Mr. Norton's fishing pole and box of tackle in the shed out back."

"Who is Mr. Norton?"

"The gentleman who owns this cabin."

Mary grunted.

"Our landlord says the fishing in that stream we crossed is excellent."

"But… it's raining."

"The best time to fish."

She grunted again.

But half an hour later, the lure of a fish supper had dragged her from their dry abode.

While Mary washed and dressed in her breeches and hobnail boots—which Miles had padded for her comfort—Miles dug up worms to use for bait.

"You've never fished?" he asked as they walked through the rain, which was still falling but gently now as opposed to the torrential downpour they'd had during the night.

"No."

"What sorts of activities *do* you do for entertainment, Mary?"

She gave him a sideways look.

Miles laughed. "Relax, darling, this isn't an examination, there aren't any right or wrong answers, I'm just curious."

She considered his question as they skirted a particularly deep mudhole in the middle of the path.

"I like my birds, of course, and I greatly enjoy working on the plans for my trade school. To be honest, I've never had a great deal of time for hobbies. At school I studied hard because there was nothing else to do. When I came home on the holidays, I nagged my father until he took me along to his work. Or at least allowed me to sit in his office and help with whatever he was working on." She paused and then said, "What about you?"

"I like to read and of course I enjoyed tearing about on my horse when I was a lad. In the summers, we'd fish and swim in the stream that runs through the property. Bev and I loved to fish and hunt." He pulled a face. "I'm not quite so keen on hunting now."

"I thought all aristocratic men loved *riding to hounds.*"

"The war taught me that all living things value their lives. And I have had a belly full of killing."

Before he looked away, she saw the bleakness in his eyes.

Mary set a hand on his arm. "Miles?"

He stopped and turned to her.

"I'm sorry, that was a flippant and clichéd comment."

"You said nothing wrong. Most aristocratic men *do* like to hunt. I used to enjoy it, myself."

"That might be true, but I said it to be provoking." She could not bear his open gaze and looked down to where her hand still rested on his sleeve. "I should not be so… combative."

He chuckled and she looked up to find him smiling—not a sad or frustrated smile, but a genuine one. "You should continue to be exactly as you are, Mary."

"How is it that you can always be so… pleasant? So courteous, even in the face of my sharp tongue."

"Trust me, it is no great hardship."

Suddenly Mary saw herself the way she could sometimes be—so scared and insecure that she struck before somebody else could hurt her first. Miles was not the sort of man who hurt other people, she knew that instinctively and had done so for some time. She was treating him unfairly.

Mary dropped her gaze again, ashamed by how she'd behaved since the night she'd met him.

He took her chin with the hand that was gnarled and scarred and tilted her face up. And then he leaned down and kissed her.

It wasn't the kiss they'd shared in the library at Coal House—hungry and angry and demanding—this was a sweet, tender exploration. Not just one kiss, but five, ten, maybe even more. Delicate and teasing, like the paws of kittens, his lips laid a trail that ran from her lips to her cheek to the lobe of her ear.

"Mary," he whispered.

The sound of her prosaic name on his tongue sent powerful ripples up her spine and she pushed up onto her toes, thrust her fingers into his hair, and yanked his head down, earning a low rumble of approval from deep in his chest.

Bucket and pole slid from his fingers, *thunking* softly to the overgrown path, and he palmed her bottom, pulling her close to grind his pelvis against her belly.

He was hard. For her.

Mary moaned, suddenly unable to take in enough air.

It was Miles who pulled away, his chest heaving as badly as hers.

"Perhaps fishing isn't such a good idea, after all," he murmured, his eyes dark and hungry.

Mary ached for him—and thrilled at the invitation in his darkened gaze. But the last thing she wanted was to undress in front of him in the broad daylight, something she'd vowed never to do again after Reginald.

And so she choked down her desire and cut him a chiding look. "You promised me a fish supper, my lord. I will hold you to it."

"Tyrant," he said, kissing her once more—on the tip of her nose this time—and then bending to collect his bucket and pole.

Miles led them to a spot on the rain-swollen stream where the water swirled into a pool.

"This looks to be the perfect place."

He set down the bucket and then fiddled with the end of the pole before saying, "Hand me one of those, will you?"

Mary looked into the can sitting inside the bucket, to where pink worms writhed in the black Berkshire soil and shook her head. "No, you can pick your own." She lifted the can.

He laughed. "Coward," he said, and then plucked out an earthworm.

Mary winced and looked away when he put the worm on the hook. "Poor thing."

"You won't be saying that when I present you with a big fat fish for dinner."

He carefully tossed the baited hook into the middle of the pond and then sat on the rock.

Mary looked from Miles to the water. "Is that all—"

"Shhh!" he hissed, and then leaned close and whispered, "The fish can hear you." He patted the log beside him.

Mary rolled her eyes but sat down beside him.

"You must be very quiet when fishing." His lips brushed her ear and his hot breath sent goose bumps prickling down her arms.

"I didn't realize fish had big ears," she muttered.

He held a finger over his lips and then turned to stare at the end of the pole.

They sat in silence.

It began to rain harder.

"Miles—"

"Shhh. Here," he said, handing her the pole. "You try it."

Mary gripped the handle and glared at him. "But I don't know how to—"

"Shhh."

Mary was just about to tell him to quit shushing her when the end of the pole jerked so hard it looked as if it might snap in half.

She shrieked and jumped to her feet. "I've got one!"

***

Mary gave a sigh of contentment and flopped back in her chair. "That is the best meal I've ever had."

Miles laughed. "Hunger seasons all dishes."

"No, it would have been good no matter when or where."

Miles stood to collect the plates, but Mary stopped him.

"You caught dinner *and* cooked it," she said. "You sit while I do this part. For once, you can sit while a lady stands, *my lord.*"

"If you insist."

"I do."

He smiled and sat back in his chair.

They were both full, warm, and even clean as he'd hauled in three buckets of water while the fish had cooked in the coals and they'd both bathed themselves behind the screen in the corner. They'd found soap and Miles had even discovered an old razor that he'd stropped until it was sharp enough to use. While it was true that they'd had to put on dirty clothing after their sponge baths, it was still better than the alternative.

"I think I could grow to like fishing," Mary said as she slid their mismatched plates and cutlery into the basin and then poured some of the hot water from the kettle over it.

"You can't claim to be a true fisherwoman until you bait your own hook and clean your own fish," Miles said.

"There's no point in *both* of us getting our hands dirty, Miles."

Miles laughed. "Well, then next time—when we fish in the stream at Avington—*you* can be the one who does all the baiting and cleaning."

She gave him a startled look, her lips parting slightly.

Miles cocked his head as he looked up from his seated position, the unusual angle giving him a different perspective. "You look so surprised." He caught her hand, which was wet from the dishwater. "Are you going to insist on our business marriage? Even after all… this?" His gesture encompassed not just the cabin, but the entire headlong journey of the past few days.

She swallowed, visibly at a loss.

Miles stood. "Leave the dishes until later," he said, lifting her hands and kissing the backs of them. She flinched and would have pulled her damaged hand away.

"No," he said. "Here, look at mine while I look at yours." He grinned. "That sounds naughtier than I intended." He gave her his damaged hand and took her left one.

For a long moment they were both consumed by their separate examinations.

When he finally looked up, he saw she was staring at him, pensive and anxious.

"Don't hide yourself from me." He reached out with his free hand and cupped her cheek, his right hand brushing the burned skin of her neck and jaw.

She closed her eyes briefly and inhaled until he thought she might burst.

"Mary," he whispered and her brilliant green eyes opened. "I'm going to kiss you."

A shudder wracked her body and she stared, the moment stretching and stretching, until she nodded.

"Yes."

Chapter 33

Mary flinched at the touch of his warm palm on her damaged skin.

"Shhh," he murmured, claiming her lips while his other hand closed around her waist and then slid slowly to her lower back.

Mary opened her mouth to him and he invaded her with slick heat while his hand came to rest over her bottom.

By the time he released her, she was breathless and dizzy, her breasts aching and heavy with desire.

Mary stared at the bulge in his breeches, trying—and failing—to force her gaze back up, hypnotized by the thick ridge, which seemed to become more pronounced with every second that passed.

Had *she* done that to him?

She blinked her eyes to clear away the haze and looked up.

Miles was waiting for her, his eyelids lowered, his sinful mouth curved in a smile of lazy amusement.

Actually, it was a smile of lazy, *knowing* amusement.

"See what you've done to me, Mary?" His hand—not the beautiful, perfect one, but the twisted and damaged one—glided over his tattered pantaloons and his fingers tightened around his shaft.

Just like in that first dream she'd had about him...

Mary was enrapt. Never had she ever seen such a thoroughly erotic sight, and he'd not even removed a stitch of clothing.

"I want to make love to you," he said, his cobalt blue almost black.

Mary nodded dumbly.

"Let's take off this gown, shall we?"

His words startled her back to herself. "But the light—the candle."

She stepped away from him and bumped into the table.

Miles cocked his head. "You don't want to see what we'll do with each other?"

He sounded so astonished that Mary almost changed her mind. In truth, she desperately wanted to see him naked; she'd pleasured herself to sleep far too often these past few weeks imagining that body without clothing. But if he took off his clothing then he'd want her to do the same, wouldn't he? And the thought of disrobing in front of this specimen of male perfection turned her stomach.

Mary shook her head. "No," she said firmly.

His lips pursed and a mulish look settled on his face. For a moment, she thought he'd argue, but he jerked out a nod. "Very well, I will extinguish all but one of the candles."

Mary glanced at the four candles and mentally calculated the light just one would produce. The bed was on the other side of the room, so it wouldn't be *too* terribly bad.

"Very well."

"In exchange I will want you naked—utterly." His eyes were stern, no trace of the playful gentleman she was so accustomed to.

Her lips parted and she swallowed repeatedly, but she couldn't force even one word out, so she gave a jerky nod.

Mary backed away from him, toward the bed, as he quickly snuffed the three candles, throwing the room into near darkness.

She gave a sigh of relief. Thank God! She could barely see him, which was terribly unfortunate, but that meant he couldn't see her, either.

He stopped a few feet away.

"Take off your clothes."

Mary startled, even though he'd spoken softly. "Take off yours," she retorted.

His low chuckle caused goosebumps to spring up all over her. "I've completed my part of the transaction. Now it is your turn."

She fumbled with the buttons that ran down her neck, wishing there were more of them.

She heard something soft hitting the floor and saw light reflected off the pale, bare skin of his shoulder and froze.

"Mary?"

"What?"

"Are you getting undressed?"

"Yes," she lied, staring through the gloom as he bent down, presumably to push off his pantaloons.

When he stood up Mary squinted.

Blast! She couldn't see anything. Certainly not the *thing* she was so curious to see.

"Do you need help?" he asked, coming closer.

"No!" Mary tugged on the last button and shrugged the dress off her shoulders.

She'd not bothered with her stays after her sponge bath earlier, so all that remained to remove was her chemise. Her hands went to the hem, but she couldn't make herself lift it.

"Maaaaaaary," he said in a sing-song voice that made her laugh. "You look… stuck. Can I help you?"

"No, I don't need your help."

She squeezed her eyes shut and lifted the flimsy garment, tossing it to the floor.

"Your stockings, too."

Mary scowled.

He laughed. "Did you just *growl* at me?"

Mary ignored him and fumbled with her garters before bending low to push her stockings to the floor.

When she stood, she was naked. And he'd come closer—close enough that she could feel his heat and smell the plain, yet oddly alluring, lye soap they'd both used to clean themselves earlier.

"Are you scared?" he asked, the words a puff of air on her bowed head.

"No."

"Liar."

"I've done this before—more than once," she retorted, and then wished she hadn't.

"I remember," he said, a smile in his voice. "Why don't you get on the bed, darling?"

The word *darling* sent a flaming ball of heat from her chest directly to her sex and she squeezed her eyes shut, the rest of her body clenching, as well, which set off a cascade of pleasurable ripples. Oh yes, she knew this feeling—she was no ignorant school miss unable to read the signs of her own body. If she were to reach between her thighs and—

"Mary?" The bed tipped on one side and she felt the brush of skin against her outer thigh as he lowered his hand on the bed. "We don't have to do—"

"I want to."

He chuckled yet again. "You don't know what I was going to say. Perhaps I was suggesting we go for a late-night swim in the stream? Or perhaps you'd like to shake your elbow with those ivories I found earlier?"

It was Mary's turn to laugh at his unexpected use of such a cant phrase for dicing. "Wherever did you hear such a thing?"

"I was in the army for over a decade, sweetheart. I may have picked up a few things here and there—especially when it comes to gambling. Where did *you* learn such a phrase?"

"My father."

"Ah."

"And no, to answer your question, I don't wish to do either of those things."

"I see." His hand moved from the bedding to rest lightly on her thigh. "You are shaking."

"It has been some time," she snapped, mortified by her missish reaction to his touch. "I daresay I shall come about once you get on with it."

"Get on with it?" he repeated.

"Yes," she forced the word through clenched jaws.

"Oh, Mary. I have no intention of merely *getting* on with it."

Mary was grateful for the darkness because it hid what was likely a very stupid expression as she gaped unseeingly at him.

"My lord?" she said.

"Yes?"

"I would have plain speaking in this matter, as well."

She didn't hear him laugh, but she felt his body shake with mirth beside her. "As you wish," he said, his hand coming up to join the first. "Open your legs for me, darling."

***

Mary was shaking like a proverbial leaf under his hands and Miles wished like hell he'd not agreed to snuff the lights. As acerbic as she sounded, her body was sending him other messages. This was not the Mary he knew—harsh, sharp-tongued, and indomitable; this was somebody else entirely. She plucked at his heart and drew out his protective instincts. He wanted to take her in his arms and give her so much pleasure she'd forget about everything else in the world. He wanted to cradle her against his chest and comfort her, soothe her worries, but that seemed to just annoy her.

So, instead, he stroked her thighs, which were so tightly clamped that he feared he might need a crowbar to force them apart. "Shhh, relax," he murmured. "I promise I will make you feel good."

Her legs parted grudgingly—too grudgingly to make mounting her either desirable or wise at that point—so he continued his gentle caressing, moving from her trim ankles up her firm calves to her knees, massaging her muscles, careful to avoid chafing the damaged flesh on her left side. "Does that hurt your burned skin?"

She stiffened for a moment, doubtless at his *plain speaking*, but then seemed to come to a decision and her body relaxed. "No." After a long moment of silence, she added, "It feels good."

"Yes," he agreed. "You *do* feel good." Miles caressed down to her calves and then kneaded the sweet curve of muscle on her right leg, more careful on her left. When she groaned, he asked, "Sore?"

"Yes. I didn't realize how much until now."

"We've walked a considerable distance."

When his hand brushed her foot, she cried out. "Ah! That tickles."

"Good to know in case you need disciplining," he murmured, earning a scoffing laugh from her. "What?" he taunted, sliding his hands back up her legs, this time not stopping at her knees but continuing upward, his fingers stroking the silky softness of her inner thighs. "You think I will be a tolerant lord and master." Before she could give some likely tart retort, he brushed his thumbs over her mound.

"My lord!"

"We're back to my lord? And here you've been calling me *Miles* so nicely."

"Wh-what are you doing?" she asked when he settled his hands on her hips and knelt between her thighs, his thumbs sliding through her private curls.

"I thought you'd done this before?"

She sucked in a breath, as if to reply, but then she paused, her silence telling him volumes about Reginald Cooper's lack of bed skills.

Damnation! But Miles wished he'd not agreed to this wretched darkness.

He gently spread her lower lips with his thumbs.

She whimpered softly but didn't try to close her legs or get away from his touch.

"Did your lover not do this to you, Mary?" he teased, caressing her slick folds but taking care to avoid the source of her pleasure.

"N-not exactly," she answered in a breathy voice.

"Do you like it?" he asked, even though her hips had begun to gently lift and roll, twitching slightly to the side, as if she could force him to graze her clitoris.

Miles smirked and allowed his thumb to caress her little bud on the next lift and roll.

She hissed in a breath. "Yes," she whispered, her hips jerking as she rubbed her sweet little peak against his thumbs.

"How about this?" he asked in a rough voice, lowering his mouth over her and covering the bundle of nerves with wet heat.

"Miles!" she shouted.

He grinned to himself at her uninhibited response. And then he proceeded to wreck her composure to the best of his not inconsiderable abilities.

***

Mary knew she should be ashamed that Miles—an *earl* for pity's sake—had his mouth between her thighs.

But it felt too good and she couldn't bring herself to care.

Reginald had never done such a shocking, pleasurable thing. He'd never even touched her *there*. Only Mary had.

Who would have believed that such a gorgeous, courteous, proper aristocrat could make such earthy, raw noises or use his tongue—and lips and even his teeth—in such ways?

Unlike the nights when she sought relief from her own hand, Mary did not want this to be over quickly—she wanted to savor it for hours. But he was too skilled, and Mary bit her lip to keep from crying out when he pushed a finger inside her, giving her something to clench around as she came apart.

After the initial sharper waves of bliss faded, Mary floated on a warm cloud of pleasure, only vaguely aware that he was still stroking and licking and murmuring sweet nothings, his hands kneading the aching muscles of her inner thighs.

"Feeling relaxed?" he asked.

"Nngh."

He laughed. "I must not be doing my job well if you can still make sounds like that," he said, and lowered his mouth again.

Mary knew she was a wanton—laid out before him, legs spread wide—but she couldn't bring herself to care.

"Come for me, Mary—just once more," he murmured.

And just like that she was clenching and shaking and barreling toward yet another climax.

Twice, she thought in wonder as she crested the rise and gave herself up to passion.

This time when the velvety darkness came for her, Mary surrendered.

Chapter 34

Mary opened her eyes and stared directly into a pair of thickly lashed blue-violet orbs.

She jolted. "Oh!"

"I'm sorry, did I startle you? I promise I've not been staring at you like a hole-and-corner pervert for the past hour." He smiled. "Only the last few minutes."

Mary glanced at the window and saw it was still dark outside.

"It's not even midnight," he said.

The room seemed lighter. Mary pushed up onto her elbows, yelped, and then yanked the bedding up over her chest. "You relit the candles."

He nodded and lifted a yellowed newspaper. "Yes. I was going to try and read for a bit, but then you woke up." He grinned and tossed the paper to the floor, propped his head on his hand, and regarded her in a way that made Mary arrange her hair until it was covering the burned side of her cheek.

Miles shook his head and reached out, catching her hand. "Don't, Mary."

"It's ugly." She wanted to bite off her tongue after the words slipped out. Not since she'd been a child had she whined so shamefully. She was alive—far more fortunate than all the others who'd perished that night—it sickened her to feel sorry for herself.

Miles pulled the sheet down, baring his torso.

Mary gasped. He'd been naked when they'd made love so of course she'd felt the scars but seeing them was a shock. She'd always believed he resembled a statute of a Greek god. Now she saw that he wasn't perfectly polished marble at all, but sinew, bone, and flesh. Not a god, but a warrior who'd been tried in battle many times over.

"Do I disgust you?" he asked.

"No! Of course not," she said, her eyes darting up from the horrific round burns that covered one side of his chest to meet his blue gaze. "You were t-tortured and survived. You are a hero."

"Tell me what happened to you, Mary. Please."

She bit her lower lip and worried it for a moment before shrugging. "It's nothing mysterious or even very interesting, just one of the thousands of house fires that occur every year in Britain. I was at my aunt and uncle's house—this was before my aunt married Reginald's father—and one of the servants must have knocked over a candle. My uncle rescued me and several servants but then was brought down by a flaming beam before he could escape. Seven people died and five of us were burned." She swallowed as she recalled Betsy Miller, the young kitchen maid who'd been almost unrecognizable.

Mary had been lucky—that's what she reminded herself whenever she thought about poor Betsy.

Miles stroked her hair back, until her cheek, neck, and shoulder were exposed. And then he gently tugged down the sheet.

Mary clutched at the only thing covering her naked body; her gaze locked with his.

"Let me see you, Mary."

She stared into his eyes, desperate to see beyond their beautiful color and shape, searching for a glimpse of the man inside. What did he want from her? Why was it important to *see* her?

"Please," he said, his brows knitting in a way that made him as difficult to refuse or ignore as a basket full of puppies.

Mary sighed and then she let go of the sheet, allowing him to bare all of her to his gaze.

"Seven people died in that fire, Mary. But you survived. You just called me a survivor. The same applies to you; your body bears battle scars as surely as mine does." His eyes drifted to her cheek and neck down to where the fire had licked the side of her breast, her belly, her hips.

And down and down.

His full lips pursed as he traced the same path with his fingers, his touch light and ghostly over some of the thicker scars, which had very little sensation.

His expression was not one of disgust or pity.

It was one of acceptance.

And desire.

When he lifted his eyes to hers, he raised a hand to cup her jaw, his thumb lightly caressing the rough skin. "We are two of a kind, Mary. Scarred and battered by life, but not broken." His lips curved into a smile. "I teased you for enjoying these past few days, but the truth is that I'm grateful we've had this time with just the two of us. We are both strong willed and it makes me shudder how easy it might have been to grow farther and farther apart, rather than closer together."

"I'm so sorry for the way I treated you, Miles. I—"

"Shhh, love. You don't need to apologize to me. I've already forgive you." He smoothed back her hair, his gaze loving as it flickered over her face. "If our positions were reversed, I can't imagine how infuriated I would have been if my father had left a clause in his will like yours did. While I'm glad his decision brought the two of us together, I regret all the pain it must have caused you, and all the doubt his demands would have sowed. But the truth is that you *are* good at what you do—more than good—and we both know you don't need a man's help to operate those businesses. But I hope you might come to need me, or at least want me, in other ways." He smiled. "Your dancing master of a husband who wishes to learn how ships are built. Will you be able to bear explaining such matters to your mathematically inept spouse?"

"I believe I can manage that." She smirked. "At least you are pretty to look at."

He gave a shout of laughter. "I always knew my appearance would be of use someday."

This time, it was Mary who kissed him first. And when she finally pulled away, several breathless minutes later, he cupped her cheek and said, "I want to make love to you again."

Mary nodded, excitement pounding through her veins at the heat in his darkened gaze.

And all for her.

"I want to leave the candles burning so I can watch while I give you pleasure, so you can watch me."

Mary nodded again.

He smiled. "Have you lost your words?"

"No," she rasped, and then cleared her throat. "I want you… Miles."

He moved over her, until his knees were between her thighs, nudging them wider and exposing her to his gaze. His breathing quickened and his nostrils flared as he stared down at her, the hungry expression on his face making her inner muscles contract.

"Does that feel good—to clench your muscles?" he asked.

"You can see that?"

He looked amused. "Yes, your body tightens externally when you do that." His gaze lowered to her sex and his throat flexed as he swallowed. "You are so pretty and pink and soft. I want to touch you—explore you while I can see you," he said, stroking up her thigh with one hot, strong hand.

"Yes," she whispered.

He slid the fingers of his damaged hand to her sex, his touch light but firm as he caressed her outer lips.

Mary's hips rose of their own accord, lifting and thrusting in time to his rhythmic caressing, his fingers drifting closer and closer to her aching core, but still not touching her.

"Yes, just like that, Mary."

She whimpered and ground against him, frustration and need swirling with desire.

"You need something inside you—don't you, darling? You need to be stretched and filled."

"Please."

His lips curved into a truly wicked smile as he penetrated her with one finger. "Tighten around me—as hard as you can."

Every muscle in her body flexed at his words.

"So beautiful," he muttered, devouring her with his eyes.

Mary couldn't decide what was more arousing: his mesmerizing touching or what that touching was doing to him.

He lifted his dark blue gaze and pinioned her while the fingers of one hand caressed between her thighs and the other pinched and tweaked and tormented her nipples, until they were hard and tight and aching.

"You like that," he teased as she shuddered and gritted her teeth to keep from begging.

He gave a low growl of approval, and then he lowered his wicked, smirking lips over her breast and sucked a nipple into his hot, wet mouth.

Mary arched her back. "Miles!"

***

Miles knew he should leave her be and allow her to rest, but his hunger for her overrode all consideration and common sense. He needed to make her climax again, to watch as her tightly laced façade slid away to reveal the passionate woman who hid beneath.

A potent, primal feeling flooded him at causing such a proud, intelligent woman to lose control. Making love to his wife-to-be was not just intoxicating, it was positively addictive.

It hadn't escaped his notice how her body had responded to his gruff, even crude, commands. Miss Mary Barnett appreciated a little aggression in the bedchamber. That didn't surprise him. He'd noticed that strong women often enjoyed relinquishing their control when it came to sex.

Miles enjoyed almost every sort of bed sport and was most aroused when he satisfied his lover. If Mary wanted a stern, dominating sexual partner, he would give it to her.

Miles felt the waves of pleasure as they rippled through her body, the spasms gradually diminishing as her orgasm washed over her.

Not until she heaved a sigh of blissful exhaustion did he rise up and position himself between her thighs, entering her with one long thrust.

Her eyes flew open and her lips parted as he sheathed himself to the root.

"Are you all right?" Miles asked, lowering himself to his elbows and keeping his weight off her while he held her full, giving her a moment to adjust.

She nodded and her eyelids lowered slightly, her lips curving into the faintest of smiles as she shifted her hips and took him even deeper.

Miles groaned. "Well, isn't that nice?"

She flexed her inner muscles, causing him to make a very unmasculine noise.

"Proud of yourself, hmm?" he muttered.

When she wrapped her legs around him, Miles sighed and gave himself up to desire, working her with deep, thorough thrusts.

He tried to go slowly—to make the moment last and last and last—but his self-control was shredded and he was too bloody aroused.

"I can't wait any longer," he said, withdrawing almost all the way and then slamming into her with every inch.

"Yes," she whispered against his neck.

The single word was enough to snap the last threads of his resistance and he rode her hard and fast, thrusting into her sweet body again and again and again before finally driving himself home.

"I'm coming," he gasped, holding her wide-eyed gaze as he shuddered, his muscles jerking and spasming to the point of pain as he emptied deep inside her.

His bones swiftly turned to jelly and he had barely enough strength to roll to his side rather than flop down on top of her.

Her faint hiss when he withdrew told him he'd sated his lusts on her with too much vigor. He would have to apologize, he thought groggily, sliding an arm around her slim body and bringing her against his chest.

Miles opened his mouth to apologize for his haste, but a jaw cracker of a yawn was what emerged rather than any words.

He *should* apologize right now, but he simply couldn't keep his eyes open a moment longer.

Chapter 35

Mary!" a voice hissed in her ear.

Her eyes flew open just as a big hand closed over her mouth. "Shhhh," Miles whispered. "We have company, sweetheart."

Mary blinked the sleep from her eyes and saw by the gray light filtering through the gap in the curtains that it must be dawn.

Miles took her hands and pulled her to her feet, which is when she saw he was already dressed.

"Hurry—I've put your breeches, shirt, and coat on the foot of the bed. Do you need help?"

"No." Her brain was sluggish but she blearily reached for her shirt first.

By the time she'd fastened the last button Miles had returned from the window and dropped to his haunches. "You put on your stockings and I'll lace up your boots."

"Who is outside?" she asked, fumbling with the thick woolen stockings.

"Two of them are the ones who searched for us in the woods."

"Donny and Petey? Or were their names Donny and Paul?" Mary asked, her memory as fuzzy as her vision.

"I don't remember their names," Miles said, looking aggrieved at himself. "I am lucky that I saw them. They would have come upon us unawares if one of them hadn't been smoking."

"What are we going to do?" she asked, pushing her foot into the boot Miles held at the ready. "Do you think Mr. Gilbert and his wife are back?"

"I don't know if he is or not, but he's got three children and I don't want him involved in this."

"So then what—

"I'm going to give myself up and—"

"No!"

"It's me they want, Mary. You can get away and go for help."

"No. I won't leave you here."

He finished lacing her second boot and pushed to his feet, glaring down at her. "You will do as you are told and—"

"I'm not one of your soldiers, Miles. So don't try and use that tone on me. We have the gun you took off that man in Blount. We can—"

"One gun against three. I don't fancy those odds."

"How good a shot are you?"

He frowned. "Why?"

"Just answer me."

"I'm very good."

"You said you can see where they're hiding. Do you think you can shoot one of them from here?"

"Probably, they are close. But that would still leave the other two."

"Do you think they know we are both inside?"

He shrugged. "Who knows? I extinguished the candle hours ago. All they can know is that *somebody* is in here thanks to that." He pointed to the crackling fire, which would be belching smoke from the chimney. He must have filled the kettle with water not long ago because it was steaming away.

Mary chewed her lower lip, her gaze darting around the single room, cataloguing what weapons they had.

He narrowed his eyes at her. "What do you have in mind."

"Here is my idea," she said after a long moment.

***

Miles cursed himself for going along with her plan but kept his gaze fixed on the door, the gun resting on the brass bed rail.

Mary had arranged the blankets in such a way that somebody coming into the small cabin would only see a messy bed.

Miles was wedged beneath it, peering through a space that was large enough for only the barrel of the pistol and one eye.

"Ready?" Mary asked.

No! This is madness.

Miles uttered one last silent prayer and said, "I'm ready. And be *careful*," he ordered for at least the fifth time.

She ignored him—for at least the fifth time—and opened the door a crack. "I know you're out there! You might as well show yourselves."

After a long pause a voice came from the direction of the cluster of trees where he'd spotted the trio. "Why? So you can shoot us?"

"With what? Lord Avington took the gun when he left."

"He left you here alone?" The man's voice rang with disbelief.

"He went for help so you'd better run and hide while you can!" That idea had been Miles's sole contribution to her plan.

"They'll never believe that you just left me here," she'd scoffed.

"It can't hurt to try."

The jeering laughter from outside told him that Mary had been right. Again.

"You'd better just come out here, Miss Barnett. We'll not hurt you. It's not you we want; it's his lordship."

"He's not here, I tell you. Why don't you come check for yourself."

"Because we'd rather not get shot."

She raised her hands, one of which held the fire poker. "This is the only weapon I have. I will not surrender it, but I will allow you to come and check for him. I will stand right where I am—right where you can see me and I can see you. But only *one* of you may come in and look."

There was a long moment of silence, presumably as the men conferred.

"Are you afraid?" Mary taunted. "Just one woman against three big, strong, *brave* men?" Her laughter was so heavy with derision that Miles found himself feeling sorry for the men.

Amazingly, her mocking worked on the fools. "I'm coming in. You keep your hands up where we can see 'em!"

"You hold your hands up, too," she shouted back.

Laughter greeted her order. "Aye, awright, lass."

This was the part of the plan that made Miles sick to his stomach—Mary standing in an open doorway with three potential captors, all of whom probably had guns.

Mary had argued that they'd not risk shooting wildly as it had ended so badly for them the last time.

As the seconds passed without the sound of gunfire splitting the air, Miles realized that Mary had once again guessed correctly.

Finally, a man came into view—his big paws held aloft—a smirk on his face.

Mary inched back slowly. "Not so quickly," she said, backing into the room and edging to the side as she did so, so that she was behind the wall, still holding up the poker.

"Don't get your feathers ruffled little miss," the man chided in a condescending tone that set Miles's teeth on edge and probably irked Mary to no end.

"Stop where you are," she ordered. "You don't need to come all the way in—you can just look from there."

"Naw, I think I'll come all the way in," he said, his expression turning ugly as he glanced around the room and saw she was alone. "Now, you put down that poker you little bitch or I'll take it from you." He reached beneath his coat, probably for a cudgel or even a pistol, and Miles pulled the trigger and rolled out from beneath the bed even as the man crumpled to the floor.

Mary was flattened against the wall as a second shot went off outside, chips and splinters of the door frame showering the room like confetti.

Miles slammed the door shut just as another bullet struck the frame.

The man on the floor was motionless, the top half of his head missing.

"Oh God," Mary said, retching while Miles opened the man's coat to find what he'd been reaching for. In his waistband were not one, but two, pistols.

Miles checked to make sure both were primed and loaded.

"Lie down over there," he said to Mary, gesturing to the stone hearth, which was off to the side and protected by a thick flagstone.

She complied without comment and Miles flung open the door. When nobody shot, he peeked around the door frame. The two men were arguing with each other rather than paying attention to the cabin.

Unlike his first shot, the second struck one of the men in the shoulder rather than the head, but it still knocked him to the ground.

The third assailant stared open mouthed as Miles charged toward him at full speed. If he'd raised the gun in his hand—provided it was loaded—he might have shot Miles.

Instead, he turned and ran.

Luckily for Miles, he was both longer of leg and in better condition than the other man, and quickly closed the distance between them.

The man flung himself toward one of three horses tethered in a nearby grove of trees. He fumbled with the reins as he tried—and failed—to fling himself into the saddle, spooked the horse, and then—far too late—he reached for the pistol in his pocket.

Miles didn't hesitate, he aimed for the head.

And this time, he didn't miss.

***

Mary shook badly as she held the pot of boiling water away from her body. She'd wrapped her hands in rags and stood ready to fling the pot if necessary.

Another loud *bang* shattered the early morning air and she jolted, hissing as scalding water sloshed over the sides and onto her boot.

Mary waited, her heart thudding in her ears.

Please be alive. Please be alive. Please be—

"Mary?" Miles called. "We are out of danger; you can come out now."

She sagged against the wall and shakily lowered the pot to the floor.

The door opened and Miles's beautiful face was grimmer than she'd ever seen it. "Are you hurt?"

She shook her head, only then realizing she was crying. "Miles!" she sobbed, and then launched herself at him. "You're alive," she babbled into his chest. "Thank God, you're alive."

He held her in a rib-cracking embrace. "Shh, shh, love. Your plan was brilliant," he soothed, stroking her hair. "Your quick wits saved us, Mary."

"And killed three men in the process," she said through her tears. She might not have pulled the trigger, but she'd killed them all the same. There must be something terribly wrong with her because she couldn't bring herself to care.

"No, only two," he said.

Mary pulled back enough to look at him. "One is alive?"

"Yes, I hit his shoulder. He is bleeding badly and will die if he doesn't receive assistance soon. His injury has made him very biddable and he confessed that Elizabeth had hired him. I am *so* very sorry—"

"Please don't blame yourself," Mary begged.

"I will always blame myself for not taking her seriously. The only good news is that several of her henchmen have apparently decamped. This gent—named Lancaster—said Elizabeth started off with close to twenty men. They started fighting after they lost track of us. Lancaster says he doesn't think there are more than three or four left, aside from he and his two associates. We are not out of danger yet, of course, but at least the word is getting out who we really are." Miles kissed her deeply and then pulled away, leaving her dazed. "I cannot say that something good did not come out of all this."

Mary sniffed. "What?"

"I can't regret this time with you, Mary." He cupped her face and some emotion—could that actually be admiration?—blazed out of his eyes. "I'm afraid I'm going to have to violate one of our terms before we've even married, my love."

My love? Her mouth opened, but she couldn't find the words.

"I can't give you a marriage without love, Mary." His gaze flickered over her face and he gave her a rueful smile. "You are far too loveable for that."

"*Me?*"

He laughed. "Yes, *you*. Loveable and brave and valiant and brilliant."

"I—I don't know what to say."

Miles grinned. "I've robbed you of words. Let me just bask in this moment." He chuckled. "I'd love nothing more than to throw you onto that bed and stay in our little cabin away from the world until this mess is over, but we should get this fool to a doctor. Not only is he a valuable witness, but he said Elizabeth is intent on hiring more men. We need to get to safety before that can happen."

Chapter 36

They stopped at the Gilberts' house before leaving, but nobody answered the door and the buckboard and horse were gone from the barn.

"They will find our note—if the woman is a midwife, she'll be able to read," Miles assured her.

Mary hoped they found the note sooner, rather than later. As rainy as it had been, it was still warm. They'd dragged the two bodies out to the shed to await the arrival of constables, but they simply hadn't had the time to clean up the bloody mess they'd made of the cabin.

Their prisoner, Thomas Lancaster, was indeed in terrible condition and lost consciousness after they'd been riding only half an hour.

Miles, who'd been leading Lancaster's horse, managed to catch the man before he slid to the ground.

Once they'd stopped, Miles checked Lancaster's wound while Mary held him in the saddle.

Miles winced at whatever he saw beneath the bloody bandage. "He'll never make it to Reading. We'll have to stop at the first village, or even a posting inn or house—anywhere somebody might know where to find a doctor."

They ended up tearing Mary's petticoat into strips to bind Lancaster to his horse.

Once he was secured, Miles glanced up at the sky, which had darkened before they'd left the cottage, the clouds that had been fluffy only a few hours before were suddenly grim and gray. "This mist will turn to rain soon."

Soon turned out to be less than ten minutes, which is when the sky opened up and proceeded to dump it contents in buckets.

"I wish we could get out of the rain for a while," Miles said, rain sheeting off his hat onto his shoulders. "But Lancaster won't make it if we tarry."

The sound of wheels rumbled behind them and they both turned, Miles resting his hand on the pistol in his waistband.

A wagon with a single, white-bearded occupant approached, moving at a near glacial speed.

"Do you think he works for Miss Everton?" Mary asked, wiping the rain from her face.

"Keep your hand near your pistol," he ordered, jerking his chin toward the gun distorting Mary's coat pocket. "Be ready to use that if necessary."

Mary exhaled a shaky breath and nodded.

The old man regarded them with obvious interest—especially Lancaster's limp form—and slowed his nag to a stop.

"We have an injured man on this horse and could use your wagon to transport him."

"Injured, ye say?"

Rather than explain, Miles asked, "Do you know of any doctor nearby?"

"Aye, 'course. But the vicarage is closer."

"This man needs a doctor, not a vicar. At least not yet," Miles added under his breath.

"Vicar and his wife take in soldiers and know doctorin'," the old man insisted.

Miles nodded, slid from his mount, and handed the reins to Mary before going to Lancaster's motionless corpse. "How far is the vicarage?"

"Less than a mile."

"Thank God."

"Do you want help?" Mary asked.

"Just hold the reins for me, love."

"Ye need help, young man?" the driver asked as Miles untied the strips holding Lancaster onto his mount.

"No thank you, I can carry him," he said, putting words into deed a moment later when he hefted their captive's limp body into his arms and laid him out in the wagon, which only held a few fence posts. "He's not got long if he doesn't get care," he said to the old man.

"Aye, only ten minutes, even goin' slow and careful like."

Miles turned back to his mount and swung into the saddle.

"You riding on ahead?" the old man asked as he set his wagon in motion.

"No. We shall stay with you all the way," Miles said. "Behind you," he added under his breath.

The old man clucked his tongue and rolled off at a gentle pace.

Miles rode up alongside Mary. "I'm sorry I can't just tell you to go ahead, but I don't want us to separate."

"I understand."

"That's my girl." Even in the rain his words had the power to warm her. He gave her one of his brilliant smiles, although she couldn't help noticing that his face was a rather sickly gray.

"Is aught amiss, Miles?"

"No. Everything is fine. Don't worry, love," he said, his words sounding almost slurred.

She nodded but kept a close eye on him.

True to the old man's word, they encountered a tidy little cottage and attendant church ten minutes later.

As their cavalcade came to a stop the front door opened and a woman in the clothing of a domestic stood on the threshold.

"Fetch the vicar and his wife immediately," Miles called out, his voice breathless and reedy. "This man is gravely injured."

The woman disappeared inside without asking questions, clearly accustomed to sick or injured people turning up on her employer's doorstep.

"Miles?" Mary asked when she saw that he was listing to one side. "Is something wrong?"

"Wrong?" Miles swayed in the saddle, blinking owlishly as he tried to pull his foot from the stirrup. "Can't say I've ever not been able to get off my horse before." He gave a strange-sounding laugh. "I must admit I feel devilish col—damn!"

"Miles!" Mary shrieked as he slid to the ground.

She dismounted in a graceless scramble and ran to where Miles had fallen. "Come help me!" she yelled at the driver of the wagon, who was staring in open mouthed shock.

A man rushed from the house. "What happened?" he asked as he crouched beside Miles's body.

"I don't know! He just suddenly fell. It was the man in the wagon we brought to you. "But please—help this man first. He is the Earl of Avington and that injured man tried to kill us.

***

The first thing Miles noticed when he woke up was that he couldn't move his hands.

The second thing he noticed was that somebody was holding them.

He turned his head with a moan and looked directly into a now-familiar—but worried—pair of gorgeous green eyes. "Mary."

"Thank God!" She squeezed his hands until the left one hurt. And then she suddenly flushed and she bit her lip. "I beg your pardon, reverend," she said, bringing Miles's attention to the other person—no, two people—in the room.

"I think the good Lord will forgive you in this instance." The man smiled down at him. "I am Reverend Talbot and this is my wife. How are you feeling?"

"A bit knocked about but not all that bad, considering," Miles lied. "What about Lancaster—er, the other man?"

The vicar's expression turned grim. "He was not so fortunate."

Miles bit back the curse that leapt to his lips. "That was our only witness," he said.

"Fortunately, her ladyship mentioned that," the vicar said. "So, my wife took the gentleman's confession before I went to give him his last rites."

"Ah, that is good news." Miles's gaze slid to Mary when he realized what the vicar had called her—*wife*. "How long have I been lying here?"

"Only a few hours."

"You haven't sent any messengers?"

The vicar smiled slightly. "Based on what her ladyship told me—and what Lancaster confessed—I thought you would wish to, er, craft your own message."

"Indeed, I would, thank you."

"Our servant stands ready for your orders, my lord."

"It is possible there are more men after us. You may be in danger merely by association."

The vicar gave him a reassuring smile. "I have called in reinforcements, so to speak. Even as we speak there are six men guarding the house, five of them ex-army. Don't worry that I've told them the reason," he assured Miles hastily. "Only that somebody was menacing the two of you."

Miles's shoulders slumped with relief. "Thank you, sir."

"My pleasure."

"Who is your magistrate?"

"Sir Lawrence Peel, my lord. Unfortunately, he is gone to visit his daughter in the north and won't return until the end of the month."

"Well, that's inconvenient," Miles muttered.

"Lord Tilney has assumed his duties while he is away. As dire as this situation is, I daresay his lordship can be convinced to meet with you tonight, if we can get word to him quickly enough."

"Then we should send word to Tilney without delay. Will you be so kind as to bring me something to write with, sir?"

"Of course, my lord." He left the room.

Mrs. Talbot approached the bed. "Do you think you could take a bit of broth, my lord?"

It was the last thing Miles wanted but he could see from the militant glint in her eyes—not to mention Mary's firm expression—that argument would be futile.

"Thank you, ma'am, that would be perfect."

Once she'd gone, he turned to Mary. "I am sorry to have left you to manage matters without me."

She scowled at him. "I wish you'd told me that you'd been shot!"

He shrugged and then winced. "It was a scratch, Mary—it just grazed me and passed through. It seemed inconsequential at the time."

"Mrs. Talbot said you'd lost a great deal of blood and she had to give you *five* stitches." She pulled an anguished face. "How was I so stupid as to not see that? I just assumed all that blood all over you belonged to somebody else."

"Some of it did," he said mildly. "You are making entirely too much of the matter, Mary." He took her hands in his. "I am feeling as fit as a fiddle now that we are not slogging through the infernal rain." He plucked at the nightshirt he was wearing. "Is this the kind vicar's?"

She nodded. "Their maid is cleaning and repairing your clothing."

"Good. I shall be able to get up and dress once she returns it."

"No, you are staying in bed."

He smirked with an insouciance he was far from feeling. "Not unless you join me, darling."

Her cheeks reddened fetchingly and she glared at him. "You have been *shot*, my lord."

"Now why do I like it so much when you call me that, with such a stern, school mistress-like expression on your face?"

"Doubtless because you've knocked a screw loose in your head at some point."

He threw his head back and laughed, and then yelped at the stab of pain.

"It serves you right," she said.

"What a bedside manner you have, my dear."

"I never claimed to have any skill in the sickroom."

"That is fine, because I shan't be inhabiting one." When she looked ready to argue, he shook his head. "There will be time to rest once this is taken care of."

Her velvety eyebrows—a far lighter shade than the hairs on her head—drew down. "Surely you don't think Miss Everton would be mad enough to attack us while we take shelter here and have the protection of several guards?"

"I think she's unhinged enough to do anything that springs to mind. Once we set the law on her tail, she will be a cornered animal and they are the most dangerous. But it wasn't Elizabeth I was talking about."

"Then why must you get up so soon? Why can't you rest? What in the world could—"

"Is my coat near to hand, darling?"

Mary frown. "No, the maid has taken it along with your other clothing." She gestured to the small sitting area in front of the fire. "But she emptied the contents of all your pockets onto that salver."

"There should be an envelope, would you fetch it for me, please."

She narrowed her eyes at him but—muttering beneath her breath—went to the table.

When she returned a moment later, he could see that comprehension had dawned as she handed him the somewhat bedraggled parchment. "Is this what I think it is?"

"Yes, it is the special license."

"Whyever did you bring it along?"

"I'm ashamed to say that I'd forgotten it in the inside pocket of my driving coat. I only remembered it when Dotty fished it out." Miles took her hand. "My darling, will you marry me?"

She looked up from the license. "Are you thinking that getting married might protect us from Miss Everton?"

"I doubt that anything will stop her except a bullet or a noose."

Mary flinched from the cold look in his eyes.

"I'm sorry," he said. "That was unnecessary."

She thought he'd been surprisingly restrained, but she didn't want to stray from their discussion. "Why should we marry now?"

"We have less than a week and—given the vicissitudes of the last few days—it seems almost criminally foolish to wait when we are sitting in a vicarage with time on our hands."

"But what about the grand wedding everyone is planning?"

"I daresay my aunts have already put out the word that the festivities have been delayed. They can hardly welcome guests when there are search parties out looking for us—which is what Lancaster mentioned."

"I am truly an unnatural daughter!"

Miles laughed. "Why do you say that?"

"Because I haven't given any thought to what my mother must be thinking. Lord, poor mama! She will be beside herself."

"Well, you have had other—more pressing—matters to deal with," he reminded her, a gleam of humor in his eyes. "I will send a message to Avington Park as well—she will know the truth before too long." He delicately cleared his throat. "Securing your inheritance isn't the *only* reason I believe we should marry now."

"Yes, I take your meaning. Spending days on end together alone, while unmarried, will give people ideas."

"Ideas that are all justified, as it turns out."

She blushed and Miles decided that—next to being flushed with passion—was his favorite look on her.

"I suppose it is far easier to ask for forgiveness than to seek permission," she said.

"I couldn't agree more, my dear."

Her stern features suddenly shifted into an impish grin. "If I'd known this was the way to get out of a grand wedding ceremony, I would have instigated something similar myself."

He laughed and then grimaced at the pain in his side. "What do you say, darling? Will you make me the happiest man in England?"

"I would be delighted to marry you, Lord Avington."

Chapter 37

By *ton* standards the ceremony that occurred three hours later in the chapel was less than grand. As far as Mary was concerned, it was a perfect wedding and—with only the Talbots and a few servants in attendance—it was just the right size.

Miles had insisted that he would *not* be married from a bed like an invalid and, after much arguing with both his nurse and betrothed, he was finally allowed to get out of bed, dress, and stand during the ceremony.

The moment after he'd kissed the bride, Mrs. Talbot and Mary marched him to his room and put him back into bed.

Although he'd protested strenuously that he hadn't needed rest, he'd fallen into a sound sleep and hadn't woken until almost nine o'clock that night, shortly after the magistrate had arrived.

It was more than a little ironic that the magistrate had come almost directly from examining the wreckage of their carriage.

"We've got dozens of men combing the area looking for you two," Tilney had said, clearly befuddled by how they'd managed to evade detection. "Your cousin among them, my lady."

"My cousin?" Mary had repeated stupidly.

"Mr. Reginald Cooper was, apparently, on the way to your wedding when he heard the news. He was quite stricken and insisted on staying to help search for you."

It had been all Mary could do not to burst out laughing. She could just imagine Reginald's *stricken* expression.

It had been midnight by the time the Tilney finally left. He'd already sent messengers to consult with the sheriff and bring Elizabeth Everton in without delay.

One of the pieces of information Lancaster had confessed was that Everton had been directing her crew of ruffians from Reading, where she was staying in high style at the Mercure George Hotel, pretending to be an American on holiday while coordinating kidnapping, mayhem, and murder.

The brazenness of the woman was truly breathtaking.

"Not much of a wedding night for you, I'm afraid," Miles said, smiling at his bride of only a few hours. "A long session with a befuddled magistrate and a hurried wedding ceremony with only our host and hostess, six guards, a cook, a groom, and one housemaid for guests."

"It was perfect. I only shudder to think of what my mother will say. She has looked forward to this wedding more, I am sure, than she did her own."

"We can let her plan another house party to celebrate, how is that?"

"Must we?"

Miles laughed and held out a hand. "Come here."

"But Mrs. Talbot said you were not to exert yourself."

"I won't do anything strenuous."

Mary narrowed her eyes at him. "Why don't I believe you?"

He just grinned and gestured for her. "Come here. I will be good. I hate to admit it, but I'm feeling a bit too rotten to be naughty just now."

She clucked her tongue. "I told you that you should have stayed in bed earlier."

"Mmm, I adore it when you scold me."

Mary rolled her eyes and took his hand, allowing him to draw her down on the bed beside him.

"There. That is better," he said, staring at her with a look that made her entire body flush with heat.

"Miles?"

"Hmm?" he said, examining her fingers and then kissing the tip of each one in a way that wasn't helping her follow Mrs. Talbot's orders.

"I know the subject probably isn't a favorite with you, but could you tell me a little about your time in the army?"

His eyebrows lifted and a wary expression settled on his face. "What do you want to know?"

"The scars you bear… they are extreme, are they not?"

"Some are." He held up his mangled hand. "This is from the soldiers who captured me and three others and spent several days torturing us to get information."

Mary stared at the round scars—so many, like the ones on his chest. "Did you give them the information they wanted?"

"No, but not because we were brave. We didn't tell them what they wanted to know because we simply didn't have the answers.

Anyone who claims they would not capitulate under torture is lying to themselves. The French soldiers who worked on us killed three of my compatriots trying to get what they wanted. They'd just started on me, and probably would have killed me, as well, when Simon—the Marquess of Saybrook—came blazing into the house where they were holding us and single-handedly killed the lot of them." He gave her a twisted smile. "I'm afraid I wasn't as grateful to him as I should have been."

"Good Lord! Why not?"

"It was his job to take crucial information back to our superiors. We'd done everything in our power to make sure he got away. Indeed, it was the reason we were captured. If *he* had been captured thousands might have died because he *did* have the information they wanted." He chewed on the inside of his mouth for a moment. "I was angry with him at the time, but after I was released from the field hospital, I realized I'd become a great deal like him."

"What do you mean?"

"Part of the reason Simon carried out that suicidal rescue plan was because he had stopped caring about anything. And a man who doesn't care about anything—including himself—is dangerous." He sighed. "I understood that I'd become what people called a loose cannon—careless and full of rage and frustration—so I sold out not long afterward and came home."

"And yet—" she bit her lip.

"And yet?"

"You seem so… happy," she marveled. "I've never met anyone else who emanates such contentment and joy."

"I wasn't this way for the first two years. Not until I'd been at the Stefani Academy—and made friends with women who'd undergone their own horrible ordeals and came out unbroken—did I count my blessings." He shrugged and met her gaze with an almost shy look. "I am grateful you didn't know me then, Mary. I was a bitter, unhappy man for a long time. I desperately wanted to return home—to Avington Park—but all I could think about when I was there was Pansy and how she'd died because of me."

"You couldn't have known what Elizabeth Everton would do."

"No, I couldn't have. I know that her death wasn't my fault… now. But back then, I was angry and in pain and so very, very bitter. Not until I met Portia and all the other teachers did I begin to let that anger go and start to value life again." He squeezed Mary's hand and then lifted it to his mouth. "And not until I met you did I discover that my heart wasn't broken, just scarred, and that it was possible not only to love again, but that it would be a deeper, more sophisticated love than I felt as a young man."

Mary bit her lower lip to keep from sobbing at his declaration. How had she been so fortunate as to find this man?

"Don't cry, darling. Come here," he said, pulling her close.

"But your side! I don't want to hurt you."

"You won't. Come and lie against me, my love."

Mary burrowed her head into his uninjured side, unable to meet his open, honest blue gaze. "It frightens me that I love you so much already, Miles. After Reginald, I swore I'd never trust anyone—I thought I *couldn't* trust anyone. But you are—" she broke off and swallowed several times before she could finish. "You are a gift to me. An unexpected gift."

His arm tightened around her and she felt his lips on her head, but then he tilted her face up, until she was forced to look at him and let him see her tear-stained face. "I'm so honored, darling. I will do everything in my power to deserve your love." He kissed her lightly on the lips.

"I must look a fright," she said in a husky voice when he pulled away.

"Yes, you do."

Mary laughed. "Why do you look glorious, even wounded?"

"Well, I've been wounded more often, so I've had more practice looking glorious."

As Mary laughed again, she realized that she'd laughed more in Miles's company these last few days—even on the run for their lives—than she had in years.

Miles wasn't only her lover; he'd become her friend—her *best* friend.

Could there be anything lovelier than spending one's life with one's best friend?

If there was, Mary couldn't think of it just then.

***

"Are you sure you wish to leave so soon?" Reverend Talbot asked them for the second or third time that morning.

305

"Our families will be beside themselves," Miles said, smiling at the warm, kindly man and his wife before climbing into the humble gig that awaited them.

"I do wish you would have agreed to use our carriage, my lord," Mrs. Talbot said. "At least to take you as far as Reading."

"You've already done enough for us and we positively refuse to impose any further. Thank you for allowing us to use your gig. I will have a servant at the Crown and Scepter drive it back to you," he said, settling beside Mary. "We'll never be able to thank you enough for everything you've done."

"You can thank us by getting home safely," the vicar said.

Miles took the reins and he and Mary waved as Miles guided the old but frisky horse onto the road. Although the day had dawned almost shockingly clear and sunny the road was still a mucky mess from the last few days of rain.

"What do you think will happen to her?" Mary asked.

Miles didn't need to ask who she meant. They'd received a message from the magistrate not long after dawn, assuring them that Elizabeth Everton had been taken into custody and that all but four of the men she'd hired had surrendered themselves. Those who were still at large, had fled the area.

"I don't know what they will do with her," Miles admitted.

"But you don't wish to pursue criminal proceedings against her, do you?"

Miles couldn't tell from her neutral expression what she thought about that. "Do you think we should?"

Mary being Mary, she gave the question the consideration it deserved before saying, "If what you believe about Pansy is true, then she has murdered once and tried to do so again. Indeed, those men who died in her service are proof of her… mania. I think the furor surrounding such a case would be dreadful and I would hate it for my sake as well as our family's. But that's not the entire reason that I'd hate to see her go to trial"

"What is?"

"I don't believe in hanging for anyone, but especially not for people who are not in possession of their faculties. I truly think she must be mad to have done all of this."

Miles thought about the cold, acquisitive expression in Elizabeth's eyes the last time he'd talked to her. "I don't know if she is mad," he admitted. "I spent very little time with her when we were betrothed. I think her father must have realized her nature and purposely kept our interactions brief to hide whatever is wrong with her. With his death she no longer had anyone to curb her."

"Do you think she had something to do with her father's death?"

"I would hate to think such a thing, but there is—"

The sound of horses—several—came from behind them.

Miles tried to twist around to look but gasped as pain shot from his side.

"What is it?" he demanded when Mary turned.

"A carriage—a private carriage, not a mail coach, but—"

"Yes?" he prodded, his hands tightening on the reins.

"Oh, wait! I recognize the carriage—it is Reginald's. The postilion is motioning us to stop," she said.

Miles eased their horse onto the grassy verge as the coach drew up beside them. He glanced over at the liveried servant who was sitting on the box and frowned as he stared at the man's face, which was black and blue, with one eye swollen shut.

And he looked familiar…

"Miles!" Mary shrieked.

Time seemed to slow as the servant on the box lifted a pistol, aiming not at Mary, but at Miles.

Elizabeth wants me dead, after all! was the thought that raced through Miles's startled brain as Mary yanked him to the side, exhibiting astounding strength for such a small person.

And then—for some odd reason—she raised her arm.

The *crack* of a pistol shattered the quiet morning air and their gig horse bolted.

Miles pulled on the reins with all his strength, but the horse had the bit and wasn't stopping. He put all his weight into pulling, but the horse's eyes were wide with terror.

"Hang on, Mary," he shouted as they rounded a corner and came face to face with a massive, lumbering dray pulled by an equally massive pair of Clydesdales.

Their maddened carthorse had enough presence of mind to avoid a head on collision and galloped off the road, straight down into a ditch without even slowing.

Miles dropped the useless reins, wrapped one arm around Mary, and grabbed the seat rail behind them just as their gig hit either a rock or a stump that stopped them cold. If Miles hadn't been holding onto the rail they would have bounced right out of the small cart and onto the horse.

The horse reared and jerked in its harness but the gig refused to budge.

Up on the road the screams of men and horses filled the air, along with the sickening *crunch* of two large wooden objects colliding.

Mary squirmed, which made Miles realize that he'd been squeezing her tightly. He also realized his wife had a *pistol* in her hand.

"Where in the world did you get *that?*" he demanded. "Not that I'm not grateful."

She stared up at him with tear-stained cheeks, her expression grim. "I shot him, Miles."

"I know. And you saved my life in the process. I didn't even realize you had the gun. I thought it was in the cloth bag Mrs. Talbot gave us."

Mary didn't seem to hear him, and her words poured out of her in a frantic rush. "I knew it wasn't over. I just knew it. I felt a heavy sort of dread all morning, even after that message from the magistrate. But I never, ever thought it would be Reginald." She swallowed convulsively and dropped the pistol onto the floorboards with a clatter. "Oh, God, Miles!" She flung herself into his arms and he held her, biting his lip to keep from making unmanly whimpers at the pain in his side.

"Shh, darling," he murmured, stroking her trembling back and shoulders. "It will be fine now." He gave a breathless, pained laugh. "Unless you can think of somebody else who might want to kill one or both of us?"

She gave a watery chuckle as she pulled away. "I suppose we should go and see if anyone needs help."

Based on the keening of animals in pain and the amount of wreckage visible even from where they sat, he knew there would be more ugliness ahead. "Why don't you wait here, sweetheart?"

She grabbed onto him—thankfully only his upper arm this time. "I'm not letting you out of my sight, Miles." She bent down and picked up the pistol which had fallen at his feet. "And before we go help, I want to reload this."

***

By the time Miles had reloaded the pistol, another wagon—driven by a farmer and his teenaged son—had stopped to render aid.

They blinked in surprise when they saw Mary and Miles appear from the ditch.

"Blimey! Any other carriages down there?" the man asked, having to shout to be heard over the moaning of men and horses.

"No," Miles said abruptly, his eyes on what was left of Reginald's coach, which had been the loser in the collision with the dray.

The farmer nodded to the pistol in Miles's hand. "Could you put those poor beasts out of their misery?" He gestured to two horses still attached to Reginald's coach, which was hardly recognizable.

"I'll take care of it once I've looked inside the coach. Stay behind me, Mary," he ordered when she began to walk toward the carriage.

"Good God, Miles—look!" Mary pointed to a pair of legs, sheathed in livery, that were beneath the crushed coach.

"Is anyone in there?" Miles called out.

A faint moaning met his question—and it sounded like a female.

"Cooper!" Miles shouted. "Open the door if you are inside. I'm armed and there are witnesses, so don't try anything foolish."

But the only response was more moaning.

When Miles reached for the door, Mary grabbed his arm. "What if it is a trick?"

"I don't think whoever is in here is in any shape to be pulling tricks."

Mary swallowed and nodded.

He needed to enlist the help of the farmer to reach the door and when he opened it, Mary saw him grimace.

"What is it?" she asked, even though she wasn't sure she wanted to hear the answer.

"It's not Cooper," he said, pity and revulsion mingling on his handsome face as he turned from the carriage to Mary. "It is Mrs. Cooper." He turned to the farmer. "I'll need your help to lift her out. She won't be moving on her own."

Chapter 38

Mary and Miles found themselves right back where they'd started only an hour earlier: at Reverend Talbot's vicarage. The expression on the Talbots' faces would have been amusing had the circumstances not been so tragic.

With the help of the kind farmer, they transported Joan Cooper and the driver of the dray—the only two survivors—back to the vicarage.

While the driver came out of the accident with a broken arm and a bad gouge on one leg, Joan Cooper's chest was crushed so badly it was a wonder she could breathe.

Mary and Miles paced the vicarage library while they waited for word about her condition from Mrs. Talbot. The vicar had sent for a doctor immediately, but Miles knew the man would not come soon enough; Joan Cooper did not have long to live.

The magistrate showed up with two armed men in response to the vicar's message.

The poor man had expected to find more of Elizabeth Everton's henchmen the cause of the carnage.

It took Miles almost an hour to explain this new threat and convince Tilney that he didn't need to leave an armed guard.

"But what about the husband?" Tilney asked, drinking his second glass of sherry even though it wasn't even noon. "Surely he is behind all this?" He looked pained and set down his glass. "I am so very confused. You say you shot the man—one of their footmen—because he was one of the two assailants who tried to capture you at the Blount fete?"

Miles nodded. "Yes, we recognized him when Mrs. Cooper's carriage pulled alongside us. He had a pistol leveled at me and was close enough not to miss had my wife not shoved me aside and shot him first."

Lord Tilney gave Mary an apprehensive look, as if he expected her to pull a weapon on *him*.

Miles squeezed his wife's hand. "She saved my life."

Before the magistrate could comment the door opened and Mrs. Talbot entered, her expression bleak as she looked at Mary and Miles. "She wants to talk to you."

When the magistrate stood along with them, she shook her head. "I'm sorry, sir, but she only wishes to speak with the earl and countess."

He blustered. "The woman is accused of conspiracy to commit murder by God! She doesn't get a say in who she will or will not speak to."

"She has already confessed everything to me, sir. I wrote it down and she signed it. I'm afraid she doesn't have much longer. Please let her speak to her family. Here is Mrs. Cooper's confession." She handed the magistrate the sheets of foolscap.

Tilney scowled but finally nodded and poured himself a third sherry before settling down to read.

Miles and Mary followed Mrs. Talbot from the room.

"She can barely speak," the vicar's wife explained as she led them up the stairs, taking them to the same sickroom Miles had occupied only the night before. "I've told her that talking is hastening the end, but… well, she is most adamant about speaking to you—both of you."

"And the driver of the dray?" Mary asked.

"He will be fine." She paused in front the bedroom door. "My husband is inside sitting with her. We will both wait right here while you speak to her."

"Er, are we interrupting his work?" Miles asked.

"She has rejected his offer of last rites." She sounded sad, but not especially surprised. And then she squinted at Miles and clucked her tongue. "My Lord, is that blood I see on your coat?"

Mary gasped. "Miles! Why didn't you say you were bleeding?" she demanded, glaring at him in a way that probably sent her shipyard and mine employees running for cover.

"It's just a torn stitch, sweetheart." He looked at Mrs. Talbot. "I'll come to you the moment we are done talking to Mrs. Cooper."

Mary scowled at him. "Yes, he will."

"We'd better go and talk to her sweetheart. Are you ready?"

Mary swallowed; her pugnacious expression replaced by dread. "I'm as ready as I'll ever be."

***

The vicar stood when they entered the room and came toward them. "She is fading fast. Please hurry so that I can be with her at the end—I hope she will change her mind and ask for forgiveness."

Mary and Miles nodded and he left them alone.

Joan began to talk even before the door shut behind the vicar. "Reg—nald nothing to do with this," she said in a horrible, croaking voice. "All me."

"Why, Joan? Why would you try to kill me?" Mary asked.

The other woman's eyes sparked with a fierce venom that surprised her; she might be dying, but she still had plenty of hatred inside her. "Y—you never deserve everything—Jealous of Reginald," she hissed. "Still want him."

"Oh, Joan. I've not wanted him for over a decade." She shook her head as a wave of sadness swamped her. "His lordship and I married last night, Joan. Even if you'd managed to kill me, nothing would have gone to you and Reginald. He put you up to this for nothing. Don't protect him with your silen—"

"No!" Joan pushed up off the bed and blood oozed from her lips. "*Not him! Only me!*" The last word was scarcely a gurgle and she collapsed in a fit of coughing.

Mary got up from her chair and held the other woman's rapidly fading gaze as she took her hand and murmured. "Shhh, don't try to talk, Joan."

"We need you, Reverend," Miles said as he opened the door.

Joan's hand tightened hard enough to make Mary's bones creak. "What?" Mary asked. "Do you want the vicar?"

"Reg innocent," she wheezed and then her eyes rolled back in her head and her body began to convulse.

"Come away, darling," Miles murmured, leading her away as the vicar took Mary's place beside the bed.

He shut the door and they turned to find Mrs. Talbot waiting.

"She confessed to you?" the woman guessed.

Mary nodded dumbly.

"She was adamant that her husband had no part in it," Mrs. Talbot said. "Do you believe her?"

Mary looked up and met Miles's worried blue gaze. "I don't know. What do you think?"

"I find it hard to believe that she did it alone," Miles said. "Not because she isn't capable of it, but because it would have been difficult to pull off without him getting *some* hint as to what she was doing. He might not have helped her, but I think he'd be a fool if he didn't guess." He glanced at Mrs. Talbot. "I don't suppose she mentioned what she was doing on this road alone?"

"She said that she and her husband had been headed to Avington Castle when they learned of your carriage accident. Mr. Cooper stayed with the searchers to look for you and sent her on to Reading to take a room at a hotel and wait for him."

Miles snorted softly. "Let me guess—the Mercator George Hotel?"

Mrs. Talbot nodded. "That is how she learned what Miss Everton had been up to. When she discovered the two of you were staying at the vicarage, she decided to overtake you on the road. The fact that there were still some men at large would have helped divert suspicion from her." She pursed her lips and added, "She did not know that you'd married until I told her."

Miles turned to Mary. "I don't know if Cooper was behind this or just suspected, but I think we should tell the magistrate everything and let him put the fear of God and the English judicial system into Cooper in case he has something else planned."

Mary nodded, even though she truly did not believe they were in danger any longer.

That morning she'd woken with the strongest, sickest feeling of dread. She hadn't known what she was afraid of, but that premonition was the reason she'd hidden the loaded pistol on her lap. She had just *known* that she'd need it.

But now the panic and fear were gone. Now all she felt was a weary sadness about Joan; what a waste her greed had been. Reginald might not be as wealthy as Mary, but he had plenty of money—certainly enough that his wife shouldn't have needed to become a murderer.

Mary looked at the man beside her and a sense of disbelief and wonder replaced her earlier fear. She was married to one of the most beautiful, gentle, and kind men in Britain and she loved him madly. Nor did she question his love, which shone out of his magnificent eyes whenever he looked at her.

Miles loved her just the way she was, plain, scarred, Mary Barnett.

He smiled at her and the expression was subtly different from all his other smiles. This one was only for her. "What is it, my love?"

Mary shook her head. Would there ever come a day when the realization that he loved her wouldn't leave her breathless with gratitude?

Mary hoped not. Because love was something worth being grateful for each and every day.

"It's nothing."

"Why don't you go and have a lie down while I talk to the magistrate and—"

Mrs. Talbot cleared her throat. "My lord?"

"Yes, Mrs. Talbot?"

"I think it is *you* who should have a bit of a *lie* down."

Mary snapped out of her love-induced daze and forced herself to shoot him a stern frown. "Yes, that is an excellent idea, Mrs. Talbot. Miles," she said glaring up at him. "You will follow Mrs. Talbot and allow her to stitch you up. And then—unlike the last time she took a needle and thread to you—you will *rest.* The Talbots have generously offered us a lovely place to stay, so we can wait a few days before we return to Avington Castle."

His eyebrows shot up. "But—"

"I think I'll have to insist this time."

Miles looked from Mary to the older woman, who was giving him a glare that Mary could only aspire to.

"But darling, I can do that after—"

"A-hem." Mary narrowed her eyes.

A faint smile played around his lips, which were paler than usual, probably from pain or a loss of blood, or both. "Of course, my dear."

Mary was startled by his sudden docility.

And then he leaned close and whispered. "I'll obey you on this matter, darling. But later—when we are alone and in bed—well, that's going to be another matter entirely."

And then he *licked* her ear.

Mary stood frozen and flushed as he winked at her and then sauntered after Mrs. Talbot wearing an expression so innocent, he looked as if butter wouldn't melt in his mouth.

She waited until he'd disappeared down the corridor and then allowed the huge grin she'd been suppressing to spread across her face as she headed toward the stairs.

Life—she thought with a joyous, almost guilty, chuckle—would never, ever be boring with a man like Miles.

Mary cut a brief glance ceilingward and whispered, "Thank you, Da!"

Her father, it seemed, had been right all along: Mary had been born for love.

Epilogue

Three Long, Wretched, Agonizing Weeks Later

Miles looked out over the ballroom at Avington Castle—a room that hadn't hosted such a magnificent event in years—and smiled down at his wife as they waltzed for the second time in one night.

"How are you holding up, sweetheart?" he asked.

Mary smiled up at him, the expression coming easier to her rather serious face with every day that passed. "I'm enjoying myself." She sounded so amazed that he couldn't help but chuckle.

"You've certainly had a full dance card."

Indeed, she'd danced each and every set.

At first Miles had worried that she was only doing it to please him, but Freddie had assured him that Mary had been the one to insist on ending her moratorium.

"It is obvious the two of you are *very* happy together," Freddie had said, blushing a little at her own audacity. "I think that has made all the difference in the world to Mary's attitude toward dancing."

"And what of your attitude?" Miles had teased. "I saw you dancing with the Duke of Plimpton earlier. I thought he was still in mourning."

Freddie's normally placid features had shifted into something that was almost a scowl. "He made an exception for me."

And that was all she'd say on the matter. Miles had his suspicions about his friend, but he was not going to start prying now. With Lori as her roommate, poor Freddie wouldn't be allowed to preserve her silence. At least not for long.

"Are you sure you don't mind removing to Bristol right after the ball?" Mary asked as Miles guided her past Gareth and Serena. Gareth was counting his steps with mathematical precision while his wife smiled with indulgent affection.

"Ah, is *that* what has been worrying you these past few days?" Miles asked. "I've seen that little notch that forms between your eyes, so don't fib."

"I'm not worried, exactly, but I feel... guilty. We've only just come home and now I'm dragging you off."

Miles liked the way she already said *home* like she meant it.

"It isn't much of a distance to ride and I can come back if needed. Besides, with Reginald selling off all his shares you need to make sure the transfer runs smoothly."

Cooper had insisted he'd never been aware of his wife's plans. Whether he had or not, Miles and Mary would probably never know. The man was clearly shaken by his wife's death and it had been his idea to sell out all his interests in Mary's companies. Afterward he was moving to France, where Mary said he already owned two small shipyards.

Miles was relieved the man was leaving the country and could only hope he'd never return.

As for Elizabeth Everton? Her sanity had taken a dramatic tumble when the executors of her father's estate had discovered what she'd been up to. Miles and Mary had agreed to forgo pursuing charges against her as long as her trustees took her into their custody and returned to Boston with her—and *kept* her there, this time.

The possibility that she'd engineered the death of her own father—not to mention that their negligent supervision had nearly cost Miles and Mary their lives—had made the trustees eager to comply when their lawyers had demanded financial restitution for the danger and suffering the woman's behavior had inflicted.

Miles didn't want to tell Pansy's parents what had happened so long ago—sharing his suspicions about Elizabeth would do nothing except unearth old, buried pain—but thanks to Mary he'd found a way to shore up the impoverished Wargrave dukedom with solid investment advice and had bolstered the duke's returns with careful infusions of restitution money.

Money could never make up for the loss of their daughter, but then nothing could.

They sent a sizeable reward to the Gilberts to thank them for their selfless help in housing them when they were in need.

They also sent Mr. Ross—Mary's inquiry agent—to deliver another gift of money to Dotty and ensure that she'd taken no harm from Gerald for helping them escape.

By the time Ross had visited their farm the newspapers had already been full of Miles and Mary's story and Gerald knew his wife had saved him from a far worse fate than the bump on the head she'd given him.

All in all, matters had been tidied up quite nicely.

"So you really don't mind going with me to Bristol for a few weeks?" Mary asked.

Miles stared down at his titian haired, emerald eyed siren and smiled. "Darling, I'd go anywhere with you." He whirled her around, employing one of the special flourishes he reserved only for her, now.

Mary giggled—yes, she really did. "Oh, I think my feet left the ground for a moment." Her giddy smile turned serious in an instant. "But you must be careful, Miles! Your side—you'll pull that wound open again. You really shouldn't exert yourself."

Miles just laughed. "Oh, my sweet, dear Mary. You have no idea how much I plan on exerting myself before this night is over."

***

Miles shut and locked the door to the master's chambers, whipped around, and leaned against the smooth slab of wood as he studied his wife.

"What is it Miles?" Mary asked, looking more than a little bit nervous. "Why are you staring at me like that?"

He stalked toward her. "Like what, darling?"

"Erm, like you are *hungry*."

"Because I *am* hungry, you little termagant. Three. Long. Miserable weeks you've made me suffer and wait." He began to unbutton his tailcoat, which fit him like a second skin.

"What are you doing? We need to go back to the—"

"It's midnight, darling. And we are a couple on our long-delayed bridal holiday. Our guests know exactly where we've gone and what we are shortly going to be doing." He struggled out of his coat as if he were wrestling with a panther and then flung it to the ground.

"Miles, that will get wrink—"

He growled, his hands already at the buttons on his waistcoat.

Mary backed toward the huge bed—a bed she'd not slept in yet. Something for which she was, entirely, at fault.

"Are you sure you feel well enough to—"

He flung aside his waistcoat and yanked on his cravat. "Don't. Even. Try. It."

Mary squeaked as he pinned her against the bed, pressing evidence of his desire against her belly as he yanked his shirt from his skintight black satin knee breeches and tossed it to join the rest of his clothing.

Mary swallowed as she looked at his battered, exquisite body, her eyes immediately dropping to the latest of the injuries he'd been made to endure.

"See?" he said, pointing to the wound which had closed nicely but was still bruised and red around the scar. "I am utterly and completely fine." He narrowed his eyes at her and ground his erection against her harder. "I've *been* fine for weeks and yet you've kept that connecting door locked."

Mary glanced at the door in question and then goggled. "Er, what happened to the door, Miles?"

He grinned and the carnivorous expression sent flares of heat shooting to her already aroused sex. "I removed it."

"I can see that. Er, you didn't need to do that. I would have unlocked it and—"

"From now on, we shall be sharing a room and you will be sleeping with me in my bed. Every. Night."

"Oh. But I thought—"

"I know what you thought—that all aristocrats kept to their own wings of the house and didn't visit one another except for the purposes of procreation on a biannual basis."

"Well, er—"

"I want your sweet little body next to mine every single night of my life, Mary, whether we engage in *carnal* activities or not."

"Oh, I do like—"

He leaned down and claimed her mouth with a kiss that shot all the way to her knees. When they threatened to buckle, he scooped her up as easily as a doll and laid her out on the bed.

Mary blinked up at him. "But... I'm still dressed."

"So you are," he said, climbing up onto the bed. "Lift your skirt, darling."

"But can't I even—"

"No." He didn't wait for her to move. Instead, he grabbed two handfuls of her beautiful rose silk gown—the loveliest gown she'd ever owned—and pushed it up to her hips along with the gossamer thin petticoat she wore beneath it.

The noise he made when he looked at her naked hips and thighs was obscene.

"Might I remove my slippe—"

"No."

He made an actual growling noise and then he shoved her stocking clad legs wide and buried his face between her thighs.

And Mary stopped arguing.

Sometime Later...

Mary heaved a sigh of utter and complete contentment. "Mmm, that was nice."

"Nice?" Miles's head popped up between Mary's sprawled legs. "*Nice?*" he repeated in an affronted tone that made his deliciously, wantonly splayed wife laugh.

"Find that amusing, do you?" he muttered, and then lowered his mouth.

Her fingers—which were remarkably strong for such slight, slender digits—sank into his hair. "I can't, Miles. I just... can*arrghhh*," she groaned, her hips lifting in a way that told Miles in no uncertain terms that she very much *could*.

His new hobby—he decided as he made his normally proud, stern, serious wife writhe and beg and sigh—was seeing just how many times he could make her orgasm in one evening.

As hobbies went, it was both economical and highly addictive.

He tormented her with his tongue until she threatened to pull chunks from his scalp.

If there was one thing in life that he'd become quite good at over the years—other than dancing—it was pleasuring a woman. But never before had he enjoyed it as much as he did with his wife.

Miles wondered, as she began to buck and grind hard enough to squash his nose, if he enjoyed making love to her so much because she *was* his wife—his, and only his, forever—or because she was such an exclusive, reserved, and difficult to know person.

Only one man in the world would ever see this side of her—this passionate, brilliant woman who gave every ounce of herself to him, holding nothing back.

Speaking of holding nothing back...

Miles pushed two fingers deep into her sheath as she began to tremble, her body tightening with her impending climax.

"Come again for me, Mary," he ordered in a raspy voice, his hips grinding into the counterpane—where he'd already ejaculated once, much to his mortified amusement. "Come for your husband like the good girl you are."

They were magic words and Miles couldn't help grinning. He adored the fact that his oh-so-severe wife liked nothing more than to be his wanton plaything when they were in bed together.

Miles savored her powerful contractions until they began to wane and then pushed up to his knees and stared down at her, gloating in a way he knew both aroused and irked her.

She cut him a sulky but sated look as he slid his hands beneath her luscious arse and entered her with a powerful thrust that made her cry out his name in exactly the loud, needy tone he adored.

Miles stared down at where they were joined. "You have no idea how beautiful you look taking me," he said, withdrawing so slowly it almost drove him mad, his ruddy shaft wet with her body's juices and so damned hard he ached to the soles of his feet with his need.

"That's a pretty frock you're wearing darling," he said in a breathy voice, slamming in deep, until his aching balls slapped against her sex. "Why don't you pull it down and show me those delectable titties you've been hiding from your lord and master for three long weeks."

Her eyes widened with shock and desire, her fingers shaking as they moved to her bodice.

Miles withdrew slowly, nodding his approval as she tugged down on the delicate silk.

"Yes, that's good," he urged, needing to exert every last bit of control to keep from riding her until they both screamed. "Show me, Mary. Show me those pretty nipples I've been fantasizing about sucking... licking."

Her inner muscles tightened around him and they both moaned at the exquisite constriction.

"So good," he rasped, reluctantly releasing her soft, fleshy cheeks and dropping to his hands, caging her body beneath his, and fucking into her hard, thrusting into her at an angle that grazed her already overstimulated bundle of nerves with each powerful stroke.

"Miles," she whimpered, her hands jerking and tearing the silk, exposing the snowy half-moons of flesh. She wore stays on her slim body and they'd pushed the small pillows high and proud, her nipples already diamond hard when he sucked one into his mouth.

Miles lost himself then, drumming into her so hard the heavy oak bed slammed against the wall.

He couldn't help laughing at the racket they must be making, and when Mary arched up against him a moment later and cried out her passion, Miles drove himself deep and let go.

***

Mary slipped out from beneath Miles's deliciously sweaty, heavenly body and quickly and clumsily toed off her slippers, yanked off her garters and stockings, and completed the destruction of her favorite, and now ruined, gown.

"Mmm, why didn't you wake me so I could admire the show?" Miles demanded as he propped his head on his hand, the very image of a debauched god.

Mary smirked. "I thought you deserved a rest after that enthusiastic performance." No matter how comfortable she'd become with his teasing and often risqué banter, she felt her face heat and knew her wretched skin would give her away.

His grin confirmed her suspicious. "Oh, darling. I hope you never stop blushing for me."

Mary fumbled with the laces on her corset, which was a pale pink to match her gown.

"Come here. You're making a muddle of that," he ordered.

"Yes, because we both know you are far more skilled when it comes to removing ladies' undergarments," Mary shot back, but turned her back to the bed.

Rather than loosening the laces his warm strong hands slid around her, one hand cupping a breast while his other hand dipped between the swollen lips of her sex.

"Mmm, feel how wet you are." He caressed her far too sensitive bud with the rough pad of a finger, the sound of their mingled juices making a mortifying noise in the quiet room.

Mary loved it. She more than loved it—she *craved* this perfect, gorgeous man who could look like a god one minute and speak as crudely as a coal miner the next.

"Did I use you too roughly?" he asked, his breath hot against her neck.

Mary sighed, spread her feet, and let her head fall back as she luxuriated beneath his magical hands.

"Hmm?" he teased, his rhythmic finger already making her forget all about removing her corset. "Did I?"

"I liked it."

His arms tightened and his finger slid inside her. "What's that, darling? I couldn't hear you?"

"I said I liked it." She gulped. "A lot."

He buried his face in her neck and sucked and licked until she knew there would be a mark on her sweaty skin. "You must tell me if I ever do anything you don't care for."

Mary didn't think that was possible but nodded.

"I find that I'm insatiable for you, Mary. I'd keep you in bed with me all day and night if I had my way, so you'll need to make sure and tell me when you've had enough of me."

She didn't think *that* was possible, either, but nodded.

He spun her around, his eyes boring into her. "Are you happy?"

The question stunned her. "Happy? Of course, I am, Miles. Can't you tell?"

He nodded slowly, his expression serious. "I want you to remember that next Season when you're cursing my name as Freddie and I force you to go to one dratted party or ball after another. I especially want you to remember how happy we are when you put on your hideously old-fashioned court gown and spend two entire weeks learning how to curtsy. You will curse my name and hate me then."

Mary smiled. "Probably."

"But at the end of next Season you will have given your sister everything you married me for and you won't ever need to exert yourself like that again. Although you'll always have to make an appearance at tiresome functions and—"

"Miles." Mary took his face in both hands and looked hard into his gorgeous eyes, catching a glimpse of that part of himself he did such an excellent job hiding—not only from the world, but from her, too.

"Yes, darling?" he asked, the shadows in his gaze already fading.

"I lied to myself for so long—telling myself I was only marrying you to satisfy that will. *You* are worth marrying for yourself. Even if Jenny never receives a single invitation to one wretched *ton* party." She smiled and ran a thumb over his plush, sensual lower lip. "And I want to have your children—several of them, not just because of our silly terms, but because I want a family with you. And I want you to learn as much or as little about my family's businesses as you like, whether it's to satisfy my father's will or because you genuinely enjoy it." Mary stared into his eyes, struggling to find the right words to express just how much he already meant to her.

"I've never been good with words or feelings, Miles. But I'm going to show you every single day how much I love you."

"I love you too, darling."

"I have something to show you," she said, her cheeks doing their best to betray her.

He grinned. "Judging by the color of your face, this is something I'm going to like a great deal, isn't it?"

Mary laughed, shoved him onto his back, and then climbed up on the bed.

"Is this one of those things you just mentioned, Mary? That you are going to show me every—*ah*! Mary! Wherever did you learn such a—*oh*, darling…"

And those were the last words of any sense to come out of Mary's beautiful husband's mouth for quite a while.

The End

Dearest Reader:

Look at this! I made it through 2022 with most of my mental faculties still intact!

I hope you loved Mary and Miles as much as I loved writing their story.

I was startled to realize the original book was one I started back in 2018. Because I never take notes or write outlines—or do any of those things which would help me immeasurably down the road—I had no idea where I was going with this story when I picked it up again. I had about 200 pages written and I ended up just scrapping all but the first few chapters and starting over.

Sometimes, I just can't remember what I was thinking when I start a book and it really is easier to just begin again.

Because I think of this series as my "gothic romances" I knew I needed a mystery. But I'd already begun the book in London, so I just couldn't think of a way to jam in a second location—the fascinating Avington Castle. That's how it ended up being a "road trip" book, which I have to admit I just love.

There is something about the "anything can happen" nature of road trips that makes writing fresh and fun again. And I also love the tightly compressed timeline such stories require.

Okay, okay! I know what you're thinking... Mary is SOOOO PRICKLY. At least that is what my husband (my beta reader) said when he read the book. Even I occasionally found myself thinking, "You must chill, Mary." But when I write I find myself sinking into my characters and the more time I spent in Mary's head the more I was forced to accept that she had EXCELLENT reasons for being such a difficult person.

Can you imagine needing to marry in order to pursue your career? Or so that you can retain money you've already earned? And then to be forced to marry an aristocrat, when they had treated you so dismissively the only time you'd been among them?

Mary's scars go very, very deep. She not only has visible burns, but she's been badly betrayed by a man she once loved.

Anyhow, the more I thought about it, the more I believed that she had every right to be furious and try to protect herself from more harm. And so her "preemptive strike" against Miles (no matter how sweet he is) seemed like a rational response for a woman who is terribly afraid of getting crushed.

In her way, she is the strongest heroine I've ever written. I think the recent trend in "strong, feisty heroines" has focused too much on crusading and twentieth century feminism, which was a long way off in 1816. Refusing to open her betrothal ball with the first dance would have been a huge deal, but not as big as insisting on holding the reins to her family's companies.

Marriage would have been a terrifying risk for a woman like Mary. Absolutely. Terrifying. Remember that no matter what her husband might promise before they tied the knot, afterward she was his chattel and he could beat her, lock her away, or do anything else he might conceive of.

So, would that make a woman like Mary prickly? You bet.

As for Miles…

Why does he hide his emotions from everyone—even the women from the Stefani School, who are the closest friends he has? Is he a "himbo"?

Well, maybe a little.

Or maybe he's the way he is because it is 1816 and not 2022.

Once again, I've tried to examine the problems of the time without using a twenty-first century lens. Miles was a POW twice and tortured one of those times. Like it or not, he wouldn't have spoken of those experiences with women. It just wasn't done. He probably wouldn't have spoken much about them with other men, either.

At this time PTSD was called "war hysteria". You can tell by the word "hysteria" that anyone who suffered from such an affliction wouldn't have received much understanding or respect.

Soldiers still suffer from the stigma today, no matter how much the medical establishment has tried to change that.

I think one of the hardest things for 21st century, post-Freudian people to believe and understand is that folks in 1816 wouldn't have just let it all "hang out" like we do today. While that reserved behavior may frustrate modern readers, I think it is part of the fascination of reading historical romance.

If you want to read about guys sharing every millimeter of their souls, read a contemporary.

If authors just project modern sensibilities into characters dressed in historical clothing, then we are depriving readers of a special experience, not to mention warping history beyond recognition.

Here are a few liberties I took with history (after my big rant above, LOL)

I jumped the gun by quite a few years by putting herons in Pen Ponds in Richmond Park. They weren't actually reported there until the 1880s, but I like to think of my bird-loving heroine seeing them.

The Baltic tariff—specifically the tax on lumber from northern European countries—wasn't eliminated until several years after the end of the Napoleonic Wars, but it would have been a huge issue for English shipbuilders, although less so as the industry moved away from wood.

The Corn Laws are a HUGE issue in 19th century British history and I only touch on some of the rocketing price issues post war people would have faced (high prices are something very much on all our minds right now!)

I use the phrase "oodles of charm" in homage to my favorite writer, Kurt Vonnegut. I've said it many times in conversation and it just felt right to use it in this book, because Miles PERSONIFIES charm. And I just love him.

What am I working on now? Well, I'm working on cooking for my family for Christmas, LOL, but after a brief break

I will move on to THE CUTTHROAT COUNTESS and HYACINTH, which are both coming right up in the new year.

Once again, I really DO pay attention to reader requests and it gets me all excited about a character when a reader is excited, so please send me an email and tell me if you think a character ABSOLUTELY must have their story told.

If you find typos, please do let me know and I will make every effort to fix them.

As always, I am grateful for reviews and I REALLY love getting emails: Minervaspencerauthor@gmail.com. Until next time, happy reading! S.M./Minerva

Who are Minerva Spencer & S.M. LaViolette?

Minerva is S.M.'s pen name (that's short for Shantal Marie) S.M. has been a criminal prosecutor, college history teacher, B&B operator, dock worker, ice cream manufacturer, reader for the blind, motel maid, and bounty hunter. Okay, so the part about being a bounty hunter is a lie. S.M. does, however, know how to hypnotize a Dungeness crab, sew her own Regency Era clothing, knit a frog hat, juggle, rebuild a 1959 American Rambler, and gain control of Asia (and hold on to it) in the game of RISK.

Read more about S.M. at: www.MinervaSpencer.com

Follow 'us' on Bookbub:
Minerva's BookBub
S.M.'s Bookbub

On Goodreads

Minerva and S.M.'s BELLAMY SISTERS SERIES
PHOEBE
HYACINTH*
SELINA*

Minerva's OUTCASTS SERIES

DANGEROUS
BARBAROUS
SCANDALOUS

THE REBELS OF THE *TON:*

NOTORIOUS
OUTRAGEOUS
INFAMOUS
AUDACIOUS (a *REBELS* novella in the DUKE IN A BOX anthology)

ANTHOLOGIES:

THE ARRANGEMENT
DUKE IN A BOX

Made in the USA
Middletown, DE
28 February 2023

25896908R00186